Promises Linger

Sarah McMarty

ELLORA'S CAVE
ROMANTICA PUBLISHING

What the critics are saying...

෨

5 STAR KEEPER! "PROMISES LINGER is by far one of the best books this year. Sarah McCarty has an incredible ability to create some of the most intriguing and believable characters. This is erotic romance at its best. Extraordinary and astounding, PROMISES LINGER will have you yearning for more of Sarah McCarty's wonderful writing."

~ *eCataRomance*

An Ellora's Cave Romantica Publication

www.ellorascave.com

Promises Linger

ISBN 9781419950100

This book printed in the U.S.A. by Jasmine–Jade Enterprises, LLC.

Trade paperback Publication July 2004

Excerpt from *Promises Keep* Copyright © Sarah McCarty, 2004

Content Advisory:

S – ENSUOUS
E – ROTIC
X – TREME

Ellora's Cave Publishing offers three levels of Romantica™ reading entertainment: S (S-ensuous), E (E-rotic), and X (X-treme).

The following material contains graphic sexual content meant for mature readers. This story has been rated E–rotic.

S-*ensuous* love scenes are explicit and leave nothing to the imagination.

E-*rotic* love scenes are explicit, leave nothing to the imagination, and are high in volume per the overall word count. E-rated titles might contain material that some readers find objectionable — in other words, almost anything goes, sexually. E-rated titles are the most graphic titles we carry in terms of both sexual language and descriptiveness in these works of literature.

X-*treme* titles differ from E-rated titles only in plot premise and storyline execution. Stories designated with the letter X tend to contain difficult or controversial subject matter not for the faint of heart.

Also by Sarah McCarty

ह

About the Author

ౠ

Sarah has traveled extensively throughout her life, living in other cultures, sometimes in areas where electricity was a concept awaiting fruition and a book was an extreme luxury. While she could easily adjust to the lack of electricity, living without the comfort of a good book was intolerable. To fill the void, she bought pencil and paper and sketched out her own story, and in the process, discovered the joy of writing. She's been at it ever since.

Sarah welcomes comments from readers. You can find her website and email address on her author bio page at www.ellorascave.com.

Tell Us What You Think

We appreciate hearing reader opinions about our books. You can email us at Comments@EllorasCave.com.

PROMISES LINGER

Chapter One

ॐ

It wasn't every day a lady strolled into Dell's. A few strumpets graced the place, but Asa was willing to bet every dollar in his pocket that the last time a buttoned-down, poker-backed lady had entered this rundown excuse of a saloon was never. One by one, the other patrons noticed the gray clad intruder. The cacophony of voices dropped until, with a resounding clank on the keys, the piano player took note.

Asa watched as the woman turned this way and that, no doubt straining to see through the murk. He lifted his whiskey to his lips, took a sip, and waited. He wondered whether it was a husband or a lover she was seeking. He hoped it was the former. A wife in search of an errant husband was bound to put on a better show.

With a sharp tug on each finger, she yanked off her gloves. Backlit as she was by the doorway, Asa had an excellent view of her silhouette. Petite and curvaceous with softly turned hips that had Asa thinking in terms of sinking deep and riding hard. He took another sip of his whiskey. As it burned the back of his throat, he tried to figure out why the sight of this woman had his cock sitting up and taking notice. Maybe it was the way she stood that piqued his interest. Kind of a cross between it's-snowing-in-hell panic and hell-bent-for-leather determination. Then again, maybe he was just the contrary sort and his cock followed suit, longing after what he could never have. Respectable women like her were the wives of bankers and judges. They were never seen within a country mile of a saddle tramp such as himself. Just because this one was perched on the doorstep of the seediest saloon in town didn't change that fact.

The sun peeped out from behind a cloud. The feeble shaft of light curved around the door, illuminating the woman's profile. His cock came fully erect and he almost wasted a swallow of rot gut choking on his surprise.

A man could look at a face like that for years and never get tired. It wasn't that she was beautiful, though she was mighty easy on the eyes. It was the way the planes and hollows came together in a delicate balance of strength, humor and bone-deep sensuality that had him gaping like a green kid. A face like that spoke of endurance and character. A face like that invited visions of naked bodies and long, lusty, leisurely nights. And her mouth, hell, her mouth was a fantasy unto itself. He couldn't begin to corral the ideas the sight of those wide plump lips had running through his head.

He shifted in his chair to ease the pressure on his manhood and reigned in his imagination. The woman might be every fantasy he'd ever had wrapped into one delectable armful, but she was about as attainable as the moon. And the sooner he forced himself to accept that fact, the better he'd be. He'd stopped lusting after what he couldn't have about the same time he had realized the son of a whore and a passing through gambler was good for only one thing in the townsfolk's eyes. Cleaning up other people's messes. He'd gotten real good at cleaning up over the years, and someday he was going to take the money he had earned bringing in robbers and murderers, and he was going to buy a future for himself and his kids. Someday.

He forced his fingers to relax their grip on his glass before it cracked under the pressure. He didn't know why this woman was stirring up old demons, but he didn't like it. He'd long since adjusted to the way the world worked, and he wasn't about to let the sight of a woman, no matter how temptingly packaged, upset the peace he'd made with life's ironies.

A quartet of poker two tables over from Asa broke into yells. A fancy gambler with his back to the door let out a hoot and leaned over the table, raking in the winnings.

As if that were the signal she'd been waiting on, the woman launched into motion. Head high, shoulders back, she crossed the cramped room with a determination that sent the working girls in her path fleeing for cover. Asa released the breath he'd been holding and tipped his chair back on two legs until his shoulders connected with the wall. Raising his glass, he toasted her grit. Not many women had the wherewithal to confront their man's shortcomings.

"Hello, Brent."

Her voice was well modulated, without any hint of a drawl.

The blond-haired gambler froze in the act of raking in his winnings. The woman moved around the table, murmuring "Excuse me" as she went, stopping when she reached the man's side. The flickering glow from the oil lamps set off the red highlights in her scraped-back hair. Those sparks were nothing compared to the fury raging in her vivid green eyes. One of which was black and blue.

"What in hell are you doing here, Elly?" Brent growled.

The name landed wrong on Asa's ear. No one that buttoned-down could ever be an Elly.

"I came for my money."

"You don't have anything I don't give you," the gambler retorted in a snide voice that just made Asa itch to feed him a few of his own teeth.

The woman didn't seem to share his irritation. Cool as a cucumber, she replied. "You're wrong." Reaching across her husband's arm, the woman snatched a pile of bills. "This is mine."

She was halfway through the stack before one of the other players thought to react.

"Hey! We're playing a game here."

13

"Mr. Doyle is cashing out," she said, not looking up from her counting.

Mr. Doyle apparently had other ideas. "Put the money back, Elizabeth."

That, Asa thought, was a more fitting name for the lady.

Elizabeth looked up from her counting. "You owe me two hundred dollars more."

"I don't owe you anything, woman." Despite the confidence in his voice, Brent's hands clamped down on the rest of his winnings. "Put it back, Elly."

Elizabeth tucked the bills she'd confiscated into her reticule. Not by a flutter of an eyelash did she indicate she heard the warning in her husband's voice. "You took four hundred dollars from my bank account this morning. Money that rightly belongs to the hands that put in a hard month's work. Two hundred I just put in my reticule. Hand me two hundred more, and we can both consider this unfortunate circumstance finished."

"Since when," Brent asked, pulling out a cheroot from his pocket and scraping a match across his boot sole, "does a man have to account to his wife for anything?"

Elizabeth placed a small circle of gold on the table. "We aren't married."

"Like hell." Brent eyed her steadily over his cupped hand as he touched the tip of the match to his cheroot.

Asa noted the distinctive band around the tip of the cheroot. Elizabeth's husband had expensive taste.

"The hell would have been if I were truly trapped into a marriage with you," Elizabeth stated flatly. "Fortunately, I'm not."

"Oh, we're married." Brent shoved his chair back. He tossed the match into the nearby spittoon. At the end of the sharp movement, his hand curled into a fist. With the tip of the cheroot, he indicated the ring on the table. "And as your husband, I'm telling you to put that ring back on and get yourself back home where you belong."

Elizabeth made no move to take the ring or hit the door. She merely stood for the span of two heartbeats, doing nothing but meeting her husband's stare with one of her own. The tension between the two was thick enough to chew on.

Around Asa, men started shifting restlessly. No mistaking it, this argument was getting ugly fast. It was easy to tell from the set of Elizabeth's shoulders that she was a proud woman. Too proud to back down. It was just as easy to tell from Brent's demeanor that he was more than willing to make the discussion physical. Asa didn't know about the rest of the men in the saloon, but he'd be hard put to watch a man take his fists to a woman. Wife or not.

With a sigh, Elizabeth, broke the stare-down. "You're such an egotistical fool."

Asa wondered if the disgust in Elizabeth's voice was aimed at Brent or herself, for it was becoming more obvious by the second that, if husbands were apples, Elizabeth's choice had been core rotten.

Brent growled low in his throat and ground out his cheroot beneath the heel of his boot. With a jerk of his chin, he indicated the remains of his cigar. "I'll be taking the price of that out of your hide tonight."

Elizabeth calmly put her gloves and reticule in the pocket of her skirt. "You won't be doing anything tonight, I imagine, besides crying into the bottom of a liquor bottle. For you see, due to what I suspect is typical ineptness on your part, yesterday's so-called marriage between us has not been consummated."

Loud hoots and ribald offers broke through the privacy of the argument to fill the saloon. Brent's pale face grew red. His gaze ricocheted between the speakers, as if every comment were a blow from an unseen fist. If Elizabeth had been looking to get a bit of her own back, she couldn't have chosen a better weapon, Asa decided. Attacking a man's mother or his privates was a guaranteed reaction-getter. Respect was a hard animal to corral here in the territory. Once a man had it roped and fenced, he didn't just open the gate and let it get away. Especially as respect had a way of turning wily once it slipped a man's lariat. Wasn't a man born who didn't know that or hadn't learned it the hard way.

From what Asa could see of the bottom line, Brent had fouled up big time as a husband, and Elizabeth had gotten a bit of her own back. While he didn't think the two had a shot at making a peaceful marriage, this game was about played out. Someone had to give, and he didn't think it was going to be Brent. Elizabeth had her husband backed into a corner. From the way Brent was sitting, shoulders squared, fists at the ready, Asa figured he was planning to come out fighting. Asa couldn't tell if Elizabeth saw, or if she was so disappointed in her choice of husband, she just didn't care, because, to his amazement, she kept driving her point deeper.

"If I were to need an annulment, Jesse Graham informs me that's all the cause I'd need."

"You went to a son of a bitching lawyer?"

Asa returned the front legs of his chair to the floor. He might have been off in his assessment. If the gambler wanted to come out of this with some skin left on his pride, he might want to withdraw and regroup in private. Elizabeth was one resourceful woman. Unwelcome admiration cozied up to the arousal humming through his blood. Damn. He didn't need to be in the middle of this.

"A woman has so few options, she can't afford to be ill informed," Elizabeth stated simply. "Especially when she has the poor sense to take up with a pathetic excuse of a man such as you."

With a roar, Brent came out of the chair. He made it halfway to his feet before a stool broke across his face, pole-axing him to the floor where he struggled to find up from down.

Like everyone else in the saloon, Asa found himself sitting in slack-jawed amazement as the pristine example of a lady dropped the remains of the stool, turned, and deftly whipped a six-shooter out of the holster of a man who was wisely scrambling for safety. With a familiarity that eased his mind, she checked to be sure it was loaded, cocked the hammer, and aimed it dead center between her husband's eyes.

"If I were you," she said in a very soft, very controlled voice. "I'd stay put."

"Damned bitch." Brent swore, holding his bleeding nose. "I'm going to beat you black and blue for this."

"No." Elizabeth adjusted the aim of the pistol a little to the left until it lined up with the freckle on the corner of Brent's eyebrow. The one she'd once viewed as his perfect imperfection. "You're not."

He was never going to touch her again. Of that, Elizabeth was sure. She'd die before she allowed that to happen.

Brent pulled out a handkerchief and wiped the blood from his nose. "Who's going to stop me?"

Her lips didn't quite make it into the confident smile she was struggling for. Elizabeth could feel them hang up somewhere in the range of a grimace. She hoped the resulting expression wasn't too pathetic. She didn't need to be showing weakness in front of this crowd. "For sixteen years before I was the Miss Elizabeth Coyote you claim to love, I was Coyote Bill's wild daughter. And, I assure you, four years back East in a fancy finishing school hasn't done much to smooth my rough edges."

"I knew she looked familiar," an old timer at the far end of the bar crowed, slapping his thigh.

Brent looked at her over the bulk of the handkerchief he held to his nose, the wad of bloody linen doing nothing to diminish his skepticism. "Is that supposed to mean something to me?"

"It means you'd best watch your back, gambler man, if you're the one who blacked Wild Elly's eye," the old timer hooted.

Brent didn't take his eyes off the gun aimed at his head. "Shut up, you old fool."

"Appears to me you ain't the one in charge right now."

"I will be."

"How very like you to be a braggart to the humiliating end." Elizabeth cut in, taking a step forward. "I cannot believe I was so stupid as to think grammar and dress made the man."

It was a mistake she wouldn't be making again.

With her elbow, Elizabeth indicated the pile of money still lying on the table. "Could someone count two hundred and twenty dollars out of that pile?"

"Hey," Brent protested as a young cowpoke hastened to help out. "You said two hundred before."

"That was before I had to reimburse the owner of this fine establishment for a chair."

"Here's your money, ma'am."

"As my hands are occupied, could you put it in my pocket? Without stepping between me and my almost-husband," she tacked on as the young man made to step in front of her.

For a few minutes, everyone watched as the kid fumbled in the vicinity of Elizabeth's right side, too shy to actually touch her skirt.

"Whatever are you doing?" Her question was sharper than she intended, betraying her nervousness. She took a breath and mentally counted to ten, maintaining her composure through sheer force of will as, with an embarrassed mumble, the red-faced kid shoved the money hard enough into her skirt pocket to tip her sideways. The guffaws following her small teeter set her nerves to screaming again. The only reason this crowd hadn't turned on her was they were enjoying the show, but that could change any second. She needed to finish what she started and get out of here fast if she intended to get out of here at all

Elizabeth took two cautious steps back. "Good riddance, Brent."

"I'll see you back at the ranch, Elly," Brent retorted. His confidence in his rights was supposed to scare her, she knew. Snap her back in line like a cur who'd forgotten its place. It just went to show how little Brent knew her that he actually thought it would work.

As the warning hung in the air, floating on the smoke-filled haze, Elizabeth knew all eyes were upon her. She could feel them, like hands reaching out of the murk. Some laughing, some goading, but all of them waiting for her to flinch or back down. She wasn't doing either. She'd been expecting the threat. Someone as blindly selfish as Brent would never take a woman seriously. The knowledge didn't prevent a shiver of fear from snaking down her spine when she thought of what would happen if Brent ever got his hands on her again. Her finger tightened on the trigger. The only thing that kept the bullet in the chamber was the scorn-laced memory of her father's voice saying, "You lose control, Elly, you lose everything."

She had no intention of losing ever again.

When her face muscles felt rigid from the effort to appear unconcerned, she pushed conviction into her voice. "If you set one foot on Rocking C land, you'll get a bullet between your eyes."

"I don't think so."

The confidence in his voice started a quiver of uncertainty deep inside. She took a breath and immediately regretted it. The smoke that had collected in the musty interior burned her lungs. She suppressed a cough and regrouped. She wouldn't cry. She wouldn't show weakness. She would, however, tighten her grip on the gun and finish what she'd started;

undoing the mistake of the day before. "Stay off my land, Brent."

She wrapped each word in precise enunciation for maximum effect. She might as well have saved her breath. Not by a flicker of an eyelash did Brent let on she'd so much as scratched his arrogance. Instead, he wiped a fresh trickle of blood from his lip with the back of his hand. His teeth bared in a savage, confident smile. "You won't shoot me, Elly."

Why did men continually believe that because she was female, she was as inconsequential as dandelion fluff?

"You're wrong," she informed him. She was close, so damned close to pulling the trigger that her fingers ached with the effort not to squeeze. She hated him for turning her wedding night from anticipation to terror. She hated him for being weak when she needed someone strong, but mostly she hated him for betraying her faith in her own judgment.

"If you kill me, Elly," he went on, dabbing at the blood on his shirt, "then you're back where you started, the ranch going to hell, the bank note coming due, and no husband to turn the situation around."

God! Had she really thought this man's clothes and speech had put him a step up on the local men? "I imagine I'll find a way."

"Not in time, you won't," Brent inserted the taunt smoothly into the conversation. "Coyote Bill loved that ranch more than life itself." The glance he shot her was calculating. "What would he think of a daughter who, in an attack of bridal jitters, lost the Rocking C?"

"I have no intention of losing anything," she responded calmly. Of that, she was certain. She wouldn't lose the ranch. She may not have been the boy her father had wanted, but she'd shed blood for that land. Worked it as hard as any man before Coyote Bill had discovered she'd had other uses as a woman. The Rocking C was hers. As much a part of her as her mother's intelligence and her father's determination. She would surrender it to no one. Least of all a wastrel like Brent. The weight of the gun made her arms ache. She raised the muzzle so it was back on target. "I have absolutely no intention of losing, period."

"If you continue with this lunacy, you will," Brent's calm equaled her own. "As your husband, I can sell it anytime I want." His voice lowered, became harsh. "Just like I can take you across that street anytime I want and teach you a woman's place."

Despite her efforts, a spark of fear slipped through her guard. Elizabeth ignored the rumblings of the other men in the bar. Her gaze focused on the widest spot between Brent's eyebrows. If he made one move in her direction, he was dead. "Are you through?"

"No. While you may want to forget our marriage took place yesterday, the law isn't so flexible." The smile he spread around the room was an open invitation for the other males to commiserate with his position.

She didn't have enough bullets in her gun to shoot the men who met Brent's smile with an understanding one of their own. Deep inside, the shuddering started. Oh God! What if they all turned on her? She searched the room with her eyes, looking for a friendly face. Her gaze collided with a dark set of eyes in the corner. The big man sat, his back braced against the wall. Despite the laziness of his posture, there was something in the set of his shoulders that told her he was as intent on the conversation as everyone else. His gaze was steady, unnerving, but somehow soothing, as if inviting her trust. She wasn't stupid enough to believe in the invitation, but if all hell broke loose, she hoped he'd be in the small contingent on her side.

"We are married, Elly," Brent pronounced, turning back to her, his position obviously bolstered by the silent communion with the other patrons. "The Rocking C is mine."

"If that were the case," Elizabeth countered calmly, allowing no uncertainty into her voice, "I'd not be wasting a perfectly good bullet by letting it sit in this gun."

She might be losing her mind, but she swore the big man with the dark eyes just gave her the thumbs up as he tipped his hat back. Even with the dim light, there was no mistaking the handsomeness of his face or the self-confidence in his expression. Since she had a need, she took some of his self confidence as her own. As a result, her voice, when she continued, betrayed nothing but strength. "Lucky for you, our marriage wasn't legal."

"The hell it wasn't! Reverend!"

Elizabeth followed the trajectory of Brent's gaze to the far corner of the saloon. A crow of a man garbed in black sat slumped over a table. When Brent bellowed again, the form shifted, moaned, and then raised its head.

"Wh-what?"

"Reverend? Was the wedding you performed yesterday legal?"

"It's as legal as the parties involved want it to be," the haggard man muttered before leaning to the side of the table and retching violently.

Beyond a flinching of her right eyelid, Elizabeth didn't let on that the sound or sight bothered her.

"Let me clarify things for you, Brent," she offered in that same controlled tone she'd used since walking through the swinging doors. "Because the circuit priest comes through here so rarely, the territory has been recognizing weddings performed by Reverend Pete under common law. As long as both parties are satisfied with the union, there's no problem." Her shoulder lifted on a shrug. "Unfortunately for you, I'm not satisfied."

Brent wiped at his eyes, stared at the blood on his pants, and looked down the barrel of the revolver. "What the hell do you think you're doing?" he finally burst out.

"I'm saving my ranch from the hands of a wastrel."

"You're saving your ranch!" He dropped his head back against the wall and laughed. "That's a hoot! The reason it was so easy to pull the wool over your eyes in the first place was because you were in such a big hurry to get married." He stopped laughing long enough to drive his point home. "Or did you forget the way the men won't take orders from a woman? Or the way the bank won't extend credit to a woman? Or the way rustlers have been swooping down on your precious ranch for the last three months ever since word got out that Coyote Bill's dead?"

"I haven't forgotten a thing."

"Then you know you need me."

"No."

"Yes, you do. You need me to run your ranch, just as I need your ranch to fund my amusements."

"What I need is a man, Brent Doyle, and I'm afraid that requirement leaves you out in the cold."

"She needs a man in more ways than one," someone interjected from the sidelines.

Elizabeth bit back the retort that sprang to her lips and let the room's inhabitants amuse themselves with speculation. She had bigger fish to fry. She searched the room for her friend. When she spotted Old Sam at the bar, she gave him the signal. Before she finished the subtle nod, he was nodding back and rising from his chair. She shifted her grip on the revolver, took a breath and started praying as she followed his progress from the corner of her eye while keeping her gun aimed on Brent. As she suspected, he headed for the table to her right. The closer he got to the stranger with the dark eyes and easy confidence, the harder she prayed. Anyone with a chin that stubborn wouldn't be easy to sway. And she so needed him to lean her way.

A tap on his shoulder took Asa's attention away from his whiskey and the show. The first thing he noticed when he turned was the hat. Battered, ragged and sweat-stained, it had definitely seen better days. The face peering from under the Stetson wasn't in much better shape. It was tanned the same mud brown as the crown and sported more creases than a ten-year-old letter from home. The gleam in the old codger's faded blue eyes was speculative, making Asa wonder if the man knew of his reputation.

"I'm thinking it'd take a hell of a man to tame a pretty little mustang like that," the old codger whispered, one lid dropping over his eye in a slow wink.

"At the very least, a brave one," Asa said by way of response. He took another pull on his whiskey, unable to keep his eyes off the woman. Damn. She was a firecracker under all that tight-ass exterior.

"Elly always did have a bit of a temper."

Asa shot the older man an amused glance. "A temper is throwing dishes at your husband when he walks though the door. This, this is…" He shook his head. "Hell, I don't know what this is."

"I imagine," the older man chuckled, "Elly has thrown a dish or two in her day." He swiped the top of his whiskey glass with a filthy sleeve, tossed back the contents, and wiped his bearded mouth with the back of his hand. "It isn't Elly's fault she doesn't let her sweet side show. Coyote Bill brought her up rough."

Rough wouldn't be the word Asa would use. Intriguing was more the way he saw her. Strong. A man could go far with a woman like that by his side. "She's something else."

"She's as straight as they come."

"Her husband's a fool."

"I won't argue the fool part, but he ain't her husband."

Asa slid his foot aside as the man punctuated his statement by spitting to the side. With his glass, he indicated Elizabeth. "Is she kin to you ?" he asked.

The old man looked shocked and then amused. "Nah, but it's not like I'd be ashamed to find out different." He looked at the last two swallows in the bottle before Asa. "Mind?"

"Go ahead." The old man didn't bother with the glass he'd set on the table. He finished the bottle in one swig, and wiped his mouth with the sleeve of his shirt before clarifying, "I worked for her Daddy for most of her life."

"And you're loyal to her." Asa didn't pose it as a question.

"Enough so that I'm giving you the go ahead."

He said it like Asa should feel honored. "I appreciate it."

Or at least he would if he had any idea what the man was talking about.

The old man glanced over his shoulder at Elizabeth, gave a nod of his head and then turned back to Asa.

"I thank you for the drink."

There was something likable about the guy, so Asa nodded and said, "I appreciated the company."

The old man's face crinkled into a smile revealing worn yellowed teeth. "I'm sure you will before long."

Damn. Was everyone in this town squirrelly, Asa wondered, shaking his head as the old man, chuckling at the joke only he understood, disappeared back into the crowd around Elizabeth. Brent's voice rose over the low murmur of bets being placed, drawing Asa's attention back to the marital drama unfolding. Dismissing the old man from his mind, he shifted in his seat to get a better view.

"That land is mine and I'm not letting you or any drunken preacher cheat me out of it."

"Give it up, Brent."

"Never. Without a man, you can't hold that ranch."

Asa sighed, knowing they'd reached the crux of the matter. As much as he admired the woman's courage, she wouldn't be able to hold the ranch without a man.

"I've thought of that." Her slightly slanted green eyes turned in his direction. "Are you Asa MacIntyre?"

He dipped his head, so his hat shielded the expression on his face. "Maybe."

"The same Asa MacIntyre who single-handedly brought in the infamous Crull gang?"

He tucked his chin a little lower, not liking the way the saddle bums in the corner were perking up. He'd come to town to relax. Not to have to battle with wet-behind-the ears kids dead set on establishing a reputation for themselves with his dead body. He was too close to his dream to risk that. "Maybe."

"The same Asa MacIntyre who headed up the Kingman Drive back in '63?"

He sighed, recognizing I-won't-give-up determination when it stared him in the face. "Yeah."

Elizabeth's voice shook for the moment it took her to ask the next question. "The same Asa MacIntyre who stopped the blacksmith from beating little Willy Jones yesterday?"

He found it interesting that her composure broke on that question. He sat up straighter in his chair and pushed his hat back off his face. "Yeah, that's me."

One shuddering breath and her face became as blank as her inflection. "Word has it you're looking to buy a small spread around here."

"If you're about to offer me the Rocking C, I got to tell you, it's way out of my pocket. I'm looking for something smaller, around a couple hundred acres."

And it'd taken him all of fifteen years to save the money for that dream. Fifteen years of working cattle, hauling in bounties, and busting his butt, doing any job that would yield close to an honest buck.

"But, if you could afford it, you'd be interested?"

"Sorry, ma'am." He tipped his hat in her direction. Lord, that woman had guts. "As tempting as the prospect is, there's no way I could stretch my earnings to cover a couple thousand acres." But he would someday. He would. And when he did, no man would look down his nose at him, spit when he passed, or keep their daughters from his company.

"What if I said it wouldn't cost you anything?"

He pushed his glass away. "Then I'd say there was something fishy about this deal. Especially as the ownership of this property is in some dispute."

"If you agree to my terms, there'll be no dispute."

"Pardon me, but I don't think you can guarantee that."

"Jesse Graham assures me that my legal husband will have full and complete title to the land."

"It would appear to me you already have more husbands than you know what to do with."

"I know exactly what to do with Brent, Mr. MacIntyre. The question is, do you know what to do with the Rocking C?"

"I know what to do with it. I'm just going to have to think on it."

"Please, reach a decision quickly."

"I'll do the best I can." He raised his glass of whiskey, noted the nearly indiscernible tremor in his hand, and took a steadying sip. Jesus, Mary, and Joseph! First, the Crull brothers and their hefty bounty had fallen into his hands like ripe plums and now this! He was on a lucky streak, for sure.

"Mr. MacIntyre?"

"I'm ruminating as fast as I can."

"Perhaps if you confided your reservations, I could help you reach a decision." When he didn't respond, she prodded some more. "It's true we've had problems with rustlers recently, but I'm sure, once the men have someone they respect in charge, the rustlers will leave the Rocking C alone and search for easier game."

"I'm not worried about rustlers, ma'am. No matter what a man has, there's always someone looking to take it away."

"Is it Brent then? I assure you he has no legal claim."

Asa smiled, shooting the now quiet man a disgusted glare. "That little piss-ant isn't worth the effort it would take to squash him."

"Surely you're not afraid of marriage?" she asked in patent disbelief.

Asa sighed. "I'm afraid you found me out, ma'am."

"But marriage is nothing more than a piece of paper to a man. It doesn't curtail any of your rights! As a matter of fact, you gain quite a few." Her fine lips thinned as she conceded. "Over me."

"And that's an awful lot of responsibility for one man to own." He looked pointedly at the gun in her hand. "You don't appear the cooperative type."

"That's your problem?"

"Yup." He took a last sip of his whiskey. Lord! If he took this woman for wife, not only would he have the biggest ranch around, but any children he had would have a lady for a mother, guaranteeing they'd grow up respected. "This territory is a dangerous place. One of the prime qualities I plan on looking for in a wife is the ability to stay put when I tell her to."

"You want my obedience."

"Wouldn't go amiss."

"You have it."

"Have what?"

"My obedience."

Still that same deadpan expression backing that deadpan voice. What would it take to rattle this woman? "Well, I thank you, and as soon as I decide whether to take you up on the deal, I'll be asking for your word on it."

"I'd appreciate it if you'd hurry up."

He wondered if she was afraid of the gambler. "Why?"

"My arms are getting tired."

And here he thought she'd admit to something like fear. He laughed at his own idiocy and rolled to his feet. In three strides, he was at her side. "Well, put the gun down, darlin'. I think I can keep this varmint contained for you."

He had her full attention. "You'll marry me? You'll take on the Rocking C?"

"You're promising me obedience if I do?"

"I promise."

"Then I'm considering it." He caught a whiff of vanilla through the smell of smoke and sweat. Like a breath of spring after a long hard winter, the scent swept from her to him, uncovering longings he'd thought permanently snowed under.

"I've always had a hankering to take myself a genuine lady for a wife," he admitted. "Always thought it'd be out of my reach, though. Sorta like a spread the size of the Rocking C."

And that was more than the truth. It'd been his furthest out-there dream, and now it was standing before him, chin up, eyes shooting fire, determination oozing from every pore, tossing out invisible challenges like swear words at a cussing match.

"But now?" she prompted.

He smiled at her hearing that "but" when he hadn't really meant her to. He took the gun from her hand, noticing what a little bit of a thing she was now that he was close. Her head barely reached his collarbone.

"Now, it appears the good Lord's working on one of those miracles I've heard tell of, but, before we shake on this deal, there are a few things you've got to understand." He uncocked the gun and emptied the chamber, using his side vision to keep tabs on her expression. "First, trouble has a way of following me."

The corners of her lips lifted in a hint of a smile. "It doesn't exactly go out of its way to miss me."

He looked at her shiner and the situation she was in. "You got a point there." He handed the gun and bullets back to its owner.

Brent obviously felt he'd been quiet long enough. He made to get up. "As touching as I find this moment, wife, you can't give away what's not yours."

Brent got to his knees. This close, it was impossible for Asa to miss Elizabeth's slight start.

With his foot, Asa shoved the man back down. "Shut up."

He slid his gloved finger under Elizabeth's chin and turned her gaze to his. "Second, what's mine, stays mine."

"I won't take the Rocking C from you as long as you do your best by it."

He smiled. She was a determined little thing. "Fair enough."

"Third," he gently traced the bruise around her right eye, "I take care of my own."

She had nothing to say to that.

"Are you hurt anywhere else?" he asked quietly, wishing he weren't wearing gloves so he could feel the texture of her skin, memorize it the way he'd already memorized her scent.

"No." Her gaze didn't leave his. Her pupils were large, nearly swallowing the green. Her breath hitched in her throat when he slid one finger down her cheek and traced the delicate underside of her chin.

"Good. Go wait for me outside the door."

Her gaze slid to his table where one of the saloon girls had taken a seat. "Why?"

"I thought you promised me obedience?" She opened her mouth and then closed it. Taking her shoulders, he turned her in the direction of the door. "Wait for me outside."

With her pride draped like a shield around her, she did as ordered. She made it as far as the door before balking. "You're taking the job?"

Asa couldn't see her face, but he bet her expression was still blank. "I'm marrying you," he replied. "Just as soon as I finish a little business here."

There was a pregnant pause. "Can I wait for you at the mercantile?"

"Outside the door will be fine."

He knew she was wondering as she walked into the sunlight if this was a test. He knew she was braced to have her pride ground into the dust. What she didn't know was that he'd dreamed his whole life of a home of his own, a lady for a wife, and the respect that came with both. He had no intention of tempting fate by mistreating either.

He pulled off his gloves, rolled up his cuffs, turned to Brent, and smiled.

* * * * *

Despite the fact that he'd ordered her to stay put, Asa was surprised to find Elizabeth waiting for him outside the saloon door. The fact that she was on the receiving end of quite a few scandalized looks didn't show in her expression. Nothing did. She was in full control of her composure. A fact that irritated Asa to no end. No woman should have such control. It was downright unnatural. He rolled down the cuffs of his sleeve.

"Thank you for waiting."

"It's what you told me to do."

He cast her a considering glance. "Yeah. It was."

He wondered if she intended to be this obedient in bed. It was an intriguing thought. Almost as intriguing as having a lady in his bed. He held out his arm. "Ready to head out?"

After a moment's hesitation, she slipped her hand in the crook of his arm. "Where are we going?"

"Depends." He tucked her in close, ignoring her effort to keep a distance.

"On what?"

"Where's the nearest yahoo that can marry us nice, tight and legal?"

"I heard Judge Carlson will be over in River's Bend tomorrow afternoon."

"Then River's Bend it is." He looked down at the top of her head, noticing a few tendrils of hair escaping her bun. They had a tendency to curl. "Where'd you leave your buckboard?"

"At the livery."

"Then the livery it is." Since the livery was two blocks down at the edge of town, he didn't alter their course.

Her gloved fingers grazed the bruised knuckles of his left hand. "Thank you."

He slid his free hand over hers before it could escape. "I may not know much about being a family man, but there's one thing you won't have to worry about."

Her "What?" was soft, almost shy. He wondered if she was embarrassed to be seen with him, or if she was regretting their deal already.

He looked down again, but he was still talking to the top of her head. "Being manhandled by strange men. I know how to take care of my own."

"I'm glad to hear it."

He'd been expecting a little more enthusiasm for his declaration. The woman made no sense, but since she was giving him the things he'd always wanted in life, he supposed he could allow her a few oddities. Things could have been worse. She could have been the hysterical type.

A fly landed on his cheek and he brushed it aside. Elizabeth flinched and he wondered if she'd truly believed him when he'd told her he'd take care of her. He did an inventory of what he could see. The hand on his arm was shaking, he realized, with tiny, nearly imperceptible tremors.

His free hand brushed his leg as he stepped around an oncoming woman with children. The calluses on his fingers scraped across the cotton of his blue denim pants, bringing to mind their differences. He supposed he couldn't blame her for worrying. There wasn't that much of her to go around and, from the looks of things, her first wedding night had given her cause to be cautious. He opened his mouth to launch another assault on her fears when she forestalled him with a proper, "Excuse me."

He stepped off the end of the wooden sidewalk. Turning, he held out his hand to help her down. The gloved fingers that rested in his were trembling. A quick glance at her face revealed it was as white as a sheet. "Are you all right?"

"Could we get off the street?"

It might have been his imagination, but he thought her grip a little desperate. He looked around. "The alley's deserted," he pointed out dubiously.

"That'll be fine."

"If you say so." He'd never escorted a lady into an alley before, but there was always a first time for everything.

As soon as the buildings blocked out the bright sun, the tremors in her hands spread to her body. "Are we alone?"

"Yes."

The tremors grew to shudders and her teeth clattered so hard they nipped the end off every word. "Are you sure no one can see?"

He wondered if she were given to fits. "The only company we've got are a couple of cats and they're too busy to pay us much mind."

"Good," she sighed, closing her eyes.

"Are you all right?"

She collapsed against him. He looked into her waxen features. He guessed he could take a dead faint as an answer to his question.

Chapter Two

** som**

For the space of two heartbeats, Asa debated what to do with the woman in his arms. His hotel was just across the street. In a matter of steps, he could drop her on the bright red velvet couch in the parlor and wash his hands of the whole mess. That was, if he could make it across the busy street without attracting attention. He had a better chance of skinning a live polecat.

"Are you sure no one can see?"

The question echoed in his head. Every syllable replicated right down to the stilted note with which it had ended.

He sighed, shifted Elizabeth in his arms, and knew he wasn't going to make a spectacle of her. A man owed his future wife that much consideration. That still left him with the burning question of what he was going to do with her.

A window rasped open above them. It was the only warning he had before the contents of a chamber pot hurtled down on the spot where he'd just been standing.

"Jumping Jehoshaphat!" he swore, shaking refuse off the heel of his boot. He glared at his unconscious wife-to-be. "These are brand new boots, woman. If you think I'm going to stand here all day, providing target practice for the folks living upstairs, you've got another think coming. Wake up!"

Elizabeth did absolutely nothing of the sort. Asa snorted in disgust.

"If this is an example of your obedience," he muttered, slinging her over one shoulder, "I'd sure hate to see your idea of acting up." He strode to an overturned crate. A quick glance up revealed no treacherous windows above. With a nudge of his boot, he chased off the amorous cats. The male hissed and arched his back as he retreated. Asa grunted right back.

"Get used to it. Life is damned inconvenient." He dumped Elizabeth on the crate. She lolled to one side and would have fallen if he hadn't set his foot on the crate to stop her tumble. "Especially when there's a woman involved."

He studied Elizabeth as she sat half-draped over his thigh. Her features were even, generous. Her lashes looked incredibly long against her cheeks. Her nose wasn't some puny thing that made a man wonder how she'd breathe in a dust storm, but rather a straight complement to her high cheekbones and pointed chin. He touched his finger to a freckle on the bridge of her nose. Yup. The woman's face definitely trotted side by side with her personality. More interesting than beautiful, but, even in a faint, strong and in control.

He frowned as he realized he'd seen the look before. He'd seen it on men who operated on the wrong side of the law. Men who couldn't afford to let their guard down. He'd never seen it on a woman. It was disconcerting and raised all sorts of hell with his soft side.

She sighed, her breath racing up his thigh and rustling the fringe on his buckskin shirt. His lips twisted as his body responded with understandable eagerness. It'd been a long dry spell between women, and if Elizabeth Coyote were a saloon girl, he'd have all kinds of interesting suggestions for her upon awakening. But she wasn't. His gaze fell to the brooch pinning the lace scarf high on her throat.

She was a lady. The lady who was going to give him everything he'd spent his life dreaming, scraping and fighting for. All because he'd been in the right place at the right time, with a reputation puffed up enough to set her fears to rest. He shook his head at the workings of fate, and maneuvered her so that, when she woke up, her cheek would be resting against his shoulder rather than his thigh.

Elizabeth came to as abruptly as she'd succumbed. It was always that way after her nerves gave out. Sometimes she swore determination alone carried her through when fear said curl up and surrender, but, once the crisis passed, all the will in the world couldn't keep her upright. Light turned to darkness and she dropped like a felled ox. Or so she'd been told. She was spared remembering that, but she was never spared the waking and the embarrassment accompanying it. Like now. Through long practice, she held herself still, straining with her senses to make out the situation before she opened her eyes and pretense faded to reality.

There was warmth under her cheek and the strong odors of smoke, stale liquor, cheap perfume and male. Of the smells, the last was the least offensive. The steady thump of a heart beneath her ear confirmed what she already knew. She was in a man's arms. Asa MacIntyre's arms. The man she'd asked to marry her on nothing more than a reputation and one act of kindness to a little boy. Lord! She wished she could keep her eyes closed forever.

"Are you feeling better?"

The question startled her into opening her eyes, rumbling as it did out of his broad chest that seemed to stretch forever. "Yes. Thank you." When she pressed to get away, his big hand curled tight over her shoulder, keeping her still. As if her wishes were of no matter.

"I'd rest a might easier if you'd just set a spell."

"I'm fine, Mr. MacIntyre."

"Pardon me if I'm not reassured, seeing as not more than three minutes ago you dropped like a log."

"I'm sorry for that, but I assure you, I'm fine now." She pushed a little and managed to get upright, but not out of his reach. She set her teeth against the quiver of anger that started deep within. A quiver that renewed itself when she realized that little bit of freedom had been attained only because Asa

MacIntyre wanted to see her expression. His finger slid under her chin, forcing her gaze to his.

"Has this happened to you before?" he asked.

"Once or twice." Whenever she had to screw her courage to the sticking point to get a job done.

"You sick or something?"

"I am in perfect health. You won't find yourself encumbered with an ailing wife."

"Encumbered?"

"Burdened."

"Oh."

She leaned further back, searching his expression. He couldn't want a sickly wife, could he? "You don't sound relieved."

She felt his shrug all through her body. "Are you given to fits often?"

"I've never had a fit in my entire life!"

"No need to get in a huff. I was just checking the lay of the land. A man has to know what to expect."

"And if I were the sort 'given to fits'? Would you still marry me?"

"Yup. I'd just have to run things a might different."

One glance at his rugged face and she knew he was serious, but she asked anyway. "Do you really mean that?"

"It's not often I say what I don't mean."

"Even if I were frothing-at-the-mouth mad, dropping like a young girl's hanky all over the place, you'd still marry me?"

A smile tugged at his generous mouth. Looking up, she saw the lines by his storm gray eyes tilted up also. The realization that he was a man given to smiling rather than snarling was unsettling. It didn't mesh with what she knew of his reputation or of what she knew of men in general.

"I'd marry you if you had one foot in the mad house and the other on a grease spill."

She shifted in his hold to better see his eyes. "Because you want the ranch?"

"Because I want the ranch."

"And what's yours," she remembered, "stays yours."

His eyes traveled a path from her head to her toes. "Always."

She shrugged off her unease. Men were a rutting lot from what she'd of her father and the ranch hands. According to her friend, Millie, that wasn't necessarily a bad thing. She swore there were ways a smart wife could turn a man's needs to her advantage. Elizabeth intended to be a very smart wife, but whether she managed it or not, in return for the use of her body and three square meals a day, this man was going to keep the land safe for her children. Any way she added it up, she had the better of the exchange.

"I think," she said, looking into his eyes and ignoring the frown on his face, "that you and I are going to deal very well together."

"Seeing as how we're planning on double teaming for life, I'd hope so."

"Double teaming?"

"Getting married."

"Oh."

He smiled. She was relieved to note his teeth were clean and strong.

"Of course," he went on, exposing those teeth in a charming smile that chased the severity from his features. "I expect we'll have a spot of trouble or two until we learn each other's lingo, but I don't expect much, seeing as how we're set on the same path."

"Keeping the ranch," she confirmed, blowing a tendril of hair off her forehead. It immediately settled on her eyelid.

"That, too."

She didn't want to know what he meant by that. No doubt it had something to do with his ridiculous desire to have a lady for a wife. The man seemed content that she was the lady of his dreams, handing him all his wishes on a silver platter. Who was she to disabuse him? As long as he didn't look too deeply or she didn't slip too obviously, they probably would get along all right.

"Mr. MacIntyre?"

His finger twirled irritatingly around a stray curl. He twisted it completely into obedience before he answered, "Yeah?"

"It's not seemly for you to be holding me this way."

"Why? We're going to be married."

She shoved against his chest. "It's not seemly for married couples to comport themselves this way in public."

He allowed her two inches of distance, but she could tell from the way his hand rested on her upper arm he wasn't allowing much more. She set to work removing his hand.

"What about in private?"

She stopped tugging at his fingers. "What?"

"What about in private? Are married couples permitted to snuggle in private?"

She succeeded in prying free his pinkie. She immediately set to work on the next digit. "I wouldn't know."

Two fingers down, three more to get to freedom.

"What about your parents? Did they snuggle now and then?"

With a yank, hard enough to pop a button on her short jacket, she gained her release. It was galling to know that, even standing when he sat, she wasn't much more than eye level with her future husband. "My parents were decent proper people and none of your business," she stated flatly.

Asa got to his feet, casually brushing the seat of his pants.

He settled his hat straight on his head. "I was just making conversation. I thought it might be a good idea to know one another before the wedding, but if you want to go to your marriage bed with a stranger, who am I to kick up a fuss?"

He turned and headed out of the alley.

"I bet," she muttered as she hurried to keep up, "it won't be the first time for you."

She didn't think he'd heard, but as her hand slipped into the crook of the arm he held out, he chiseled her gaze away from a knot hole in the rail three store fronts down by sliding his finger under her chin. "But I bet it will be for you, and that was the whole point."

No, it wasn't. They both knew it. And the urge to point that out was nearly overwhelming, but she held it in check. She'd love to let him know her brain functioned as well as her corset, but she recited multiplication tables in her head instead, until she could make her expression blank and the words leaping on her tongue still. Men didn't like to be corrected and ladies didn't cause scenes, in public or in private. Keeping quiet was hard to do with his gaze memorizing every nuance of her expression, but four years of grueling comportment lessons came to her aid.

"You're a prickly little thing," he sighed, shaking his head over her success.

"I'm not the least little."

She was back to deadpan, Asa noticed. A flash of relief, then a flash of anger, colored by a hint of vulnerability, and the woman was back to her poker face.

"At least you didn't deny being prickly," he sighed, wondering if his life from here on out was going to be a continuous trek over egg shells.

"You're entitled to your opinion."

He turned in the direction of the livery, then stopped. "Are you sure you're up to this?"

"I assure you, Mr. MacIntyre, I'm perfectly fine."

She was going to hold to that story. He could tell from the set of her chin. "Did anyone ever tell you that ladies are delicate creatures? In need of soft words and tender touches?"

Her step faltered. "No."

As they entered the warmth of the livery, he motioned her to a bench. "Now, that's going to be a problem."

She gingerly sat on the rough wood, her back so straight it dared a sliver to lodge in her backside. He had to wait until her hands were properly folded in her lap before she asked, "Why?"

"Because, I've had it drummed into my head so much, I've grown quite attached to the idea."

"Of ladies?"

He kept his face as straight as an arrow as he answered, "Nah. Just the part about touching them tenderly."

* * * * *

"Repeat after me. Do you, Asa MacIntyre, take Elizabeth Coyote to be your lawfully wedded wife? To honor and protect…"

The words to the ceremony droned in Elizabeth's ears like so many gnats at a picnic. She supposed she should take more notice, but it wasn't like she hadn't been through this before. And there was nothing in Asa's voice as he repeated his vows to cause unease.

He was confident, sure. He'd been that way since Old Sam had pointed him out in the bar. "A man to hitch her wagon to." That's what Sam had said. And since her own taste in men had proven so flawed, she'd burst into Dell's Hair of the Dog, declared herself free of Brent and gambled her future on this one.

From the corner of her eye, she studied his profile. Her soon-to-be, locked-up-as-tight-as-two-dogs-in-a-barrel husband was a handsome man. His square face with that jutting chin would never be called pretty, but there was a no-nonsense strength from within that she found infinitely more appealing than Brent's carefully groomed confidence. Where Brent had strutted, Asa strode. Whereas Brent brayed his successes to all who would listen, Asa wore his experience and strength like an invisible cloak.

She let her gaze wander the dusty courtroom with its tiny tables, makeshift podium and scattering of chairs, and silently chastised herself for a fool to have mistaken Brent for a man. She should have known Old Sam wouldn't have steered her wrong when it came to a husband, and he'd hated Brent on sight. She sighed. Old Sam was an excellent judge of character.

She snuck a peek at Asa again. She really was going to have to work on her judgment. Even if the man hadn't proven his intelligence by stopping by the lawyer's office and confirming her story, her identity, and her rights to the land before heading out of town yesterday, one look into his eyes should have told her he wasn't a man given to foolish risk. That he was a man to count on. The judge's droning took a more staccato note, bringing her out of her reverie. "Do you Elizabeth, take Asa MacIntyre as your lawful husband. To love, honor and obey?"

That was her cue. All she needed was to say two little words, and her ranch had a fighting chance, but God help her, the words wouldn't slide past her lips. She had absolutely no idea if she could love this man. Wasn't even sure she wanted to.

Two, three seconds crept by. Her groom's hand, so casually holding hers, began to tense. She caught her breath, nearly choking on a dust mote. If she didn't promise to love, honor and obey, she'd fail. MacIntyre would disappear to wherever men of his ilk went. She'd lose the ranch, and she'd become the one thing she abhorred. A silly, helpless female. Good for nothing more than tatting pillow trims and waiting on a man's good will. Incapable of doing the most basic thing a son could accomplish; keeping the Rocking C in the Coyote family. She moistened her lips, took a deep breath and tried again. To her dismay, the only thing that came out was a blatant hedge.

"I can promise to try."

"I beg your pardon?"

Well, she'd succeeded in shocking the judge. His fat cheeks were quivering with outrage. Without looking at Asa, she repeated herself. "I said I can try."

She hoped her groom's frown wasn't as heavy as the Judge's, but she wasn't going to draw his displeasure by checking.

"Young lady," Judge Carlson censured. "It's a woman's place to look to her husband for guidance, to follow his lead. It clearly states in the Bible—"

"It'll do." Asa's deep drawl cut the judge's tirade.

"What?"

"I said I'd take an honest try."

Judge Carlson drew himself up to his full height. "Young man, I cannot proceed with this ceremony in good conscience without having my say."

"You serious?" Asa asked in that low drawl that just goaded a listener to react.

Elizabeth shot him a glance. A blind man could see this bloated fool of a judge was serious. He practically vibrated with indignation and moral outrage.

"I most certainly am. I've married more than two hundred couples in my ten years of serving God and country, and I can assure you while the fervor of love that brings a man to the altar can make him overlook the basics, it's always in the best interest of the marriage to start as you mean to continue."

"Seems like that's what we're doing."

The judge cleared his throat, shifted his Bible in his plump hand, then snapped it closed. "I'm afraid, young man, that your bride's reluctance to promise love and obedience bodes ill for your union."

His censure elicited amusement rather than anger in her husband as evidenced by his bland response. "Ever heard the expression, 'you can lead a horse to water but you can't make him drink'?"

"Of course."

"Then I suggest you hitch us up, and let me worry about who'll be wearing the pants in this outfit."

Elizabeth thought the judge was going to refuse. She thought she'd have to lie. Midway to the attempt, her husband's hand tightened painfully on hers. He caught her gaze with his darkly silver one and gave one shake of his head. It was an order to keep silent. She pressed her lips together and swallowed her resentment.

"It's highly irregular and I feel ill-advised, but I'll go along with this request." Elizabeth let out her breath on a sigh of relief, only to suck it back in outrage as the good judge felt compelled to add, "But only because I feel you're a man capable of keeping your wife in line."

"I appreciate the vote of confidence, Judge."

Elizabeth would have dearly loved to kick Asa MacIntyre in the shins. She had to settle for unobtrusively digging her nails into the back of his hand.

His retaliation was swift. "Lift your face, darlin', like a good, obedient wife."

She didn't miss the emphasis on the word obedient. Cursing her promise and the desperateness of her situation, she did as ordered. His lips were planted on hers before she could gasp. She dug her nails deeper. His lips pressed harder. He clearly wasn't going to give ground. Well, neither was she.

Through gritted teeth, she muttered, "The judge."

"Isn't seeing anything he hasn't seen before," Asa drawled, barely removing his lips from hers. "Open your mouth."

Her eyes flew wide at that. Her gaze collided with his. This close, she could see the flecks of slate gray splattering the lighter irises. She could also see Asa MacIntyre was a determined man. She kept her mouth closed.

His finger touched the corner of her mouth. "Open."

"I don't want to."

He drew back a quarter of an inch. His breath intermingled with hers. "I don't remember asking if you wanted to."

It was an order. Clear and simple. Only obeying wasn't simple with the judge watching, and, with the space between their lips yawning like a chasm, almost too great for her modesty to cross. She thought of her ranch. She thought of her father and the duty he'd left her with when he'd died. Her lips parted a hair's breath.

Asa's nose touched hers. "A little more, darlin'."

As soon as the ranch was flourishing, she'd kill him. She opened her mouth a fraction more. If he wanted it any wider, he'd have to get a pry bar.

She soon discovered he didn't need one. Only his tongue, which he slid through the slight opening with shocking smoothness. Her breath caught in her lungs as his taste flooded her mouth. She wanted to hate it, him, but he tasted of coffee and cinnamon. And it wasn't unpleasant. She closed her eyes as he nibbled at her lower lip, sending sparks shooting through her body.

"Kiss me back."

The words drifted into her mouth, his breath becoming hers as he tipped her head back, arching her back over his arm so the suddenly sensitive tips of her breasts pressed into his chest. Against her stomach she could feel the hard ridge of his erection. His tongue traced the full curve of her lower lip, taking her gasp as his own as she caught his shirt front in her grip and tentatively touched his tongue with hers.

"Damn, darlin', I love your mouth," he whispered for her ears alone as the judge cleared his throat.

"May I remind you two that I haven't gotten to the part of the ceremony in which you kiss the bride?"

Asa lifted his head and loosened his hold. "Just getting in some practice."

He didn't look the least embarrassed while Elizabeth wished for a hole to crawl into.

"I'd say you're finished practicing and ready to move on."

Elizabeth opened her mouth to tell the judge what she thought of him. With a tip of his finger, Asa forestalled her plan, shutting her mouth and answering the judge. "Then I suggest we get this wedding underway so the moving on is nice and legal. Ready, darlin'?"

There was absolutely nothing in the man's voice to make her think he was amused, but as sure as she was choking on frustration, she knew Asa MacIntyre was having a good old time. She searched his face for confirmation, but the only indication to his mood was the way his eyes crinkled at the corners.

If he dared laugh out loud, she decided, she'd kill him, and the ranch be damned. She'd found two husbands in as many days. Surely it wouldn't be that hard to locate a third. He didn't laugh, more the pity, and his vows were clear as a bell.

Never hesitate, girl, or you'll show yourself for the weak female you are.

Her father's voice rang in her ears. She locked her gaze with MacIntyre's and made sure her vows were just as clear. She didn't let herself think of anything beyond the moment, otherwise she knew she'd crumble into a useless ball of waffling indecision. Just when she didn't think she could stand anymore, Judge Carlson snapped his Bible shut.

"I now pronounce you man and wife. You may kiss the bride."

As Asa placed his lips on hers, a shiver went down her spine.

The ranch was safe. Now there was only the price to pay.

Chapter Three

ജ

They arrived at the ranch at sundown. Even to Elizabeth's loving eyes, the two-story ranch house looked bad. The place was in such a dire need of white wash, it was the dingy gray of poorly washed linens. The repair she'd made on the front steps fell in a shadow, which only served to enhance how much she'd botched that particular job. Someone had left the supplies on the porch, and chickens were now pecking at the dried corn scattered over the wood porch. One of the dogs or a coon had gotten into the bag of bacon, and, in search of more, had torn open the rest of the sacks. She wanted to cry. Instead, she squared her shoulders, and said, "I'm sorry."

"It's a nice setting with those mountains in the background."

The tactful response surprised her.

"Father said my Mamma called those mountains our Guardians. That they loomed over us like that to scare away evil."

"Yup. They could sure do that."

The buckboard stopped at the watering trough in front of the barn. The thirsty horse blew over the water. Asa's horse, tied behind, whinnied hopefully. Asa jumped down and strode around front.

"Could you hop down and bring Shameless up with old Willoughby here?"

Catching her skirts in hand, she did as asked. "I didn't know his name was Willoughby."

"Occurred to me on the ride here that he had the look of a Willoughby."

49

As she brought his horse up beside the other, she couldn't help asking, "What does a Willoughby look like?"

He handed her the reins of the horse harnessed to the buckboard. "Like this."

He didn't smile as he said it and, this close to the trough, she could see why. The water was brackish with bits of green slime drifting across the surface. She wanted the ground to open up and swallow her.

"I gave orders..."

She let the disclaimer trail off as Asa headed for the well pump. What did it matter if she gave orders? The fact that her hands had allowed the horse's water to stand this long was humiliating testimony as to what they thought of her authority.

He returned with two buckets and set one in front of each horse. She tightened her grip on Shameless' reins. Whatever angle her husband wished to attack from, she had no defense. The ranch was a mess. She'd failed to control anything.

His finger tipped her face to his in a gesture that was becoming familiar. She fought the urge to close her eyes. She deserved this.

"You scooting my gaze because you're embarrassed?"

"Wouldn't you be?"

"Yeah, but I'm not a woman trying to keep a ranch together by myself."

Willoughby jerked his head free to reach the water. She jerked her chin out of Asa's reach with no less urgency. Grinding her teeth for control, she shoved the reins into his hands. Useless. The man saw her as useless. "From the quiet, the men haven't ridden in yet."

"How many are there?"

"Ten when I left."

His left eyebrow rose. "Should I be expecting more or less?"

She pulled off her gloves one finger at a time before answering. "I have no idea. Would you like me to introduce you when they get here?"

"Morning'll be soon enough."

She took a deep breath, shoved her gloves in her reticule, and wished he were given to excessive speech. At least that way she'd know what he was thinking. And where she needed to bolster her defenses.

"Why don't you head into the house and rustle up some dinner while I get Willoughby and Shameless settled?"

Resentment swept over her in waves at his dismissal. But what did she expect? Respect? When his first view of her home showed the level of her failure?

"Would you prefer steak or ham?" she asked carefully as he led the horses away.

He stopped so quickly, Shameless bumped him with his head. He went forward two steps before asking, "You got any syrup to go with that ham?"

"I think so."

Shameless bumped him with his nose, anxious to get to the barn. Asa didn't budge. She remembered his tactful reaction to the shambles of the ranch and softened despite herself. "Would you care for anything special?"

"Mashed potatoes?"

Mashed potatoes were as common as day old bread, but he made the request with the same awe a miner would demonstrate when confronted with the specter of a two-pound nugget. She ran her gaze over Asa from his head to his toes. He was a big man. Last night, he'd had a dinner equal to hers in size. She remembered how quickly he'd demolished it. How closely he'd watched her finish hers. She remembered how he'd taken on Brent.

"I could probably manage potatoes."

His free hand went to the front of his body. "I'd be obliged."

She studied him with new eyes. His chestnut brown hair, long overdue for a cut, curled over the collar of his shirt. His clothes were practical, but, on closer scrutiny, worn threadbare in places. He was tall and big-boned, no doubt about it, but now she wondered if his leanness came naturally or from lack of proper food.

"If the coons didn't get to the good corn, I could probably put together some Johnny cake," she offered, wondering if the reason she couldn't see his hand was because he was clutching his stomach.

This time it was Willoughby who bumped Asa. Again, he didn't budge. She might have been imagining it, but there seemed a vulnerability to his stance as he mentioned casually, "Red-eye gravy would sure taste good with that Johnny cake."

"Gravy might be possible." Provided she could find some leftover coffee.

"I'll be looking forward to it."

He still didn't face her, but instead of lumbering, the horses had to trot to catch up as he headed for the barn. Some of her frustration faded to amusement as it became apparent that Asa clearly viewed her as invaluable in one area of the ranch.

"You're taking an awful risk, MacIntyre," she called out, "assuming I can cook."

"I'm hoping, darlin'. I sure am hoping."

With a smile on her face, she spun on her heel and hurried to the house, deciding the blackberries she'd picked before she'd left could go into a cobbler. That way, she'd at least have dessert to offer.

* * * * *

Elizabeth used the hem of her apron to wipe the water from her hands. Supper was set and simmering. And so was she. Despite the breeze coming through the open door, the kitchen was a humid inferno. A glance out the window revealed dusk snuggling up to the empty yard. Past the thick trunked oak tree, she spotted the chicken coop. No hens pecked outside. As was their habit, they were probably inside, waiting for her to lock them in safe for the night.

She wished she had the same option, but, come nightfall, the first payment on her debt would begin. No matter how much she told herself it was no big thing, that women all over the world did this every day, she was nervous. Scared spitless as a matter of fact. And it wasn't just because she didn't know if MacIntyre was mean in bed or not. That was actually the least of her worries. More than anything, she was terrified that, in her ignorance, she'd do something on her wedding night so totally stupid, the man would be laughing for months to come. Lord, she hated appearing incompetent.

She checked the simmering potatoes, poking them a little harder than necessary. The fork bounced off one without even gouging a hole. She replaced the fork on the table next to the stove and scanned the yard again. She had a good fifteen minutes before she needed to slide the corn bread in the oven. In that time, she could gather the morning's eggs and have them on hand for breakfast. Of course, getting the eggs meant crossing the yard, which, since her father's death, was tantamount to entering enemy territory. The trickle of fear that sent her heart tapping in her throat renewed her determination. Dammit! She would not be made a prisoner in her own house.

Grabbing the egg basket from a peg by the door, she stepped onto the back porch, pausing to let the evening breeze caress her cheeks. The sounds of the approaching night enfolded her and she relaxed into its embrace. Here and there, a cricket chirped. Soon, the night would be filled with their loud chorus, but for now, the sound was calm. Peaceful. Almost like a promise of better things to come.

She closed her eyes, wallowing in the remnant of a promise that enfolded her like the memory of her mother's hug. Lord, she hoped things were going to be better. She'd never been so scared or gambled so high as when she'd walked into Dell's and asked Asa Macintyre to marry her. She still couldn't believe she'd done it, but desperate times called for desperate measures.

The only consolation was that, unlike Brent who'd lied and hidden his true personality behind a polite facade of manly attributes, Asa was the real thing. Whatever else he turned out to be, she knew he had the ability to run this ranch. Asa MacIntyre had the heart, the determination, and the reputation to take the Rocking C back into prosperity. At least, she hoped so.

Doubt swirled from its hiding place deep inside, sneaking up on her blind side. For a second, every decision she'd made came back to haunt her, swamping her in insecurity, until, with a relentless maneuver born from long practice, she shoved it back down. She opened her eyes and surveyed the yard and outbuildings. This was her home. The place her mother had called her sanctuary. The place where she, Elizabeth Ann Coyote, had been born.

On this porch, she'd stood as a small child with her mother, holding hands, staring at the small oak sapling, and listened with wide-eyed wonder to the story of how, with love and nurturing, it would grow into a tree capable of protecting them and guiding them. Her father had said it was going to die and that they were wasting time babying it along, but her mother had merely leaned down and whispered in her ear to believe. She'd watered that tree every day from then on, wanting to do just that. And it had grown. Year after year, a living testament to love and determination.

She ran fond eyes over the oak's silhouette, remembering and smiling. As a child, she'd been frustrated with its slow progress. As an adult, she'd been in awe of what its steady determination to thrive had accomplished. Today, it stood a good thirty feet, and where it had once thrown dappled shadows, it now delivered full shade.

Whenever life got complicated, she remembered her mother and that tree. Both had faced the odds and made a place for themselves. So had she, and it wasn't back East or in a fancy town. Her roots were firmly sunk in the Rocking C with its wide-open spaces, constant challenges, and relentless demands. Like that tree, she thrived here.

And she was going to stay. She was determined. Marrying Asa had been the right thing to do. She knew it in her gut. All she needed to do to succeed was to believe her course was right, and to be strong enough and determined enough to see it through. She looked at the basket clenched tightly in her hand. That strength and determination included getting eggs from the hen house so she'd have something to offer her husband for a wedding breakfast.

Peace faded to unease. She searched the yard again. It appeared empty. Still, she hesitated. Ever since her father had died, the ranch foreman had been playing with her like a cat with a mouse. Cornering her when no one else was around, taking liberties, each time going further than the last. At first, she'd thought she could handle it, but he'd gotten worse. She'd thought of complaining, but removing Jimmy wouldn't remove the threat. A woman alone, unfortunately more often than not, was seen as a target, so she'd done the sensible thing. She'd stepped up her search for a husband.

Her haste, however, had cost her. By not questioning Brent close enough, she'd created a bigger disaster by buying into his pack of lies. Hopefully, she'd cleaned up that mess because, if not, her goose was truly cooked. No one, she thought, as she peered into the darkness under the tree, was going to quietly sit back and watch her pluck a third husband from the scanty pile of eligible men passing through town.

She nearly dropped her basket when she thought she saw a shadow move beneath the spreading arms of the huge oak. The hairs on her nape leapt to attention. She took a breath to still the butterflies in her stomach as she carefully scrutinized the area. Nothing moved except the leaves swaying with the light breeze. About the time her lungs threatened to burst, she decided she'd confused the motion of the wind with the malevolent mannerisms of the ranch foreman.

She released her breath on an audible sigh. Relief from the constant threat of Jimmy Dunn was one of the benefits she hoped to reap from having Macintyre as a husband. Whatever his faults were, she was sure Asa wasn't the type to ignore a man bothering his wife. Even if the man was a big, blond, belligerent, fighting type.

No, she decided, recalling her husband's reputation and broad shoulders. Jimmy wouldn't scare a man like Asa. She tightened her grip on her basket, stepped off the porch, and reminded herself again that she'd done the right thing in marrying Asa MacIntyre. He was big and mean, and more than capable of handling threats to the ranch, whether they came in the form of rustlers or overly familiar foremen.

Her steps slowed as she skirted the shadows stretching from the oak. She sucked her lower lip between her teeth and chewed as she realized there was no reason for Asa to believe her if she screamed and he caught her in a compromising position with Jimmy. They hadn't had enough time to establish any trust or knowledge of each other. If the opportunity ever came up where she needed to explain her difficulties with the foreman, she'd have to choose her words carefully. She didn't need the complication of a husband jumping to conclusions.

Two steps from the hen house, a heavy hand slapped down on her shoulder, driving her teeth into her lip. She didn't have time to toss retrospection aside in favor of alarm before she was pulled against a large, male body. As the scent of liquor and sweat assaulted her nostrils, reality hit. For one crippling moment, she didn't know what to do.

"Hello, Elly." His voice, as always, was a soft drawl of sound. Low and intimate, as if there were only sweet secrets between them. It was as much crap as the chicken droppings she stood on.

"Let me go, Jimmy."

His answer was scary in its brevity. "No."

She looked into his bloodshot, blue eyes, felt his fingers biting painfully into her upper arm, and understood one truth with crystal clarity. Whatever her future held with Asa, it had to be better than this.

"I told you I'd be here for you," Jimmy continued his parody of a lover's voice.

Elizabeth tugged on her arm. Instead of letting go, he tightened his grip. She could have shot herself for wincing when his smile broadened.

"Did you miss me?" he asked, his eyes narrowing, the lines beside them fanning out in an evil mockery of laughter.

She swallowed back a "Hell, no." Above all, she knew she needed to keep control. She couldn't let the shaking inside spread to anywhere he could see. Oh, God! She was so sick of this. His fingers sank deeper into her flesh. Pain constricted her throat as his thumb ground into her collarbone. She wanted to scream blue murder. She wanted to rage and swear. Instead, she had to settle for forcing an off-putting "Excuse me," through her pain-clogged throat.

Jimmy's smile expanded to let her know it wasn't enough. It was never going to be enough.

* * * * *

Asa came around the side of the barn, drawn to the kitchen's back door by the tantalizing odors drifting on the evening air. He hadn't tasted a home-cooked meal in a coon's age. He'd dallied a couple of hours in the barn, trying to give his wife some time alone, but a man could only hold out so long against aromas like that. At least he'd put the time to good use, checking the lay of the land. It was clear the hands had been slacking off, just as it was clear Elizabeth had been doing her best to pick up that slack. Two things he could say for sure about his wife. She wasn't lazy, and she wasn't worth a plugged nickel when it came to carpentry.

A very controlled "Excuse me" from the other side of the hen house pulled him up short.

He'd recognize that icy tone of voice anywhere. His wife was in a snit about something. He decided to keep the coop between them until he discovered what it was. His stomach growled, agreeing that they didn't want any backlash that might affect the quality of their meal.

"Move out of my way, Jimmy."

A slow curl of anger unfurled that the person his wife was facing was a man.

"I don't think so, Elly."

"That's Miss Coyote to you."

He made a mental note to remind her she was Mrs. MacIntyre now.

"I like Elly a lot better." The man's voice dropped to an insinuating whisper. "It's more…friendly."

"I told you the last time you cornered me, Jimmy, that if you ever did it again, you'd be fired."

"But you're married now, Elly." A soft thump announced something landing against the other side of the hen house. "You don't have the power to fire me."

"My husband does. He'll be heading this way any minute."

"That little piss-ant gambler isn't going to do squat. And you know it."

"He will!"

"Then why don't you scream for him?"

That's what Asa wanted to know as he headed to the rescue. He heard a gasp, then a man's muttered curse of pain. "Bite me, will you, hellcat?"

Asa was around the corner of the hen house before the last syllable died, and what he saw drove reason from his head. The cowhand had his fingers dug into his wife's breast. He was using it to hold her pinned to the rough wall. The other arm, he was shaking, trying to dislodge her teeth from his wrist.

With a sharp blow of his hand, Asa broke Jimmy's grip on his wife. Before he could follow with a second, Elizabeth was between them. She drove the hard toe of her boot into her tormentor's groin and Jimmy doubled over. Elizabeth was on him with the ferocity of a badger. Her hair tumbled out of its bun as she grabbed a chunk of firewood and walloped the man on the back. Her breath hissed between her teeth, punctuated with violent mutterings. As Jimmy dropped to his knees, Asa took a step back.

His wife clearly had the situation in hand.

He shook his head as she walked in front of the convulsed man. The move clearly showed her a green horn at this kind of thing. He caught her arm. When she spun around, wood raised, he plucked it from her hand.

"Shh," he soothed, pulling her into his arms. "It's all right."

Instead of fainting with relief like he expected, she struggled. "Let me go."

"Why?"

"I want to kick him in his filthy mouth."

Asa eyed Jimmy. "Not now you don't."

"Yes, I—"

The sounds of violent retching cut off her claim.

She stood stiffly in his arms. "Well, maybe not now."

"I'd be saving it for later." He looked down at the undulating waves of hair that fell over his arms, reinforcing the impression of dainty femininity his body was responding to. He smiled. "Were you planning on leaving a piece of him for me to whale on?"

"No." The answer vibrated dead center below his breastbone.

"Good thing I stepped in then."

That brought her gaze to his. Instead of the tears he expected, he saw an open challenge that baffled him. He turned his attention to something he did understand.

From the sound of things, Jimmy was about done puking up his guts. Asa set Elizabeth carefully away from him. He kept his hands on her shoulders until he was sure she wasn't going to keel over. She was as steady as a rock, leaving the comforting words he intended to say sitting awkwardly on his tongue.

"You came out here looking for eggs?"

She nodded, catching the fall of hair into her hands and twisting it into a knot at the base of her neck. He didn't miss her wince as she moved her right shoulder. The bastard had probably hurt her good.

"Why don't you go get them while I clean up around here?"

He grabbed Jimmy by the collar and hauled him to his feet. As she straightened from retrieving her basket, he called her name. She paused and looked up.

"Next time you even think some yahoo's backing you into a corner, I want you screaming loud enough to do a banshee proud."

She merely nodded.

"And Elizabeth?"

"Yes."

"You're Mrs. MacIntyre now."

Beyond a thinning of her lips, she didn't respond.

Asa wondered if he'd ever understand his wife. Yanking Jimmy in front of him, he headed for the barn. Besides teaching this yellow bastard some manners, he needed to let loose some frustration.

* * * * *

Supper wasn't the friendly meal he'd been hoping for. By the time Asa finished his third helping of cobbler, he felt like he sat in the middle of a powder keg. To make it worse, Elizabeth kept shooting him glances he didn't understand. He couldn't tell if she was angry or upset, but remembering her temper, he sure as shooting didn't want to risk it being the former. Not on his wedding night, so if his mouth wasn't chomping on food, he kept it closed.

"Would you care for more cobbler?" she asked from her side of the table.

"No. Thank you." He placed his napkin beside his plate, wincing as he did so. Two fights in one day were hell on his knuckles.

"We have an ice house," she offered.

"What?"

"I said if you'd like to soak your hands, there's probably enough ice for you to do it."

He'd heard of ice houses, sure, but he'd never experienced the luxury of ice in August. He wasn't about to pass it up. "That would sure be appreciated."

Ten minutes later, she was back. In her hands was a large tin basin that made bell-like tinkles as she walked. He kept his expression bland, not wanting to appear a bumpkin. She placed the basin before him on the table. Before he could lift his hands, she had them in hers. Each one was carefully inspected before she placed it in the basin. Her face was tight as she pushed his right hand under the chilled water and said, "Thank you."

Since there was no telling what she was feeling from her expression, he replied with the truth. "It was my pleasure."

Within a couple of minutes, the cold water was doing its job. "Damn, this is good," he groaned on a complacent sigh.

She reached around him to collect the plates. "They don't hurt anymore?"

"No."

Her breast, plump and tempting, came into view as she removed her cup, reminding him of her injuries. He cleared his throat, not sure how to bring up the subject. She stared at him, waiting for him to speak, his dirty dishes in her hands.

"What about you?"

"Excuse me?"

"Did you soak your…er…did you treat your…uhm."

Her face flamed bright red, leaving no doubt she understood. She shrugged, grimaced and muttered a hasty, "I'm fine."

The bruise around her eye showed a revolting green against the bright red of her cheeks. It didn't take schooling to know the woman hadn't treated her own injuries. Hell. When had she had the time? She'd cooked him dinner with all that he'd asked for and then some. She'd fetched ice for his hands, and now she was cleaning up. Damn. As a husband, he wasn't exactly outshining the competition.

"Put those dishes down and come here."

"If you don't mind, I'd rather get to them before the gravy hardens."

"I mind."

Her back to him, she dropped the plates into a basin set beside the stove. "That's probably because you won't have to scrub them in the morning," she muttered.

He heard even though he bet he wasn't supposed to. "I wasn't making conversation, darlin'."

She faced him, daring him.

"Come here."

He'd seen grubs cross meadows faster than she got to his side.

With his foot, he snagged a chair and hauled it kitty corner to his own. "Sit down."

She did with stiff-backed reluctance. "I'm fine, you know."

"You're sore."

"Of course, I'm sore."

"I'm sorry I didn't act sooner."

"You got there soon enough."

Not in his opinion, but he was grateful she wasn't screaming to point that out. One thing was for sure, his wife wasn't bearing out the rumor that ladies were delicate. Hot on the heels of that thought came the image of Jimmy's hand against Elizabeth's breast. The cruelty on the bastard's face lingered in his mind. Damn! No telling how much harm had been done. He pulled his hand out of the water and gingerly touched her breast. She gasped and shrank back into the chair.

"What are you doing?" If her face got any redder, she'd explode.

"I'm taking care of you."

"I can take care of myself."

"You have a husband now. You don't have to." He stood, using his height to keep her from bolting. "What in hell do you have on under this dress?"

"It's called a corset."

He traced the ridges until they stopped at her waist. Hell! She was trussed up tighter than a Christmas goose. "You got a broken rib or something?"

"No. It's an...unmentionable."

He wouldn't mention it either if he were dumb enough to let someone harness him into anything as uncomfortable as what he was touching. He didn't claim to have many dealings with decent women, and the women he did sport with normally weren't wearing anything that got in the way of business, but common sense said a body didn't cage itself to the point of pain.

"You wear this often?"

"No decent woman would leave the house without it. Could you please remove your hand?"

He looked at her closely. "Am I hurting you?"

She swallowed twice before she managed the lie. "Yes."

He moved his hand gently under her breast. It probably labeled him a bastard, but the feel of that soft resilient flesh curving into his palm had his cock painfully hard and straining. Near as he could tell, the iron-like contraption she called a corset wrapped under each breast, imprisoning it. He remembered Jimmy's grip, the way he'd ground her flesh around. "Shit. Why didn't you tell me you were hurt that bad?"

She didn't offer an answer. "Please take your hand away."

He did, but only to set to work on the buttons of her dress. Her hands caught his.

"Please."

"I aim to see how bad that bastard hurt you."

"I'm fine."

"Prove it."

She closed her eyes. When she opened them, the wildness was gone. Poker-faced, she asked, "Is that an order?"

"Yes."

In the controlled voice he remembered from Dell's, she asked, "Do you mean to strip me bare in the kitchen or could I move to the privacy of the bedroom?"

His neck heated as he realized, with the kerosene lamps burning, anyone could see into the kitchen. He cleared his throat. "The bedroom is fine."

"Could I be allowed a moment of privacy or would you like to tear my dress off yourself?"

The disdain in her voice flicked him on a raw spot. He was tempted to strip her just to prove who was boss, but then he remembered she was a woman married to a stranger and this was her wedding night. To top it off, she'd just been accosted.

He nodded to the bedroom. "I'll be there in five minutes."

* * * * *

Instead of five minutes, he gave her ten. From the expression on her face when he walked into the room, that might have been a mistake. She looked like a cornered wildcat, ready to lash out at the least provocation. Considering the direction his thoughts had taken while waiting for time to pass, he'd probably give her provocation aplenty.

"It's been longer than five minutes," she growled from the rocking chair where she sat hunched, a sheet clutched so tight in her hands, her knuckles were white.

"Must be my watch stopped."

Her chin came up and her back straightened. "Do you even own one?"

"Nope." He closed the door behind him. A glance at the window revealed the yellow drapes were pulled tight. Three strides brought him to her side. She took a shuddering breath. Pity touched his heart. "You know, if a stranger walked up to me and asked me to drop my pants, I'd be hard put not to put a bullet between his eyes."

Her smile was feral. "Apparently, we're alike, Mr. MacIntyre, because, at this moment, I would very much enjoy putting a bullet in you."

He snagged a finger under the sheet where it touched the bottom of her chin. "I imagine you would." He tugged gently. She took one deep breath and never let it out. The sheet slowly expanded, sliding off her shoulders. When it pooled around her waist, he ordered, "Breathe."

"I could hate you for this."

"I bet you could." Truth was, she didn't have much to hate him for. He couldn't see beyond the frilly bits of material that cupped her breasts, the ruffled lace shuddering against her pale skin as she fought to keep her breathing even. He touched a ridge of what he supposed was her corset. "I thought I told you to get rid of this."

She glared at him. "You told me to take off my dress so you could see my bruises."

He smiled at her hair splitting. "So I did."

He slid his finger under the bit of lace. She stared at a point beyond his shoulder as he pulled it away from her skin. The exposed nipple puckered immediately. It was a very tempting sight. He touched the tip of his finger to the tip of her breast. "I'm not going to hurt you."

"It wouldn't matter if you did."

"No. I suppose it wouldn't." And that was a hell of a note on which to start his wedding night. He pinched her nipple delicately. Her eyes flew to his and her lips shaped around a soundless "Oh."

He made a mental note of her sensitivity while his free hand coaxed her lower body closer to his. It was his turn to groan when her soft belly cuddled his cock. The heat of her skin scorched him through his denim. As a result, his grip on her nipple tightened. She jerked in reaction, her body surging against his creating an exquisite friction that had him clenching his teeth. He wanted that nipple in his mouth. Between his teeth. He wanted his cock buried deep in her sweet cunt, relishing her climax as he bit down lightly. He twisted her nipple gently before reluctantly letting her go to tug on the edge of the corset.

"This contraption is going to have to come off." His voice was a hoarse parody of his normal drawl.

She sucked in another shuddering breath, but didn't pull away. "Why can't you take my word for this?"

"I'm not the trusting sort." And he very badly wanted to see her breasts.

"Just my luck," she answered sarcastically.

He smiled, regaining his voice. "You married a very thorough man, darlin'."

He snuggled his finger into the valley between her breasts beneath the corset. A quick tug emphasized his order to stand up. His opinion of his bride went up as she did as he ordered. Were their places switched, he didn't know if he'd have been capable of such control.

"Let go of the sheet."

He could tell she tried. He took pity on her. After all, modesty wasn't a bad quality for a man's wife to possess.

"Cotton can be a bit mule-tempered, can't it?"

Instead of soothing her, the softness of his voice set loose her temper.

"Damn you! Stop torturing me." She threw the sheet to the floor. He only had a second to appreciate the generous curves emphasized by her undergarment before she was muttering, twisting this way and that, yanking on ties he couldn't see and tossing the corset in this face.

"You wanted the corset? There it is!"

He pulled the stiff garment away from his face. The spot where it had struck above his eye stung. "I guess if you can move like that, you weren't hurt too bad."

She stamped her foot, causing her breasts to bounce enticingly. "I believe I already told you that."

He brought the corset to his nose, breathing her scent. "So you did." He tossed the garment to the floor.

He knew the precise moment her anger gave way to caution. It was when he sat on the bed and took off his left boot. When it dropped to the floor, her pulse took to racing in her throat, but she didn't move to cover herself with her hands.

"I don't suppose there's any point in asking you to wait until we get to know one another?"

"Nope. Seeing you get rid of one husband due to lack of performance doesn't incline me in that direction."

She sighed and clenched her hands into fists. "I was afraid of that."

He dropped his other boot to the floor and tugged off his socks. "Anything else you're afraid of while we're on the subject?"

Her chin came up. "Would it make any difference if there were?"

He stuffed his socks in his boots and patted the bed beside him. "Come here."

Her chin came up another notch. "Is that an order?"

"Nope. That was more in the line of a request."

"Why?"

"Because I thought you might like to talk a bit."

"I wasn't aware talking was part of," she waved her hand descriptively, "this."

"Now that we're on the subject, just what do you know of 'this'?"

"Enough." Her arms crossed over her chest. "I've seen animals procreating."

He could imagine what that impression left her braced for. "Any chance you caught a glimpse of your folks?"

Her response was an emphatic, "No."

"Any chance you've done any of this before?" he asked as he unbuttoned his shirt.

"Are you calling me loose?" She looked ready to throw the wash basin at him.

"Hell, no! I was just checking the level of your experience."

"Any gaps in my experience are more than made up through observation and practical intelligence."

The woman was holding onto her composure through sheer willpower, but he'd eat boot leather if her "observations and practical intelligence" had her anywhere near the reality of his lovemaking.

Her "Could we just get this over with now?" interrupted his thoughts.

He got to his feet, dropped his shirt to the floor, and pulled her into his arms. She stood stiff as a board. He smiled at the silent protest. "Going down fighting, huh?"

He wasn't surprised when she didn't answer. He stroked his hand down her hair, working it loose from its makeshift knot.

"I won't lie to you, Elizabeth," he said as her hair spilled down her back and over his hand like liquid silk. "I am going to make love to you tonight. Most of the things I'm going to do will embarrass you. Some of them, hopefully, will make you feel good. A few might scare you, but nothing I intend is supposed to hurt. If it does, you have my permission to wallop me and scream blue murder."

He thought the snort that preceded her "A lot of good that will do me," might have been laughter. He tugged on her hair, hoping to see her face. She had damn strong neck muscles.

"I'm not looking at you," she informed him when he tugged again.

"Why?"

"Because I want to talk."

"About what?"

"I want to know about the scary things."

"Not the ones that'll make you feel good?"

"If they feel good, I'm not going to mind them, am I?"

"No arguing your logic, darlin'."

"So?"

"Well, it's going to be tough to pick them out random-like."

"I'd prefer if you didn't need to hit me."

Aw, shit! He rested his chin on top of her head, remembering what the gambler had done. "I don't hit, darlin'."

"Then what do you do?"

He rocked them subtly, enjoying the drag of her pert nipples across his skin, amazed she was still in his arms, terrified as she must be. Facing down a man in a bedroom wasn't something most ladies were schooled in. "I usually start with kissing."

"On the mouth?"

"Yeah, but I imagine I'll work my way down to your neck and then your…" He couldn't think of a word that wasn't offensive, so he just plunged in with the truth, "your breasts."

"You want to put your mouth on my bosom?" Her scandalized whisper seared his skin.

"Yeah," he confirmed huskily. "I'd definitely want to do that."

Her forehead rubbed back and forth against his chest as she thought on that. "You wouldn't bite?"

Lord above! What kind of animal did she think he was! "You might feel my teeth a time or two, but no. I'm not the biting kind."

He thought she relaxed a bit. "How would you do it?"

She was killing him with the images she brought to mind. His cock was so hard, he was afraid he'd shatter. He couldn't resist dragging his thumb across the plump nipple so close to his hand. It might have been his imagination, but he thought she pressed closer. "I'd start out real gentle-like, brushing my lips across your nipple. A woman can be very sensitive there."

She slapped him on the chest. Not hard enough to hurt, but it definitely got his attention. "I meant how would you do...'it'."

He remembered her reference to animals and smiled despite himself. "There are many ways for a man and woman to enjoy each other, but this first time, I think I'll settle on the standard."

"I don't know what that is."

Tenderness overwhelmed him. It must've just about killed her to admit that. His wife was a proud woman, and he was a jackass for teasing her. He resumed his stroking of her hair. "Basically, you lie on your back and I come over you." He cleared his throat, feeling the back of his neck heating. "Between your legs," he clarified.

"Oh."

"Do you have anymore questions?"

She nodded.

"What then?"

"Are you sure you wouldn't rather wait?"

After talking about it this long, she'd be lucky if he waited until he got to the bed. "I'm positive."

"Then could we just get it over with?"

He slid the straps of her camisole off her shoulders. "I hate to burst your bubble, darlin', but a thorough man doesn't hurry on his wedding night."

If he hadn't found it so amusing, her softly uttered "rats" would have ground his confidence into dust.

Chapter Four

❧

No, Elizabeth decided as Asa stared at her bosom, he definitely wasn't a hurrying man. She'd had her eyes closed for three counts of fifty, and he still hadn't progressed past the looking part. She took a deep breath. It caught halfway down her parched throat and sent her into a coughing fit. She would have latched onto the distraction if her husband hadn't decided to cure her fit with well-placed slaps between her shoulder blades, the first of which sent her straight into dangerous territory. The bed.

She hovered on the brink of indecision. The second slap sent her plopping down onto the mattress. The corn husks rasped in tune with her labored breathing. From the corner of her eye, she saw Asa's concerned frown and upraised hand.

"Water," she managed between chokes.

"Of course." He was out of the room as quickly as he'd entered. In the seconds before he returned, she managed to yank up her camisole and wrap the coverlet around her torso. She took the glass he offered. The cool water eased her throat. She wished it could do the same for her nerves. "Thank you."

She would have held onto the glass for whatever protection it offered, but he took it from her. "You're welcome."

His gaze fell to the coverlet hiding her bosom from view. She couldn't read his expression, but not for one minute did she want him to think she was afraid. "I was cold."

The way his lips quirked made mincemeat of her ruse. "Then why don't you slide under the covers, darlin'?"

Because she was stalling, and they both knew it. "I wouldn't want to start another coughing fit."

"No," he agreed, setting the glass on the bed stand. "We wouldn't want that."

The quirk of his lips was definitely a grin. She didn't care. He could laugh at her all he wanted as long as he was willing to indulge her.

"Well," she began, only to decide she didn't know where to go with the conversation. She shifted her weight on the mattress. The corn husks whispered a protest. Asa took it as an invitation. Their protest was twice as loud when he sat beside her. Her breath caught when he slid an arm around her waist and she forced it out as he tugged her against his side. She would not be a coward about this. She'd made a deal and she'd live up to her end. She held perfectly still for his next move.

"I don't suppose you'd feel any better if I told you that what's going to happen between us is perfectly natural? That our bodies are made to fit together?" he asked.

"No."

The side of his chest pushed against her shoulder as he sighed. "I didn't think so."

His hand pressed against her head. She resisted, but he kept at it until her cheek found the hollow of his shoulder. She didn't know why the man thought that holding her close was going to soothe her, but he did.

"I'm not comfortable," she said.

"Then relax."

Since it was either that or have her neck snap, she did. A quick peek showed his gaze fastened on the flame of the oil lamp. His hand began stroking her hair. Gentle, light touches that started awkward but soon changed to comfortable. The silence stretched as tight as her nerves.

"I don't have any choice in this," he said, an apology coached in the bald statement. "You could wake up tomorrow and change your mind."

"Yes." And the ranch would go to the bank next month. She wouldn't have her home. She would have failed in her duty, and she would have failed herself. Lord, she was weak enough to think, as a solution, it wasn't so bad.

Beneath her ear, Asa's chest rose and fell with his even breathing. His fingers slid from her hair and explored the tops of her bare shoulders. She controlled the urge to cringe.

The rhythm of his breathing broke as he sighed, "Damn, I'm a selfish bastard."

"Why?"

"Because I could chance that you won't change your mind and give you time."

She looked into his face. His grim expression squashed her small hope. "But you won't," she concluded out loud before asking, "Why?"

He had to know she was looking at him, but he didn't take his gaze from the steady flame of the lamp. "Three reasons. First off, if I do get killed holding onto this ranch, you'd be back where you started with your ranch up for grabs to whoever lands you at the altar."

"I don't understand what that has to do with consummating our vows."

His free hand cupped her belly through the bunched up quilt. "If you had a baby, the child would inherit when he grew up, not your next husband."

"If there was anything left to inherit," she pointed out.

The pressure of his fingers increased. For absolutely no reason, she found it protective. "There's always risks, but it's the best odds you've got."

As he was the best bet she had against losing it all. The similarity in their thinking was comforting. "You said there were three reasons?"

No mistake, the hand on her stomach was protective. And possessive. "The thought of a little one of my own has been nagging at me."

"You want a son." That she could understand. Her father had spent his whole life on two pursuits; building the ranch and getting a son.

"I'll admit you dropping a delicate little girl first time off scares the beejezus out of me, but I expect I'd manage."

She just bet it scared him. Men were obsessed with sons. "I'll have you know, Mr. MacIntyre, women do not do anything as indelicate as 'drop' babies."

"Well, you tell me the correct word and I'll use it."

"It's not something that's discussed."

That got his attention away from the lamp. "If we're not to discuss it, how am I to know when you get in the family way? Or if you need something when you do get that way?"

It was obvious he found the situation amusing while her cheeks were burning from the direction of the conversation. "I'm sure something will occur to me if the time ever comes," she said through gritted teeth. "You mentioned a third reason?"

The corn husks rustled as he shifted to face her. His hands contracted in the quilt. "The only thing I've been thinking about since you laid out that fancy gambler is the way a man gets a woman pregnant." The quilt started to loosen as he pulled. "And how much I wanted to do that with you."

She closed her eyes. The time had come.

The tugging stopped. The loose hair on her forehead parted on his slow exhale. "That," he admitted in a low voice, "and how much a bastard I feel for forcing this issue."

She opened her eyes. Her gaze collided with his. He was going to stop. Instead of the relief she expected to feel, there was only an onslaught of terror. She couldn't lose her home! Just as she couldn't lose her last chance, because it suddenly occurred to her that, come morning, she wasn't the only one who could walk away. While she loved this place with an intensity that went back to her grandfather, Mr. MacIntyre's ties were only cemented in the nebulous hope of future profit.

She wet her lips and schooled her expression to calm. "You aren't forcing anything."

He shook his head and touched his index finger to her knuckles. "Darlin', were you willing, you wouldn't be popping the stitches in that quilt."

She looked down. Her knuckles showed white through her skin. "I'm just nervous," she explained. She counted to ten, and one by one, willed her fingers to relax. "I'm perfectly willing."

He tugged on the quilt. She reflexively tightened her grip.

"I can see that." His lips quirked again.

She straightened her spine and released the quilt. "I'm perfectly ready to uphold my end of the bargain, Mr. MacIntyre. I just don't see why you insist on disrobing."

His left eyebrow quirked up. "Because it's more fun that way?"

She tossed her head. The quilt started to slip. "I fail to see where extreme mortification would be fun." By widening her elbows, she was able to stop the quilt's decent. "Until we get to know one another, do you think we could perform our duties modestly clothed?"

His expression went from amusement to shock and then back to amusement in the time it took her to take a hopeful breath.

"I see no reason why we need to abandon decorum," she growled, piqued.

"Decorum?" he asked, his right eyebrow lifting to join the left.

She cautiously waved one hand between them. "Decorum. You know, a polite respect for each other's sensibilities?"

"No. I didn't know." He rubbed his hand across his mouth. Elizabeth had a sneaky suspicion he was hiding a grin. She set her chin a bit higher. She fully intended to hang onto her dignity and, the sooner he accepted it, the better.

He removed his hand from his mouth and rubbed it on his thigh. "Let me get this straight. You want me to perform my 'duty' fully clothed, holding onto my modesty and yours, and remembering my manners all at the same time?"

"You needn't make it sound so implausible."

"Darlin', when a man sets to pleasuring a woman, he's got enough to chew without adding more to his plate."

"I have no idea what you're talking about."

"That's clear enough."

She ignored his interjection. "But I'm sure we can get through this with our dignity intact if we concentrate on the necessities."

"I'm thinking our ideas of what's necessary are about as far apart as a body can get."

"I don't think so. We both want this ranch. Like you, I'd like children." She hoped her cheeks weren't as red as they felt. She needed to keep the upper hand and she hadn't a prayer if she came off as namby-pamby. She cleared her throat and continued. "At Miss Penelope's Academy for Young Women, the subject of marital duty was discussed."

"This Miss Penelope's Academy is a school?"

"Yes."

"And this is where you got the notion that a man and woman bring their manners to their wedding bed?"

"You needn't scoff, Mr. MacIntyre. The Academy is very respected. All the best families send their daughters there with complete confidence that, when they graduate, they'll take their place in society as the wives of respected men. Why are you laughing?"

"Was this Miss Penelope a dried-up prune of a woman?"

"I always thought of her as properly reserved." She recalled Miss Penelope's impeccable dress, upswept hair, and modulated voice. "Dignified."

The corn husks rustled louder as Asa shifted closer. "I hate to upset your apple cart, darlin', but, if I aim to pleasure you, that dignity you're so fond of is going straight out the window."

His hand gliding around her waist dislodged the quilt. No matter how she widened her elbows, she couldn't halt its descent. His fingers brushed the side of her breast. His calluses dragged across her flesh. She wished the floor would open up and swallow her as he nudged the edge of her camisole off her nipple. She closed her eyes.

"Mr. MacIntyre…"

"Damn, you're as pretty as a wildflower."

"Mr. MacIntyre."

Amusement colored the rough tones of his drawl. "Seeing as I'm looking at your charms, don't you think you could call me by my first name?"

"Asa!" His name ended on a high note as his finger traced a circle on her bosom.

"Right here, darlin'"

"Surely this isn't necessary!"

"If by 'this', you mean my touching you, nothing could be more necessary."

She caught his wandering hand by the wrist. When she opened her eyes, his face was inches from hers. For all the amusement in his voice, his expression was intense. Intimidating, but she clutched her conviction like a lifeline. "I don't believe you."

His resistance to her tugging halted. "You calling me a liar?"

She'd never be so idiotic as to call a man a liar to his face. "I believe you're laboring under a misconception."

"Want to lay it out a little clearer?"

"I don't feel it's necessary for you to touch me so intimately in order to perform your duty."

"You don't?"

The incredulity in his voice sparked her anger. "You tell me. Is it necessary for you to touch me so intimately in order to...complete the act?"

"Not for me—"

She cut him off. "Then I'd appreciate getting it over with."

"It won't be nice for you if I just 'get it over with'."

"It's not supposed to be nice," she muttered. Her bravado giving out, she redirected her gaze to the oil lamp. "It's a duty, like any other chore, and I intend to get through it the same way I get through the wash."

"Shi—I mean, shoot. I don't think I want to hear this, but just how do you plan on getting through it?"

"At Miss Penelope's, they suggested occupying our minds during monotonous chores by designing a new dress or planning a party."

"And this Miss Penelope is an expert on the duty between a husband and wife?"

She heard the doubt in his voice. How dare he scoff at her education! The man had probably never attended school a day in his life. She gritted her teeth. "Miss Penelope would never lie. She's a very responsible woman, dedicated to the education of the young women at her school."

"And you're dead set on sticking to her teachings?"

She met his gaze and that slightly raised eyebrow defiantly. "Nothing to date has made me question my education."

"And you're willing?"

"Perfectly."

He motioned to the bed. "Then drop your death grip on that quilt, darlin', and let's get to it."

Get to it? He wanted to get to it? Just like that? "Now?"

His eyebrow went up a notch, but he didn't laugh at her stupid question. "Seems like as good time as any. And you were the one who wanted to just 'get it over with'."

"I may have been a little premature in my decision."

He tugged on the sheet. "Nope. Seeing as how the night's getting away from us and morning comes early, I think now is about perfect."

For all of the seriousness of his expression, he was laughing at her. She knew it. And the knowledge stung.

"Let go the sheet, darlin'."

"Not until you blow out the lamp."

"I like the light on." A quick tug on his end of the quilt had it slipping from her grip. She tried to catch it, but he tweaked it away. Damn. He was fast.

"I am not participating until you blow out the lamp," she informed him as she lunged for the trailing corner of the quilt.

"Seems to me you're not the one calling the shots here."

She caught the quilt, but leaned too far over and Asa caught her. She was forced to continue her argument from an undignified sprawl across his lap. "I mean it, Mr. MacIntyre. I'm not participating in anything with the light on."

"Too much light interferes with your planning?" His hand passed across her posterior and she yelped. She squirmed to get up, but his forearm across the small of her back kept her pinned.

"I have no idea," she gasped as he touched her intimately again.

"Then I think we'll leave it on."

"No!" The heat from his hand permeated the thin cotton of her pantaloons. She didn't want to picture the image she presented in her current position. "Let me up."

"I like you like this."

As if to prove his point, his hand moved in a circular motion. He traced the seam of her buttocks with indecent accuracy. Her protesting wiggle only served to give him more ideas. On his next pass, he pressed harder, causing the material to catch embarrassingly between her cheeks where his finger probed. She froze, mortification drying her protest in her throat.

"Damn, you're something, darlin'."

"Let me up," she hissed. His finger traced the crease he'd created. Despite her determination to lie still, her hips bucked, driving his hand firmly between her legs.

His "not just yet" sounded alarmingly gruff to her straining ears. Something poked her in the side and, ranch girl that she was, she knew what it meant. Her husband was aroused. The hand across her back shifted so his elbow had her pinned and he could use that hand to separate her thighs. His fingers wedged deeper, until he could cup her woman parts.

Oh God, she thought, there was no reprieve. He took his hand from her back, slipped his forearm under her chest and turned her across his lap. His fingers between her legs supported her weight. The hand across her chest kept her pinned against his arm. As he moved it to cup her breast, she looked into his face. There was no softness. No sign that he shared her distress or even noted it. There was only an intense concentration as he watched his hand engulf her breast.

"The light…" she whispered, blinking to fight back tears. He didn't seem to hear.

"Part your legs," he ordered.

"I can't. The light."

His gaze met hers. No mercy there. "You promised me two things—willingness and obedience."

She closed her eyes, counted to ten, and then kept on going.

"That's an order, Elizabeth."

How could the man expect her to keep her word in circumstances like this? She parted her legs a spare inch. He took a mile. When she felt his fingers slide through the slit in her pantaloons to slip between the folds of her female flesh, it was too much. She turned her face into the hollow of his throat and prayed for her Maker to take her then and there. Beneath her cheek, his chest rose on a shuddering breath.

"Guess I'm going too fast for a student of Miss Penelope's, huh?" he asked on the exhale.

She guessed he was going too fast for the women who lived over Dell's, but she wasn't going to risk losing his compassion by saying so. "I'm sure it would be easier on both of us if we blew out the lamp."

In response, he stood, leaned over, and blew out the lamp. The fact that he didn't moan or even shift his grip convinced her that struggling would be useless, even if she wanted to forsake her word. As darkness enveloped them along with the stench of kerosene, he gave her a little toss that switched his grip to her waist.

She dangled in his arms as he asked, "You still planning on making a dress while we do this?"

"Yes." He had no idea what her complacency was costing her.

"You're going to cut and stitch while I do whatever I want?"

"You said you wouldn't hit," she hastened to remind him.

"We've already established what I'm set on doing. What's up for grabs is whether you plan on joining in."

Was he questioning her integrity? "I know my duty, Mr. MacIntyre."

"Asa," he reminded her.

"Asa," she dutifully repeated. She crossed her arms over her chest as a compromise between encouragement and obedience. "Could we please get on with this?"

"You in a hurry?"

"I'm scared to death."

"I can feel you trembling."

There was a long pause in which he did nothing.

"Is there something wrong?" she asked.

"I'm trying to figure a way to make you less nervous. Any particular worry you're gnawing on?"

She thought about it. "I don't like not knowing what you're going to do next."

"Seeing as how I'm a talker, I could probably manage a warning or two."

Having her inch, Elizabeth decided to go for a mile. "I also don't like it when you handle me sooo...intimately."

"That," he said, a smile in his voice as he brought her breasts back against his chest, "you're going to have to get used to. Any more questions?"

It was hard to think with the threat of his big body so close to hers. Through the lingering odor of kerosene, she smelled his scent. She wanted to dislike it, but he smelled of soap, fresh air and blackberries.

"Well?" he prompted in the wake of her silence.

"I guess not."

"No need to sound so discouraged, darlin'. We're going to do just fine. Put your arms around my neck."

"Why?"

"Because I want to feel your breasts against me."

Shock at his bald pronouncement held her frozen for the two seconds he waited before pretending to drop her. Reflexes threw her arms around his neck. She felt his smile against her hair. "That's the way."

"I'm not sure my sensibilities can take any more warnings," she admitted grudgingly.

"Then why don't you stuff them under the mattress?"

"What?"

"Your sensibilities and all that other starchy stuff Miss Penelope taught you."

"I can't." The words ended on a small squeak as he tossed her again in order to shift his hands to the backs of her thighs.

"Then, darlin', you'd best get to stitching because the fun's about to begin. Wrap your legs around my waist."

She was too smart to ask why this time. She just did as ordered. He took a step back and sat on the edge of the bed. If she thought the humiliation of having him touch her was bad, it was nothing compared to the humiliation of straddling his lap. When he suggested she move to the right, she had no illusions as to why. His manhood pushed heavily against her inner thigh.

"I can't," she confessed. "I'm not breaking my promise, I swear. I'm doing my best. I just can't."

"Guess that stitchin' isn't getting you too far, huh?"

She shook her head. It might have been her imagination, but she thought his lips brushed her hair. "Could we just get this over with?" she asked.

"You always in this much of a rush?"

"Please? I'll beg if you want. I—"

His finger across her lips cut off the rest of her plea.

She pulled back. "Is that a yes?"

"A man wishes his whole life for a woman to beg for his lovemaking. Guess when she does, the least he could do is honor the request. Lie on the bed, darlin', while I shuck these clothes."

For a man about to get his wish, he didn't sound enthusiastic, but she was too beset by her own problems to care. Nausea rolled in her stomach, her hands shook, and, as she scrambled to do as he asked, she thought she'd further humiliate herself by throwing up. Remembering his earlier explanation of what he preferred, she lay on her back. After careful consideration, she placed her hands at her side. Lying in the dark, she listened to the rustling of his clothes. A soft thunk indicated his belt hitting the floor. She took three deep breaths, swallowed her nerves and said, "I don't suppose you could remain dressed for this?"

He cursed beneath his breath. The chair legs rocked as he threw something over the back. "I'm willing to forsake a lot of things out of respect for your sensibilities, Elizabeth, but I'll be damned if I'll come to my wedding bed dressed for work."

The disgust in his voice flicked her pride like a whip. "It was only a suggestion."

The mattress sagged as he knelt on it. Over her. His breath blew across her face as he growled, "Well, it was a damned poor one for a wife to be making."

The fact that he swore in her presence told her more than she wanted to know about his feelings. His legs slipped between hers. The planes and curves of well honed muscles were rock hard and alien against her softer flesh. With his knee, he pushed first one thigh and then the other to the side. Instinct had her resisting, but his strength brooked no denial. He wasn't satisfied until she was spread wide, more open and more vulnerable than she had ever been in her life. The feeling was alien, but in the dark of the night, with the heat of his body reaching out to cover her in an intimate blanket, not as terrifying as she'd expected. His breath blew across her cheek. The sheets rustled as his hands shifted near her shoulders. Fear and a foreign sense of anticipation caught her breath in her throat as he slowly lowered the length of his strong body over hers. He was all muscle where she was soft. Rough where she was smooth. And hot. Very, very hot.

She released the sheets from her death grip and slowly brought her hands up to his forearms. The dark was kindness itself, giving her courage she couldn't find in the light. Tentatively, she curled her fingers around the hard flesh. He was so very different from her. The hairs on his arm were more prominent than hers, denser. They tickled her skin.

Experimentally, she slid her palms up and down, playing with the sensation.

Asa moaned. "That's right, darlin'. Hold on."

She didn't see where she had much choice. Especially when he brought his mouth to the side of her neck. His lips were soft where she'd expected them to be firm. As she contemplated the newness, they found a spot beneath her ear that sent goose bumps spreading out from her neck, over her torso and amazingly, shockingly, concentrating in her breasts. The longer he nibbled at her neck, the more intense the feeling became until her breasts felt swollen and her nipples actually ached. Instinctively her torso arched up, pressing those sensitive points into the solid wall of his chest. The relief was exquisite. Asa's chuckle vibrated against her ear. New shock waves shivered down her spine. The heat seemed to transfer from his body to hers, pooling between her legs. When his tongue trailed from her neck up to her ear, swirling around the edges, she gasped out loud.

She held her breath until he did it again. And again. Her hands slid higher, her fingers skimming his flesh, following the muscled grooves in his upper arms until they naturally embraced the solid bulk of his shoulders. Muscles she didn't know she had clenched between her legs, and her insides wept with a hungry longing that demanded relief.

It came in a manner she wasn't expecting. Something broad and large wedged against her intimate flesh. Asa soothed her initial start with a soft murmur. His left shoulder slid out of her grasp as he leaned away. His teeth nipped her earlobe. The pain was sharp and swift, and unbearably pleasurable. The ache between her thighs blossomed into full-fledged need. He reached between their bodies and began rubbing his penis up and down the wet folds of her woman's flesh. She tried to hold still, but it was impossible. With each glide of that large head across her flesh, the sharp bite of need was soothed and nudged higher. On the next pass, he did something way up that drove a spike of ecstasy through her body. Her moan was uncontrollable. His response was immediate.

"Let's try that again."

With slow deliberation, he pushed his manhood against that special spot. The breath she'd been holding whooshed out. He held himself there, just massaging that special spot until she thought she'd go mad if he continued. Suddenly he stopped, and she knew she'd go mad from that alone. She strained upwards with her hips, seeking the connection she needed, but she struck only air. Following the demands of her body, she wrapped her legs around his thighs, using all her strength, she pulled, wanting him back. Needing him now.

"Easy, darlin'," he whispered against her ear. "I'll give you what you want."

His manhood probed between her thighs. Not where she wanted it, but lower. He slid easily through the wetness there, seeking, searching, until he nestled into a soft welcoming valley. A whole new host of sensations immediately clamored for attention. And her body tensed in eager anticipation. Bedding a man was nothing like she'd been told.

At first, the pressure was light. Little pulses that tripped lightly over her skin in an intriguing invitation. Following his lead, she pushed up when he pushed forward. It was pleasurable, but it wasn't enough. Maybe not for him either, because beneath her hands, his skin became slick with sweat and his breath was no longer controlled and even.

His "Hold on" was enticement itself.

His thigh muscles bunched beneath her grip before he surged against her.

Suddenly what had been pleasurable verged on pain. She couldn't prevent her instinctive flinch. "Easy, darlin'."

On the next surge, she gasped.

Asa swore.

On the third attempt, she pushed against his shoulders and twisted away. This was worse than anyone had warned her about.

Asa threw himself to the side. The mattress rocked and his curses echoed through the darkness.

It was only when she felt him throw his legs over the edge of the bed that she realized what she'd done.

"I'm sorry," she apologized as she heard the rustle of his denims. "I'm ready."

"Forget it. This whole idea is crazy."

Panic of a different sort took root in her chest. "No. It's an excellent idea. I'm just more nervous than most, I guess."

He shifted away. Her panic burgeoned into full life. "I can do this."

"It's okay, Elizabeth." He sounded utterly weary. "A yahoo like myself had no place hooking up with a lady."

He was leaving. Walking away from her and their deal. Oh God, she had to do something! She couldn't let him leave. She had to prove to him she could be a wife. More than that, she had to do it now. Immediately in a way he couldn't ignore. She remembered what Brent had tried to make her do. How he'd wanted her to put her mouth on his manhood, hitting her when she refused. He'd said it was what all men wanted. What they craved. The lust on his face as he'd forced her mouth toward his groin had made her believe every word he'd said. Maybe Asa was like Brent in this one way. Maybe if she did this, he'd reconsider. There was only one way to find out. If she were wrong, it wouldn't be anymore embarrassing than having to face the town people when husband number two up and left.

She scrambled to her knees as Asa stood. Reaching out, her hands connected with his bare chest.

"I can do this, Asa. I can."

His hands caught hers. "It's all right. I don't think any less of you."

But he did, otherwise he wouldn't be leaving her bed. Other women did this daily. It was only her own cowardice that held her back. She would not lose everything to cowardice.

With a moan, she launched herself at Asa, trusting his grip to keep her from falling. The air left his lungs in a surprised "oof" as her nose smashed into his hard belly. His arousal brushed her cheek, and she offered a prayer of thanks that he still wanted her. All was not lost. Before she lost the opportunity, she opened her mouth and turned her head. Her aim was off. His manhood brushed the corner of her mouth. So was her estimate of his size. She forced her jaws as wide as she could, and took him into her mouth. To her surprise, it wasn't repulsive.

He lay heavy and hard against her tongue, with that breathless immobility that signified deep horror or agonizing anticipation. With the tip of her tongue, she experimented tracing the flared head. The flesh was hard and yet intriguingly resilient. She pushed tentatively in the center. The effect on Asa was like a bolt of lightning striking his body. He jerked upright, almost unseating his manhood. To keep him trapped, she wrapped her lips as tightly as she could around his impressive width and sucked hard.

"Jesus, Mary and Joseph!" Asa's curse rang harshly above her head. His grip on her hands tightened painfully. She fought the upward pressure. She had his attention. For once, Brent had been right about something. Asa wanted this. With a bob of her head, she took him deeper. While his hands pushed her away, his hips followed wherever her mouth led. The helpless surge of his hips as he pressed his manhood deeper was a balm to her pride. She could do this. She flicked the tip of his manhood with her tongue. His hips jerked reflexively. When she swallowed him deep, he moaned and pushed harder. Obviously wanting more. And she took it. Every thrust, every moan, every hard surge because this was what she wanted, too. To know she was woman enough to hold him. To keep him. To do what needed to be done. To know she wasn't hopeless.

The battle of wills ended before she was ready. Her strength was no match for Asa's, and the battle for supremacy was over when he said it was. One second she was winning, and the next she was flat on her back, trying to sort up from down as Asa dragged her to the edge of the bed. Her legs dangled helplessly. His hands anchored hers at her shoulders. She held her breath as he wedged his huge manhood between her legs. Like before, he nestled into that sensitive valley. The only sound in the room was his labored breathing as he rubbed the thick head over her moist flesh. His movements were rougher now. Less controlled. His push was more of a shove. She bit her lip against the pain. She wrapped her legs around his hips and whispered, "Make me your wife, Asa."

As if she'd applied spurs to his flesh, he swore and jerked against her. His fingers dug into her hips as he yanked her toward him. Once, twice, and then his hot seed poured over her woman's flesh. With a groan of her name, he fell against her, his chest squashing her with every labored breath. It was done, she realized, shifting under his weight. The marriage was consummated. Waves of relief swept over her. She'd pushed aside her feminine weakness and done what was necessary. Asa was no more free to walk away than she was. The land was safe, and so was she. She shuddered and let the darkness come.

Chapter Five

⅏

Morning came damned early when a man had regrets about the night before. It wasn't the first time Asa had realized this, but it was the first time he'd felt the regret so keenly. It might have something to do with the way Elizabeth was bustling around the small kitchen, a picture of wifely contentment. Damn, the woman was so green she didn't even know she'd been shortchanged. He sipped his coffee and listened as she hummed. How the hell was he supposed to explain to her she was still a virgin? That he'd been so hot for her, he'd gone off like a firecracker? Hell, what man in his right mind even confessed something so humiliating to his wife?

Then again, how could he not? The first time they made love for real, she was bound to take note. Especially if first times were as painful as he'd heard. He looked Elizabeth up and down from her white shirtwaist to her black shoes peeking from beneath her navy blue skirt. Hell, there wasn't enough of her to play in a strong wind. He'd probably about kill her if they ever did get around to a real first time.

Which brought him to another question winging around his mind. Where in hell had she gotten the notion to use her mouth on him? No woman had ever done that for him before. He didn't expect it of whores, and he sure hadn't planned on asking for it from a lady. Especially one as proper as his wife. Brent popped immediately to mind. The man was a bully, all right. He wouldn't think twice about putting his own pleasure above a woman's. Even on their wedding night.

Asa shot Elizabeth another sidelong glare. That was another thing he planned on his wife learning. He wasn't a selfish man. Last night hadn't been normal for him. She'd caught him by surprise, that was all. He blamed the novelty for his mad rush to the finish line.

He leaned back when Elizabeth came to the table to remove his plate. The sweet high curves of her breasts came into view. He imagined he could see her nipples through the material of her dress. He remembered how they'd felt against his tongue, round, hard, demanding. And realized he was aroused. Again.

He groaned under his breath. He was pretty sure Miss Penelope had all sorts of rules against husbands and wives coming together while the sun still shone.

He grabbed his coffee in disgust. He moved so fast, some sloshed over the brim. "Shit!"

The curse exploded into the air. Hearing it, Elizabeth took a steadying breath. Dealing with an angry man took patience. Control. Calm. Everything she didn't feel at this moment. As far as she could see, her husband had nothing to be cursing about. That being the case, she'd much rather bring the frying pan down on his belligerent head, but, as she expected all she'd accomplish would be a denting of her best pan, she needed to come up with another plan. She turned away from the stove. It was immediately obvious why Asa was mad. He'd spilled hot coffee down his shirt.

"Are you okay?" she asked with what she hoped was an appropriate amount of wifely concern.

"I'm fine," he snapped.

As if she hadn't heard the anger in his tone, she handed him a napkin. "This may help."

"Thanks." He took it and had the grace to look ashamed for his curt answer in the face of her courtesy. At least, she preferred to assume it was shame. Thinking he had some sense of common decency made it easier to hold her temper. The man had been a bear ever since she'd brought him warm wash water this morning. He'd gone from astonishment when she'd carried it into the room to anger by the time she'd left with his dirty clothes. Her hopes that he was just grumpy when first up had been dashed when he'd come downstairs. He'd been pensive and snappy through three helpings of breakfast.

She watched as he tossed back the last of his coffee. She hefted the pot and carried it to the table. Maybe more coffee would improve his mood. "Would you like more?"

"No." Apparently, coffee wasn't the solution for Asa as it had been for her father.

She drew in another breath. The towel she'd wrapped around the speckled handle of the coffee pot fluttered as she strove for patience. "Would you care for more breakfast? There are home fries left and it would only take a few minutes to fry up—"

"I'm not hungry," he interrupted.

"Are you sure? It's no trouble." At least, not as much trouble as his growl.

"I'm sure." He shot her a look she couldn't decipher, heaved a sigh that echoed hers, and then expanded in a more natural tone. "After three helpings, I'm not even sure I can move, let alone walk to the bunkhouse and meet the men."

His attempt at humor came out more forced than funny, but she didn't care. At least he was making an effort. It was a step in the right direction. "You probably have time for another cup."

He probably had time for two or three. "No thanks. The day's not gonna wait for me to get a start on it."

He didn't have much to worry about, Elizabeth thought, as she headed back to the stove. Especially if he was worried about meeting the hands. One thing was for sure, whatever time he got to the bunkhouse, there would be men aplenty for her husband to meet. Not one cowboy was going to miss meeting the man who'd put Jimmy in his place. A man who could take down a bully commanded respect.

A woman who accomplished the same goal commanded nothing. Bitterness seeped past her guard like a bad habit. She forced the anger back. She'd made her peace with the world when her father had died. From here on out, she was calling the shots in her life and, as the woman in charge, she didn't want to be at war with her husband. She settled the coffee pot on the iron burner without a clank. "I imagine Jimmy informed everyone that there's a new boss man and it isn't Brent."

"I had plans along those lines, but, if last night's message didn't get through, I'll repeat it this morning."

Was he planning on beating every hand on the ranch?

She replaced the towel she'd had wrapped around the pot on a peg over the stove. "You could still have problems." The towel threatened to fall. With a deft move, she flipped it back in place, wishing she could fix everything so easily. "If you'll wait a minute, I'll go with you."

"No need," he answered. "I'm not so feeble that I need to hide behind a woman's skirts before passing on orders."

She gritted her teeth against the humiliation of being dismissed. "I merely thought the common courtesy of an introduction was called for."

"You women may put a lot of stock in formal introductions, but I'm not courting a gal, I'm running a ranch. Any how-de-do's that needed saying, I took care of last night."

"When you beat Jimmy?"

"When I taught Jimmy a lesson on what's tolerated around here."

"Jimmy was never tolerated around here." At least by her. Her father had been a different story altogether.

"Apparently, he didn't get the message."

"Apparently." She grabbed the skillet full of bacon grease and poured the fat into the lard can. The action gave her an excuse not to look at Asa while she tried to make her point without getting him growling again. "Still, there may be some trouble. The men might not take you at your word. If I come with you, I could make sure they know you have my backing. It might ease things."

"The bunkhouse is no place for a woman."

She placed the skillet in the wash basin. Patience, she reminded herself while she counted to ten, was a virtue. "I've been down to the bunkhouse plenty of times."

"You have a husband now, darlin'." A loud grating squeak announced his chair shoving back. "What kind of man would I be if I married up with you and then left you to handle my job as well as yours?"

She bit her tongue. She gripped the cutlery, struggled to hold onto her patience, and tried again. "I don't mind this one last time."

"There's always some testing of the new boss. Might as well get it out of the way."

"I don't doubt you're a capable man—"

"Capable enough that you don't have to take time from your work to do mine," he stated flatly.

The last of her fragile hope died that he might want her as a partner. The cutlery hit the dishpan so hard, the sound echoed around the room and water splashed everywhere.

The chair squawked again as he shoved it back under the table. "You mind telling me what you're so mad about all of a sudden?"

Instead of turning, Elizabeth started wiping up the water. "I'm not mad."

Not that she was admitting, because then he'd want to know why, and she didn't think she'd be able to keep from killing him if he laughed when she told him she was as knowledgeable as a man when it came to the ranch. Or worse, that he might want to listen to her opinions. She set to scouring the skillet with zeal.

"Glad to hear it, darlin', but would you mind gentling your grip on the cookware until I see if we can afford the trip to town to replace it?"

She *was* banging the pots. Anger, she realized, was a devil of a hard habit to break. She immediately relaxed her grip. "Of course."

"Now, would you mind facing me and answering my question?"

"No." Not until she got herself under control.

"No, you don't mind facing me, or no, you don't want to answer my question."

No to both, but she supposed she couldn't evade either.

The face she presented as she turned around was totally composed. As put together, Asa decided, as her dress and ruthlessly smoothed back hair.

"Are you ordering me to answer your question?" she asked calmly.

Now there was a thought. "You know, darlin', when a woman's as trussed up tight as you are, she shouldn't walk around picking fights."

The only hint that his comment annoyed her was an almost indiscernible tightening of her lips. "I asked you a relevant question," she said calmly.

"That wasn't a question, that was a dare," he answered just as calmly.

"It was and is a question which you've still failed to answer."

"There you go again, daring me." He couldn't resist. The more sweet calm she threw his way, the more he wanted to devil her. This act she had of always being sweet and unruffled was so much bull, it practically reeked manure. She was as mad as all get out. If he needed proof, he'd find it in her chin. If that sweet, stubborn curve got any higher, the woman would be stuck with a permanent crick.

"I fail to see, Mr. MacIntyre, why you'd want to turn an innocent question into a battle."

He folded his arms across his chest and settled his weight onto his good hip. "It does make a body wonder why anyone would set out to do that, but, sure as shooting, you're itching for a fight." When she didn't rise to the bait, he continued. "Seems all I did was ask what had you slamming pots around and, you went all poker-backed on me."

"I did not go poker-backed on you, MacIntyre, whatever that means—"

"Poker-backed means you couldn't pull that spine any tighter unless you wanted to pop it in two."

"I simply placed the pots in the basin to be washed," she continued as if he hadn't spoken. "If that doesn't meet with your approval..." She ended on a shrug.

The way she stood, all sweet and gentle, looking as calm as a daisy sitting in a meadow of sunshine, was irritating as hell, but knowing that she was doing it on purpose to aggravate him took the edge off his bad humor. It was a strange and new thing, not having a woman run from his scowl. Kind of fascinating in an irritating sort of way. "So, I'm supposed to believe you were placing pots in the sink hard enough to crack 'em because you like the way the sun's shining this morning?"

"You, Mr. MacIntyre, can believe whatever you want. No doubt you're eminently capable of handling any testing sent your way."

"You got that right." Asa smiled. "Which brings us to the question of why any new wife would want to test her husband?"

"I have no idea what you are talking about."

And pigs would fly before noon. "You don't?"

"No." Her weight shifted slightly, suggesting she might be digging in for another round.

"Seems to me it all started when I didn't need you to introduce me to the hands." He shook his head. "But that doesn't make sense as one of the reasons you married me was to handle the ranch."

"The men," she corrected a little too quickly to be polite.

He hid a smile and pretended he didn't hear. "My part of the deal was that I took over the men so you could get back to your needlework." He hadn't seen any needlework around the house, but, from talk he'd heard, needlework was a woman's passion.

Just maybe not Elizabeth's, he decided as her face immediately turned beet red.

"I assure you, Mr. MacIntyre, there's more to a woman than needlework."

"Hey, don't be embarrassed. It's no never mind to me if you can't make those fancy little pillows."

"I'm perfectly accomplished at needlework!"

"I didn't mean any slight," Asa continued in the face of her anger. "I'm a plain man and plain pillows suit me fine."

The man was anything but plain, Elizabeth thought, unless she considered him plain aggravating. "If you want a house full of fancy pillows with cute sayings on them, I'll make them for you."

"That'd be nice. I always had a hankering for one that said Home Sweet Home."

"Fine, then that'll be first on the list."

"Well, I thank you. Now, do you want to tell me why you're so angry?"

"No."

"Then come here." He pointed to the floor in front of him. He didn't give her time to budge before he repeated himself. "I said, come here."

She would have, too, if he hadn't snapped his fingers. Instead, she planted her feet, arched her chin up, and matched him stare for stare. In a pissing contest, he had an advantage, but, when it came to a battle of wills, she could hold her own. "I'm not a dog, Mr. MacIntyre."

"You call me Mr. MacIntyre one more time, and you're going to wish you were."

"Oh, for heavens sake!" She threw up her hands before slamming them down on her hips. "What possible objection can you have to being called Mr. MacIntyre?"

"Plenty. I'm your husband."

"And I'm your wife." She bet he used that frown to scare people. Well, not her. "It's a sign of respect for me to refer to you as Mister."

His right brow took wing, landing somewhere in his hairline. "Who in hell told you that?"

"All proper—"

"Is that another one of those idiotic rules you learned at that da—darned school?"

"It's not an idiotic school."

"Jesus, Mary and Joseph! Let's get something straight! I don't care what you learned in that fancy school. I don't want a wife who walks around trussed up tighter than a Christmas goose, who wears more clothes to bed than she wears around the house, and I definitely don't want a wife who calls me Mr. Anything!"

When he was done shouting, she was right in his face, matching him yell for yell. "Well, what do you want me to call you?"

"How about honey, or sweetheart, or hey, here's a thought..." He pushed his face in hers. "What the hell is wrong with Asa?"

On that note, he shoved past her and slammed out the door.

Elizabeth stared at the closed door. "Nothing's wrong with Asa. I just find jackass preferable."

The door flew open so quickly, she dreaded he might have been listening. From the set of his shoulders, she guessed the few seconds of fresh air hadn't improved his mood. "Did you forget something?"

"Yes."

"What?"

"This."

He stepped into the room, bringing the fresh scent of morning with him. Beneath his hat, his storm cloud eyes glittered with emotion. Her heart dropped into her stomach. She searched the small kitchen for a weapon. Unfortunately, in order to secure a pot or knife, she'd have to come within his reach. Where was her brain this morning, angering a man to the point she'd needled Asa? If she wanted to be so stupid, the least she could have done was to arm herself while she was at it.

He stopped when they were toe to toe. Her feet betrayed her resolution to show no fear. She took a step back. Asa took a step forward. Her rear collided with the kitchen table. His hand reached out. She closed her eyes and braced for the blow.

It was the longest time coming. In the eternity in which she waited for his fist to make contact, his scent surrounded her. The heat of his body scorched her nerve endings. His chest brushed against hers. The briefest of contacts and then nothing. No pain, no bruises. Just nothing. She opened her eyes.

"I forgot my lunch."

"Oh." For the life of her, she couldn't think of anything. A bead of sweat trickled down her forehead. She felt her heart pounding. No doubt her pulse was visible in her throat.

"I forgot something else." Slow and easy, his drawl made a mockery of the fear that parched her throat.

"What?"

He shifted the sack containing his lunch to his left hand. His right came up to slide slowly around the back of her neck. His smile was as lazy as his drawl. "I forgot my goodbye kiss."

"Oh."

He tugged and she went. His thumb tipped up her chin. His head came down. She closed her eyes when his lips touched hers. There was none of the force she expected. No probing with his tongue. There was just the sweet, light rubbing of his lips on hers. He eased back. Disappointment at the separation tripped over her defenses. Opening her eyes, she looked into his. His gaze was intent. His thumb pulled her lower lip free of her teeth and slid across the moist interior. "You want to kiss me back?"

Did she? She slid her arms around his neck as her breasts swelled and plumped in anticipation. "Yes."

His thumb slipped into her mouth. Her lips closed reflexively around it. His groan vibrated against her hardened nipples. His eyes were glued to the sight of her lips wrapped around his thumb. "Damn, I love your mouth."

"You said that before."

He smiled, moving his thumb in and out of her mouth, sending tingles down her spine. "You'll probably hear it a time or two more."

She caught his thumb with her teeth. Holding his gaze, she sucked lightly on the salty flesh.

"Damn!" There was a soft thump as his lunch hit the floor.

He didn't look mad anymore. Elizabeth couldn't contain her smile as she swirled her tongue around the rough pad. It wasn't her imagination that he jerked against her.

"Jesus! Do that to my cock and I'll be your slave for life."

Two things hit her at once. Shock at his wording and satisfaction on finally knowing what men called their things.

"You liked it last night when I kissed you there?" The question obviously threw him for he stared at her open mouthed, but not a word passed his suddenly tight lips. She dragged her hands to the buttons on his shirt and slipped her fingers between the flaps. The hair on his chest tickled her fingertips. "You liked my lips on your…cock?"

His breath drew in harshly. He released it on a rough laugh. "Yeah."

"Then why did you pull me away?"

She popped the top two buttons of his shirt and her smile broadened as he seemed to freeze into a statue. Against her stomach, his cock pressed demandingly. Above her head, his breath sawed in and out of his lungs in desperate anticipation. His hands fell from her face. They landed by his sides, briefly touched her hips, and fell back to his sides again. He clearly didn't know what to make of her boldness. She kissed his chest through the vee of his shirt. She decided she liked him off balance.

With the tip of her tongue, she tasted his flesh. He tasted as fresh as he smelled. He tasted of pure, unadulterated, clean masculinity. His big hand came up and cupped the back of her head, pressing her against him.

"You're killin' me darlin'."

"I'm just kissing you back."

"You're playing with fire."

She cut him a glance through her lashes. "Not yet, but I intend to."

His hand never left her head as she kissed her way down his torso on her slow drop to the floor. Until her knees hit the wood planks, she wasn't really sure she was going to go through with it, but when she saw the extent of his desire for her, remembered the night before, the power that had been hers those few brief moments she'd had him in her mouth, she knew what she wanted. His fingers clenched in her hair, stopping her from moving forward.

"You don't need to do this."

It was a long trip up to his face. A long pleasurable trip. Her husband was one finely put together man. She moistened her lips with her tongue. "Don't you like it when a woman kisses you there?"

His eyes closed and his head tipped back like he was struggling for control.

"I've never asked a woman to do that."

She paused, returning her gaze to the front of his pants. "I was the first?"

She might have imagined it, but his cock seemed to be reaching for her through the heavy denim.

His "yes" was a harsh hiss of sound.

She liked knowing that. With one finger she reached forward and traced the contours of his shaft. His hips bucked helplessly beneath her touch. A woman could get addicted to having a man react to her like this, she decided.

"I liked it," she confessed in a barely discernible whisper.

"What?"

A quick glance determined she had his full attention. She didn't know if he truly hadn't heard or was shocked at what she'd said. She did know, however, that she wanted to taste his cock again. This time at her pace, without his interference.

"I liked it," she repeated clearly.

She was lifted from the floor by two large hands on her upper arms. She looked up to find his dark eyes glittering with emotion, the dark almost swallowing the silver.

"What?" she asked on a twinge of unease.

"I'm thinking I might like it, too."

In the time it took her to blink, he had her up and sitting on the table top. It was going to be tough to accomplish what she wanted from here. It took all her composure to point that out without stammering or crumpling into a ball of embarrassment. He didn't appear to notice. He merely flashed a grin and chuckled when she groaned. For once, he didn't argue her avoiding his gaze. It should have warned her, but she was too caught up in mortification to pay attention until it was too late.

She nearly jumped out of her skin when his cool hands captured her ankles. As she scooted back, she asked, "What are you doing?"

With a tug, he undid her efforts and had her posterior teetering on the edge of the table.

"Thought I'd have a bit more breakfast," he answered, stepping between her calves, completely unconcerned with her skirt riding up past her knees.

She tried to push the material down, but she wasn't too effective as she had to use one hand to balance on the table top. "This isn't seemly," she pointed out desperately as he stepped between her splayed thighs. Her skirt continued its upward climb.

His "I wasn't going for seemly," was completely unconcerned with the fact that her skirt was now above her thighs and sunlight was highlighting every wrinkle in her pantaloons.

He paused. "Now there's a problem."

What on earth could he be seeing as a problem. Down there?

On second thought, she didn't want to know.

The jiggle he gave her legs as he reached for something in his boot upset her balance. With a gasp, she felt her arm give out and she landed on her back.

"Now that's a sight."

She was sure it was. It wasn't every day a woman found herself laid out on the kitchen table in broad daylight, with her skirts hitched up around her waist and a fully dressed man standing between her thighs staring at all there was to see. She squeezed her eyes shut. The one corner of her soul that wasn't writhing in mortification wished heartily she'd put on her fancy underwear this morning. The silk ones with the expensive lace.

Something cool and narrow touched her thigh. She jerked upright only to immediately fall back. "Is that a knife?"

"Yup." His drawl was unconcerned. His hand on her midriff stopped her next lunge.

"Just lie still darlin' and we'll be getting this problem out of the way."

"I assure you I don't have any problem down...there." At least, she hoped not.

The knife began an upward slide. She heard the hiss of material parting, and suddenly had an excellent idea of what he thought was a problem.

"Are you crazy?" she gasped.

"Nope."

"I can't be naked in the kitchen!" There was a light tug as the knife hit the thickness of the drawstring waistband, and then the cool waft of the morning air on her hip.

"I wasn't shooting for fully bare assed."

As if that was some comfort. "I absolutely refuse to allow this to continue." The knife slid under her opposite leg and slid through the cotton like it was nothing.

"It's a little late to be complaining."

Not in her book. While he was distracted returning the knife to its sheath, she wiggled toward the side of the table and freedom.

He stopped her simply by using his grip on her legs to pull her hips back toward him. "Hold still, darlin'. I've never done this before and I'm real interested in getting it right."

She glanced at his face and immediately wished she hadn't. He was looking at her. There. She squeezed her eyes tightly closed as if she could somehow block out the image of his expression. Hard. Intent. Lustful.

Nothing could block out the sensation of his calloused fingertips drifting up her sensitive thighs until they reached her hips. She couldn't suppress a shiver and the goose bumps that sprang up along the path his hands had taken. His thumbs drew circles around her hipbones, grazing the creases in her thighs. With each pass, little sparks of sensation migrated inward from the spot. Her woman's flesh felt tingly and started to swell. The only thing that saved her from complete mortification was the fact that her pantaloons still preserved her modesty.

She hadn't even gotten the prayer of gratitude formed in her mind before that thin cotton was whisked away. Her eyes sprang open. Out of the corner of one, she saw the white fabric drift to the floor.

"Oh my God!" she gasped in shock, her hands flying to cover her privates. "What are you doing?"

As she watched, he lowered himself to his knees. His face was just above her hips, within inches of her most private place. Between the curves of her breasts, she met his hot gaze. Before her scandalized eyes, he tipped his hat back, and smiled. "Why darlin', I'm planning on getting acquainted with your sweet little pussy."

"You most certainly are not!" She jerked to a sitting position, aided by the way his big hands anchored her thighs.

He glanced up as she propped herself up on her elbows. "You planning on watching?"

"Oh my...no!" She took a swing at him. All she accomplished was to knock off his hat.

"A pity." He was totally unrepentant. "I think I might have enjoyed that."

As she glared at him, he leaned forward. She felt his breath on her...pussy a second before the touch of his tongue.

He touched, swirled, and then slid through the soft folds in a leisurely lap.

It was like watching a train wreck happen. Her dignity and reputation were going to hell in a handbasket, and all she could do was stare. Fascinated.

She thought he would be repulsed, but instead he seemed enthralled. Looking up at her, he ran his tongue around his lips, as if collecting every morsel of her flavor. His gaze was serious. He held hers as he leaned forward again. And very slowly, deliberately, he stuck his tongue out. It seemed to take forever for his tongue to reach her. Her breath caught in her throat as he rested it against the pink flesh swelling at the top of her pussy. She stopped breathing altogether when he fluttered it there, shooting a maelstrom of sensation from her groin through her body. She tried to shift away, but he followed, sucking the flange of flesh into the heat of his mouth. Her world reduced to a spiral of sensation that started out narrowed and intense, and spread outward like wildfire throughout her body. She wanted to pull away. She wanted to shove closer. She settled for a combination of the two, alternately pushing toward his mouth and then pulling away when the feeling got too intense.

"What are you doing to me?" It took a tremendous amount of concentration to get the question out.

He lapped at her pussy, delving, swirling and dipping through folds as if searching for every drop of moisture. "I'm making you feel good."

Lord was he making her feel good. "This has got to be a sin."

"Maybe." He slipped his big hands under her rear, and pulled her down until her hips rested on the edge of the table. "Come here."

"Why?" She should have known the man would answer with complete embarrassing honesty.

He tilted her hips up. "Because I want to lap up all the delicious cream I can convince you to give me."

"Oh God." The back of her head made a soft thunk as it fell back to the table, just one more sensation in the cacophony going off in her body. "You can't be serious."

She'd barely survived what he'd done so far.

As if to prove he was serious, he ran his tongue from the base of her pussy to the top. Once. Twice. On the third pass, he paused here and there to wiggle, press and nudge. His voice, when it came to her, was muffled. "Never been more serious in my life. You, Mrs. MacIntyre, are one tasty treat."

And he proceeded to eat her from top to bottom. One excruciating inch at a time. She should have been appalled at what was happening. At the hot words he muttered against her creaming pussy. At the whole indecency of the situation. At the way she wanted him to go on. Instead, she closed her eyes and decided she was going to go up in flames. Her skin felt stretched too tightly to contain her body, while her woman's flesh throbbed and ached with an unrelenting emptiness.

His focus went from nibbling at her entire pussy to concentrating at the top. His tongue lashed a particularly sensitive spot, and the breath left her body in a soundless scream. He did it again, a firm wet tap, and she jerked up straight to fall back and writhe as he lashed it over and over. With every pass of his hot tongue, molten need poured through her body, until she was gasping his name with each breath. Pleading for something he kept withholding from her.

"Just a minute darlin'," he soothed, kissing her creaming flesh gently.

She wasn't waiting for anything. With a burst of strength she latched onto his hair and pulled his face back to her aching, sopping pussy. Acting on instinct. His laugh vibrated just to the left of where she needed it. She wiggled frantically, needing his lips and teeth to release her from this torment.

His big hands stilled her hips. "No need to snatch me bald. I get the idea." He blew against the sensitive knot of flesh.

"Please..." He was killing her, leaving her stretched out on this burning, unfamiliar ledge.

"I like you like this," he murmured, lapping delicately at her folds, swirling his tongue in the thick juices weeping from her hungry slit. "All soft and generous." He lapped again. "Needing."

He pressed his tongue against that one spot high up. Lightning streaked through her body arching her back off the table, driving her pulsing flesh closer to his face. Closer to paradise. Her hands clenched on the side of the table as he did it again. This time, her scream was a strangled plea for more. He didn't give it to her. When her spine reconnected with the table, he pulled back and asked, "You liked that, huh?"

Later, she'd smack him for sounding so smug. Right now, she needed him to do it again. "What was that?" she gasped, her hips helplessly lifting and searching.

He stroked her softly with his tongue, as if to soothe the flesh he'd just driven insane. "That was your clit."

She could barely feel those tantalizing sweeps of his tongue. "My what?"

He rested his chin on top of her mound. His morning beard pricked her sensitized flesh. The relentless demand in her body subsided to a dissatisfied howl.

His smile was pure male satisfaction as he explained. "Your clit. A very tasty, sensitive little button that, apparently, likes to come out and play."

"Oh." Now that the furor inside had died down, she was beginning to feel embarrassed again.

Her feelings must have shown on her face, because he got a real determined look and said, "Oh no you don't."

She didn't get a chance to ask what he meant, as he moved his face. His prickly, bearded chin brushed her clit, and she almost leapt out of her skin.

"Asa!"

She only had time to register the surprise in his eyes as he paused. The tiny pricks of sensation were excruciating. Locked somewhere between pain and pleasure, she held her breath.

"Easy, darlin'."

Asa trapped her hips tightly in his hands before he cautiously shifted his chin again. The effect on Elizabeth was immediate. Her fingers clenched tighter in his hair, dragging him closer.

"Like that?" he asked.

"Harder," she begged. "Oh please, harder."

He did it again, tentatively adding a bit more pressure. He could tell from the way her head tossed that it wasn't enough, but damn, her woman's flesh was so delicate, he didn't want it cut up.

Catching him by surprise, she yanked on his hair and threw her hips up at the same time, driving his chin into her swollen clit. "Yessss!"

He almost came at the sound of her gratification. Using one hand to steady her hips, he slid the other down to his pants. He let her ride his chin however she wanted, while he pulled his cock free. He paused for a heart beat to smear his hand with her copious juices. Wrapping his fist around his painfully aroused flesh, he started pumping while grinding his rough chin against her hard clit. He worried about hurting her, but she liked it rough, and anything less had her sobbing in frustration. Suddenly, with no warning, her body convulsed and she arched her hips into his face, grinding and screaming, her body jerking in powerful spasms. It was all he needed for his own orgasm to crash over him. As his seed jetted out onto the floor, he twisted his face into her pussy, capturing her little clit between his lips, holding it firmly as he sucked it while the crashing waves of pleasure took him out of himself. He felt her struggle to get away, but something primitive in him refused to let her deny him anything. Least of all, the taste of her satisfaction, the way he wanted it.

He sucked harder. She screamed again and the spasms began again, throwing her cunt against his mouth before she tried to jerk away, but he wasn't letting her get away. He clamped his lips down and followed the bucking of her hips. He would never let her leave him. She was his.

It was her sobs that got his attention. And her pleas for mercy. He came back to himself to find her jerking under his mouth.

"Shhhh, darlin'," he murmured, reluctantly releasing her clit. It made a little popping sound as it sprang into the air.

She groaned and shuddered.

He pulled back and assessed the damage. Her beautiful cunt was swollen and red. Her entire pussy looked well loved. Her scent enveloped him. A combination of satisfied woman and vanilla.

He stood. She curled onto her side. Her ribs heaved with her efforts to breathe. It was almost a rejection. He pulled her dress down and leaned over the table to see her face.

"You okay?" he asked, stroking her wild tangle of hair.

She groaned again, and then grabbed his thigh. Before he could figure out what she had planned, she dragged herself around until her mouth was lined up with his groin. His knees buckled when she took his softening cock into the heat of her mouth.

He froze, not knowing what to do. She seemed content to hold him in her mouth, suckling him gently while her breathing slowly returned to normal. He stroked her hair and murmured soothing nonsense, until with a soft sigh, she released him. His cock waved enthusiastically in the air, clearly up for another round. She stroked him lazily with her hand.

"When you put him in my mouth, what's that called?"

Of all the things he expected her to say, that hadn't been it. "You're sucking my cock."

She frowned, squeezing him lightly and smiling when his cock jerked in reaction. "No. What's it called when you do it to me?"

He cleared his throat. "Fucking your face."

She looked him straight in the eye, her gaze slumberous and heavy lidded. She tugged his eager cock toward her and said, "Fuck my face, Asa."

Chapter Six

❧

The one bad thing about having a husband who could handle things was that it left no excuse for avoiding housework. Dipping her white rag in water, Elizabeth swatted at a few drifting dust motes before going back to wiping down the parlor lamp's milk glass dome. She tried very hard to keep her eyes on the job, but the late summer sunshine kept taunting her through the lace curtains. Every now and then, a rose scented breeze would waft in, fluttering the curtains and stirring up all kinds of longings. She scrubbed at a soot mark and tried not to imagine how good it would feel to be riding into the mountains, maybe stopping at the swimming hole for a dip.

She paused, sighed and then took herself to task. There'd been a time when her impulses had ruled her life, but not anymore. Being impulsive could cost a person their home, family and everything they thought true about themselves. She wasn't an immature child, incapable of understanding the consequences of her actions or the depth of her responsibilities. She was a lady and a ranch owner. Ladies didn't cavort around the countryside unescorted, let alone take dips in swimming holes. They tended to the house, pretended they didn't sweat, and smiled, even if they were melting in the heat faster than a candle on a stove.

She sighed again and used the end of her apron to wipe the sweat from her brow. She looked at the smudge and winced. Being a lady was going to be the death of her. Unfortunately, it was part of the deal she'd struck with her husband. Since the man was willing to borrow the kind of life-threatening troubles that came with the Rocking C, she was locked into the role of lady. It was a matter of honor to give him what he wanted. At least for her.

Dipping her rag in saleratus, she rubbed anew at the last vestige of the smudge. When it came off, she breathed a sigh of relief, put her hands in the small of her back and massaged her aching muscles. She would have loved to stretch her whole back but the darned corset negated any such pleasure.

She stepped over to the window and inhaled the fresh breeze, letting it sweep the boredom away along with the scent of beeswax and saleratus. Glancing over her shoulder, she decided it wasn't all for nothing. The parlor looked good. Warm, inviting, subtly gleaming. Now, if she could keep folks to the parlor and the kitchen, she could call it quits for the day. She smiled wryly and shook her head. Like that was going to happen. Asa was definitely going to want to take over the study. With all the work that had waited since her father died, she'd never gotten around to keeping it clean. Dust piled every corner along with three months of neglected bookkeeping.

A whinny outside returned her attention to the outdoors. A rider came through the arch over the gate. Even if she hadn't recognized the blood bay gelding, she'd never forget the man riding in. Aaron! She straightened her hair, whipped off her apron and stuffed it into the umbrella stand. By the time she heard the porch step creak under his foot, she had her hand on the doorknob. She counted to three, and then swung it open, smiling at his misstep when the door wasn't there to stop his hand from knocking.

"Hi."

His response was a laugh. "One of these days, you're not going to catch me with that."

His laughter warmed her. "I've been catching you for fifteen years. If you were going to wise up, I think you would have done it by now."

His "you would think" made her smile. For the fifteen years she'd been catching him, he'd been giving her the same answer. It was like an anchor for her soul. The rest of her world might be in chaos, but this part was the same. Aaron was always there. They fought more often than they agreed due to his tendency to think he was always right, but, as they'd grown up as close as brother and sister, somehow it seemed right.

She stepped back to usher him into the relative coolness of the foyer. "What brings you here?"

"Heard in town you married up a couple times this week."

She winced. "Once was a mistake I corrected. The second time was for real."

He removed his hat and tossed it onto the hat rack. His brown hair was ruthlessly smoothed back from his square face. There was no mistaking the concern in his blue eyes as he swept her from head to toe. "Well, I guess you could say I'm here to check whether wedding number two was a mistake."

It wasn't going to be a pleasant visit, Elizabeth decided. He was obviously on one of his protective I-know-better-than-you missions. She motioned him into the parlor. "I have no complaints and I'm not expecting any."

He glanced up after settling himself into her father's chair. "Right."

The one word came out so scathingly patronizing, for a second, the image of her father imposed itself over Aaron's face. She blinked to dispel it. "I'm satisfied with my marriage."

"So you're happy?"

"For goodness sake, Aaron!" she protested as she reminded herself to sink decorously into the wing-backed chair across from him. "I've only known the man twenty-four hours. I can't tell you what he likes for breakfast, let alone whether we're going to suit!"

"But you married him."

There was censure in the statement, as if her decision had been anything but the only choice available. It was also in his blue eyes and his posture, making her realize why he reminded her of her father. His big, stocky build was a fair image of Coyote Bill's. Combined with him sitting in her father's chair, delivering condemnation in a quiet, polite tone of voice, the situation was enough to resurrect the dead.

"Of course I married him." She arranged her skirt into straight folds. "If you remember correctly, it was your suggestion that I marry."

"I suggested you marry one of the local boys. I didn't say to pick a man with a reputation dangerous enough in itself to be a threat." He said it as if she'd failed to follow his directions.

"Your suggestion that I marry was perfectly valid, and I considered it fully before making my decision."

He sat back in his seat and regarded her coolly. "So, why didn't you consult me when you went husband-hunting?"

"Why would I?"

"Because I could have guided you past the most obvious bad choices?"

She brushed a piece of lint from her skirt and grabbed hold of her patience. "Who would you have suggested I pick that I haven't already thought of?"

"Willy Samuel?"

"Willy Samuel is sweet on Jane Hendricks."

"He'd throw her over in a heartbeat for this ranch."

That said about all she needed to know about his honor. "And spend the rest of his life comparing me with the love of his life? I don't think so."

"Jason Miller?"

"He's fonder of whining than of working."

"But you could control him."

"So could anyone else with enough wits and a big enough bribe."

He sighed. "Yeah. I guess you'd never be able to trust him. He's also a bit of a mamma's boy."

"Between the two of them, I'd spend my marriage sleeping with my eyes open." He opened his mouth to trot out another suggestion, and she forestalled him by holding up her hand. "We've already eliminated half the eligible bachelors in the vicinity, but just let me go through the remaining two. Jeremiah Palmer drinks when he's not working and I will not take up with a drinking man. Brian Pallante hates the territory and has every intention of going back East as soon as he gets his sister married to someone who'll take that puny spread of his. Offering him the Rocking C would only be an incentive for him to sell more of this territory."

"Can I speak now?"

"Of course."

"I wasn't going to suggest either of those men."

"Well, if you were going to suggest one of the hands, I have to say it's a poor choice. Most of the men couldn't stand a tie if it came with whiskey and saloon girls attached."

"Elizabeth!"

Damn! She'd forgotten in the ease of long companionship that ladies didn't know of saloon girls, let alone mention them. Especially with Aaron, who had rigid ideas about women and their roles. "I'm sorry."

"You should be." He gave her one of those I-expected-better-of-you looks and then sighed. He waved his hand. "Sometimes, I forget who your mother was."

So did she. She glanced at her hands in her lap. Her grip on her fingers was so tight, her knuckles were white. She hoped her mother had attained some fun out of life before she died. She counted to ten and eased her grasp. "My mother was from a respectable family back East."

"My pa said she was beautiful, but wild as a March hare."

"She wasn't crazy!"

"You know the stories as well as I do. What would you call her?"

Desperate. She'd call her mother desperate. Living with her father had a way of provoking that reaction in a woman.

"My mother, for all her supposed faults, was my mother." She met the pity and censure in his gaze without flinching. "I prefer to think of her as a good woman who made some bad choices."

The first one was thinking her father was lovable. The second was thinking she could save him. The third one had killed her — thinking she could escape him.

"I'm sure you would, but people around here have long memories." Aaron reached over and placed his hand on hers. His palm was rough and hard. "You've got to be careful, Elly, or your reputation will go the way of hers."

She freed her hand under the guise of smoothing her skirt. "I prefer to think people will accept me as I am. I've done nothing to be ashamed of."

"Marrying two men in the space of two days has set a few tongues wagging."

She was sure it had. "No matter who I married, people were going to gossip."

"They'd gossip a lot less if you hadn't plucked your latest from that cesspool Dell's!"

"At the time, I didn't have any choice."

"You could have come to me."

"It was a situation that required my personal attention."

"Any situation that requires entering a saloon requires a man to solve it." He sat forward in the chair, his hands digging into the upholstered arm. "Dammit, Elly! If you don't want to end up like your mother, you need help. You're running wilder than she ever did!"

His anger, his opinion, hit her like a fist in the gut. "Is that what you think of me?" she asked in a whisper.

"Ah, hell, runt." He ran his hand through his hair. "Of course not. You just get me so mad, I forget what I'm saying."

She didn't think he forgot a thing. She wondered if Asa shared Aaron's opinion of her character. She wondered if he was just waiting for the moment when she dropped her ladylike demeanor and shamed him. She'd have to be careful, she decided. Very careful not to mess up. Asa had bargained for a lady. If she saw to it that's what he got, he'd be satisfied. He wouldn't leave.

"I shouldn't have said that," Aaron apologized.

"No. You shouldn't have."

He sank back into the upholstery. "I shouldn't have brought up your mother at all. I know how much it upsets you."

It didn't upset her, it infuriated her, but no one seemed to recognize that. She made her "thank you" properly polite.

"How did we get on the subject in the first place?"

"You were expressing your displeasure with my taste in husbands and suggesting marrying one of the hands would have been a better alternative."

"I did no such thing," he countered wryly. "You went off on a tangent before I could point out that Jed Simmons would have made you an excellent husband."

"Your foreman?"

"Don't sound so shocked. He's single, knows ranching like the back of his hand, and is as dependable as the day is long."

She couldn't help sounding shocked. She was. Jed Simmons had never entered her head as a choice.

"He's only a few years older than me, and not bad looking to boot," Aaron continued.

"I never considered him."

"If you'd sought my counsel before impulsively rushing into a solution, you would have."

"The man is a dictator."

"Jed knows what needs doing and he expects it to get done. My ranch has never run smoother."

"I don't like the way he treats his horse."

"That buckskin he rides never got past green broke, but that just means Jed doesn't shy away from a challenge."

"Or from an opportunity to dominate something."

He considered her point for a moment, his head tilted slightly to one side. "I don't think you'd need to worry about Jed being heavy-handed. He's a fair man. As long as you handled the house and minded his rules, he'd be a good husband."

"Can you honestly see me calling a man who's taken orders from me when you've loaned him out as Mister?"

Aaron shrugged. "I don't see the problem. You'd be calling any husband Mr."

What the hell is wrong with Asa?

The memory of Asa's question came shooting to the fore. She'd been mad at him because he didn't expect overt subservience. She mentally shook her head. No doubt about it, she owed the man an apology. "Well, whether Jed would make a suitable husband or not, is rather a moot point. I'm married now."

Thankfully, to someone else.

"I came here to talk about that."

"I thought as much, but your concern is unnecessary."

"I was thinking along the lines of a solution."

"Excuse me?"

"For the right amount of money, Judge Carlson would be willing to set aside the marriage. He wasn't content on how it proceeded anyway." His glance said he was aware the judge placed the blame on her. It also said he knew her well enough not to disagree.

"On what grounds, for heavens sake?" she asked, exasperated. "The marriage has been consummated!"

Aaron's neck went beet red, highlighting the red in his brown hair. "With a man of MacIntyre's reputation, I assumed that would be the case." The red spread to his cheeks as he doggedly pursued his point. "It's...commendable that you're up and about, attending to your duties today, but your continued sufferance is unnecessary."

He sounded as if he'd fully expected to find her gushing blood this morning in the wake of her husband's assault. "I assure you, Aaron. I'm fine."

"You're a lady and you have to say that. I'm also aware of your stubborn nature that makes it impossible for you to admit you made a mistake. But, the bottom line is, a woman of your sensibilities has no place taking up with a gunslinger."

That was going too far. She stood up. "I did not take up with a gunslinger!"

"If he isn't one already, MacIntyre's one slip from it!"

She didn't know much about her husband, but instinct told her Asa was far from slipping. She shook out her skirts, and said coldly, "I think this conversation has gone far enough."

Aaron caught her wrist in his hand, chaining her in place. "Hear me out."

She tugged, but he didn't let go. Since she had little choice, she listened, but inside, anger fermented.

"Judge Carlson is willing to set aside the marriage due to it taking place under false pretenses." She suffered another gaze full of criticism before he explained, "Apparently, you failed to promise to love, honor, and obey."

"Asa and I worked that out between us, not that it's any of your business."

"I'm sure MacIntyre agreed to a whole lot of nonsense to get his hands on this ranch, but he's no one a lady such as yourself should put up with."

She'd about reached her limit. "For heaven's sake, Aaron! We grew up together. Am I so good at pretending that you've forgotten I ride and shoot better than you?"

The fingers on her wrist tightened imperceptibly. She reigned in her temper as he continued. "How you were raised wasn't your fault. For all his mistakes, your father made up for his error in raising you wild by sending you back East to learn the things a mother would have taught you."

"He was a saint."

"There's no need to be sarcastic. I was there when you were growing up. I know the mistakes the man made. How frustrated he got when you weren't the son he wanted, but, in the end, he did right."

By banishing her from everything she loved? By taking away her heart and soul and condemning her to four horrible years of monotonous lessons in frivolous deportment? He might as well have sent her to jail.

"And that makes up for everything?" she asked.

"It makes up for one hell of a lot."

Not in her book. Never in her book. She jerked on her arm. "Let me go."

He did reluctantly. "As soon as you calm down, Elizabeth," Aaron assured her, "you're going to see the sense in what I'm saying, so listen up."

"Do I have a choice?"

"Not really."

She sighed. Whether she agreed with him or not, Aaron truly believed he was protecting her. "Then go ahead, just know I'm not changing my mind."

"Being the person he is, I'm sure MacIntyre will take a cash offering not to contest the divorce. It'll take a few months to push through, but Jed can come over here and keep things running until you're free to marry."

His plan had more holes than a moth-eaten sweater. "Let me get this straight," she said, untwisting her shirt sleeve as she clarified. "All I've got to do to make life perfect is to come up with enough cash from a bankrupt ranch to bribe a judge and a gunslinger, keep the bank from foreclosing while I sort out my personal life, and learn not to anger my next husband?"

"Not perfect," he countered, "but workable. As I mentioned before, if you hadn't been so impulsive and consulted me before taking it into your head to marry, things wouldn't be so complicated now."

"The only reason things seem complicated is because you refuse to acknowledge my plan is a perfectly good one."

"Dammit, Elly! I would have married you myself if Patricia hadn't trapped me into marriage already."

She couldn't resist the taunt. "Must be a failure in your superior planning abilities that made it possible for her to trap you."

"She wanted it!"

"Apparently, so did you. Enough to risk getting her in the family way."

"I did the right thing!"

"You met your responsibilities beautifully, but my point is that *your* plan was to have a little fun. You worked for months to get it. You got your fun, but, in all your planning, you never once glimpsed the lifelong commitment attached to the back end."

"What exactly are you getting at?" His blue eyes narrowed as he stared at her, daring her to say what she felt.

Without a qualm, she did just that. "I feel, in light of past circumstances, that your plans lack long-term considerations."

"I was young and a man!"

"As that was only two years ago, you're still young and it goes without saying that you're still a man."

His hands raked through his hair, springing free the curls he hated, proving she'd made her point even as he denied it. "I fail to see that my marriage to Patricia has anything to do with you."

"Exactly. As your marriage to Patricia is none of my concern, my marriage to Asa is none of yours."

"But you don't have to stay married to him."

"No, I don't, and I thank you for pointing that out, but I want to stay married to Asa MacIntyre. From all accounting, he's an honorable man. He doesn't lean to excessive drink and he has more than enough knowledge and experience to get the Rocking C back on its feet, so, while I appreciate your concern, I have no need of it."

He looked ready to argue. If there was one good thing about being a lady, it was the ability to end unseemly conversations. She patted Aaron's hand, and took over the conversation. "Quite honestly, I'm content with my choice of husbands." She squashed his argument with a friendly smile. "Now, would you like some blackberry cobbler before you head back to your place?"

Aaron stood. He slapped his hand against his blue denims. "You're going to be stubborn about this, aren't you?"

"I made a sound decision. There's nothing stubborn about it."

He reached out and squeezed her shoulder. "I care about you, runt. Don't let your pride get in the way if you need help."

"I won't."

"In that case, I'll have some of that cobbler."

As she led the way to the kitchen, Elizabeth breathed a sigh of relief that her father's plans for her to marry Aaron had never come to fruition. They were good friends, but they would never have suited as husband and wife.

Chapter Seven

ॐ

If he were a man who took killing lightly, this might be the moment for it, Asa decided as he watched Elizabeth through the kitchen window. As sure as God made little green apples, there was a man sitting at *his* kitchen table, chatting with *his* wife, eating the last of *his* blackberry cobbler. As the man was neither old nor wearing a collar, he figured he'd get off lightly if the law ever caught up to him.

Part of him couldn't believe what he was seeing. He hadn't believed it when the guard he'd placed on the road had said there was a rider heading for the ranch. He hadn't wanted to believe it when the guard had said it was a friend of Elizabeth's, but it was hard to ignore when "it" sat at his kitchen table making free with his cobbler. Elizabeth was the first decent thing he'd ever obtained for himself, and already someone else was moving in.

Asa saw the man swirl his finger around the plate, cleaning crumbs off the edge. He said something. Elizabeth laughed, touched his hand with hers, and then got up to pour him some more coffee. The same as she'd done for Asa that morning. More than he resented the last of his baked goods going to the interloper, Asa resented Elizabeth fussing over the stranger. She was his wife, dammit.

Before he moved in to establish his claim, Asa took one last look at the stranger, noting his clean clothes, clean hands, clean everything. He remembered Brent's fancy dress and lily white hands. He looked down at his own, caked with dirt and grime. While Elizabeth had married him because of his reputation, she obviously had preferences in a man. He watched as the stranger efficiently used the napkin before him, and winced when he couldn't remember using his this morning. Clearly, given her druthers, Elizabeth liked a man clean and well-mannered. He knew enough not to wipe his mouth on a tablecloth, but was sure there were enough holes in his education for a woman with a fancy Eastern education to take note of. As for the dirt…he swatted at the dust on his denims. That came with the territory, but he guessed he didn't need to track it daily into the house.

He stepped back from the window. Elizabeth seemed safe enough, and, as hunkered in as the stranger was, Asa figured he'd stay put for the time it took him to visit the pump.

* * * * *

Five minutes later, damp from the washing up, Asa stepped through the back door. As soon as he entered the kitchen, the laughter stopped. Elizabeth jumped up. It could have been due to guilt, or, more probably, to the way the door slammed in his wake.

"Evening." He took off his hat, wincing when dust puffed out. His face and hands were clean, but a day's labor clung to his clothes. The stranger was clean, presentable and comfortable. It irked Asa almost as much as the drop of water that slid down his neck.

Elizabeth came immediately to his side. "You're home early." She took his hat from his hands.

"One of the men said he saw a stranger headin' this way."

Elizabeth started, and then smiled. "It must have been the new man. Everyone else knows Aaron's horse about as well as they know Aaron."

Actually, it'd been Sam, and he'd recognized the horse, but Asa hadn't found the knowledge that a male friend of Elizabeth's was visiting any more calming than if he'd been a stranger bent on mischief.

Asa looked over Elizabeth's shoulder at the man wiping his mouth on the napkin. He was probably in his early twenties and about as comfortable as a man could get.

"That blood bay gelding yours?" Asa asked.

"Yes."

"Nice horse. Shame he's gelded."

"That's what I thought when I bought him off an Easterner." The man pushed back his chair. The same squalling chair Asa had been sitting on that morning. The darned thing didn't even squawk. Asa took the irritation in stride as the man extended his hand in greeting. "Aaron Ballard."

"Asa MacIntyre."

"You have quite a reputation."

Asa settled his weight onto his heels as he exchanged a civilized handshake. "People like to talk, especially when things get boring."

Ballard didn't let go of the subject as easily as he released Asa's hand. "Any truth to the rumors?"

He shrugged. Out of the corner of his eye, he noticed Elizabeth fussing with his hat. "Enough so you needn't be worried Elizabeth's been left short-changed and flat-footed."

The man opened his mouth, probably to grill him more, but Asa cut him off by saying to Elizabeth, "You know, darlin, I kinda like that hat just the way it is. I've got the dust settled just so. Keeps it nice and balanced in a strong wind."

Elizabeth immediately stopped fussing with the brim. "I'm sorry."

He smiled, liking how sweet she looked, how respectable. How wifely. "No harm done."

Instead of putting it away, she smiled uncertainly. There was a soft side to her smile that had him wondering if she was glad to see him?

"Did you really post a guard on the house?" she asked. She was staring at him like he'd done something more extraordinary than taking care that his wife was safe.

His "Yes" was drowned out when the stranger said, "Of course he did, Elly! What man worth his salt wouldn't make sure the ranch house was safe? This is where you keep the money."

Asa wanted to shoot the yahoo when Elizabeth's smile dropped from sweet to disappointed. "Of course."

Though her expression was poker-faced, he knew he'd never get the brim of his hat to recover from the death grip she had on it. In the most practical voice he'd ever heard her use, she told him, "You haven't seen it yet, but there's a safe in the office. It'd take dynamite for anyone to get money out of there."

Now, there was a picture to soothe his nerves. Strange men with dynamite in the house with Elizabeth. He shook his head, reached out and removed his hat from his wife's hands. "Well, if I ever get to the point in my life where I worry more about money than my family, I'll be sure to keep that as a comforting thought."

Asa would offend the devil himself to hear that uncharacteristically shy "thank you" of Elizabeth's. Darned if she didn't look as if she didn't know what to do with his concern. He drew her gaze with a touch to her cheek. "Everything's okay?"

"Oh, yes." Her gaze clung to his. She was nervous, startled and happy. All because he'd done the decent thing? Damn! The woman needed someone whether she showed it or not.

"Aaron is a long time friend and neighbor," Elizabeth said, as if to fill the silence that sprang up.

Which could explain the possessive air the man had about him.

Elizabeth waved her hand between them. "Aaron, this is my husband, Asa MacIntyre."

"Elizabeth," Ballard sighed with exasperation. "We already introduced ourselves."

"Oh, yes."

To Asa's way of thinking, Aaron didn't have to point out the obvious, but since he had, and since Elizabeth was looking like she'd love a hole to dive into, Asa passed his hat back into her keeping. As she grabbed it and darted to the peg by the door, he asked Aaron, "You say you live here about?"

"The Bar B runs the length of the Rocking C's western border." Ballard took a couple of steps forward and intercepted Elizabeth on her return. He put a proprietary hand on Elizabeth's shoulder. "Elizabeth and I are more like family than friends as we grew up together."

The man was looking to lose an arm, that much Asa could see. Elizabeth stepped away. Asa slapped a smile on his face as congenial as the one Aaron was sending him. "Then I guess I need to thank you for helping her out after her father passed on."

"Everyone did what they could."

Which, from what Asa could determine, was about nothing. "Well, I'd like to pay you for your time."

"That won't be necessary."

"I insist. You just tally up the work and send the bill over."

"Why don't we just say you owe me like for like?"

"I reckon I can settle for that." Easily.

"It's settled then."

Elizabeth stepped between them. Her hands kept smoothing her skirt over her hips in a nervous gesture. Asa figured it was a habit she'd be breaking herself of if she knew how it drew a man's imagination to wander.

"Could I get you a cup of coffee?" she asked him.

"That would taste good. Just let me signal the men everything's fine and get Shameless settled, then I'll be back."

"I could do that for you."

"Signal the men?" He smiled. "Darlin', if you tried to shoot off that gun of mine, you'd be dirtying the back of your skirt, not to mention sporting a bruise the size of Texas on your shoulder."

"Elizabeth's a darn good—" Aaron interrupted.

"I'm sure it can't be that hard," Elizabeth cut off the neighbor's interjection. "But I was referring to putting Shameless away."

She was wearing that perfectly calm expression which Asa was beginning to realize meant she was annoyed. He reached out and plucked his hat off the peg by the door where Elizabeth had put it. "I reckon I got just enough energy to settle Shameless as long as you set out some of that cobbler from last night to go with that coffee."

"Sorry, neighbor. Elizabeth was kind enough to share the last piece with me."

The words were polite, but the man wasn't sorry about anything. Asa settled his hat on his head. "Well, now, that is a shame. The thought of that cobbler kept me going all day."

"One area where Elizabeth never makes a mistake is the kitchen."

The implication being that there were areas where she did mess up. One of them in her choice of husbands? Asa waited a heartbeat for Elizabeth to lay into the man, but, to his surprise, she just stood there. Mouth shut, face tight, accepting the barb. Was she that fond of the yahoo?

"Funny," Asa drawled, keeping his annoyance in check. "The one thing I picked up right away is that Elizabeth is one capable woman. Makes a man stay on his toes so as not to be outshined."

It might have been his imagination, but he thought Elizabeth sidled his way a bit. He slid his hand to her back in silent encouragement in case she had a mind to take an actual step.

Aaron laughed. "You only say that because you're newly married. Just wait around a bit. As a man who's watched her grow from diapers to pinafores, I'd say you've got a few surprises coming."

"I'm looking forward to them."

"She has more than a bit of her mother in her."

Beneath his fingers, Asa felt the start go through Elizabeth's body. In the wake of the ripple, her muscles pulled taut. He didn't know why, but it didn't take a genius to figure out the barb about her mother hurt.

"If her mother was half the woman Elizabeth appears to be, I'll count myself lucky."

Aaron's mouth twisted into a rueful smile. "It's that appearance that's going to do you in."

Elizabeth's small gasp cut through all Asa's pretensions toward manners. He slid his hand across Elizabeth's back until he could curve his fingers around her shoulder and pull her into the protection of his side. "Mister, I don't know what you were looking for when you came here, but, if it's trouble, I think you just found it."

The bastard had the gall to look offended. "Excuse me?"

"I never knew Elizabeth's mother. I never met her father. But I've met Elizabeth and I've met you, and, from that, I'm willing to lay money that you figured I was too ignorant, and Elizabeth too much a lady, to comment on an insult you slid into the conversation like it was just another how-de-do."

"I only meant to say—"

"I have no interest in what you say. I'm more interested in how you say it." Asa stroked his fingers down Elizabeth's arm. Damn the son of a bitch! Her muscles were still hauled up as tight as a bowstring. "Where I come from, if a man plans on picking on a woman, he damned well better expect her husband to come calling."

"I wasn't picking on Elizabeth."

"Uh-huh." Beneath his hand Elizabeth's muscles pulled tighter. Probably because she could feel the tension in his own muscles and figured he had more to say on the subject. She'd be right, too. No one was going to take pot-shots at her while he was around. "So, why exactly are you here?"

Asa watched as Aaron bit back his hostility before admitting, "I came to check on Elizabeth."

No way that was the only reason he was here. "And?"

She assures me she's fine. The look he sent Elizabeth said he had his doubts.

"Good." Asa tipped his hat at Aaron. "Then, seeing as you've got what you came for, you can be on your way."

Beside him, Elizabeth gasped. In front of him, Aaron smoldered. In his eyes, Asa read his fury. He also read, for whatever reason, he wasn't going to push things. That was a pity. Asa would have loved to gut-punch the yahoo. For what he'd said to Elizabeth, and also for eating the last of his cobbler.

"I'll see you later, Elizabeth." The man nodded to Elizabeth.

"Thank you for stopping by," she answered calmly as if the two men on either side of her weren't bristling with hostility.

The woman had style. She was also quick on her feet. She'd managed to shift so any blows he and Ballard wanted would have to happen over her head.

"I'll see you out," Asa volunteered, putting himself between Elizabeth and Ballard.

"That won't be necessary." Ballard tipped his hat to Elizabeth. "I know the way to the door."

Asa smiled. "I wouldn't dream of upsetting Elizabeth by not showing you out. She sets store by good manners."

Instead of bristling obligingly at the shot, Ballard visibly relaxed and sent him a glance of what could only be called approval. Asa shook his head as the man retrieved his hat from the rack by the front door. Didn't anyone around here react predictably?

"If you need any help, don't hesitate to call," Ballard offered as he settled his hat on his head. "We're only an hour's ride away."

"I'll do that." When hell froze over.

"Say hi to Patricia and little Ron for me," Elizabeth jumped in.

"I will."

Affection softened the other man's face as he looked at Elizabeth. Asa wanted to break the man's fingers as he brushed them down the side of her cheek and said, "Take care, runt."

Her "I will" was just as soft, sending knife blades of jealousy ripping into Asa's guts. Was there more than friendship between the two?

Ballard stepped out the door. Elizabeth quietly shut it behind him. When she turned back to Asa, it didn't take hard looking to see she was mad as a wet hen. The hands on her hips and the angry flush on her cheeks were dead giveaways. And he knew exactly what she was mad about. She didn't like the fact that he'd threatened her friend.

"That was completely unnecessary."

"That yahoo had no right coming in here and hurting you."

"He's my friend."

"Then, honey, you need a new set of friends, 'cause with friends like that, you sure don't need to go hunting up enemies."

"Is that an order?"

"What?"

She folded her arms across her chest and asked him calmly. "Are you ordering me to not be friends with Aaron?"

He'd forgotten about requiring her promise of obedience. "Hell, no."

As he headed down the hall toward the back door, she fell into step beside him, and asked, "Where are you going?"

"I've still got to signal the men and put my horse away." He paused at the door. "Unless you have objections?"

He hadn't expected her to come with him, but as she showed no signs of slowing when she reached the door, he held it open for her.

Her nose lifted two inches. "Of course not."

As she passed, her scent of vanilla, beeswax and tantalizing woman drifted up to tease his nostrils. When she reached the top step and started to unwrap Shameless' reins, he said, "Is there something you want to say to me?"

She turned, reins in hand. He stepped off the porch, cleared his rifle from the saddle scabbard, and fired off two shots that signaled the all clear. As he slid the rifle back into the scabbard, she answered, "Yes."

He took the reins from her hands and slid his free arm around her waist. "Keep me company to the barn and you can tell me all about it."

As if she had any choice, Elizabeth thought. The man wasn't a bully, but he sure had a laid back way of getting what he wanted, which, apparently, was her company. As he shortened his strides to match hers, she felt his fingers slide up her side.

"I thought I told you not to wear one of these." His fingers tapped the bone of the corset. It made a slight "tick" sound.

She took a steadying breath. His scent filled her nostrils. She braced herself for the repugnance she usually felt at the way a man smelled. It didn't come. Asa smelled of horses, leather and the outdoors, but he also smelled pleasantly of something else. Something elementally him. Something she liked. "You didn't tell me not to wear a corset. You asked me not to wear one."

He sidestepped them around a manure pile. "You don't feel that's a bit of hair splitting?"

"No." She glanced up in time to see a smile flirt with his lips. The man was an enigma, taking offense at the slightest things, and at others, having the patience of a saint.

"You want me to order you not to wear it?"

"Not hardly."

"Why not? The thing seems darned uncomfortable."

"It is."

"Then why wear it?" He stepped aside to let her through the barn door first.

"No proper lady would be without one."

"Uh-huh."

"What does that mean?" The warm scent of the barn enclosed her in a welcoming hug.

"That's polite for 'I've never heard such bull in my life'."

"It's true. Being seen without a corset would be scandalous."

"My reputation could probably survive the scandal."

"Mine wouldn't."

He tied Shameless to the hitching post and made short work of the cinch. He had nice hands, Elizabeth decided. Long-fingered, broad across the back, and very agile.

"Correct me if I'm wrong, but, now that we're married, isn't your reputation mine?" He swung the heavy saddle clear of the gelding's back.

"Sort of." It was a blatant stall. His teeth flashed white in the sun-dappled interior, letting her know he was aware of it.

"Well..." He tossed the saddle onto the wooden support leaning against the wall. "Seeing as how my reputation doesn't give two hoots about anyone else's opinions, I guess you could chuck that contraption into the old well tonight."

"I don't think so."

"Why not?" He picked up a rag and started to wipe down Shameless.

"Because none of my dresses would fit." She grabbed a curry comb and moved in beside him, currying where he'd finished wiping. Beyond a quick glance in her direction, he didn't say anything.

"Hadn't thought of that." He moved to the other side of the horse and repeated the process. "Might be time for you to get a new wardrobe."

"You truly don't mind if I don't wear one and everyone notices?"

He folded his arms along the horse's back and regarded her across the breadth. "Let me put it this way; if you needed to move in a hurry, could you get the job done with that thing on?"

"Not hardly." She was lucky to manage bending over to get biscuits out of the oven.

"Then I don't mind a bit." He flicked his finger at her nose, and went back to wiping down the horse.

It took her a minute to put it together, it was such a novel concept. "You're concerned about my safety."

"It's a husband's job to take care of his wife."

As he was wiping the sweat from Shameless' underbelly, she couldn't see his expression, but that was just as well since he couldn't see hers. The man didn't give two hoots about convention if it meant her safety. She was flabbergasted and, well...warmed.

She bit her lip, weighing the pluses of never again having to have those bone stays cut into her flesh against her moral obligation to protect her husband's reputation. "People would talk."

"I'd survive." He tossed the rag into the corner. He grabbed a water bucket, and slapped Shameless' shoulder. "Bet you'd like some water, big fella."

He headed to the pump just outside the barn door. Elizabeth watched him go, words hovering on her tongue. She moved around the other side of the horse and started currying. Shameless let out a huge sigh. She patted his neck. "Feels good, huh?"

In response, he nibbled at the sheaf of hay on the floor. Over his neck, she watched Asa pump the handle that would bring up the water. It took a fair amount of effort. Through his shirt, she imagined she could see the play of muscles. Her husband was a strong man. The thought didn't dismay her the way it had yesterday. As a matter of fact, it was kind of intriguing, watching the way his shirt stretched and clung to the muscles bunching beneath. The sight caused a funny sensation in her belly. He turned to bring the bucket back in, and she hastily dropped her gaze, which was silly as he couldn't see into the cool interior from the bright sunshine. He set the water in front of Shameless who promptly blew suspiciously across its surface before drinking.

"I have a compromise to suggest," she said.

"I'm listening." He picked up the bristle brush and smoothed the hair on the opposite side of the horse.

She stopped currying, bit her lip, then took the plunge. "I'll only wear the corset when we go into town."

He glanced at her. "You sure?"

"As long as you make me a promise."

"Thought there might be a catch."

"If it ever starts to bother you, I'd like you to let me know before you make any decisions."

"Decisions?"

"Yes. I'd like the opportunity to rectify the problem before you draw the obvious conclusions."

He straightened from checking Shameless' hoofs. "Conclusions?"

She felt the heat creeping into her face, but she held her ground. "Yes, before you decide my lack of corset indicates a lack of moral character, I'd like the opportunity to commence wearing it again."

He laughed. "Darlin', if finding you entertaining good-looking men in my kitchen in the middle of the day doesn't get me thinking along those lines, I doubt your not strapping yourself into that contraption is going to get me doubting your 'moral character'."

"Aaron just stopped by to make sure I was all right."

He came around to her side of the horse. He picked up Shameless' front hoof and set to work with the pick. "He heard the rumors you married up again."

"Yes." She wished she could see his face. "He was concerned."

"He was jealous."

She laughed. That would be the day! "Aaron and I are just friends. He has a wife and a two-year-old son."

He shot her a knowing glance over his shoulder. "Those things have nothing to do with his wanting you."

"You misread the situation."

She stepped back as he slid his hand down his horse's side to get to the rear hoof. "I'll allow one of us has a hold of the wrong end of the stick."

It was clear from his tone that he thought it was her. "Does this mean you're going to forbid me to continue our friendship?"

He dropped Shameless' foot back to the ground and stood to his full height. "Everybody's got to make those kinds of decisions for themselves."

He put the pick back in the tack box behind her. She turned with him, wanting this settled. "What exactly does that mean?"

"It means," he said, reaching out to tuck a strand behind her ear, "that time has a way of making clear who your friends are." He took a step toward her. Suddenly, he was too close. She took a step back and came up against the warm barrier of Shameless' side.

"You're going to smell all horsey after this," he informed her.

After what? she thought desperately while saying aloud, "I like horses."

"I can see that."

His hand cupped the back of her head. His fingers were doing something to her nape that sent chills down her spine. She couldn't tell from his expression whether he was angry or amused. All she could tell was that he was very intent.

"You burrowing into Shameless' side because you're afraid?" he asked.

"I don't understand you!" she burst out.

He smiled a slow smile that captured her attention, it was so lazy and full of promise. "You'll figure me out eventually."

She'd prefer now. He stepped forword, until the toes of his boots touched the toes of her shoes. Her heartbeat throbbed in her throat. Was he trying to get even with her for Aaron's arrogance? "I'm sorry Aaron said what he did."

He stroked his finger around her ear. She couldn't hide the shudder that went down her spine.

His smile broadened. "Why?"

"Why what?"

"Why are you apologizing for Aaron? He's a grown man."

"He's a little protective."

"I have a good idea who Aaron is and what he's up to."

She swallowed as he shifted forward a bit more. "I don't think you understand the situation."

"As I said before, time has a way of clearing up these matters."

His breath whispered across her brow. It suddenly dawned on her that he was planning seduction, not retaliation. "You're going to kiss me!"

She wished the words back as soon as they popped out of her mouth.

His lazy smile spread to a full-fledged grin. "Like I told your neighbor, you keep a man on his toes."

She wasn't sure if she wanted his mouth or not. She expected him to pull her away from the horse. That's why she wasn't prepared for his kiss when it came, because, instead of pulling her into his arms, he slid up against her, easing her into an embrace. His mouth brushed hers as his chest settled onto her breasts. Her gasp puffed against his lips. His chuckle vibrated against her chest.

"You got any objections?" he asked as his mouth slid across her cheek.

"Yes. No." Was he actually nibbling on her neck? Goosebumps chased down her arms. She squeezed her eyes tightly closed and confessed on a high squeak, "I don't know."

She felt him pull aside the collar of her shirt. "That's what I figured."

He kissed the spot where her collarbone met her neck. She never knew anything could feel so good. She felt his whole body shift as he draped his arms over Shameless' back. The move brought his entire body the length of hers. The sensation was so sublime as to be sinful. "Are you sure we should be doing this?"

"Absolutely."

"I meant here."

"This barn's off limits for a couple of hours."

"A couple of hours!" What in the world did the man intend to do? Last night hadn't taken more than a couple of minutes!

"Yup." He shifted his torso from right to left and then back again. "A newly married man gets to make all sorts of requests."

She opened her eyes to find his face eye-blurringly close. "You knew I'd come down to the barn with you?"

"Gotta admit you made that part real easy."

"Why the barn? Why not the house?"

His features blurred to nothing as he kissed the tip of her nose. "You're such a practical thing."

"That didn't answer my question."

His shrug did strange things to her equilibrium. "Always wanted to spark a girl in a barn." His mouth brushed hers again in one of those teasing touches. "You ever been sparked?"

"No." It was a humiliating confession to be making at her age.

He leaned back. "Now, that's a darned shame. How old did you say you were?"

"I was twenty-two last April."

His fingers brushed her temple as he clicked his tongue. "Just a baby."

"A lot of women have four or five kids at my age!"

"I'll get to work on that right away if you're set on competing."

He tilted his head and pressed a gentle, yet strangely intense kiss on the side of her neck. "I was just making a point," she gasped.

His lips parted. She felt the touch of his tongue before he sucked softly, and her knees turned to jelly. "Oh my God!"

"Easy, darlin'. I've got you."

His "got you" was the insertion of his knee between her thighs. With a hitch, he lifted her until she was suspended there, straddling his hard thigh, the horse at her back, Asa's mouth on her neck. It was the most astounding moment of her life.

"You like that?" he asked. His breath on her neck sent a new spray of goose bumps down her arms.

She bit her lip and nodded.

"I'll keep that in mind." She couldn't begrudge the smile she heard in his voice. Her neck felt bereft when he left it to place his mouth on hers.

"Open your mouth, darlin'."

She didn't hesitate.

"That's good." The words breathed into her mouth didn't prepare her for the sheer pleasure of his kiss. "Put your arms around my neck."

She dragged her arms up from her sides. She felt so lethargic it was hard to do, but she found it much more satisfying when she did. It gave her the leverage she needed to prolong his kiss when he would have pulled away. When he paused for a moment, she tipped her head back, hoping he'd resume his attention to her neck. His response was a chuckle and a total commitment to the task. A restless feeling filled her. Her stomach pulled taut and the area between her thighs felt equally tight and aching. She shifted, trying to ease the sensation. Or increase it. She was no longer sure.

His big hands splayed over her hips. "Like this," he whispered in her ear.

He arched her back, pressing her hips into his thigh while her head rested against Shameless' side. The sensation as she slid down his leg was breath-stealing. Though his hand in the small of her back kept her as he wanted, his lips on her neck were a far better anchor.

"What are you doing to me?"

"Just a little innocent sparking."

There was nothing innocent about what he was doing to her. It was as sinful as all get out and it was probably a lack in her moral character that she demanded more. "Do it again."

"You do it."

"I don't know how."

"Like this." He nipped her neck. The sharp jolt of pleasure ricocheted through her torso up into his. The jerk of her hips dragged her pussy across the rough denim of his pants, abrading her sensitive flesh deliciously.

"That's right," he drawled in her ear when she threw her head back and moaned. His hands on her hips encouraged another slide against his thigh. "Just like riding a horse. Move with me."

She'd been riding since she was three. Catching his rhythm was as natural as breathing. His mouth returned to hers, less gentle, more demanding. More in tune with the sensations charging through her body. Her breath came in gasps. Her grip tightened around his shoulders. Her hips took over the rhythm, freeing his hands from the obligation. Her pussy swelled and pouted, increasing the pleasure, the ache. The fire consumed her, spiraling higher. She tore her mouth from Asa's. She needed air. She needed the freedom to express the feeling exploding through her body She'd have been embarrassed by the moans escaping her if he hadn't been whispering in her ear how he liked them. How he wanted more.

His fingers climbed her torso, counting the ribs of her corset. When he reached the fullness of her breast where it swelled over the top of the garment, he flipped his hand and used the tender point of her nipple to count the ladder of his fingers.

She buried her face in the curve of his neck, afraid of where this was leading. Afraid she wouldn't care. "Asa!"

He released her hips. His hands cupped her breasts, weighing their fullness. With a squeeze, he tested their resiliency. "You're doing fine, darlin'."

His thumbs rubbed her nipples, gliding over her cotton shirt in a caress so light, it was almost illusionary. She needed more. She froze when he grasped both nipples simultaneously between his fingers and thumbs. For the space of two heart beats, he did nothing. In those two seconds, she discovered anticipation could be agony.

When she opened her eyes, he was watching her. The blush started at her toes, but she didn't look away. She couldn't. All the feelings she struggled to contain, he wore openly. Proudly. And she wanted to release all that passion, to experience it. To feel it pour over her in a sensual rush. She slid her fingers into his hair. The strands were cool and soft against her flesh. A balm to her over-stretched nerves. "Please," she whispered, holding his dark gaze with hers.

The pressure on her nipples increased, stopping just short of pain, holding her on the edge.

"Just lean back and trust me," he drawled.

She couldn't. She wanted to, but she couldn't give up the pleasure she'd attained. If she moved back, it would be gone.

He bent his head. A sharp twinge in her breast immediately blossomed to pleasure, surprising her enough to scoot back. She stared into Asa's face. His smile was sensuous. His expression intense.

"You bit my bubbies!"

His breathing was as labored as hers. "Lean back and I'll do it again."

She did, and he did. Gently. Thoroughly. It was almost too much. He squeezed and tugged her nipples with his lips as his hands worked her on his thigh. She tossed her head from side to side, trying to find release from the agony within. "Asa!"

"Jesus!" He was lifting her, tugging at her clothes, pushing her skirts away from between them. His hands were hot under her thighs. Even through the thin cotton of her pantaloons, she could feel their power. He lifted her. His teeth on her breast through her shirt distracted her from the intimacy of their position. She wrapped her fingers in his hair and forced his mouth harder on her breast.

"Put your legs around me."

She did, mindlessly obeying. The hard ridge of his cock burned hot and huge against her crotch. The pulsing pressure took her higher. Every nerve stretched to the breaking point. Reaching for release. "I can't stand it," she gasped.

"Not yet," he ordered, his face inches from hers, every plane etched with the passion taking them both.

"What?"

"I want to see."

She had no idea what he was talking about, but when his mouth left her breast, she groaned and pulled, but he didn't respond. His hands gripped her hips anew. With relentless force, he slid her pussy over his cock. From top to bottom, he let her slide. Her pantaloons, slick with her juices, caught at her pussy lips, tugging at her already sensitive flesh, adding another biting element of sensation. She moaned and twisted, pressing harder. Striving.

"That's it, darlin'. Ride me. All the way."

He repeated the motion, elongating the contact, forcing her to take more. Their combined gasps filled the barn, drowning out the soft sounds of horses shifting and pigeons roosting. The world dwindled until it only consisted of his touch, his breath, his will. She locked her ankles and pulled closer. It wasn't close enough. Every thought, every sensation, her world focused on the point where her hips met his. The pleasure built until it was too much. Something was happening.

"Help!"

"Go with it," he whispered hoarsely. She opened her eyes. His gaze locked with hers. Had she not been so far gone, his expression would have frightened her. He shifted their bodies until his hand could reach between them. His fingers grazed her swollen flesh, tracing the curves lightly, sending whispery darts of delight weaving through the heavy drive of pleasure grinding through her loins. With a firm tap on her clit, he forced all the sensation rampaging through her body to coalesce in one burning, aching, unbearably sensitive point of agony.

"Now," he ordered. At the same time, he thrust his hips into hers, grabbed her swollen clit in his fingers, pinching and tugging with relentless demand. One she was helpless to refuse. Her senses shattered on a scream that echoed forever.

Chapter Eight

က

He knew the minute the reality of the situation hit her. Her body, leaning so softly against his, stiffened one muscle at a time, starting at the base of her spine and spreading outward.

He sighed. "I suppose this is where you start fretting on my reputation?"

"Would you think me horribly selfish if I admit I'm more concerned with my own?"

He laughed softly. "I suppose I could make allowances."

Her "thanks" was a dry husk of embarrassment.

His stomach chose that moment to rumble loudly. She leapt on the sound like a kitten meeting a grasshopper. "You're hungry."

Her words vibrated against his chest.

"I told you, darlin'. I've been dreaming on that cobbler since sun-up."

"I gave the last to Aaron."

"You don't sound guilty."

The jerk of her shoulders under his hand could have been laughter. "I'm sorry."

"That's the most insincere apology I've heard in all my days."

"Would I be redeemed if I admit I baked a cake this morning?"

"Depends on what kind."

This time, he knew it was a laugh. Husky and sweet, slightly smothered by his shirt. "You're not fooling me, you know."

"Not fooling you how?" he asked.

"I heard your heart jump a beat when I mentioned cake."

"That's cheating."

She looked up from his chest. Despite the redness of her cheeks, she met his gaze squarely. Not much kept the woman down. He admired that.

"I bet I could ask for anything right now and you'd give it to me," she told him.

"That'd be a sucker's bet, so I won't be taking you up on it," he countered. "But it doesn't have anything to do with that cake you baked."

He didn't think her face could get any redder, but she proved him wrong. "I'll make you a deal."

She about strangled on the words, but he admired the fortitude that kept her fighting when she was so obviously handicapped by modesty.

"Shoot."

"You don't mention my outrageous behavior here, and I'll put frosting on that cake."

Saliva filled his mouth. "Chocolate cake with frosting?"

"Yes." She pushed out of his arms, collided with Shameless' side, and sidestepped out of range as if she expected him to be getting ideas again.

"You drive a hard bargain." He was hard put to hold his laughter in. Did she really think stepping out of his arms would make him forget how good she felt?

"Is it a deal?" she asked, swatting her skirts as if the wrinkles were responsible for her lapse from proper behavior.

"Depends," he drawled.

"On what?"

"On whether you plan on doing it again."

"Mr. MacIntyre!"

He stared at her. Her skirt was hopelessly wrinkled. Her hair was half down. Her neck sported a small love bruise. Her lips were swollen. On the whole, she was the spitting image of a woman who'd been tumbled in the barn. And she was back to calling him Mister? He reached out and straightened her bun. It immediately lurched to the other side. "Don't you think you could bring yourself to call me Asa?"

Her hands flew to her hair. "Oh, my goodness!" She centered the knot of hair on her head and held on for dear life. "I must look a fright."

"I like it."

She glared at him while clinging to her hair as if it alone had the last grip on her dignity. "I can't believe you let me stand here, carrying on a conversation, while totally, totally…unpresentable!"

"There's not a thing wrong with your looks."

If glares could kill, he'd be dead for his teasing. She released her hair and started fussing with her clothes. Small gasps of dismay punctuated her twisting this way and that. Finally, the burst of energy ended in a total stillness. "I'll never make it back to the house."

Her voice was as accepting as her expression. He had no idea why she put such stock in being 'presentable' but she did. "You promise to put chocolate frosting on that cake and I'll get you to the house without anyone being the wiser."

All the hope of a green horn betting his last dime rested in her gaze. "I don't see how—"

He clicked his tongue. The woman was the most suspicious critter he'd ever come across. "Getting you inside is my side of the deal. You just need to ante up."

She held out her hand. "Done."

He took it in his, the novelty of shaking hands with any female making him smile. "Done." He nodded with his chin. "You get that hair under control, and I'll get Shameless settled in his stall."

Her gaze flew to Shameless. Her cheeks flushed scarlet anew. It wasn't hard to follow where her memory traveled as she uttered a strangled "okay" and fled to the opposite side of the barn.

Damn! Asa thought. Who'd have thought having a wife would be so much fun? He looped a lariat around Shameless' neck and led him to his stall. From the corner of his eye, he saw Elizabeth fussing with her hair. Her arms were raised, her body partly turned so the curve of her breast flowed into the curve of her hip like the elemental sweep of a river. It was a purely feminine pose that caught him by surprise with a wave of possessiveness. Along with some pure lust. The woman was his. No one else's. And he wasn't going to lose her. Not for any reason.

Which meant he had to find a way to make her want to stay, he decided, as Shameless clopped placidly behind him on the way to his stall. The scene in the kitchen with Aaron had given him some bad moments. She'd been so at ease with the other man. Truly confident, not that fake stuff she kept tossing his way. He hadn't liked the feeling of standing outside looking in while she entertained the other man. He'd spent too much of his life that way.

He sighed. Apparently, this marriage business was trickier than he'd been led to believe. To hear married men tell it, a man got married and chains started locking tight as if by magic. Nights on the town were curtailed. Evenings were spent at home in front of the fire or carousing in the bedroom. A man had a wife to account for and to account to. Eventually, he had kids and his obligations expanded. A married man had responsibilities. He had obligations. He had people who cared about him. A married man was part of a bigger community. A married man belonged.

He nudged Shameless away from the grain bucket. The horse's grunt echoed his own feelings. It was getting pretty obvious that he needed to work on his husbanding, because, married or not, he couldn't be freer if he floated on a breeze. Elizabeth made no claims on him, chained him with no demands. She just let him be. He tossed the halter onto the hook with disgust. If that didn't beat all. Here he'd waited his whole life for someone to sink their claws into him, and he married up with the only woman who couldn't care less if he came home at night.

Maybe he was the only married man in history looking for the chains others whined about, but dammit, he was getting tired of drifting through life with no one caring whether he showed up at dusk or at dawn. He eyed Elizabeth using his corner vision. She was scrubbing at a smudge on her shirt. Damned if she didn't make him smile. Too proud to want the world to know she'd been sparking with her husband, yet hot-blooded enough to have enjoyed it.

A smart man would find a way to make himself matter to a woman like that. If he did, he'd never be on the outside looking in again. Elizabeth wasn't a woman to let someone she cared for go wanting. All a man had to do was to look at how far she'd gone to save this ranch to know that.

He stepped out of the stall, and latched the door. Yup. The key to nailing down this marriage was in finding the key to Elizabeth's loyalty. She was a straightforward woman. It couldn't be that hard to put a handle to. He'd just have to think on it some.

Elizabeth watched as Asa came ambling her way. His stride shouted pure confidence as he crossed the distance between them with that deceptively lazy way of moving he had. Once again, she realized he really was a fine figure of a man. Broad-shouldered, slim-hipped, and strong. Both inside and out.

Lord, how was she supposed to hold someone like that? Especially someone who simmered with such intensity. She shook her head at her own denseness. How had she fallen for his just-a-cowpoke act? Common sense alone should have clued her in to his real personality. No one accomplished what he had by the time he was thirty-two without a will of iron and the intelligence to put it to good use. Lord, sometimes she was too stupid to breathe. Thank goodness the qualities he was opening her eyes to were strengths, not weaknesses.

She smoothed her hands down the front of her dress. No matter how tightly she tucked in her blouse or how hard she stretched the fabric of her skirt, the material insisted on returning to its revealing pattern.

She still couldn't believe she'd acted as she had. Even though it had been her husband she'd been "sparking" with. The constant reminder in the way her clothing lay was hard to take. He probably thought she was loose. Especially after this morning. While he claimed he didn't mind it now, the first time he got his suspicions up, he'd be throwing it back in her face. She'd have to be very careful in the future that she didn't give him any reason to be suspicious.

"You ready?" he drawled as he came abreast of her.

She was going to hell in a hand basket for sure. Just the sound of his voice was enough to evoke memories of other words just as slowly spoken. Hot on the heels of those memories came the unladylike sin of lust. Maybe she was just like her mother. She took a breath, straightened her shoulders, and mentally pulled her dignity around her. Just because she was the contradiction of everything ladylike inside didn't mean she had to let it show. "I'm ready."

His right brow shot up. "This isn't going to work if you poker up on me."

"What isn't going to work?"

"Our stroll back to the house."

Stroll? She'd been thinking more along the lines of a mad dash. "You plan on strolling?"

"Yup." He held out an arm. With the free one, he motioned her into the crook. "Quicker you slide over here, the quicker I'll be getting to that chocolate cake."

Mentally clutching her pride, she stepped to his side. His arm immediately slid to her waist, under her arm. "Relax," he ordered.

"I am relaxed."

"Uh-huh."

"I am!"

"Darlin', when a man has his arm around a woman and she's relaxed, there's some natural accommodating that goes on."

It took her a second to figure out what he meant. "And you're an expert on that?"

"I've had my arm around enough to be sure on the subject."

She made her voice as prim as she could. "I'm sure you feel you are, Mr. MacIntyre, but I'm relatively certain your accommodating expertise took place outside proper circles."

"Excuse me?"

"As we've already established, no decent woman goes about un-corseted."

She knew as soon as he made the connection because his neck turned slightly red and the hand resting on her hip reflected the same tension she saw in his jaw. She'd only meant to get the upper hand. To get a bit of her own back. She hadn't meant to insult him, but she had. She knew it. She touched her hand to his where it rested on her waist. "I'm sorry."

"Nothing to be sorry about." He steered her out the barn door.

"I didn't mean to insult you."

"I never made a secret about where I came from."

But he hadn't advertised it either. As they stepped into the sunlight, she raised her hand to shield her eyes. "Still, I'm sorry."

He didn't say a word, just kept walking across the yard, his path taking the route least likely to bring them into anyone's path. His arm around her waist a natural barrier to anyone seeing the wrinkles in her shirt. She looked down at the hand resting on the flare of her hip. It was a big hand, all but spanning half her hip. A hand he'd never touched her with except in gentleness. A hand she knew in her bones he wouldn't hesitate to sacrifice to keep her safe, not because he bore her any great love, but simply because he believed a man protected what was his.

Every man she'd ever known who'd claimed to be honorable valued respectability whether they lived up to their concept of honor or not. Asa's honor ran bone deep. He had to value respectability to some degree. And she'd just as much as told him she didn't see him as respectable. Sunlight blinked to shade as they reached the spreading branches of the old oak tree by the back door. She planted her feet and jerked Asa up short. She took advantage of his surprise to twist out of his grip and face him.

"I said I was sorry."

"I heard you."

His expression was so unconcerned, she started thinking she'd been wrong. "And I heard you say it doesn't matter, but it does if you think I don't think you're a respectable man."

"You're making it hard for me to keep my end of the deal." He waved his hand in the direction of the back door. "Ten more steps and I'll be earning that chocolate cake."

She brushed aside his hand. "You're not distracting me from this."

"From what?"

She slammed her hands on her hips in exasperation. "From you thinking I don't think you're respectable!"

He sighed and met her gaze evenly. She found no solace for her frustration there. "Darlin', if you were hoping to marry with a man society would admire, your choice fell far short of the mark."

"I don't think so."

"My mother was a whore who'd lay down for any man, no matter how drunk or diseased, if it meant she could get more opium. My father was one of the thousand who'd found relief between her thighs." This time, he brushed aside her hand before she could touch him. "In case you don't know what that means, I spent my first years in a cat house in San Antonio, fetching and carrying for the women who worked there. Later, I hustled the streets, searching for food and sleeping in alleys. The nicest thing that ever happened to me was my mother's death when I turned thirteen."

He delivered the facts of his birth in an unemotional drawl. No doubt it was in an effort to make her believe it didn't affect him. She could understand that need to protect oneself. She did it herself. "Are you trying to shock me?"

He sighed, whipped off his hat, and ran his fingers through his hair. "No."

"Good, because Old Sam already told me what he knew about your background."

"I never pegged you for a liar."

"Okay. So all he said was your beginnings were rough, but you were as honest as the day was long, fair in a fight, and a man to hitch my wagon to."

"Uh-huh."

"Will you stop that?"

"What?"

"Stop acting like you know what I'm going to say before I say it. It's a most annoying habit."

"You weren't going to say my background didn't matter? You weren't going to say what interested you were my other sterling qualities?"

He had the gall to look amused while he stole her thunder. She wanted to smack him. "For an intelligent man, you are incredibly stupid!"

She spun on her heel and marched into the house. Let him stew on that. The screen door gave a satisfying thump as she let it slam behind her. Halfway into the kitchen, she stopped to let her eyes adjust to the dimness. She near jumped out of her skin when the screen door slammed again. She turned and made out Asa's silhouette. Apparently, he wasn't a man given to stewing.

"You needn't look so scared. I didn't come in here to whale on you, though I'd be well within my rights for that crack."

She tipped up her chin. "Stupid is as stupid does."

"You're pushing it."

Yes, she was. And she had no idea why. "I'd like to be alone."

"You owe me some chocolate cake."

She marched to the cupboard. Opening the door, she pulled down the cake. She resisted the urge to toss it on the table. Instead, she gently set it in the middle. What she really wanted to do was to smash it in his face. How dare he take her apology and make light of it!

"I've never welshed on a bet in my life." Scooping the dirty dishes from her visit with Aaron into a pile, she moved them to the wash basin. Returning to the table with a plate and a fork, she plopped Asa's place setting before him. Aligning his fork on the napkin, she took the knife and plunged it into the center of the cake. Stepping back, she waved Asa to his seat. "Enjoy."

Asa looked at the precise place setting. The beautifully frosted cake. The knife still quivering in its center. No doubt about it. His wife was beginning to lose a bit of her starch. "It's already frosted."

In that carefully precise voice he was fast coming to hate, she said. "Yes, it is."

"You tricked me."

"It's not my fault you chose to bargain without ascertaining the facts."

"If that means I get what I deserve for bettin' blind, I guess you're right." He pulled the knife free and waved it at the single plate. "You not planning on having any?"

"I don't want to spoil my dinner."

He caught a glob of frosting on his finger before it could splat on the checkered tablecloth. As natural as breathing, the frosting made its way to his mouth. The rich flavor spread through his mouth, seducing him with its promise. "Darlin', you sure can cook."

"Thank you."

"Are you sure you don't want some?" he asked as he cut through the cake.

"No. But you go ahead. I'll just go upstairs and make myself presentable."

That quick, she was out of the room. And it was just him and that mouth-watering chocolate cake. He should have been thrilled. He'd only had chocolate cake a few times in his life, but it'd been enough to know it was his favorite. Now he had an entire cake in front of him. It hadn't cost a week's wages and he had all the time in the world to enjoy it. He should have been hopping with glee.

Instead, all he could think of was how Elizabeth had looked when Ballard was here. The kitchen had seemed a cozy place. Warm. Almost seductive. He leveled a chunk of cake onto his plate. It sat in the middle of the white expanse, dark, moist and slathered with frosting. It should have sent his mouth watering anew. Instead, it seemed lonely somehow, sitting on that stark white plate. Like something was missing.

The whole kitchen felt that way, he realized. Almost unwelcoming. Definitely neglected.

Maybe it was the pile of dishes waiting to be washed. He left the cake and filled the basin with water from the warming pan. Working up a lather on the cloth draped over the side, he set to cleaning the mess. When he was done, he glanced around. The dishes drying on the sideboard was an improvement, but things still didn't feel right. He looked about, but couldn't put his finger on what was wrong. No doubt about it, he wasn't going to fully appreciate that cake without everything being just perfect.

"You didn't eat your cake."

Elizabeth was back. He turned to find she'd changed into a red-checked dress that made her look so prim and proper, he itched to nudge her bun askew.

"Thought I'd get these dishes first." He tossed the dishrag into the basin. Water slopped over the side. He suppressed a curse as he fished out the rag to wipe it up.

She came rushing to his side as if it had been an emergency. "Oh, my goodness! You didn't have to do that."

"It's just a little water."

"No." She stood to his left, wringing her hands and fidgeting. He got the distinct impression she'd shove him to the side if she thought she could get away with it. "I meant the dishes. I would have gotten to them. Just when I was about to, you came in and I haven't had a chance to clean up."

"It's all right."

"No, it isn't. I really am responsible. I would have gotten to them."

He caught her by the shoulders. She flinched. "Elizabeth, I did the dishes because I was standing here and they were sitting there. I reckon we'll all survive."

"But you didn't eat your cake!"

Apparently, that was supposed to mean something. "It's not going anywhere."

She glanced at the table and wrung her hands anew. "I didn't even pour you coffee!" She bolted for the stove, halted halfway there, and turned to apologize again. "It's no excuse, but I was so worried about being presentable—"

The way he remembered it, she'd been mad because of his teasing. "I can pour coffee."

The look she shot him said "don't you dare" louder than if she'd screamed it. She motioned to the table. "Go sit down and eat your cake. I'll get the coffee."

"You don't have to heat it up. Cold is fine."

He might have saved his breath for all the mind she paid him.

He sat at the table. It must have been his imagination because the piece of cake seemed to have perked up in his absence. His mouth watered immediately on sight. When Elizabeth came over, coffee cup in hand, he was a little embarrassed to note he'd put a full third of the cake on his plate. She took a look at the size of his helping as she placed his coffee before him. Instead of shooting him a frown, she seemed to relax.

She waited expectantly for his first bite. He'd be damned if he was going to take it with her hovering like a waitress at a restaurant. He pushed the adjacent chair out with his foot. "Have a seat."

"Just let me get supper on."

"Does it need to be done now?"

"No."

"Then have a seat."

She sat kitty corner to him. Her hands folded primly on the table as if she didn't quite know what to do. He cut a piece of cake with the side of his fork. Her gaze followed every inch of the short journey it made to his mouth. Her eyes stayed glued to his face as he chewed. When he made to go for another bite, her eyes followed the fork.

"Sure you don't want some?" he asked.

"My father killed my mother."

The words lay between them like stone. A crumb lodged sideways in his windpipe. He grabbed for his coffee. Thank the Lord it wasn't piping hot or he'd have been short a throat come morning.

She went on as if nothing were amiss across the table. "I just thought you should know, in case you thought in marrying me, you were obtaining a respectable wife."

He blinked tears from his eyes and stared at his wife. Sure enough, she'd just dumped a lit bundle of dynamite in his lap. He wasn't touching it until he garnered a few more facts. He waited until he took another bite of cake, chewed and swallowed, before he asked, "Why?"

"When I was about eight, he caught her with a neighbor. The situation was compromising enough he felt it necessary to kill her."

"He couldn't have just sent her away?"

"Apparently not. She had a habit, I've been told, of less than ideal behavior."

He ate a bit more cake. "That's what Aaron meant when he said there was some of your mother in you?"

"Yes. People don't forget easily."

That he understood. There was always someone in every town the folk made fun of. The system worked for the majority of the folk, unless you were the one on the receiving end of all that scorn. Then it was hard to take. "Yeah. Folk's memories are a bit long when it comes to something like that." He dipped his finger into the frosting clinging to the edge of the plate. "Your father ever go to trial?"

"No. There was some dispute of the actual events. Some said it was really the other man who shot her. In the end, her death was declared accidental."

Jesus! "You stayed here with your Pa after?"

"Yes. I was lucky that he didn't feel I was doomed to the same path."

He guessed people had different views on lucky. As much as he'd hated his mother, he'd have taken a gun to whoever had killed her if she'd gone that way. "Well, if it'll set your mind to rest, I'm not one for holding the past against a person."

After an initial start of surprise, her expression relaxed a hair. "No. I guess you wouldn't. Not with how it must have been for you."

The woman blew hot and cold for sure, but he was beginning to figure her out. The more proper her demeanor, the more unsure she felt.

He got up and fetched another fork from the wash pile. He sat, pushed the plate across the table until it rested between them. He held the fork out to her. "Dig in."

"I couldn't."

"Why not? I'm sharing."

She looked surprised, and then embarrassed. "I don't really know."

"I've always figured, if you can't say why you can't do something, then maybe there isn't a reason to hold back." He placed the fork in her hand. "I'll meet you in the middle."

She stared at the plate for awhile. He had the impression she was thinking on something. Finally, she tapped the plate with her fork. "You've got all the frosting."

"You got a problem with that?"

There was a brief hesitation. He was beginning to expect them. Seems the woman wasn't too well acquainted with good-natured teasing. She eventually reached a decision. "Yes."

He smiled at her hesitancy. Very un-Elizabeth-like.

He heaved a huge sigh. "You drive a hard bargain, woman." He turned the plate until the frosting crossed an imaginary dividing line. "Happy now?"

Her smile was tentative, but there. Her "I'm working on it" was a fair imitation of his own speech. His chuckle jerked up short when she beat him to the first bite, securing for herself the glob of icing he'd marked for his own. He wasn't going to be beaten by anyone half his size. Especially when it came to chocolate cake!

The next choice bit ended up in his mouth. The third was a dead tie.

His "remove your fork, woman" was all play growl.

Immediately, she separated her tines from his. "Of course." There wasn't even a click of displeasure as she placed her fork correctly on the edge of the plate with great precision.

"Hell."

"I'll thank you not to swear in my presence." A neat folding of her hands on the table punctuated the proper reprimand.

Obviously, handling wives was a tricky business. Especially one as jumpy as Elizabeth. Staying on the good side of a man suspected of killing your mother had to make for a bumpy ride. She'd described her upbringing as lucky, but he thought he'd hold back his opinion on that subject. A lot of the woman didn't ring true. She couldn't take a joke, panicked at the least hint of offense, defended herself with the ferocity of a badger against a man twice her size, and burned like fire in his arms. How the hell was he supposed to figure her out if she kept breaking all the rules?

He pushed the cake until the disputed piece crossed to her side. "I was only joking."

"You clearly ordered me to release the cake."

"We were playing."

There was no doubting her seriousness as she said, "What has that got to do with anything?"

He sat back in his chair and studied her closely. Nope, she was serious. "About everything, I'd say."

"Mr. MacIntyre, I gave you my promise to be obedient. It would help tremendously if you'd just say what you mean."

"You can't tell the difference between when I'm serious and when I'm fooling around?"

"No." One word, yet it summed up everything.

He reached for his coffee, took a sip, and pondered the moment. As the rich flavor merged with the taste of chocolate, he came to an understanding. "You don't trust me."

He watched her fingers as the question sank in. Her grip grew white-knuckled.

"I want the truth," he advised.

Her grip relaxed and she gave it to him. A little defiantly, but still the truth. "No."

"Because you don't know me?"

Her chin came up. He guessed he was in for another pride-busting revelation. "Yes."

He tried a stab in the dark. "And you don't have a whole lot of use for men?"

"To date, I haven't met many who deserve the respect they demand."

He hazarded a guess. "Or the obedience?"

"Yes." She pushed back from the table. "I've got to get supper on."

He was willing to be diverted for the moment. "What are we having?"

"Venison stew with biscuits."

"You're going to make me fat."

Her gaze traveled him head to toe from where she stoked the stove with more wood. "You could use some weight."

"You won't be saying that a month from now if you keep feeding me like the last two days."

She straightened, grabbed an apron off the peg on the wall. As she tied it around her back, she said, "I'll cut back if your horse turns up swayback."

He chuckled. "I appreciate you keeping an eye on things."

Elizabeth moved the big pot of stew on the counter to the front of the stove. The man had her so off balance she didn't know what to do or say. First, she'd think he was serious and then he'd turn joking or bark an order that had her shivering in her shoes. She was tired, embarrassed, and confused. "No problem."

She gave the contents a stir, then moved to the counter to get to work on the biscuits. The silence behind her stretched. She could feel his eyes on her. Willing her to do something. She mixed the flour, baking powder and added a touch of sugar. When she was cutting in the lard, he spoke. "I guess I make you nervous."

She jerked and slopped flour over the side of the bowl. "Yes." She scooped the flour and lard back in.

A scraping sound caught her attention. She looked over her shoulder and saw he was spinning his cup on the table, studying the movement as if it contained deep secrets. She turned back to her biscuits before he could catch her staring.

"You mentioned in the barn that you've never sparked in a barn before."

Lord! Did he have to bring that up?

"Did you just mean in the barn or ever?"

Oh God! How had he known?

"I am not loose if that's what you're asking." Despite how she'd behaved the last twenty-four hours.

"I thought I was pretty clear on what I was asking."

Heat swamped her cheeks. Did the man have no sense of privacy? "I fail to see what my past experience has to do with anything."

"Don't go getting mad."

"I am not mad." She slammed the biscuit dough on the board.

"Tell that to those biscuits."

"The biscuits are fine." She caught herself before she could knead them past the count of ten. If they came out like rocks, he'd never let her live it down.

"Fine. You're not mad."

She grabbed the rolling pin and flattened the dough. "Mr. MacIntyre, I get the impression you're trying to make a point."

"I liked it between us in the barn."

She almost strangled on her embarrassment. "Asa!"

"Well, leastways, I know how to get you to use my first name."

"You promised you wouldn't mention that."

"I didn't. You're the one who hopped down that path. I was talking about how we worked to get Shameless settled." He looked as innocent as a saint sitting there, but she knew he'd done it on purpose.

"Though the other was nice, too," he added outrageously.

"Oooh!" Her cheeks burned like fire.

He held up his hand. "I'm sorry, but that was too good to pass up."

"Why do you insist on humiliating me?"

"I'm deviling, not humiliating. Deviling you is fun. It's supposed to make you laugh."

"Well, it doesn't."

"Yeah. I've about figured that one out. And a darned shame it is, too, but I think I've found a solution."

"You have?"

He tilted his chair back on two legs. "Occurs to me that you're always jumping on things I say because you don't know me well enough to spot when I'm deviling you."

"It couldn't be because you bring up the most inappropriate subjects?"

"We're married, darlin'. We can't go dancing around the things we want to say just because some prune-faced lady told you they weren't proper." He shook his head at her. "No doubt about it, you've got to loosen up."

"You could always—"

She almost spit when he cut her off with another head shake "Nope. I'm too old a dog to be learning new tricks. Sure as shooting, we've got to get you used to my ways."

"I see." Just like every other man, he wanted everything his way. She accidentally chopped a biscuit in half while cutting them out. She tossed it back in the bowl to include it in the second batch. "And how am I supposed to do that?"

"I've been thinking on it."

She was beginning to recognize the long drawl as a warning. "You have a plan?"

"Yup." He took a sip of what had to be stone cold coffee, yet he didn't wince. She couldn't stand cold coffee. She brought the pot over. He held up his cup.

"How do you feel about being courted?"

Chapter Nine

ഇ

She missed the cup completely and poured the hot coffee straight into his lap.

"Jesus , Mary, and Joseph!" The chair crashed to the floor as he jumped to his feet.

She stared in dismay at the steaming front of his denims. Dear God, he was going to kill her. "I'm sorry! Are you okay?"

"Hell no! I think you just took off some pretty important layers of hide!"

She backed hastily out of his reach. She measured the distance to the door with her eyes.

"Don't you dare run out of here," he warned.

"I was just, just…"

He pulled his pants away from his thighs as best he could. The glance he sent her was wry. "Do you always burn the men who come a courtin'?"

"You mean *you* want to court me?"

This time, he was the one to look startled. "Well, who'd you think?" Realization dawned mid-sentence. His brows dropped low. "You didn't think I'd be bringing in strangers?"

He didn't need to say it as if it were the furthest thing from possible.

"How am I supposed to know what you think? We're already married. The marriage has been consummated and you ask me if I want to be courted. You're the most contradictory man!"

"That's a heck of a leap you made there." He grabbed a napkin and swiped at the spill.

She took another breath, clinging to her patience and ladylike demeanor. "Husbands do not court their wives!"

He stopped wiping his pants with the napkin and stared at her a good long minute. His expression was inscrutable. "Darlin', we're further behind than I thought."

"I have no idea what you're talking about."

"I can see that."

She was beginning to believe he delighted in keeping her off balance. She wiped her hands on her apron. "Are you badly hurt?"

His expression was wry as he shifted gingerly. "There are parts of me that have been happier."

She inched closer to the door. "I didn't spill the coffee on purpose."

"If I thought you did, you couldn't sidle to that door fast enough to save your backside a warming."

She stopped. The door was only two feet away. "It was an accident. You startled me."

He sighed. "Come here."

"I could get you some cool well water."

"Quit stalling and come here."

Before she took the steps to bring her within reach, she shifted her grip on the coffee pot. Her plan was for nothing. She'd forgotten how much taller he was. As soon as she got close enough, he plucked the pot from her hand.

"You won't be needing this."

"I—"

His finger over her lips cut off her protest. "I don't want lies between us. It was a smart move, thinking to use that coffee as a weapon should I turn ornery."

"Thank you." She didn't know what to say and since he did seem to be complimenting her—for thinking about tossing coffee in his face?—the response seemed appropriate. Dear Lord, he was addling her brain. "I don't understand you."

"You've said that before." He reached out and pushed a loose piece of hair back from her face. She felt foolish for flinching. His touch was nothing more than an infinitesimal brush of skin, incredibly gentle. Soothing.

"It's clear as day you've met with a few ornery types. You're as nervous as a cat with its tail under the rocker, always waiting for me to turn on you." He shook his head and curled his hand around her head. She felt engulfed. Threatened. She conjured up an image of a huge stone wall and mentally shoved her fear behind it. Not for anything was she going to let him know how much he frightened her.

"I can feel your muscles tightening." His gaze was sharp on her face. "You're scared now."

Her lips were dry. So was her mouth. She had to lick her lips before she could get the words out. "It was an accident."

"You're thinking this is a trick and I'm planning on getting my own back."

It took everything she had to stand still under his hand when she heard the accusation in his low-voiced drawl.

"I know you're mad," she said. She wanted that in the open. Mad she could deal with. Mad she understood.

His "Ah, darlin'," was incredibly soft, almost sad, but the hand that pulled her against his chest was relentless. He wasn't satisfied until he had her head resting over his heart and her body wrapped in his arms. She stood awkwardly, not knowing what to do. What he expected of her.

"Listen."

She waited. He followed the order with nothing. After a minute or two, she couldn't stand it anymore. "What?"

"Listen." Something touched the top of her head. His cheek? "What do you hear?"

"I can't hear anything except your heartbeat."

"Is it beating slow or fast?"

She pressed her ear slightly closer. "Slow."

He took her hand and placed it on his jaw. "How does it feel?"

With the barest of movements, she explored. "Rough and prickly."

His chest bounced her cheek on a chuckle. "Guess I'll be upping my shaving to twice a day." His hand covered hers and pressed her fingers into his skin. "How do my muscles feel? Hard and tense or relaxed?"

"Relaxed."

"Exactly." His hand left hers. She dropped it to his shoulder. This close, she didn't have anyplace else to put it.

He tipped up her chin with the side of his finger. "I'm not mad."

"I burned you."

He'd started shaking his head before she finished speaking. "I startled you and you spilled the coffee. There's a world of difference between the two."

She was shocked to her toes that he saw the difference. She was afraid everything she was thinking showed on her face. She tried to duck her head, but his finger under her chin kept her face exposed to his gaze.

"No more hiding."

Could he read her mind?

"I made you a couple of promises back at the saloon. Do you remember what they were?"

"You'd keep my ranch safe and you'd keep outsiders from hurting me."

"You married me with that being your understanding?"

From the way his head jerked back, she got the impression that she'd shocked him. Did he think she was so dimwitted she couldn't remember their deal? "Yes. It was more than I expected."

"You promised me obedience not thinking that I'd keep my hands off you?"

"It's not illegal for a husband to hit his wife." Though it should be.

"Darlin', little as most women are and as big as most men are, it darn well should be." It was a shock to hear his words echo her thoughts. He eyed her up and down, seeming to miss nothing in the examination. "If I ever took a notion to whale on you, there wouldn't be anything left but a greasy spot."

"I'd survive."

His finger was no longer required to hold her chin. Pride alone kept her gaze locked with his. He shook his head. No doubt he thought she'd crumble at the first hint of pain. Well, he'd soon find out he had another think coming. Her father had made sure she was strong.

"It never occurred to me that you've been waiting for me to sock you one," he continued. "Heck, no wonder you were so interested in my stepping between the blacksmith and that little boy."

She took immediate offense. He made it sound like she was some beaten cur, crawling with its tail tucked between its legs. "I haven't been waiting."

"It hadn't occurred to me," he went on, ignoring the interruption, "because I don't hit women, I don't kick dogs, and I don't beat on little kids."

Did he think she was going to swallow that line of bull? "Everyone gets mad."

"Yes. They do. When I get mad, I yell." He winced. "A lot. When I get so mad I think I'm going to lose it, I slam doors and storm out of the house. I don't take out my bad humor on things littler than me."

"I'm sorry."

"You apologizing because my heart's beating fast and my muscles are tightening up, or because you believe you've been insulting me regularly for the last day or so?"

She ducked his gaze, not wanting him to read the truth in hers. "Both."

"How about we make a deal?"

"What?"

"Bring your gaze back up here, darlin'."

She figured if she didn't, he'd be pushing it up with his finger. That and the fact that she didn't want him thinking she was a coward were the only reasons she met his serious gaze with hers.

"How about we put aside the thought that we're married and you let me court you with all the courting rules in place?"

"What's the point in that?"

"The point is that I don't like having to walk on egg shells, and I don't imagine you do either. It means that I like the way we worked together in the barn a whole lot more. I'd like to have more of those moments rather than those stiff formal ones I keep running up against. The only way you're going to be comfortable with me is to get to know me without feeling pressured."

"Courting couples don't share a bed."

"I'm aware of that."

"But men want," she paused, decided this wasn't the time for modesty, and plunged on through her inhibitions. "You'll want to share a bed."

He shook his head as if she were dimwitted. "I'm not saying I won't want to spark, but I got to be honest, darlin'. The next time we go to bed, I'd like to feel I'm making love to my wife and not forcing her."

What game was he up to now? His eyes were a mellow gray. His chest relaxed against hers. There was no sign this was a trick, but she knew it had to be. If Asa weren't so much a man, she'd have started thinking he was one of those sissies in the dime novel she'd read once. She'd stopped believing that nonsense the day her father had caught her in the hayloft reading one. He'd spent the next month showing her the way of the real world. She'd come to understand quickly the only use a real man had for soft womanly emotions was to use them as a weapon against a woman. Like Brent had used them against her.

"Courting me isn't necessary," she told Asa. "You didn't force me and it's ludicrous to feel like you did."

His head was shaking before she got to the last syllable. "It doesn't set well with me. I don't want to be telling my son that I all but raped his mother."

"You didn't rape me!" He wasn't going to lay that guilt on her.

"I know you gave permission, but it still isn't a night I'm building fond memories on."

"I did my best. If you'd told me what you wanted…"

"I'm not placing blame." He put his fingers over her lips, halting her instant retort. "You did what you had to do to save the ranch. I did what I had to do to keep the ranch. We did what was necessary to seal a business deal. But we didn't begin a marriage."

"I don't know what you're talking about."

"Yes. You do."

"Mr. MacIntyre…"

"Asa."

She took a breath and counted to ten. She had to talk him out of this lunacy. "Mr. MacIntyre, I fail to see what's wrong with what we have now. It's a clear-cut business arrangement based on mutual understanding. You know where you stand and I know where I stand. That we enjoy each other occasionally is an unexpected plus."

"There you go again, getting all formal on me. It was good between us in the barn. And I'm not talking about grooming Shameless, but the minute it was over, you started making me out to be a stranger."

"I don't think of you as a stranger."

"I'm not going to argue with you. I'm ordering you to think on some courting rules. I want you to think on what you need to be comfortable, and then I want you to pass that on to me."

"You want me to direct the course of our...courtship?" Why hadn't any of the rumors that preceded the man indicated he was loonier than a bed bug?

"Yup."

"What if you don't like what I've decided?"

He flashed her a grin. "Then, like every young buck who's ever come a courtin', I'll do my best to change your mind."

"You're serious." My God, she couldn't believe it!

"Yup."

"Why?"

"We're married. To me, that's a once in a lifetime thing. I've seen other couples who've made a marriage work. Seems the one thing they have in common is they're comfortable with each other. We got the cart before the horse here, but it's fixable."

"So your plan is to fix it by courting me?"

"Yup."

"According to my rules?"

"You got a better plan?"

"No." But she wasn't sure she liked this one. There were too many risks. All on her side.

"Then I say we go with mine."

"How much time do I have?"

"For what?"

"To come up with a plan."

"Do you think you'll be needing more than a day or two?"

There had to be a way his offer could work for her. If she thought on it hard enough, she'd come up with a plan of her own. "I think two days would be sufficient."

"Good." He took a step back. For the first time since he'd touched her, she felt like she could breathe. "I'm going to change clothes."

"I'll finish the biscuits," she told him as he stretched. His shirt caved in over his stomach. She decided to make up another batch. The man was still awfully lean.

He brought his arms down. "After supper, I'd like to take a look at your records."

"They're in the study." She watched as he strolled to the door. The depth of his tiredness showed in the set of his shoulders. "Would you like some salad greens with supper? I think there are still some in the garden."

"That'd be fine."

She watched as he left the room. A slight limp indicated his discomfort. Whether she'd really burned him or if it was the fact that the wet denim clung uncomfortably, she wasn't sure. She felt guilty either way.

She turned her attention to supper. She had some buttermilk left from this morning. She'd make a special dressing for the salad. Buttermilk was supposed to be very nourishing.

Wiping her hands nervously on her apron, she went back to the biscuits, her mind in turmoil. She only had two days to figure out how to handle this. She couldn't lose anymore ground. She couldn't.

* * * * *

175

Two days later, Asa sat in the study, going over the books for the hundredth time, but the facts didn't change. The ranch was on the edge of bankruptcy, that much was clear. What was a surprise was that someone had clearly had a hand in putting it on the edge. Every time a bank note came due, there'd been a disaster with the cattle. A well had been poisoned. Rustlers had struck. Cattle had been driven off. Hands couldn't be hired. It had been going on for the last year, not just the last few months. Someone wanted the Rocking C to go under. If he wanted to pull the place out of bankruptcy, he was going to have to smoke out the sneaky, yellow-bellied S.O.B and show him the error of his ways. He was in the process of making a list of suspects when the knock came at the door.

He closed the account books and pinched the bridge of his nose. No doubt it was Elizabeth coming to deliver her rules. While most women would be thrilled he'd given them time, Elizabeth was appalled. It was hard to miss. The last couple of days, she'd been as skittish as a newborn deer. If he had a penny for every I-don't-understand-you glance she'd sent his way, the Rocking C would be solvent. Every courtesy he'd extended, like sleeping in another room, seemed to give birth to more confusion until he'd thought the woman would explode, she'd gotten herself so worked up.

God help him, he was beginning to suspect that Old Sam's statement in the bar that "Coyote Bill brought Elizabeth up rough" hadn't referred to a lack of dresses. The woman's distrust of men and any kindness they extended went bone deep. Asa had a feeling Brent's part in Elizabeth's distrust was more along the line of confirming rather than creating. He placed his pen on the desk top, checked to make sure no incriminating notes were lying about, and called for her to enter. Last thing he wanted was for her to start worrying he couldn't pull the Rocking C out of this mess.

The door opened and she sailed in, head high, shoulders back, a sure sign she was ready to fight. She nodded her head. "Mr. MacIntyre."

She was using his full name again. He wondered if she knew how it made his blood heat. When she said it all prim and proper like that, he wanted to lay her down and kiss her until she admitted he was Asa, her husband, someone she cared about.

"I thought we'd settled on you calling me Asa?"

She wrung her hands, seemed to realize what she was doing, and stopped. "I'm sorry. This whole marriage is taking some getting used to."

He relaxed into the high-backed chair. The stuffed leather seat welcomed his weight like a lover. Taking over the Rocking C did have its compensations. "In time, we'll get used to each other."

From the look she sent him, he guessed she didn't agree. She licked her lips. "I've come to a decision."

"You sure you took enough time?"

"Two days was plenty."

"Let's hear it then."

"You've been very considerate in keeping your distance."

He smiled, hearing it put like that. Sounded like he was a real gentleman, instead of being drowned in work, spending twelve hours a day eking as much out of the daylight as he could before coming home and dropping exhausted into the spare bed, only to repeat the same procedure the next day. "Thank you."

Her hands commenced to clench and unclench in the folds in her skirt. "But I don't feel that's the best way for us to proceed."

She had his attention now. "You don't?"

"No." If her fingers picked up any more speed, she was going to spend an hour pressing that skirt.

"What do you suggest?"

Her gaze seemed to lock on a point just to the right of his shoulder. "I'm well aware men have needs that need to be met regularly."

"You are?"

"Please, don't make fun of me, Mr. MacIntyre. This is a very embarrassing subject and I'm doing my best to get through it."

"My apologies."

"I can't see where refusing you my bed will accomplish anything except to increase tension between us."

"You can't?"

If looks could kill, he'd be dead. "No. I cannot."

"Because I have these needs?"

"Exactly." She was viewing him with a bit more favor now. "While I'm aware a man doesn't exercise all his needs with his wife—"

"He doesn't?"

She looked down her nose at him. "I may not be experienced, Mr. MacIntyre, but I have a good working knowledge of how the world works."

"I'm beginning to see that." At least, he was beginning to see how she thought his world worked.

"As I was saying, while I understand you won't be faithful in body to me for the duration of our marriage, I'd like to make it a term of our 'courtship' that, for one month, you confine your needs to my person."

"You would?"

As her chin tipped higher, the look down her nose took longer. "Yes, I would."

"Why?"

"Why what?"

"Why a month?"

Her face abandoned pink for a bright red hue. "My reasons are private."

"Well," he drawled, "Seeing as how I'm giving up all those other women, I feel I've got a right to know the why of it."

"It's only for a month."

He pretended to consider it. He sighed and looked regretful. He bit back a smile as her hands stopped their desperate clenching. When she spoke, her voice was perfectly precise.

"If you must know, I'd like the opportunity to get to know your preferences."

"I get the feeling you're not talking about how I take my coffee."

"No. I'm not."

He waved her to a chair. "You sure you don't want to sit down?"

"I'm fine."

He rose from the chair and came around the side of the desk. He was pretty sure it wasn't his imagination that she seemed to hold herself so still, it appeared she'd stopped breathing. He hitched his hip on the corner of the desk. "Let me get this straight. As part of our courting, you expect me to come to your bed and educate you in precisely how I like my loving?"

Her nod was stiff. A bare jerk of her chin.

"And I'm to keep my attentions confined to you?"

Another jerk.

"After the month, however, I'm free to sport where I want with no complaints from you?"

This time, she managed a hoarse whisper. "Yes."

"Well, now, that's darned generous of you."

"I'm trying to be reasonable."

No, Asa thought, she was being clever as a cat and just as practical. She was planning on holding him with sex unless he missed his guess. Failing that, she was planning on relegating him to the role of scoundrel, insuring that he never got a chance to hurt her. Her cleverness made him smile. He wasn't going along with her plan, but he could work with it. "How often?"

"What?"

"How often am I allowed to come to your bed?"

The total look of dismay on her face clued him to the fact she hadn't thought of that. She rallied though. "I'd think that would depend on the frequency of your needs."

Every time she referred to his needs in that prissy tone of voice, he wanted to laugh and kiss her at the same time. "Well now," he drawled, "needs are funny critters. A man doesn't rightly know when they might sneak up on him."

"You don't know how often…?" She waved her hand between them in a descriptive arc. This time, her dismay showed clearly on her face. He nearly burst a gut holding in his laughter. She was so sweet to tease. As if he was going to let her get away with neatly stashing him into a single corner of her life.

"Nope."

She sat in the chair. "I hadn't considered the possibility…" For the first time since entering the room, she looked him squarely in the face. "This is going to be a problem."

Not for him. "I don't see where it could be too tough. If we shared a bed at night, you'd be convenient if I got struck with the notion."

"These needs come upon you mostly at night?"

He could actually see her brain ticking away at the options. He shrugged and admitted, "A fair number of them."

"We could move your room to the one across the hall."

He shook his head. "I'm not liking the thought of crossing that cold floor."

"It's not that cold yet."

He shook his head again. "I can see how set you are against the idea. Why don't we just drop that line? I'll settle things as best I can."

He shifted back to his feet. She sprang to hers, placing her hand on his chest to stop him. "No. It's all right. I was just reluctant to give up my privacy."

He raised his eyebrow at that blatant lie.

"No," she hurried on to assure him. "It'll be fine." She nodded her head as if he'd done something other than just stand there. "It's settled. You'll share my bed and I'll be convenient for your...well, I'll be convenient."

"For the next month."

She nodded, visibly relaxing. "Yes."

"And then?"

"We'll revisit our decision."

He touched her cheek, thinking how pretty a green her eyes were today. He wondered how long it would take her to realize he had no intention of behaving like she wanted him to. Sure enough, if she wanted to pigeon-hole him, she was going to have to raise her expectations. "Fair enough."

He slid his hand around the back of her neck. He was dead tired, but he wasn't so tired that he didn't want to steal a bit of her nervousness. "Come here." He pulled her into his arms. As always, she stiffened up first and then relaxed. "You got anymore rules?"

"Yes." There was a pause. "Is there any reason we have to stand like this?"

He chuckled. "Not a one." Without another word, he scooped her up and sat on the chair. When he had her settled in his lap he asked, "Is that better?"

"I meant, was there any reason you had to hold me for us to converse?"

"Yup." He scooted down and resettled her against his chest. "I like holding you."

She didn't seem to have an answer to that.

He rested his head against the back of the chair and closed his eyes. "What are your conditions?"

"I'd like you to come home for lunch if possible. And I'd like for us to attend church together on Sunday."

"I'm not much of a churchgoer."

"You said you wanted us to do normal things."

"Best I can tell, y'all don't have a regular preacher, so I can't see how going to church on Sunday is normal."

"We have a preacher that comes through every other week."

"Uh-huh."

"Are you saying you won't go?"

"I promised you could set the rules and, if you insist, I'll go."

She sat up stiff in his lap. "There's no need for you to go to church. I can go by myself."

He cracked one eye and took in her mutinous expression. "You're not riding all the way to town on your own."

"I'll get a ride with Aaron and his wife."

He closed his eyes. "Like hell you will."

"Mr. MacIntyre!"

"You don't want me swearing, don't go throwing that neighbor in my face."

"I didn't throw him anywhere. And, even if I did, Aaron is a childhood friend, a perfectly respectable member of this community, and a married man."

"Darlin', I don't care if he's one of those saints, he's not escorting my wife anywhere."

"You have no right to be jealous."

He tried to tug her back against his chest, but she was in a snit and her backbone was iron tough. "You hinting I got call to be jealous?"

"I most certainly am not." He cracked both eyes and saw she was serious.

She shifted until she ferreted out his gaze with hers. "I haven't done a thing to deserve your jealousy. Even when Aaron told me he'd help me obtain a divorce, I stuck to our bargain."

Asa sat up straight, almost dislodging her from his lap. "That son of a bitch offered what?"

She patted his chest as if she thought that would calm him. "He'd heard the rumors and he wanted to reassure me that I didn't have to stay married to a gunslinger."

He just bet he'd offered her that. "And what did you say?"

She met his gaze calmly. "I told him I was satisfied with my choice of husband. I thanked him for his concern, and then I changed the subject."

He could see her doing it, too. All prim and proper. Elizabeth was loyal. She'd stick by her word. Some of his anger slipped, but not his unease. "I imagine that offer was a bit tempting."

"No, it wasn't. Divorcing you would land me back where I started. Aaron's a nice man and very concerned about my welfare, but he's not practical."

And Elizabeth was.

"A man's got to be practical out here," he agreed.

She sighed. "It would help."

"No doubt." He rubbed her back, urging her against his chest. He liked the way she felt resting against him. Soft and sweet. She gave up the unequal struggle and lay her head on his chest. He let his mind wander over their conversation. The part about where she referred to being back where she started set a warning chill down his spine. Aaron's ranch bordered Elizabeth's. If it went bankrupt, Aaron would be the one most likely to want to take over. The drought was hitting everyone hard. He wondered how hard it was hitting Aaron's spread. He made a note to check it out. Just not tonight. Tonight, he was just too doggone tired.

He let his head drop back. Under his hand, Elizabeth's shoulder muscles relaxed. He smiled and closed his eyes. She was skittish, but he'd coax her around. He recalled her summation of his 'needs', and his smile broadened. No doubt she considered herself an authority on the subject, but she still had a lot to learn about him. He didn't like discord in his life. He had no intention of having anything other than a sweetly willing wife in his bed. Other men could waste their energy looking for excitement outside the marriage. With the proper approach, he was willing to bet Elizabeth was more than capable of delivering all the excitement he could handle. It was going to take some ruminating, but he'd find the key. Only a fool wouldn't.

Elizabeth's even breathing and lax muscles told him she was asleep. He decided to hold her a bit longer and enjoy this rare moment of peace before he carried her up to bed. He imagined her discomfort with the kindness and smiled anew. Courting Elizabeth was looking to be the most fun he'd had in a month of Sundays.

Leaning his head back on the chair, he relaxed, letting the quiet overtake him.

Chapter Ten

જી

Elizabeth cast a harried glance at the sun streaming through the window. If she didn't hurry, she was never going to get Asa's lunch to him. He wouldn't wait before heading into town either, because he wasn't expecting her. He'd grabbed some cheese and biscuits and told her not to worry, but, well, darn it! She hadn't cooked herself into the ground the last two weeks, filling out his lean frame, just to see the man drop back to scrawny from eating hard tack and cheese.

She put the last of the fried chicken in the basket. She wrapped two fresh loaves of potato bread in a towel, packed four ears of corn over it and carefully balanced an apple pie on top. She was halfway to the door before she remembered silverware. Muttering under her breath, she tucked some in the side. At the door, she grabbed her shawl. It would heat up as the day wore on, but right now there was a nip in the air. Before she fastened it, she took a moment to finger the pin. A feather could have knocked her over when Asa had brought it home from town the other day. It was a simple rendering of a bunch of wildflowers tied with a bow. It was silly and impractical, and she couldn't stop touching it. He hadn't said anything beyond it had made him think of her.

She'd spent hours pondering about that, but she hadn't asked. No doubt to him, it had been an impulse. The thought forgotten as soon as he'd made the purchase, but to her, it was the first present anyone had gotten her since she was eight, and it had meaning. She just couldn't figure out what.

As soon as she stepped onto the porch, the breeze tugged at her shawl. She tucked the loose ends under her arms, held the basket tightly, and dashed to the barn. It was warm in there, humid and thick with the lingering odor of the animals that'd spent the night here. As she passed Shameless' stall, she blushed as she had every day for the last week. She couldn't think of the horse without remembering her husband and the license he'd taken.

Or her response whenever he was near.

She'd been worried that he'd think less of her, but it didn't seem to matter to him that she'd enjoyed his touch. Fortunately or unfortunately. She sighed. That was another thing she hadn't decided upon since he hadn't touched her like that again.

She shook her head at her silliness. She should be grateful she had a husband who was capable and respectful, who didn't make demands and gave her little presents. Even though she didn't understand the man, these last weeks had been the most peaceful she'd had in her entire life. She tied the basket to the saddle horn. Part of her didn't want it to change. Another part of her wanted her husband to do something besides kiss her gently on her forehead and fall asleep on his side of the bed.

If she were brutally honest, she wanted more. Of it and him. She wanted to be the wild woman again who'd taken his hard cock in her mouth and sucked him to mindlessness. Only this time, she didn't want him to pull out at the last moment. She wanted to taste him, to feel him come over her tongue. To swallow his seed. To own him in that intensely intimate manner. She just wasn't sure about how to get back to that moment. Then she'd been out of her head with need, her body on fire from repeated orgasms. It had seemed right and natural at the time to beg him to fuck her face. However, she couldn't imagine just sidling up to him and asking for a repeat performance out of the blue.

The way he cuddled her was nice, though. She bit her lip as she untied Willoughby's reins. She flat out didn't understand the man. Asa'd been eager enough before. Maybe his needs weren't that frequent. Willoughby shifted to the right as she slid under his neck, knocking her bonnet to the barn floor.

"Darn it."

"Can I help you, ma'am?"

She looked up to find a brown-haired, brown-eyed ranch hand standing respectfully with his hat in his hand. She scooped up the bonnet, self-conscious that he'd know from her ease of movement that she wasn't wearing a corset. "I'm fine."

His hat lazily spun in his hand. Without missing a beat, he tossed it in the direction of the horse. "Going somewhere?"

She expected to see the hat hit the floor. At the last possible second, he caught it in his hand. There wasn't even a break in rhythm. While his expression didn't change, she swore she saw a smile in his eyes. "I was just riding out to bring Asa his lunch."

"I'll keep you company."

Her stomach dropped in dismay. Which was really silly as she was only bringing her husband lunch. Not plotting a way to get him naked and hard and in her mouth. "That's not necessary."

"He's out a piece. Pretty little thing like you might get lost."

She gritted her teeth. Pretty little thing, indeed. "I assure you Mr...?"

"Clint, ma'am."

"Surely you have a last name?"

"Just Clint will do."

"I assure you, Mr. Clint, that I know every inch of this ranch."

Had she hired him? She looked at him closer. A lot of men came west to forget things. Going by a first name wasn't uncommon, but still, she had to ask. "Are you running from the law, Mr. Clint?"

He spun his hat in the air. It seemed to take on a life of its own and flipped onto his head. While she stared in amazement, he said, "No, ma'am. Just don't hold much with formality."

Where had she heard that before? "Well, Mr. Clint, I really want to catch my husband before he heads for town. While I appreciate the offer of an escort, I don't have time to wait for you to secure a mount."

He emitted a short whistle between his teeth. Before her ears could recover from the blast, he was swinging lazily into the saddle of a beautifully proportioned palomino that appeared from one of the stalls. "No problem."

She swung up onto her own mount, adjusting her skirts so they covered as much as possible. She eyed him as she adjusted the reins. "A true gentleman would have helped a lady onto her mount."

He flashed her a slow, easy grin. "A true gentleman would have been eating your dust."

Gads! Was she really so transparent that every man around could read her like a book? She touched her heels to Willoughby's flank. As she passed the cowboy, he inclined his head respectfully.

"I gather you've been assigned to keep an eye on me?" she asked.

He didn't bother to deny it. "Asa was worried you might need help around the place."

How dumb did he think she was? "Seems to me Old Sam would be a better choice to help close to home rather than a capable man in his prime."

His sleepy-eyed palomino pulled up along Willoughby. The horse, she decided, was a lot like his owner. While he seemed to be as lazy as all get out, he seemed to have no trouble keeping up.

"Asa sets a store by you, ma'am. He's not one for taking chances."

"So he's assigned me a guard?" Willoughby's snort was an eloquent summation of her disgust.

"It wasn't like that."

"How was it?"

"This might be something you'd be better off asking your husband."

"It's a long trip to the back range. I might as well spend it productively."

"Somehow, I knew you were going to say that," he answered as forlornly as if she'd assigned him a week of well digging.

He stared straight ahead, but while his lips didn't move, his eyes crinkled at the corners in amusement. Elizabeth realized for the first time he was an attractive man. "So, how exactly was it?"

"It came to Asa's attention that you're not much of a homebody."

"Excuse me?"

"Seems like you like to spend the afternoons gadding about."

"I do not gad."

"Well, Monday, you went up the mountain."

"Asa wanted blackberry pie."

"And I'd like to be the one to speak for the rest of the hands, ma'am, and thank you for the pie you sent down to the bunkhouse. It was a welcome addition to Old Sam's idea of cooking."

"You're welcome." That was the longest speech she'd heard the man make. She suspected it was along the lines of a distraction. "So how does my picking blackberries on the mountain constitute gadding about?"

It really was the most irritating term.

The way the crinkles left the corner of his eyes told her he'd caught onto her annoyance. "It just made the boss nervous, ma'am."

Her gaze dropped to the rifle in its scabbard and the revolver riding on his hip. "So nervous he insists on an armed escort?"

He shifted uncomfortably in the saddle. "You really might be more comfortable discussing this with your husband, ma'am."

"I'm perfectly comfortable discussing it with you."

"Tuesday, you went up to the Hennessy spread."

"The Hennessy's are people of modest means. Calling it a spread is a bit of a stretch."

"I didn't want to be impolite enough to call it a shack."

"Why? I do."

He shot her a glance. "I can see that."

"If Jack Hennessy would lay off the bottle and attend to his family, his wife might just have a decent place to winter in."

"You seem a bit emotional on the subject."

"I dislike Mr. Hennessy intensely."

"But you like Mrs. Hennessy?"

"Jenna Hennessy is a sweet woman. She deserves better than a honeymoon freezing to death in the mountains." And she deserved better than to be knocked around daily by her husband.

"I think I saw her in town. She's blonde, very young and pretty?"

A horrible combination for a woman. Elizabeth struggled to keep the disgust out of her voice. "She is."

"Word is Hennessy's a mean son of a gun."

"He is."

Clint tipped his hat back on his head. "Might have to take me a wander up the mountain one of these days."

Elizabeth glared at him. Typical man. One whisper that a young, unhappy woman might be ripe for the plucking, and they couldn't wait to go check it out. "You leave Jenna Hennessy alone or you'll be looking for another job!"

His gaze, when it met hers, was cold, sending a chill down her spine. For all his lazy nonchalance, Elizabeth realized that Mr. Just-Clint was a very dangerous man. "Pardon me, ma'am, but what I do with my free time is my business."

She bit her lip on the argument that leapt to her tongue. Jenna's face came to her mind. Too thin, full of pride, struggling to cover the misery of her circumstances with flashing smiles and a belief that all would be well. "Please, Mr. Clint. Leave her alone. She doesn't need any more trouble."

"As I said, ma'am, what I do with my free time is my business."

He was right. She made a mental note to warn Jenna. "We've lost the topic of our conversation."

"Gotta admit, I was kind of hoping it would stay lost."

"No doubt as you've been assigned the role of spy."

"I'll allow it might seem that way to you."

"There's no other way to see it."

"I'll be letting you take that up with your husband, ma'am. If I'm not mistaken, that's him heading our way."

She looked where he pointed and, sure enough, Shameless crested the hill at a canter, Asa on his back, in a seamless silhouette of grace and power. He looked like a man capable of ruling the world. And he was her husband. A little trill of what could only be pride went through her.

Clint dropped back as Asa pulled up beside her. "Anything wrong?" Asa asked.

She shook her head, another thrill chased through her at the concern in his voice. It was unusual having someone care about her. "I brought you lunch."

His face creased into a smile. "That's a nice surprise." He turned toward Clint. "Thanks for escorting her up here."

"No problem."

"Did you have any trouble?"

"None. You want me to head over and see how the boys are coming with rounding the strays out of the back canyon?"

Shameless sidled alongside Willoughby as Asa answered, "No doubt they'd appreciate the help."

"Then I'll be getting over there." Clint tipped his hat to Elizabeth. "Ma'am."

She nodded back. "Mr. Clint."

She felt a disturbance at her side. She looked down. Asa was rummaging through the food basket. She smiled. "If you don't get your hand out of there, you're going to mess up lunch."

"Just thought I'd see what you brought."

"You weren't looking forward to hard tack and cheese?"

"I'd get by on it, but it can't hold a candle to..." He sniffed. "Apple pie?"

"You can smell that over horse and leather?"

His hand settled on her thigh. It was warm and heavy through her skirt. Comforting. His smile was lazy. She couldn't see his eyes as they were shadowed by the brim of his hat.

He shrugged. "Would I go down in your estimation if I also confess to smelling bread and fried chicken?" She laughed and his hand squeezed her thigh. "Were you planning on keeping me company?"

She couldn't tell from the tone of his voice whether the question was resentful or hopeful. "I could head back if you'd rather be alone."

"What man in his right mind would pass up the opportunity to dine with a beautiful woman?"

She felt the blush rise to her cheeks. Sometimes, she actually felt like he thought her beautiful and wasn't just playing with words.

"I passed a little meadow on the way here," he continued, obviously taking her blush for acceptance. "It sits down a bit, so we'd be protected from the wind."

He removed his hand from her thigh. She missed the contact immediately. Lord! The man was the most touching person she'd ever met and, what was worse, she was getting used to it.

She motioned with her hand. "Lead on."

He caught her hand midway. Shameless hugged Willoughby's side tightly as they rode, Asa's leg continually brushed hers. Butterflies fluttered in her stomach, bringing to mind the previous time they'd fluttered. In the barn. She needed to break the tension before she did something embarrassing.

"Why do you have Clint spying on me?"

If she wasn't mistaken, the hand on hers tightened briefly before he answered. "He's not spying on you. He's taking care of you."

"I've been taking care of myself for many years now."

He brought her hand to his mouth and brushed a kiss across the back. The butterflies in her stomach took flight. She couldn't suppress a gasp. She dared a look at him. He pushed his hat back. The smile on his lips left her in no doubt that he'd heard. "I take care of my own, Elizabeth."

"I'm not a child who needs to be watched."

"You're my wife and I have a duty to protect you."

"From what?"

"Outlaws. Indians. Wild animals. Jack Hennessy."

She had no trouble meeting his gaze now. He was obviously serious.

"There haven't been any outlaws around here in ages. The Indians have all been driven away, and I have yet to run afoul of a wild animal."

"Elizabeth, you're acting like I've been unreasonable."

"I don't like being watched."

"That's too damned bad. Either you stick by your escort or you don't go out."

"You can't tell me what to do!" She bit her lip. He could and they both knew it. All he had to do was order her to stay home, and her world would dwindle to the walls of the ranch house. No more riding. "I don't like it."

"Neither do I, but with the railroad coming, there's a rough crowd passing through Cheyenne. There're also those rustlers you had trouble with. With one source of money cut off, they could turn to others."

"Are you trying to scare me?"

"If I thought you'd have the good sense to scare, I sure enough would be."

"There is nothing wrong with my sense."

"Sure enough, darlin', you're a poor judge of people."

"I chose you, didn't I?"

"Nope."

The smug smile on his lips clued her in. "Darn it! Old Sam told you, didn't he?"

"I don't know what you mean."

"That rotten skunk. He promised he'd keep the fact I'd asked between us."

"How do you know he didn't?"

"The way you're smiling at me, as if you're the only cat in the barn that's got cream."

He chuckled. "Guess I'll have to work on my poker face."

If he did, she was down and out for sure. Willoughby slipped on the way down the slope. She shifted back to accommodate his descent. Shameless stepped aside to avoid a tree. Asa didn't let go of her hand until the last moment. Just when she was sure they were going to end up hugging the big spruce, he let go.

She knew he'd be smiling when she caught up to him. Nothing seemed to panic him while he took endless delight in tormenting her. He was like the wind, blowing hard or whispering in soft teases. Never from one moment to the next could she say what he'd do. He kept her guessing. He kept her...smiling.

She watched the smooth way he dismounted. The muscles in his back stretched his shirt tightly across his shoulders. He was all man. Well-muscled, honorable, with enough punch to his name to make men clear out of his path, and yet, he seemed to look for laughter the way her father had searched for flaws. She shook her head. She didn't know which she preferred. One was familiar. The other intriguingly different.

She hadn't admired much in her father with the exception of his devotion to purpose. She admired a lot in Asa. Mostly his ease with everything he faced. Like now. She'd been staring at him unknowingly for the last three minutes. No doubt he felt uncomfortable, but rather than squirm, he simply stood there and waited her out. No censure. No impatient "let's get going". Just acceptance that she needed a minute.

"I'm sorry. I didn't mean to stare."

He held up his arms to help her down. "No harm done."

"It was rude."

"Not as long as you didn't uncover any warts."

"What?"

"I said I didn't mind as long as you didn't find anything you want removed."

"You have to know you're a very attractive man."

"I haven't had many kids run screaming," he admitted as he swung her down. "But this face has seen better days."

Could he be uncertain about his appearance? There was a bump on his nose that said maybe it had been broken. A small scar bisected his right cheekbone.

"You're staring again." He caught Willoughby's reins in his hand. "Picking out the flaws?"

He said that as if he'd been through this before. She wondered if he'd been rejected. "I like your face." It came out fiercer than she'd expected.

He turned and smiled at her from where he was tying Willoughby beside Shameless to a fallen log. "I like yours, too."

"You're very handsome."

She said that as if it mattered. Asa wondered if she thought he was worried about his looks. He patted Willoughby on the neck, gave Shameless an affectionate pat, and headed back to his wife. There she stood, her fists balled at her sides. He realized she thought his feelings were hurt and she was ready to defend him. He stopped when he was two feet away from her. "I'm glad you like my face."

"I don't want you to think I'd rather have a smooth-faced boy for a husband. Someone who didn't know how to handle himself in a fight. Someone who didn't have a broken nose and a scarred cheek."

He caught her hands in one of his. "I don't think my pride can take any more of my flaws trotted out."

"Dear God!" Her eyes widened with dismay. "I didn't mean to make you self-conscious."

"Relax." He kissed the tip of her nose, laughing when her eyes crossed. "Do you like the way I look?"

"I just said so."

"Then that's all I need to know."

She stepped back, freeing her hands. She took the food basket from him. "I really made a mess of that."

"Oh, I don't know," he said, ambling along beside her. "Depends on what side of the glass you're looking from."

"Why?"

"A man likes to know his woman isn't battling an urge to run screaming when he steps into the light."

His reward was a shy chuckle. He pulled her up short when she showed every intention of crossing the glade and heading into the woods beyond. "I thought here would be a good place."

"Oh?" She stopped, blushed a bit, and nodded her head. "Yes, it would."

She was clearly flustered.

Asa took it as a good sign. Maybe all the restraint he'd been practicing for the last week was coming 'round to reward him. She was beginning to trust him. He'd been heading home today at lunch. Wanting to see her too much to stay away like he'd planned, then he'd seen her riding toward him with Clint. About made his day. She'd actually sought his company. And managed a compliment in the bargain. Yup. Things were definitely looking up.

She spread the blanket on the mossy ground. Overhead, spruce boughs gave a fragrant canopy. If it weren't this cool, it'd be a darn sticky place to eat lunch, but this time of year, it provided an intimate haven from the wind and prying eyes. A haven he was intent on using to his advantage. Truth was, he was about starved for a kiss. Not one of those uptight come-around-to-my-way-of-thinking attempts he'd utilized before, but an actual kiss with interest on both sides. That was something he was looking forward to all right.

Before he sat beside her on the blanket, he twitched a stick from beneath it. If dessert went the way he planned, he didn't want any rude intrusions. "Looks like quite a spread."

"A man your size needs to eat."

She looked him up and down and added another piece of golden fried chicken to his plate before passing it over. He placed it on the ground beside him. "Trying to fatten me up?"

"You could use a little weight."

"You're welcome to try, but I gotta warn you, I've always been lean."

"That's good to hear."

"It is?"

She smiled and daintily made a plate for herself. "That means I won't have to spend time this winter letting out your pants."

He laughed, eyed the ladylike amount of food on the plate she put beside her, and shook his head. Couldn't keep a bird alive with that piddlin' amount. "Lord, darlin', there's hope for you yet."

"There is?"

"Yup." He snagged another piece of chicken and added it to her plate. "You made a joke."

"I wasn't aware you felt I lacked a sense of humor." She placed the added chicken back in the basket.

"Oh, I had my suspicions." He took a leg off his plate and added it to hers. "I was just beginning to doubt you'd loosen up enough around me to let it shine."

"What a colorful way to put it." She reached for the piece of chicken.

"That's me. All color. No refinement." He let her get the piece halfway back to his plate before he shook his head.

"No?" Her tone went all prissy.

He edged her hand back until it hovered over her plate. "There isn't enough food on that plate to keep a gnat alive."

"It'll be fine."

"Yeah." If, by fine, she meant ready to drop at the first sign of exertion.

"Mr. MacIntyre, a lady does not bring an appetite to the table."

He closed his eyes and counted to ten. "What does she bring?"

"Refined conversation, companionship and manners."

"How about you drop the first and last and bring a healthy appetite instead?"

"That wouldn't be proper."

He closed his eyes and counted to ten. Again. He'd never heard such horse hockey in his life as Elizabeth spouted as gospel. "Well, I guess that explains it then."

Her eyebrows arched quizzically. She took a nibble of her chicken. "Explains what?"

"Why you don't see too many ladies hereabouts." He waited until her mouth was full of drink before he continued. "No doubt, they all passed out mid-lecture on a ridiculous rule some poor girl was expected to follow next."

Lemonade spewed all over the blanket as she laughed and choked at the same time. Only quick reflexes kept him free of the spray. Equally quick reflexes scooped her into his arms and pounded her on the back. The first slap might have been a bit hefty as she flipped half over his arm. Darn. He kept forgetting how slight she was. As soon as she caught her breath, she was back to lecturing him.

"You, Mr. MacIntyre, are a miscreant of the first water."

He tipped up her chin so he could see her red-cheeked face. "You insulting me or complimenting me?"

"All books on proper behavior insist that I should be insulting you. At the very least, taking you to task for your disrespect."

"But you're not?"

She shook her head. "No."

"Any particular reason?"

Her smile was bright and cheery, startling him with its openness. "No, because I've often had the same thought myself."

He pondered that and all its ramifications. "That mean you might be open to some negotiations as to what ladies can and cannot do?"

"I cannot speak for all women, sir."

"I'll settle for you speaking for yourself."

"Very well."

"You think you can bring yourself to call me by my first name? Sure 'nough, darlin', every time you call me Mister, I'm checking over my shoulder to see who you're talking to."

"I thought you'd gotten used to it."

"I confess to the fact I've been waiting you out."

"And now you're not content to..." Her eyebrows rose again. "Wait me out?"

"A smart man keeps an eye for negotiating opportunities."

She leaned her head against his shoulder. "And you're a very smart man."

"Whoa, darlin! Two compliments in one hour. Better ease up or I'll start thinking you're buttering me up."

Her body grew tense in his arms. He leaned his cheek against the top of her hat. Something poked him in the ear. "Ouch!" He rubbed his ear. "Any chance you could see your way to disarming that hat?"

She smiled. A soft smile that set his neck hairs on end in warning. She lifted the hat off her head. She held it above her head as she shook the ties free of her chin. Seated as she was in his lap, he had a bird's eye view of her breasts. And it was a mighty nice view.

He must have stared too long, because she dropped her hands suddenly. The little hat landed with a plop on her folded legs. "I'm sorry."

Now it was his turn to raise his eyebrows. "For what?"

"I didn't mean to shock you."

"Shock me?"

"You said it was all right."

"I did?"

"I won't do it again."

She wouldn't? "Whoa, darlin', do what?"

"I said I was sorry."

"I heard that, darlin'. Problem is, I was still eating dust on the first sorry." He tipped up her chin. "What are you apologizing for?"

She told him, but he had to ask her to repeat it, her voice was so faint. "I'm not wearing my corset."

"And you think that's worth losing a smile over?"

"It appears I misunderstood your dismay."

He had to turn the words over in his mind two or three times before things made sense. "You mean my staring?"

Her hands clenched in on one another. "Yes."

"Darlin', we're going to have to work on your education some. That wasn't dismay. That was plain old admiration." He met her shocked gaze. "You have the prettiest breasts I've ever seen."

He had to give her points for pluck. While her cheeks turned cherry red, she kept her eyes open. "If you think that, why haven't you touched them?"

Whatever response he'd been expecting, that wasn't it. The one she gave him left him so weak-kneed, she could have knocked him over with a feather. For the third time in his life and the second time this month, he felt heat scorch up his neck. Along with it came laughter. "Dammit, woman! How am I supposed to come off as strong and capable when you've got me blushing like a school boy?"

"You look good in red."

"You'd best hope no desperado comes upon us now, 'cause armed or not, I wouldn't be putting anything into the man but laughter."

"I like you, Asa MacIntyre."

Soft as a feather, that whispered confession put an end to his laughter. "I like you, too, Elizabeth."

"So why haven't you done anything about it?"

It was a good question. He just wasn't sure how directly he wanted to answer.

Chapter Eleven

ဢ

"Are you going to answer?" Elizabeth asked, watching his expression carefully. The man was as changeable as a fall day.

He touched her cheek. "Yeah."

"With the truth?"

"I hadn't decided that, but I suppose you're going to insist?" His right eyebrow quirked as punctuation to the question.

"Yes." She definitely wanted the truth. She shifted off his lap to her knees.

He sighed from his toes as if it were a great sacrifice. "Well, then, I guess I'll have to." She waited and counted ten breaths before he finally said, "I was waiting on a sign."

"As in a miracle like Reverend Griffin talks about in church?"

His chuckle was deep, intimate, coaxing. As seductive as his come-hither lazy grin. It ought to be illegal, she decided, feeling the pull, for a man to toss about charm as easily as Asa did.

"Nothing that earth-shattering."

His gaze dropped to her lips and she felt it like a touch. Yet,he made no move toward her. She folded her hands in her lap. She clutched her composure as tightly as she did her fingers. There was no hope for it. She was just going to have to bring it out in the open. "I was wondering why you were going into town today?"

"I have some business to take care of."

That was no help. A pine needle rested on the blue serge of her skirt. She flicked it away. It sailed clear off the blanket. "Will you be coming home for dinner?"

"I told you this morning I wasn't sure if I'd get everything done in time."

She smoothed the crease created by her overzealous flicking. "Will you be stopping by the saloon?"

"Ahh."

She wished he were more vociferous. That 'Ahh' could mean anything, and there was only the slightest chance one of them wasn't correct. Her cheeks felt like they were on fire.

In no apparent hurry to clarify his exclamation, Asa drew his knee up and rested his forearm across it. His legs were so long, his knee was level with her mouth. It wasn't any effort at all for him to reach out and hook his finger under her chin. She'd never met a man so devoted to face-to-face conversation. Hadn't his mother ever told him that demure ladies kept their eyes downcast? It was something a man was supposed to look for. He tugged and she had no choice but to meet his knowing gaze. Couldn't he even allow her any of the few advantages available to being a lady?

"You want to know if I plan on being overcome with manly needs while I'm in town?"

She gritted her teeth against the amusement in his voice. "The thought had crossed my mind."

His finger dropped away from her chin. "You forget our deal?"

"No." Lord, this was embarrassing.

"I gave you my word."

"I know. I didn't mean to insult you. It's just that…"

"Just what?"

"Two weeks have gone by."

"Yeah?"

If she didn't die of mortification, there wasn't a God. "You haven't come to my bed."

"Darlin', I've been there nightly."

"I was speaking figuratively."

"Uh-huh."

He was being deliberately obtuse. She took a steadying breath. If she didn't get a hold on her emotions, she was going to wrap her fingers around his neck and throttle a direct answer out of him. "Then why…?" She filled in the blank with a descriptive wave of her hand.

His right eyebrow kicked up. She heeded the warning and braced herself. "Why haven't I exercised my marital privileges?"

She gritted her teeth again in the face of his amusement. "Yes."

"I've been waiting for an invitation."

Anger and relief swept through her like a wave. She held up her hands as if to ward off his idiocy. "I invited you two weeks ago."

He was shaking his head before she finished the statement. "Not to my way of thinking."

It was a struggle, but she managed to contain her anger and frustration so her voice lost its high squeak and came out in a more even-toned threat. "What exactly do you consider an invitation?"

If he smiled, she was going to go over to his horse, wrench that rifle out of the scabbard, and shoot him in a place guaranteed to get his attention.

He didn't smile. He picked up a piece of chicken instead.

"Now, today was a nice start," he said, taking a bite of chicken. He hummed in his throat as he chewed. She had to wait for him to swallow to continue.

"What was so nice about today?"

"This is the first time in two weeks you've done anything but stare at me when I do something nice. Today, you wanted to spend lunch with me and you paid me two compliments. Right now," he took another bite of chicken, "I'd say things are looking up."

"You wanted me to…approach you?"

"Don't go bug-eyed on me. I told you forcing a woman wasn't my style."

She pressed her fingertips to her forehead. "Mr. MacIntyre, I'm afraid you're going to have to be clear as to what you expect from me."

"Calling me by my first name would be a start."

As much as she wanted to, taking that step was very…frightening. "I know." She opened her eyes to find his face level with hers. There was no avoiding his eyes this close. "I'm trying. I really am."

His hand slid behind her neck. With a slight pressure, he pulled her forward. "I know, darlin'. You haven't heard me complaining."

He was going to kiss her. She knew it, she just didn't know if she wanted it because she'd likely go up in flames, and she couldn't converse when she was burning.

She bit her lip. "But you were going into town."

"And you think I'm looking for something I can't find at home?"

"The thought crossed my mind."

This time, he did smile. "There's nothing I can get in town that I don't have better at home."

She sighed. "I don't know if I can be as…willing as you seem to want."

"That's one worry you can hand over to me. I won't be going to town for women." His lips brushed her nose. "I'm not a green boy. I can wait for what I want."

The supposition being that he wanted her. "But I've only got a month…"

He shrugged as if time slipping away were nothing. "You were the one who put a time limit on things."

"But you agreed!"

He kissed one eye closed and then the other. "I said I could live with your rules." His voice was as soft as his lips on her cheek. "You were so intent on boxing me in. Truth was, I never had any intention of my manly needs taking me anywhere outside your bed."

"You let me worry!"

"Darlin', you were the one who said you were an expert. You didn't want to hear anything I said, so I figured the easiest way to clear things up was to let you see for yourself."

"I could just kill you."

"How about kissing me instead?"

"That wouldn't be nearly so satisfying."

"How do you know?"

He was completely outrageous, but he was right. How did she know that killing him would be more satisfying than kissing him? She'd never really kissed the man. Her eyes dropped to his mouth. Quirked in that half smile she was coming to like, it looked eminently kissable. Like, if she placed her mouth on his, she could snatch a bit of his laughter for herself. She made to move forward, and then stopped. "Would you mind?"

"You thinking on kissing me?"

"Yes."

"Heck, no. Why would I mind that when I've lost more sleep these last two weeks speculating on that very thing?"

"You've wanted me to kiss you?"

"Yeah. I've wanted it."

How…intriguing. He'd wanted it, and he hadn't taken it. He'd waited for…her.

She leaned a fraction of an inch closer and placed her lips against his. Her first thought was that her instincts were right. As soon as her lips tested the texture of his, his smile wandered onto her own mouth. She liked the way his lips were soft and his afternoon whiskers tickled the edges of her lips.

She moved her mouth experimentally. It felt equally good. She stole a bit more of his smile before pursing her lips lightly and kissing him as she'd heard talked about, tentatively running her tongue around his mouth. Exploring the hard edge of his teeth and the slippery soft glide of his inner lips. When she would have pulled back, she ran against the barrier of his hand on the back of her head. She opened her eyes and found his closed. The expression on his face mirrored the feelings inside her. Pleasure. Wonder. Maybe even a bit of impatience?

He was enjoying this as much as she was. He was also anticipating where it would lead. She liked that. She moved her lips back to his. She pressed them there for a while, but it wasn't close enough. She sighed at the pleasure. His lower lip felt fuller than his top lip. Softer. She touched it with her tongue. He hummed in his throat.

"I like that."

His words whispered across her face. She did it again. He hummed again.

The vibration traveled from his lip to her tongue. The butterflies she'd noticed earlier sprang to life in her belly. This time, when she touched his lip with her tongue, she lingered, testing his resiliency. His breath escaped in a puff of air. She smiled and succumbed to an urge. She nipped his lip. Instead of jumping like she expected, she felt his lips stretch in a smile. "Hell cat."

"I'm sorry."

"Don't be. I felt that all the way to my toes."

"I didn't hurt you?"

His response was to nip her lower lip. Sensation flashed through her body like a grease fire. "Oh!"

"Feels good, huh?"

"Oh my."

"Hmmm."

She eyed his lips with new respect. They obviously possessed talents she hadn't considered. "What else feels good?"

He laughed, gave her a quick kiss, and pulled back. "Lots of things."

She licked her lower lip and tasted him there. A shiver went down her spine.

"Tell me."

Asa smiled. For a woman who preached convention, she sure was unconventional. "I'd rather show you."

Before she could get around to asking the question he could see in her eyes, he wrapped his arm around her shoulder and tumbled them to the blanket. Before she could rethink her decision, he scooped her onto his chest, and pulled her thighs over his. She didn't look at him while he positioned them, but he could feel the expectancy in the careful stillness of her body. He pulled the pins from her hair, letting it glide like silk over his hands. She didn't say a word either as he gathered her skirt up over her thighs, but her gasp as he tucked the material under her told him she felt his arousal against her thigh. She wiggled her hips, ruining his alignment.

"You want to scoot around," he drawled, stuffing a loop of the material into the sash on her skirt. "I'd be mighty partial if you moved down and to the left."

Her brow creased. Her eyes widened as she figured out what he was saying. To his surprise, she slowly moved down until his manhood pressed her intimately. Her heat and moisture teased him through both their layers of clothing. His cock jerked and lengthened, fighting the restriction of his denims. When she pressed her hungry cunt against him again, he couldn't prevent a thrust of his own.

"Good God, darlin'! You're going to be the death of me."

"I'm sorry." That quick, she scooted away.

"Damn!"

She picked up on the dismay in his voice. She straddled him again.

It was a struggle to find a normal tone. "Darlin', would I be right in guessing you're not unwilling anymore?" He stopped her hips from pushing against the head of his shaft.

"I never was."

"That's not strictly true, but I'll keep that discussion for another day." He took a breath as she rubbed against him again. His drawl wasn't the steadiest as he asked, "Do you want to make love with me?"

"Yes."

"Then lift up a minute."

She did. He made short work of his belt and the buttons on his pants. He slid his hand inside and freed his aching cock. It sprang into the warm sunlight, straight and strong, reaching for her thinly clad pussy. He didn't take his hand immediately away. She was staring at his cock, her eyes wide. Her tongue peeped out, moist and tempting. She ran it over her lips. His cock twitched and pulsed against his palm, lengthening further, wanting that moist heat wrapped around the sensitive head. He wanted that tongue stroking over the flared expanse, lapping the pre-come from the tip, sliding beneath the head to tease the sensitive underside. With a leisurely movement of his hips, he pumped in time with his mental image, driving his shaft upwards through his hand so it grazed the slit in her pantaloons, tormenting them both with the teasing contact.

She followed him down on the descent.

Light as a butterfly, she settled her dry warmth onto his shaft. He jerked when her small hand attempted to encompass his cock, and then stilled as she positioned him to the delicate opening of her pussy. She rocked on him, not hard enough to force a union, but hard enough to wedge the tip into the moistening valley. He slid his hands around her buttocks and stilled the relentless pushing of her hips.

She bit her lip, and shot him a confused glance. "It won't go in."

He could feel the tension building in her. It didn't take a genius to see she was trying to do this perfectly. She was just too green to know she wasn't ready or that he was supposed to have some fun getting her there.

He ducked her gaze, crossed his fingers, and then church-serious said, "I'm embarrassed to admit this, darlin', but I'm not ready."

"You were before." She bounced a little. He kept her from doing damage by catching her hips in his hands.

"Men aren't like women," he explained. "They need kisses and sweet-talk before they can, well, perform."

"You want me to sweet-talk you?"

"It would help."

"If I kiss you, you'll be ready?"

He struggled to hold onto his laughter. "I'd be warming up."

Her fingers on his chest brushed his nipples; the tip of her nail snagged one before moving on. Fire flashed through his body. He couldn't suppress a groan.

She latched onto the sound like a starving dog faced with a steak. She eyed his nipple, his lips, and then her breasts, discreetly covered in white. "You said before you'd want to kiss my bubbies?"

"No lie, I'd like to do that again. But, right now, I'd settle for a kiss."

She leaned forward and pressed a kiss to his lips. Close-mouthed and dry, he didn't find it much inspiration to anything except his amusement. He didn't hide his disappointment.

She sat up. His erection glanced off her buttocks. He bit back another moan. She was sweet and earnest, and she was driving him crazy.

"I'm not doing this right." Her voice was an agony of self-disgust.

He made an immediate decision to shake her of that worry. "How about we make a deal?"

"What?" Sharp as a tack, the woman had the intelligence to be suspicious. He'd have to be equally sharp if he didn't want this afternoon dissolving into chaos.

"Seeing as how you're green at this, why don't we come to an agreement?"

"What?"

He combed her glorious hair through his fingers. It curled and bounced back into its previous pattern over her shoulders. Lord, he thought, even her hair was stubborn. "Why don't we agree that I'll tell you what I want, and then you'll do it if you feel like it."

Her relief was palpable. "You promise to tell me if I do something wrong and you don't like it?"

"You have my word of honor."

He figured it was an easy promise, he didn't even need to cross his fingers when saying it. He couldn't imagine her using that luscious body in any manner he didn't like.

She pushed back, hands against his chest, face set in lines of rigid determination and demanded, "Tell me what to do."

He rolled so that she was beneath him on the blanket. That would be his pleasure.

Chapter Twelve

ഔ

He propped himself up on his elbow so he could look down on her. "First thing I got to ask is, do you have your heart set on being proper?"

"No. I've pretty much given that up around you."

"Good." Despite the readiness of her reply, he could see she was nervous. Her eyes were huge in her face, and faint lines of tension shadowed her brow. The little lace ruffle at her throat fluttered with her pulse. He reached up and stilled it with one finger before slipping buttons from their holes. No doubt Elizabeth's nervousness was going to get worse before it got better. The woman did not understand the meaning of the word relax.

"Come here, wife," he ordered.

"That's the first time you've called me that," she whispered, wiggling to a more comfortable position under him.

"It is?"

"Yes."

"That a problem?" Might as well address these worries as they came, he decided as he admired the play of sunlight and shadow over her upper chest. With the tip of his index finger, he traced the line of her right collarbone as it arced away from the hollow of her throat.

She tipped her head back. Goosebumps sprang up along the path of his finger. "Not if I can call you husband."

He trailed his finger back along the path just taken. When he reached the hollow of her throat, he pressed. Her pulse beat a rapid tattoo beneath his touch. He smiled. "You won't find any complaint here."

She said "husband" again. There was a wealth of possession in the tone. He found he liked it. Almost as much as he liked her next words.

"You belong to me."

"That's what we promised before God. To cleave unto each other…"

"Forsaking all others," she completed.

The breeze blew a strand of hair over her chest. It fell forward across her shoulder and caught in the open front of her shirt. He traced its path as it curled down over her breastbone and into the cleavage just visible over the lace edge of her undergarment. "Why am I not surprised you latched onto that part?"

"Wishful thinking?" she offered.

Her breath caught as he pulled her camisole away from her skin and stared at the unfettered fullness of her breasts. He didn't know whether that catch was from embarrassment or excitement. He didn't really care. The white curves with their rose colored tips shivered enticingly with her roughened breathing. As he watched, the nipples crinkled and pulled into a slight pout. He wanted to feel them harden against his tongue.

"More than likely," he agreed. He released the camisole and looked up. "You settled?"

"I believe so."

"You have any objections if I kiss you?"

"None I can think of."

None that she was admitting to, he corrected silently as the tension started in her neck and spread down her body. He sighed, knowing there was no cure for her nervousness but experience. He leaned over. Her eyes closed. He touched his lips to hers. Her brow creased.

The lips under his were rigid. He moved his lips to the corner of her mouth. She kissed the opposite corner of his. He touched the corner of her mouth with his tongue. Her tongue shot out and tapped the corner of his mouth. He pulled back a breath to get a gander at her expression. The crease between her brows indicated high thinking. He sighed.

"Darlin'?"

Her eyes popped open. "What?"

He shook his head. "No need for panic. I just had another question."

"What?"

He chewed on the best way to address the subject, then decided nothing but the blunt truth was going to get the job done. "You wouldn't be thinking of memorizing everything I do, would you?"

"Uhm, well, maybe."

"Don't get me wrong." He undid two more buttons on her camisole and spread the material so it was open from chest to waist. "That'd be a great approach if I were teaching you to rope a calf."

She leapt right into the space left by his delicacy. "That's exactly how I learned!"

Lord help him, she looked ready to do battle in the middle of his seduction. He worked the little bow free at the waist of her camisole. "And I bet you're a top-notch roper."

"Good enough I don't toss a lariat twice," she boasted while casting a nervous glance at the amount of skin he was exposing.

He kissed the end of her nose. Mutiny dissolved to indignation. "Stay with me here because this is important."

From the dead-on way she met his gaze, it was clear he had her attention.

"Romancing a woman, well, that's a touchy subject for a man."

"It is?"

He ran his finger down the length of her nose, his heart stumbling over a slight catch when her eyes crossed trying to follow his movement. "Uh-huh."

He smoothed her right eyebrow and then moved to the left. "A man has a lot on his mind the first time he lays down with a woman."

"Are you saying you're feeling apprehensive?"

He could have sighed with relief that she was making it so easy for him. "Sure enough, I'm getting all het up thinking about how you're studying every move I make."

"But how am I supposed to learn?"

"Let me try to explain it this way. Will you agree that a good teacher is confident in what they're teaching?"

Her "yes" was cautious.

"Well, truth is, I'm not confident enough about what you like to teach you what I like."

She frowned. "That doesn't make any sense."

Oh, no, he thought. They weren't getting into an argument now! "It does, and before you argue with me, let me remind you that I'm the one with the experience."

"You just said that you didn't have any."

He grit his teeth. "With you," he clarified. "I don't have experience with you and, as every woman is different, I'm a bit unsure here."

"Too unsure to teach?" The fingers on his forearm clenched as she exclaimed, "Then what are we going to do?"

It was as close to a wail as he'd ever heard her utter.

"I was kind of hoping, this time out, you could just lie there and let me know what feels good."

"To me?"

"Uh-huh."

"But I'm supposed to be making it good for you!"

216

He cupped her cheek in his hand. "Remember in the barn, you moaned when I kissed your neck?"

Her blush started at her breastbone and spread outward to her face and, intriguingly, her nipples. "Yes."

He couldn't resist tracing a reverse path, following the curve of her cheek down the length of her throat, over the planes of her chest and then up the rise of her breast until the tip of his finger rested against the tip of her nipple. "I felt ten feet tall then."

"And that would make it good for you?" She stared at where his finger met her flesh.

"This one you're flat out going to have to trust me on." Using his nail, he gently scraped the plump nipple, rewarding her flinch and gasp with a repeat caress. "Nothing makes a man feel better than when a woman feels good at his touch."

"But later?" Her lower lip sucked in between her teeth as he let his fingertip hover over her expectant flesh.

"Later, I'll take great pleasure in teaching you to make me howl." Her nipple rose fat and sassy from her breast, vibrating with the tension with which she held still.

He flicked it lightly in reward for its impudence. Her entire body jerked up in response.

"Providing..." he drawled as if she hadn't just come off the blanket at his touch.

She looped her arms around his neck and arched her torso toward his hand. "Providing?"

"Providing, this time, you relax enough to let me make you howl."

She frowned. "I don't think ladies howl."

He smiled, watching the pulse in her throat do some fast-stepping as he, slowly, deliberately took her nipple between his thumb and forefinger. He milked it rhythmically as he settled his chest over hers. "You will, darlin'. You will."

He brushed her mouth with his. "Do you like that?" he asked.

She frowned, as serious as a preacher confronting the damned. "It's all right."

He stroked his tongue over her closed lips, keeping the touch featherlight. She jerked her head back.

"No?"

She hesitated, then admitted, "That felt funny."

"Funny good?" While she thought about the answer, he increased the pressure and speed with which he teased her breast. He wanted her nipples aching and sensitive to his slightest touch.

"I don't know."

"Let's find out then." He did it again.

She jerked but, this time, pressed closer rather than away.

"Good?" he asked against her lips.

Her "yes" was a sigh.

He placed his mouth on hers, rubbing lightly against her contours. He'd never set out to seduce a woman more deliberately. He'd never had the need, but then, he'd never known what he was missing. Breaking through Elizabeth's defenses was a delicious game of cat and mouse. Her honesty jolted his senses.

There was no coy trying-to-please. He'd asked her to be honest and she was brutally so. She found a no-nonsense surge of his tongue past the barrier of her lips 'unsavory' to use her word, but if he preceded it with a few tentative forays, her toes curled against his thigh and her chest rose against his. Clearly, she was a woman who wanted to be seduced.

He held back his need, striving for gentle, but her sensual honesty all but destroyed his good intentions. Never had he had a woman who enjoyed his touch so much. Never had he had a woman so open. That it was his wife who rose to the touch of his hand on her breast was an aphrodisiac in itself.

She was his and no other's. Only his hands would touch her. Only his lips would coax hers into a mating dance. Only his thighs would settle between hers. Only his lips would wrest a broken cry from her throat when he nipped her neck. Only he would know he could reduce her to sobbing his name by teasing, then suckling her pert nipples. Only he would hear the moaning scream she issued when he nipped one with his teeth. Only he would be gifted with the sweet dampness between her thighs when he delicately explored her silken folds.

The scent of her arousal surrounded him. He slid his hand down her waist. Over her hip. Between her thighs. He found her swollen. Wet. Hungry. For him. She was his. Totally and completely his. By God's word and her own choice. To a man who'd grown up with nothing, she was his own personal paradise. For however long he could hold her, he would, milking every drop of pleasure from their time together.

He shifted his position so he could reach her other breast. The scent of evergreen rose up to surround them as his elbow dug into the spongy ground. He pulled his hand reluctantly from between her thighs. Her juices clung to his fingers, mingling with the scent of nature. She had the ripest, most succulent nipples when aroused. They perched atop her breasts begging for his tongue, his teeth. His attention.

He didn't make her wait. He spread her thick cream onto her nipple until it glistened a deep rose in the sunshine. With his thumb, he tested her slickness, her readiness. He replaced his finger with his mouth, gently at first, scraping his teeth over the turgid bud, pressing harder as her flavor exploded through his mouth and her hips rose to his touch.

He struggled to keep his approach gentle as he delved between her thighs, seeking the swollen bud of her clit. He coaxed it out of its protective cover with pulses of his fingers that exactly matched the rhythmic suckling of her breast. When it pushed, satin smooth and proud, against his fingers, when her hands dragged his head against her straining breasts, he pinched it hard and strong. Her strangled scream confirmed something else for him. While she liked the gentle approach at first, when aroused, she wanted him to push her to the limit. To take her. To make her his anyway he wanted. He pinched her clit again and wrested another pleasured scream from her.

"That's it," he whispered against her nipple. "Tell me how you like it."

Her answer was a shaking of her head. He set his teeth to her engorged reddened nipple, letting her feel their edge. Her hips thrust in unconscious demand. Asa bit down gently, and she froze. Even her breathing stopped. Against his hand, her pussy clenched and wept. Her clit, if possible, swelled even fuller. He could feel her pulse against his finger. She was on the verge of an orgasm.

He ground his cock beneath him. The pain took the edge off his pending release.

"Not yet, darlin', not yet."

Elizabeth opened her eyes. And then promptly closed them. She struggled to get air into her lungs as her body coiled from the inside out, tighter and tighter. She wanted, needed him to continue what he was doing. To feel his teeth rake her flesh, to feel his fingers wrestling that surge of sensation from her clit, but he was just holding still, promising everything but doing nothing. She couldn't stand it.

"Open your eyes," he ordered.

She did, seeing nothing but a blinding flash of sunlight.

"Look." His voice was a hoarse grating of sound as he tapped her breast. She did as ordered. Watching as his mouth encompassed her breast. Feeling the suction as he worked his way back to her tip. The jolt of lightning that blazed into pleasure when he nipped her, forced a cry from her throat. As he did with every other sound she made, he smiled. The pleasure on his face left no doubt that she was making him happy.

With the tip of his tongue, he soothed the point of her nipple. To her disappointment, she felt nothing. She wanted the fire she'd felt before. The propriety-stealing pleasure he'd taught her to like. She curled her fingers in his hair. As before, the cool strands soothed her overheated flesh.

"Do it right."

She couldn't believe it was her voice huskily ordering him.

His answering smile was feral. His face hard with desire. A sensible woman would have been afraid. She was discovering she wasn't the least sensible because she tugged his hair and repeated her demand, horrified as soon as the words left her mouth. Asa didn't share her reaction. Instead, he threw back his head and laughed.

His "Ah, darlin, you're one in a million" was a balm to her conscience. She only had time for a deep breath before he made love to her, holding nothing back. And she adored it. He let her feel his teeth, nipping and scraping gently in an erotic dance of claiming that was as elemental as her response. The force of which started a quiver of fear.

"Asa?"

"Oh God, darlin', don't be pulling back now." His cock nudged her thigh as he shifted position.

"I don't know." She wanted to tell him what she was feeling inside, but she couldn't find the words. Not now when her body was clamoring for appeasement.

"I do, darlin', and, right now, I'm a very happy man."

"But no one told me…"

He kissed the side of her neck, nipping her flesh and sending shudders of pleasure down her spine. "How could they know you're one-in-a-million?"

"You don't mind?"

"Darlin', you've got me so fair to bursting, I'm afraid of embarrassing myself."

"Where?"

He took her hand and slid it down his body. "Here."

He closed her fingers around his manhood. Beneath her palm, he throbbed with energy. So much energy, it was amazing. She propped herself up on her elbow and curled her fingers around him, surprised as always by his size. His strength. Her fingers didn't meet. She measured him from shaft to tip. She doubted she could hold him with both her hands. Especially at the base. He was much wider there than he was at the top, though she doubted her fingers could meet around him even there. He flexed in her grip as she squeezed experimentally.

"Easy there."

Above her, his weight shifted back and away, giving her more freedom. She kissed the flat male nipple that was suddenly within reach. His manhood jerked in her grasp as she did, surging with life. Enthusiasm.

She explored the hard-soft flesh under her command. He moaned and arched his hips. He slid through her fingers. She retreated to the tip, feeling him jerk and shudder as she did. He liked this, she decided, glancing at his face and seeing the deep lines carved there. She swirled her fingers around the top, gauging the different shape and texture. He caught her hand in his, his expression one of anguish.

"What's wrong?" she asked.

"There are certain things about a man's body," he broke off, clearly torn before admitting, "I'm pretty excited."

She pondered that for a moment. Then squeezed gently. He moaned and jerked her hand free. "You're ready," she deduced.

His chuckle was a raspy shadow of its normal deep-voiced self. "Yeah, I'm ready."

She flopped to her back and spread her legs. "So am I."

He rolled onto one elbow and shook his head, frustrating her. "Not yet, you're not."

If her "Why not?" was petulant, he had no one but himself to blame, she decided, blinking against the sunlight streaming through the pine boughs.

"Truth is, darlin', I'm enjoying the getting ready part too much to give it up just yet."

"You are?" She wished she could see his expression clearly, but backlit by the sun as he was, it was impossible.

"Yes. Now, why don't you bring those pretty breasts back here and I'll show you how much."

She didn't think about hesitating. Wrapping her arms around his neck, she arched her back in compliance.

"Lord, you're something," he murmured, before sliding his hand under her breast. Cupping it in his callused palm, he urged her flesh into his mouth. When he started to suckle, he settled in, not giving her any time to think. No respite in which to do anything more than ride the waves of pleasure he created. The tension inside her built to near exploding, until he slipped his hand between her thighs to probe gently.

The tip of his finger slid into her with indecent ease when she moved her hips. The feeling was as sublime. "Am I supposed to be like this?"

He paused. "Like what?"

"Sooo…wet," for lack of a better word.

He stroked between her legs again. She fought the urge to move against his hand. "You mean here?"

"Yes."

"Oh yeah," he sighed and dropped his forehead to hers. His fingers penetrated deeper as he explained, "A woman's body prepares itself for a man's that way. If it didn't, it would hurt you when I come inside."

"It didn't hurt last time." She shifted her hips. His finger felt strange inside her, soothing yet irritating at the same time.

"Well, last time, a whole lot of things weren't done right." He stilled her hips with his forearm. He pushed harder. She felt the resistance and the release as his finger slid knuckle-deep into her pussy.

"Darlin, I want you to relax."

"I am."

Another finger prodded her pussy. "Here."

She buried her face in his neck, bumping his nose along the way. "Oh God."

She placed her hands on his chest.

"Just concentrate on my fingers and relax."

He pushed against her again. After an initial resistance, her flesh softened and then relaxed. His second finger sank to the first knuckle before stopping.

She concentrated on the feelings that kept shooting through her. Not as hard as when he'd been kissing her breasts, but still nice.

He fucked her with the tips of his fingers for a minute, slowly increasing the pace, the friction. She found herself spreading her thighs and lifting her hips. His second finger slid to the second knuckle. She now had two fingers inside her pussy, pushing and pulling at her intimate flesh, sparking sensation in areas she didn't even know had nerves.

He smiled. "That's it," he whispered against her neck. The palm of the arm he was bracing himself up with flattened across her stomach, just over her pubic bone. He pressed down. Immobilizing her hips. The pressure on her pussy increased. A steady demand for entrance.

"No, don't tense up," he whispered. "Just relax."

She forced herself to unclench her fists. The pressure increased to near pain.

"Easy, darlin', just a little more." There was a sudden give and an incredible feeling of fullness.

He now had two fingers completely inside her. It wasn't comfortable. She tried to shift away.

He pulled his fingers out before forging them back in. "Damn, darlin', you're tight." When they were seated to the hilt, he pressed harder, almost convulsively probing for more.

"Am I supposed to be?"

He kissed her quickly as if to shut her up. "You're perfect, darlin'. Just perfect."

He pulled his fingers all the way out before forging back in again. The feeling was strange, not quite painful, but on the edge. The third time he didn't pause before reinserting them. He just fucked her hard and steady, and relentlessly. Her pussy burned with the friction. A tingling breathless shiver of sensation started at her toes and snaked over her body, making her hair stand on end.

"Asa?"

"Just relax," he ordered again.

She didn't have any choice. He had her pinioned. He paused on the next withdrawal, then he was back, and there was more than before.

"Asa! That hurts."

"I'm sorry." He didn't sound sorry. He sounded driven. Desperate. He pushed again. Harder. She gasped at the bite of pain and pleasure that rolled over her as he managed to wedge three fingers into her pussy.

"Damn. You haven't taken..." He bit off whatever he was going to say. His voice was rough and gravelly as he asked, "Is it too much? Can you take more?"

There was no doubt he needed her to take more. She felt overstretched and too full, and her pussy burned where it struggled to accommodate him, but a more primitive part of her enjoyed it. Wanted more. Wanted to see exactly how much she could take.

The upward thrust of his fingers made her moan, as her sensitive tissue clasped and clung to his fingers.

"Easy now. I can fix it."

Before she could ask what he meant, he was sliding down her body. His hands stayed where they were, but his mouth moved scandalously low. She grabbed his hair and tugged.

"Leave be, Elizabeth."

"But?"

"Trust me, darlin'. You'll like this."

She already knew she liked this, but she wasn't sure it was okay to be doing it in the open. That was before she felt the hot, moist pressure of his tongue on her over-stimulated clit. Fire streaked through her loins. She bit her lips and gasped.

His chuckle vibrated on her clit, reverberating through her body. Her hands no longer tugged. They pressed his mouth closer. He responded by lashing her with his tongue, and then gently capturing her aching, hungry bud with his teeth. When she was writhing, he pushed with his fingers. The pain was nothing compared with the pleasure.

"That's it," he encouraged through the lust boiling through her. "Open for me, darlin'."

He stretched her wider, then slid his fingers free. She felt bereft. Empty. Aching.

His teeth and tongue were relentless on her clit as his fingers were merciless on her pussy. He kept her poised there, empty and aching, before he pressed his fingers against her again and began a steady fuck. She took all three fingers to the hilt, hard and deep over and over, her pussy struggling to accommodate the demands he made on it while her body struggled to control the maelstrom of sensation overwhelming her. There was no escaping the feelings that built. She gasped, begged, but he didn't stop. He merely drove her higher until her body arched like a tightly strung bow. One more lash of his tongue, one more thrust of his fingers and she knew she'd shatter forever, never to be the same again.

He pulled back, depriving her of all sensation.

"Asa!" It was a sob. A plea for mercy. She wiggled against him.

"Hold on," he ordered, pushing her hips down with his arm.

He was not going to leave her like this!

"No more teasing," she demanded, struggling to renew contact with his body.

"I've got something better if you'd just stop fighting me," he growled.

Something hard and warm brushed her starving pussy. Lightning streaked up her nerve endings. She twisted upwards. "Oh, yes!"

"Jesus!" He sounded like he was laughing and moaning at the same time. His hands on her hips held her still. His fingers grazed that sensitive spot as he spread her, and then there was a delightful pressure against her openly weeping pussy.

"Oh, yes," she sighed again, closing her eyes against the sunlight, wanting to concentrate on the feeling of him against her. Hot. Hard. Huge and eager.

"Put your arms around me." The order was a harsh imitation of sound.

She obeyed immediately. He reached between their bodies. His fingers took over where his tongue had left off, gliding over her clit, circling, teasing. It was too much. Her whole body exploded and then re-centered on that one central point of bliss. She sobbed, the pleasure was so beautiful, and over and over her body spasmed. Each throb had her whole concentration until the last one dropped off. So caught up in her bliss, she barely noticed the pain as Asa breached her pussy with the wide head of his cock.

She opened her eyes. "That was heavenly," she whispered as the aftershocks vibrated through her.

"Glad to be of service." The lightness of his tone was belied by the strain in his expression. Sweat beaded his brow.

She felt the trembling in his arms. The throbbing of his body in hers.

"Asa?"

"Stay relaxed, Elizabeth."

"I don't know if I can," but she knew she would. For him. For herself. Because she wanted his hard cock. No matter what.

"You can." He told her, increasing the pressure. "You will."

He crept in a bit more. The lining of her pussy pushed against him, gripping and dragging. Sensitizing.

"Why wasn't it like this before," she gasped as he bore down on her.

He closed his eyes and groaned as her flesh gave and he sank an inch deeper. "You're still a virgin, darlin'."

"But the other night…"

"I'm not one for force."

She felt his muscles gather as he prepared to push. She caught her breath in preparation. Again the pain. Again the frustration.

"Put your arms back around my neck," he instructed her.

She looked up at him. There was no doubt he was in agony. "Does it feel good to you?"

"That's the hell of it, darlin'. Men like it any way it comes, whether the women are enjoying it or not."

And he felt guilty about that. She saw it in his eyes and understood he was a giving man, but she didn't want to be a taking woman. She wanted this thing between them to be the same as everything else. Open. Honest. She arched her breasts toward his mouth.

He bent and suckled her. By the second, his actions grew rougher, more primitive, dragging her along until he was alternately biting and sucking. She could feel the tension pounding beneath his skin, shaking his muscles, dampening his flesh with perspiration. An equally primitive reaction built in her. She felt him pulsing just inside her. It wasn't enough. She didn't want to be something precious and worshipped. She wanted to be his.

She took the decision out of his hands. She braced her feet under her hips and arched upward, impaling herself, biting her lip against a cry.

Like glass facing the blow of a hammer, her action shattered his control. As if he couldn't stand anymore. He growled low in his throat, sank his fingers deep into her hips and pulled. She felt him tear deep. Before she could register any pain, he'd pulled out and was surging anew. On the third thrust, she thought he'd break her in two. On the fourth, she didn't care.

She twisted, whether to get closer or away, she didn't know. This was too wild. Too elemental. It excited and scared her at the same time.

"Mine," he growled as he thrust deeply into her, his hips slamming against hers, his mouth working her breasts.

"Yes." A growl rose in her own throat.

He lifted her feet until her ankles were hooked around his hips. "Mine," he growled again, holding himself against her as she worked to get the last inches of his hard cock inside her. She couldn't and the frustration almost had her crying.

He took the initiative out of her hands. He slid his arms under her thighs and flipped her legs over his shoulders. He walked his hands up her side. The air was filled with the scent of their lovemaking and the spruce when she lay completely open and vulnerable to his touch. She could do nothing but receive him as he drove his cock into her pussy, grinding his hips against her clit on the downstroke, forcing her to take the last two inches, ignoring her gasps when she thought she couldn't, sharing her exultation when she, finally, finally did. Then he, as she lay impossibly stretched beneath him trapped between heaven and hell, he caught her gaze with his. She couldn't look away as he said, "Mine." As if to prove it, he pulled all the way out. And in one, mind-boggling lunge, re-seated himself to the hilt.

The air left her body, her nerves screamed, and everything in her pulled up tight. With quiet, deliberate, ruthless persistence, he did it again, but this time when he growled "mine", she confirmed it, her body jerking in helpless spasms as reality shattered and she gave herself over to his possession as her orgasm took her. As if her climax triggered his, Asa's control snapped. His cock jerked within her, caressing her walls anew as spurt after spurt of his hot seed filled her eager pussy. Wrapping her arms around his neck, she held him tightly while his body shuddered and emptied into hers.

For the first time in her life, she felt like she belonged.

* * * * *

"Who'd have thought Miss Prim Elizabeth Coyote was such a wildcat in bed?" Asa mused with deep contentment minutes or hours later.

She was draped across his body. Warm sunlight heating her skin. Completely boneless. Sated. "That's Elizabeth MacIntyre," she corrected into the curve of his neck. He smelled of man and sunshine. She took another deep breath just because.

"So it is." His fingers played gently with one of her nipples. His toes stroked the bottom of her foot.

Against her thigh, she felt a stirring. She shifted her hips. "Hmmm."

"Just ignore him," Asa instructed. "He has no sense."

She didn't want to ignore him. She reached between them. "I like him," she said. And he liked her if the way he swelled at her squeeze was any indication.

"You're too sore." It was a halfhearted protest. She loved him for making it.

She eased down until he was in position. "No, I'm not."

She couldn't imagine ever being too anything to turn away from her husband.

"I can wait."

"I can't." No matter how she tugged, he wouldn't roll over. She raised her eyebrow at him. "This isn't going to work if you don't do your part."

He laughed, shook his head, and urged her into a sitting position where she straddled his hips. "You do it," he ordered. "I'm too tired."

He wasn't too tired, she noticed, to stroke her breasts the way that caused the goosebumps to chase up her spine. He did it again, encompassing each breast in one of his big hands, sliding from the fullness of her chest up to the crest with a featherlight touch that had her nipples pulling taut. When he reached the very tip, he lightly, gently grazed her nipples. Just hard enough to get their attention. He did it again. And again. On the fourth pass, she dug her nails into his chest and bit her lip to keep back her cry of protest. She needed more. So much more. She shifted against his cock, experimented, then found just the right angle.

Her breath caught as he pressed against her. She was sore and he was bigger than she remembered.

He stroked the inside of her thighs. "Nice and easy, darlin'."

His hands glided up until they spread across her hip bones. His thumbs met at the juncture of her thighs. As she eased down, so did his thumbs, until they connected at the swollen nub of her clitoris. She gasped, jerked and pressed. He stroked her clit again, and she felt the natural giving that allowed his cock to slide home. She didn't take him all, she couldn't. She was too sore, but it didn't matter. They moved as one, flesh gliding together, intimate parts brushing in rhythm, asking silent questions, garnering quiet responses. It was a courting. A mating.

It was exquisite, sensual and oh, so gentle, this loving. She cried when the end came and the illusion drifted to reality. She wanted it to last forever. She wanted the emotions to be real.

Asa held her while she cried, offering her his shoulder and asking no questions. Somehow, that made the reality all the more wrenching.

Chapter Thirteen

Town was a rude awakening from the quiet of the ride in. People bustled about. The streets were a muddy mess of excrement from the ceaseless parade of cattle, horses, and buggies. Occasionally, boards were strewn across large puddles in order to facilitate crossing the street. The air was full of the scents of food and animals. The din of voices and music from the saloons overpowered the quiet conversations of residents, while the rowdy shouts and laughter of cowboys and railroaders out for a good time dominated all else.

"Believe it or not," Elizabeth said as they walked down the boarded sidewalk, "Cheyenne used to be a peaceful place."

"Uh-huh." Asa steered her around the third drunken man in the same amount of minutes. "Some say the railroad is going to be the salvation of Wyoming—put it on the map—but I've got my doubts when you see the crew that's putting it together."

"They are wild," she agreed.

"Uh-huh."

A man careened out of the door ahead of them. He landed on the wooden sidewalk with a bone-slamming jar. Another man came flying after him, prepared to carry on the fight.

"This is worse than I remembered," Elizabeth admitted.

Her grip tightened on his arm, telling Asa she was nervous. He just didn't know if it was the prospect of getting caught up in a gunfight or whether it was being seen with him that had her nerves strung tight. He sighed and thought it was probably the latter. He wasn't much of a catch, even if he was handy in a fight. "If you have friends in town, I could drop you there before I go to the bank."

"I'm fine." She glanced up. "After all, I have the notorious Asa MacIntyre by my side. No one would dare bother me."

"You'd best be hoping they ask who I am before they swing," he answered, not sure if her lips were twitching because she was fighting a smile or a frown.

"Don't worry, I've got bragging rights and I'll be sure to use them if a miscreant seems too impetuous for his own good."

"I'll hold you to that." He wasn't exactly sure what she meant, but he liked the bragging rights part. Might mean she liked being his wife. Truth was, he kind of liked being her husband. She had a quick wit when she wasn't trying to be ladylike. She didn't cling, but she had ways of showing she wanted him around.

He tipped his hat to a lady and gentleman passing on the right. His mood lightened when they both nodded back. That was something he'd have to get used to. Being respected for something other than his reputation was new. He and Elizabeth had garnered their share of glances crossing town. Most of them speculative, but not once had a woman swept her skirt aside when he passed. With Elizabeth on his arm, he belonged somewhere and it showed. "You want to get something to eat at Millicent's before we head back?"

He'd eaten there once before he'd met up with Elizabeth. Next to his wife's cooking, it was the best he'd had.

"Can we spare the cash?" Elizabeth asked, sounding hopeful.

"If we can't, there's not much point in me stopping by the bank."

Gun shots erupted behind them.

"Down!" In a flash, Asa had Elizabeth down on the ground, covering her with his body while he aimed his revolver in the direction of the shots. "Son of a bitch!" If he could have reached them, he would have strangled the cowpokes firing exuberantly in the air. The shots ended as abruptly as they started.

"What happened?"

"Just a couple of yahoos letting off some steam." Asa got to his feet. He grimaced as he helped Elizabeth. Her blue jacket and riding skirt were covered in dirt. "Darn, I'm sorry."

She glanced at him as she brushed off her skirt. "It's just a little dust."

It was more than that. He tucked a stray curl behind her ear. "I didn't hurt you, did I?"

"My dignity is a little smudged."

He winced. "I was kind of hoping not to embarrass you this first trip in after the wedding."

"Who says I'm embarrassed?"

He pushed his hat back. "You're not?"

"No." She tugged her jacket straight. "I'm not." She brushed the dust off her left elbow. "Truth is, I'm probably the envy of every woman in town."

He put his hands on his hips. "Let me get this straight. I throw you down in the middle of the sidewalk, get your outfit covered with Lord knows what, and you couldn't be happier?"

She beamed at him like he was a particularly bright pupil. "Exactly."

He was never going to understand the woman. "Glad to be of service."

But it wasn't his imagination that her step was lighter as they made the last three storefronts without incident. There wasn't anything an average Joe could pick up. Her expression was still composed, but there was a hint of pink in her cheeks brought on by excitement. There was also a satisfied tilt to her lips. He shook his head again, held open the bank door, and followed her into the cool interior. The place smelled of ink, leather and wood polish. He didn't care for the smell any more than he cared for the man standing by the teller cage.

It was too much to hope that Elizabeth wouldn't see Ballard, but it rankled that she spotted him right off and almost made a spectacle of herself trying to get his attention.

"Aaron!" she called, waving her hand. When he didn't turn immediately, she called his name again. Aaron turned and said something to the teller before coming over.

"Elizabeth! It's wonderful to see you."

He took her hand in his. Asa waited for Elizabeth to withdraw it. She didn't. That slapped some of the good out of his mood. Manners dictated he acknowledge the other man. He nodded his head. "Aaron."

He might as well have saved the energy for all the attention the man paid him.

"What are you doing here today?" Aaron asked Elizabeth.

"Asa had some business to attend and he was kind enough to invite me to come along."

Aaron looked his way. "Are you finished?"

"No." Asa didn't figure he owed the man more than one syllable.

"Well, then, why don't I take Elizabeth off your hands? You can meet us at the restaurant at the Ballroom Hotel when you're done."

For once, Elizabeth wasn't opening her mouth, she was waiting patiently for him to do the husbandly thing and make a decision. Unfortunately, this was one of those damned if you do and damned if you don't decisions. If he said no, not only would Elizabeth think him petty, she'd be here the whole time he met with the bank president while missing a fancy meal. On the other hand, he didn't want his wife spending the afternoon chatting and dining in a fancy hotel with a good-looking neighbor.

He slipped his arm around Elizabeth's waist. "Well, that's right nice of you. A couple of years from now, I might look more friendly on that offer, but right now, I find I'm partial to Elizabeth's company."

Damn! He was a selfish S.O.B. Elizabeth would probably enjoy a chance to have an expensive dinner in a fancy hotel. But, before he could set his mind to backtrack, she leaned into his side. Her "Thank you" was aimed at Aaron and showed no sign of discontent.

"Are you sure?" the other man asked. "Banking business could take a while."

Asa had to give the man points for persistence.

Elizabeth's hand settled over his where it rested on her waist. Though her touch was as light as a feather, he had a distinct impression she was trying to soothe him as she said, "I've already made plans with my husband, but I appreciate the invitation."

The relief that went through him was unwarranted. What else could she say? He hadn't left her any option. He felt like a dog in the manger, but he couldn't bring himself to rescind his statement. He neither liked nor trusted Aaron. He didn't want him within a mile of his ranch, let alone his wife.

"It was nice to see you again, but..." He stepped back so Aaron could pass. "Don't let us keep you from your business."

The show of manners was lost on Ballard but earned him another stroking from Elizabeth. "Maybe you could come over for Sunday dinner?" she asked.

She'd better plan on doing a heck of a lot more than stroking if she expected him to sit down to the dinner table with their neighbor, Asa thought. He was saved from having to turn down the invitation by Aaron himself.

"Unfortunately, I have plans." He took his hat from under his arm. "Maybe another time."

The man hadn't cleared the door when Elizabeth's "thank you" reached Asa's ears.

"For what?" he asked.

"For being polite."

"No need to go looking for trouble." Not when he had a feeling it was going to come to his door anyhow. Looking down, he noticed she was clenching her hands. "Something wrong?"

"No, I'm just thinking."

"About what?"

She shrugged. "Things."

He had his mouth open to press the issue when a neat, rotund older man came around the counter. "Mr. MacIntyre!"

He stepped away from Elizabeth. "Mr. Dunn." He held out his hand. "It's good to see you again."

"Glad you could make our appointment." He shook his hand twice in a very precise movement. "Have you been waiting long?"

"Nope. Got waylaid by an acquaintance of Elizabeth's."

"That's right." He smiled. "Mrs. MacIntyre and Mr. Ballard grew up together."

"So I've been told." Asa answered as the banker ushered Elizabeth to a wide-backed leather chair by the potbellied stove. "Why don't you have a seat here while your husband and I conduct our business?"

She sank into the chair like a feather drifting onto a pillow, her spine straight, her hands folded in her lap, head tilted in perfect feminine deference. "Thank you."

The banker's whole demeanor softened, his voice patronizing. He clearly saw Elizabeth as nothing of consequence. To Asa, who'd watched her pole-axe a man with a bar stool and face down private demons without batting an eyelash, it was a revelation of the depths of stupidity to which a man could sink.

"Could I get you coffee or tea?"

Elizabeth raised a hand to her throat. There the slightest flutter to her fingertips. "Oh, could you? It was a chilly ride in."

Chilly, hell. She'd spent most of the trip napping, cocooned in his duster.

The banker lit off to get her beverage with the walk of a man on a mission.

"What are you up to?' Asa asked Elizabeth.

"I didn't realize you were coming here when you said you were coming to town."

"No. I believe you had in mind a trip to the saloon."

She cast a quick glance in the banker's direction where he was barking directions to some poor, wet-behind-the-ears kid. "Don't trust him. He's as slimy as they come."

"His opinion of you is a lot higher."

She dismissed the discrepancy with a wave of her hand. "He's just a man."

And what exactly was he?

She seemed to realize her mistake. "I mean, he's not a very intelligent man. He thinks women have no brains at all."

"I can see where that would make him fair game."

"That's always been my opinion," she replied dryly. "Especially since I think he's taken advantage of a widow or two."

"Seriously?" He really didn't need to ask. Elizabeth was nearly always serious.

"Yes."

Mr. Dunn was coming back. Elizabeth caught his hand. She tugged him down and kissed his cheek, damned near shocking him out of his boots. No doubt Mr. Dunn saw it as a demonstration of wifely emotion, but the whispered "watch your back" lingered in his mind as he straightened. Elizabeth wasn't a woman for dramatics.

"Mr. Higgins will bring your tea." Mr. Dunn said in a cheery voice as he approached.

"Thank you so much." Elizabeth breathed in a proper ladylike expression of appreciation. "You're such a considerate man."

Mr. Dunn puffed up fatter than a chicken with the chills. "I hope you find the tea to your satisfaction."

"I'm sure it will be fine," Elizabeth answered.

A wildcat posing as a lap cat and Mr. Dunn was falling for it hook, line and sinker. Asa shook his head. It was enough to make him wonder at the wisdom of letting the man handle anything, let alone his money.

"I'll try not to keep your husband too long," Mr. Dunn continued. He bowed slightly. "Now, if you'll pardon us, your husband and I have business to conduct. It shouldn't take long. I'll do my best to have him back to you as quickly as possible."

Elizabeth blushed and nodded. "Thank you."

He turned to Asa and held open the door. "Mr. MacIntyre, if you'll just step into my office?"

"You got the transfer?"

"Oh, yes, the funds came through just fine. There's just one little detail that needs to be ironed out…"

Chapter Fourteen

છ

On a cloudy day, the blue of Millicent Foster's Boarding House and Eating Establishment was bright. On a sunny day like today, its bright blue and pink assaulted the senses. Stepping through the door didn't alleviate the visual disarray. Millicent decorated to suit her impromptu likes and dislikes with complete disregard to style or even color coordination. Every table in the place sported a different table cloth. The attack continued with the sounds generated by the diners crowded into the small restaurant.

No one commented, though, because of the scents that teased ones nostrils. They were heavenly and only chaotic because the customer had to make a choice from the dinner menu. Millicent Foster could cook.

"Looks like quite a crowd tonight," Elizabeth offered.

Asa looked around. "She'll make a pretty penny off this crew."

"Do you want to wait for a table?"

"Are you kidding?" left no doubt he wasn't budging.

"Hey!" That's my order! A blond man shouted from the table in front of the window. Elizabeth saw he had the waitress by the arm, prohibiting her from setting a plate on the adjacent table.

"Is not," came the immediate response from a rough-looking man seated at the neighboring table.

"She might make some money," Asa amended as both men jumped to their feet, "if the customers don't bring the place down around her."

Elizabeth smiled as the waitress, a young girl, hightailed it to the back, taking the disputed food with her. "Not if Millicent's here."

As she finished the sentence, an orange-haired tornado appeared among them, wielding a huge wooden spoon.

"Millicent?" Asa asked, the corner of his mouth kicking up in that familiar grin.

Elizabeth nodded, taking a step back from the door. Asa followed suit.

"You two have the manners of trash," Millicent yelled. She punctuated her statement by bringing the wooden spoon down on their unprotected skulls. When they grabbed their heads, she pointed to the door. "Take yourselves out of here right now." When they didn't move fast enough, she whapped them again. "Out!"

"What about our dinner?"

"Yeah," the other man hollered. "We paid for it!"

"Bessie!" Millicent yelled, brandishing her spoon and backing the men toward the door. "Bring these gentleman's orders out here."

Bessie handed the tray over. Millicent scooped it up in one of her hands. As soon as the men cleared the threshold, she pitched the entire tray after them. Food and curses filled the air. "You want to act like pigs in my establishment, then I'll be slopping you like hogs." She stood in the doorway, her six-foot tall frame blocking the light. "Don't you dare set foot in this place again."

"Aw, Milly!"

"Where we gonna eat?"

"Maybe that fancy hotel up the street will serve your kind." She turned and slammed the door, almost running over Elizabeth on the way back to the kitchen.

"Elly!"

Her smile was as familiar as sunshine to Elizabeth. "Hi, Millicent."

"This your new man I've heard talk about?"

"Yes." Elizabeth smiled as Asa's eyes widened in shock. Millicent had the husky voice of a siren when she wasn't screeching. It was so incongruous with her build, it never failed to shock people. Mostly men. Millicent slapped him on the shoulder with a vigor that belied her fifty-plus years. "How ya doing?"

"Just fine."

Elizabeth caught Asa's hand "Asa MacIntyre, this is Millicent Foster."

He brushed the brim of his hat with his fingers. "Pleased to meet you, ma'am."

Millicent's hearty laugh filled the room. "Hear that, gents? Elly's done married a man who knows how to address a lady." She took two steps to the counter, scooped a fresh baked pie off the shelf and waved it under Asa's nose. "This here is for you after you get done with supper."

Asa smiled that lazy, drawn out smile that inevitably made Elizabeth's heart go pitter-patter. "Apple pie! My favorite. Haven't had that in a coons age."

Millicent beamed ear-to-ear. Elizabeth forgave him the lie. Millicent was one of her favorite people.

"Aw, heck, Milly," the Sheriff called from the back of the restaurant. "I called you ma'am last week and I didn't get no apple pie."

Millicent snorted inelegantly as she waved Asa and Elizabeth to the table vacated by the blond railroader. "Who you think you're kidding, Sheriff? You only called me ma'am cause you were being sarcastic."

"Be fair, Milly."

"Letting you eat my cooking is as fair as I'm getting!" She turned back to Elizabeth and Asa. "Now, what'll you be having, Elly?"

Elizabeth unfolded her napkin across her lap. "I'd love a sweet potato."

"As an appetizer, that'll do, but what are you planning on for the meal?"

"I'm really not hungry."

"Child, we've been over and over this. You won't start putting meat on your bones unless you start putting food in your belly."

"I'll eat a big breakfast in the morning," she promised, excruciatingly aware that Asa watched the exchange.

"So you say now, but I won't be around to witness it." Millicent heaved a sigh from her toes. The men at the next table got up to leave. She started piling their dishes onto her tray. "I know your daddy had a thing about how he thought a woman should look, but you gotta let it go."

Elizabeth felt the old tightening in her belly. The churning nausea. She was aware of Asa's eyes on her. "I'm just not hungry, Millicent."

If she ate anything now, she'd be violently sick. She pinched the napkin between her fingers.

"Hrrmph!" Millicent wasn't buying her excuse.

Elizabeth felt warm callused fingers slide over hers and found Asa looking at her. He nodded his head once and gave her fingers a soft squeeze. As his fingers wove between hers and loosened their grip from her napkin, he said, "I'll take care of her, Miss Foster."

This earned him a disbelieving snort and a hard glare. With a practiced hitch of her shoulder, Millicent balanced the loaded tray. "I've heard that before."

"Not from me."

Millicent stood and stared at Asa, saying nothing. Elizabeth felt the tension like a knife. She wanted Millicent to like Asa. After what seemed an eternity, Millicent proclaimed abruptly, "I've a feeling I'm going to like you."

"Well, now, I was just having the same thought," Asa replied. His hand now rested calmly on Elizabeth's.

Millicent let loose with her booming laugh, causing all heads to turn their way. "Just for that, you get my chicken and dumplings to go with that pie."

Elizabeth breathed a sigh of relief. If Millicent and Asa had taken to feuding, she couldn't have borne it. Millicent was as close to a mother as she'd ever had. "You're being honored," she informed Asa as Millicent wove her way back to the kitchen.

Asa's smile was gentle as he said, "I'll reserve judgment on that until I taste her dumplings."

* * * * *

The plate Millicent placed in front of Asa was laden with food. "You eat all that and I'll get that pie."

If he ate all that, Elizabeth decided, he'd be over to Doc's getting medicine for a stomach ache.

"Check back in about ten minutes," Asa said, his voice laced with confidence and anticipation.

Millicent beamed. "I do like a man who can eat."

"In that case, ma'am," Asa said as she placed a glass of water before him, "we're going to get along fine."

Millicent chuckled and turned to Elizabeth. Elizabeth braced herself for the disapproval she knew was coming. It landed in the thud of her sweet potato before her. "Here's your order."

Millicent jerked her thumb in Asa's direction. "How you expecting to keep up with a man like that, let alone hold onto him, when you don't have an ounce of meat on your bones?"

"Mr. MacIntyre is free to leave anytime he wants." Elizabeth's stomach clenched even as she made the statement.

Millicent could be brutal with her disapproval. "What kind of —"

Asa's low drawl cut her off. "Don't suppose she's too worried about it, because she knows I'm not going anywhere."

Millicent spun on him. "It's a man's nature to wander." Her ever present wooden spoon punctuated the statement.

Asa calmly took a bite of dumpling. His expression melted into one of pure bliss as he chewed. "You sure can cook, Miss Foster."

The spoon waggled ominously. "Don't try to get around me with that slow-talking sugar."

Asa wiped his mouth on his napkin. "I wouldn't dream of it."

"Harrumph!"

She was going to whap him, Elizabeth just knew it. He was going to provoke Millicent with his teasing ways, and then she was going to whap him. If she did, he'd be nursing a headache for days. Elizabeth stabbed her fork into the sweet potato, fragrant with butter and a touch of cinnamon. "You're right, Millicent. I've got to start eating more now that I have a husband."

She put a bite of the potato in her mouth. It sat like a lump of dirt. She didn't know how she'd force it down her throat without choking.

Millicent eyed her suspiciously. Elizabeth managed a weak smile. It didn't appear to reassure the other woman, but she seemed to be relaxing. Just when Elizabeth was sure Millicent was going to let it go, Asa spoke up.

"She's not right."

If she had a shotgun, she would have loaded his backside with buckshot. She watched fatalistically as the light of battle reentered Millicent's blue eyes.

"You saying I don't know what I'm talking about?"

Behind Millicent's back, Elizabeth made frantic motions for Asa to shut up. He ignored them. "I'm saying that if you're trying to convince my wife I'm hankering for something else, then you and I have a problem."

The restaurant grew quiet as the patrons realized a standoff was in the making.

Millicent put her hands on her hips. "I notice your problem is with my convincing her, not the truth of it."

Elizabeth groaned. Millicent loved to argue.

"What truth would that be?" Asa asked, calm as could be.

"Men don't like skinny women." Millicent said with complete authority. "They get tired of being poked and jabbed by all them bones."

"That so?" Asa asked, interested.

"Gotta say she's right about that," the Sheriff hollered. That got hoots and hollers as it was the worst kept secret in town that the sheriff was sweet on Millicent.

"I wouldn't say that," Jed Stuart countered. "I like 'em trim and sleek like soft pussy cats."

Elizabeth wanted to sink down in her seat as the argument of men's preferences grew and swelled with little regard for the decency of the topic. Millicent and Asa paid it no mind. Their gazes were locked onto each other, their discussion private unto themselves.

"That's so," Millicent retorted, echoing Asa's response with all the force of her considerable personality.

Elizabeth knew how it felt to come up against that force. It always left her feeling like she'd survived a hurricane. Asa didn't even look like he'd been ruffled by a breeze.

"Well, I hate to argue." He took another bite of his chicken. "But a man has a right to his tastes."

"And yours are?" Millicent had the persistence of a fly. Elizabeth wished that, just once, Millicent wouldn't focus on something pertaining to her life. She really didn't want to know Asa's preferences. Hearing he liked plump blondes would be torture.

"I'm happy with my wife."

He said that as if he meant it. No smile. No prevarication. Just a straightforward statement of fact. Some of the tension left Elizabeth's throat. She took another sip of water and discovered she could swallow the bite of sweet potato.

Millicent's toe tapped hard on the floor for about ten beats before it stopped. Some of the stiffness left her back. Her spoon dipped to a less menacing position. "Darned if I don't believe you."

"Glad to hear that, 'cause I'd sure hate this fine meal to go cold while we debated the point."

Millicent laughed. "You're a character, Mr. MacIntyre."

He nodded once. "I'll be taking that as a compliment."

Millicent nodded back. "You do that." Her attention swung back to Elizabeth. "You got yourself a good man. Don't mess it up with any of your nonsense." She frowned at the sweet potato. Elizabeth wished she'd managed to choke down another bite.

"You eat every bit of that," Millicent ordered. "If I have anymore than the skin to slop the hogs, I'm going to take it personally. You'll be nine-years-old all over again."

"I'll eat it all," Elizabeth promised. Somehow, she'd manage.

Millicent paused and sniffed the air. "Gosh, darn it, Bessie! Did you take that corn pone out of the oven?"

"I meant to," Bessie wailed in a clear indicator she hadn't.

With a curse word that singed, Millicent forged a path to the kitchen.

"What happened when you were nine?" Asa asked.

Trust him to latch onto that. "My father and I were having a discussion."

"How did Millicent get involved?"

"It started here."

"Uh-huh." He pointed to her plate with his fork. "You going to eat that potato?"

"I suppose."

"So the argument with your father started here?"

She sighed, recognizing he wasn't going to give it up. She poked the potato with her fork. "Father thought I was too puny. He thought, if I ate more, I'd be able to handle ranch work better."

Without guilt, Asa made free with her potato. "Your father overlook he was dealing with a little girl?"

"He had hopes the problem could be overcome."

On an "Uh-huh", another bite disappeared. "Your Pa have a tendency to drink?"

Her fingers clenched in her lap. "No. He just believed he could...change things."

"Can't see the logic in trying to change a sweet little girl into a strapping boy."

"I wasn't sweet."

He paused in his theft of a third bite. The fork hung, fully loaded about six inches above the potato. "Now there, darlin', I've got to disagree." She knew she was going to regret it, but she met his gaze anyway.

"You melt as sweet as honey on a man's tongue. Gotta believe you started that way to end that way."

She tried to protest, but all that came out was a strangled, "Asa."

The man at the next table seemed to lean their way. She'd be mortified if she thought he'd heard what Asa had said.

Her husband was blithely unconcerned. "On this, you'll have to take my word."

"I'll take your word, not because I agree, but because this conversation is highly improper."

The glint in his eyes was devilish. "Guess that means I'll have to prove my point in private."

If he did, she'd probably strangle on the embarrassment.

"What happened when Millicent stepped in?" he asked as he made the last of her potato disappear.

She didn't know whether to be offended or relieved that he'd eaten her dinner, so she answered his question instead. "She interrupted my father and told him she'd get me to eat the meal before the morning was out."

"Did she?"

"Many times over."

His right eyebrow kicked up. "She wasn't satisfied with once?"

"I kept getting sick."

"And she kept making you eat?" That was the first time she'd heard a man growl.

Elizabeth remembered the day vividly. The pain from the beating her father had given her almost crippling her when combined with the nausea inspired by the smell of meatloaf. Millicent's desperate pleadings. Her father's angry discovery that she'd gotten sick. His fury. Millicent's intervention. "She didn't have any choice."

"Appears to me she had a hell of a lot of choices." He slammed the napkin on the table.

She caught his hand with hers before he could slip away. "You weren't there. I'm very grateful to her."

He stared at her, first, like she was nuts, then in confusion and, finally understanding dawned. Of what, she didn't want to know. Just as long as he didn't go after Millicent with that look in his eye, she was happy.

"I love Millicent very much."

"I can see that." The look he shot her was a warning. "Someday, you're going to tell me the whole of it."

"Thank you."

"Uh-huh." He went back to his chicken and dumplings. "You're racking up quite a debt for someday."

She wasn't worried. Someday was a long way off. A clever person could postpone someday forever. "I'm a procrastinator."

"A what?"

"I like to put things off."

"I guess I'll learn to live with it."

"I'll try to keep it to a minimum."

"I'd appreciate it." He looked to the right. "Here comes Millicent. If you want her to think you ate that potato, you'd best wipe your mouth with that napkin and pretend you enjoyed it."

As she did as he instructed, the truth hit her like a steam train, running over her defenses with blinding speed. He'd eaten the potato so Millicent wouldn't lecture her. Just like he'd deflected her criticism. Just like he'd thrown his body over hers when the bullets had started flying. Just like he'd put Aaron on notice when his thoughtless comment had hurt.

I take care of my own.

She'd heard him say it many times. But she'd dismissed his comment as dog-in-the-manger male bragging, but—

She pulled the napkin away from her mouth. It seemed to actually matter to him that she was happy. And he was doing his best to discover what those things were and that she didn't run into any discord. Hot on the heels of understanding came dismay. She didn't know what to do with someone like him.

"You ate," Millicent observed happily as she came abreast of the table.

"You added just the right amount of cinnamon," Elizabeth commented, not willing to lie outright.

"You remember now, it's just a pinch."

"I'll remember."

"Something wrong with your meal?" Millicent turned and asked Asa. "For a man who was talking seconds, you sure are picking."

"Nope." He took a hearty bite. "I just got sidetracked talking to my wife."

"You really like her that much?" She said it as if it amazed her that anything could distract a man from her chicken and dumplings.

She was a fool but Elizabeth found herself holding her breath for the answer.

"Yes. I really like her."

Millicent snorted. "Newlyweds! Not a lick of sense. Think they can live on love alone." She motioned to a table by the window. "Just like those two over there."

Asa obligingly looked. "You mean the table with the big man in buckskins and that lady all dressed in pink?"

"That's the one."

"That's Cougar McKinnely, isn't it?" Elizabeth asked.

"Yeah."

"I don't recognize the young lady."

"That prissy bit of nonsense is Emily Carmichael. Ever since she found out Cougar's got more money than God's got little green apples, she's been set on hooking him."

"He doesn't seem unhappy with the arrangement," Asa added.

Millicent snorted in disgust. "He's too straightforward a man to see he's being taken for a ride." Her scowl deepened as her thumb jerked over her shoulder in Emily's direction. "She bats her eyes and coos, and he mistakes it for real interest."

"You don't think she's serious?" Elizabeth bit her lip. She didn't know Cougar very well. He was a half-breed, and her father hadn't had anything good to say about him, but Cougar was the adopted son of Doc. Whenever she'd had to go to Doc for care of her wounds, Cougar had always been kind. He'd brought her soup once when her mouth had been too sore from a calf's kick to chew. He'd stood in the pouring rain and said he knew how it felt and handed her the crock. He'd stayed. Talked. She'd been too astonished by his kindness to take precautions. Her father had come upon them, accused her of leading McKinnely on. Cougar had stood up for her. Her father had taken his fists to him despite the fact he'd been not much more than a boy.

Doc had had a lot to say about that. The sheriff had come out. In the end, her father had apologized to Doc and Cougar to stay out of jail, but he hadn't meant it. After that, she'd done her best to stay away from Cougar McKinnely. But she hadn't forgotten his kindness.

She looked at the couple. "I hope you're wrong, Millicent. Cougar deserves a woman who loves him."

She ignored the sharp glance Asa sent her way. His jealousy over Aaron was enough to handle. She wasn't adding Cougar McKinnely to his list.

"So do I, honey," Millicent said on a sigh, "but I'm not. You just watch those two. Cougar's smitten, all right. He's fallen for the girl, but she wants nothing to do with him. She practically cringes when he touches her."

Just then, Cougar reached with a lover's tenderness and a gentleman's regard for protocol and laid his hand atop Emily's. She immediately found a pretext to slip her hand free.

"That girl sure wants no part of that man," Asa observed.

He was so positive. Elizabeth wondered with guilt how Asa felt in the wake of all the times she'd pulled back from him? Was she equally obvious?

"It's as plain as the nose on your face," Millicent agreed, "but Cougar can't tell the difference between maidenly modesty and repugnance." She shook her head. "I never thought I'd say this, but I wish that man had more of a penchant for saloon girls."

Both Asa's eyebrows flew up. Elizabeth couldn't restrain a gasp.

Millicent had the grace to look embarrassed. "Well, it's the truth! Tough as he is, mean as he had to be before Doc and Dorothy got hold of him, that boy's been holding out for true love."

Elizabeth looked across the room and studied Cougar more closely. Cougar McKinnely a romantic? Just then, he threw back his head and laughed at something Emily said. His long dark hair swung across his shoulders, giving his profile an exotic cast. For the life of her, she couldn't see it. He exuded danger, confidence and life, yes, but...romance?

"I hate to start the disagreements before I get my hands on that pie," Asa interjected, "but that's one man I wouldn't want to come up against in a fight. That being the case, I'm having real trouble believing he's the sort to read poetry and sigh over true love."

Elizabeth bit back a smile at Asa's accurate summation. "He is awfully big and mean-looking," she agreed.

Still, she couldn't forget the image of a nineteen-year-old riding six miles in the rain to bring her soup.

"I didn't say he's a sissy boy," Millicent growled, setting her hands on her hips. "I said he believes in true love. It's all Doc and Dorothy's fault, making out that there are others who believe in such a thing just because they found it."

"Maybe he'll figure it out for himself," Elizabeth said hopefully.

Millicent snorted. "No way in hell that girl's going to let onto the truth until she's got a wedding ring on her finger."

Asa was strangely silent. Was he thinking on the similarities between his situation and Cougar's? Guilt and dismay washed over her in waves. She owed him better.

"Here, now, don't eat that!" Millicent ordered, sweeping the half-eaten plate from under Asa's nose. "It's cold."

"Still tastes good," he argued around a mouthful of food.

"No one sits down to a cold meal at my table."

"It was hot when it got here," he pointed out.

Millicent bristled and Elizabeth wanted to laugh. She'd been on the receiving end of Asa's humor enough to empathize.

"And I kept you gabbing, so now it's cold," Millicent countered his argument. "I'll bring you a fresh plate. When you clean that, I'll bring your pie."

Asa groaned as she strode away. "Now I'm in a pickle."

"Why?" Elizabeth asked, knowing full well how his plan had backfired.

"You heard her." He shot a despondent glance at the pie on the counter. "I've got to clean the plate to get the pie. I might have managed to finish that plate and still had room for pie, but if she loads me down again, I'll never make it."

No sooner had he finished the sentence than Millicent came back with a plate groaning with the load it bore. She placed it in front of Asa with a flourish. On a "Dig in", she was off to clean another table.

His sigh must have originated in his boot heels, it was so deep and drawn out. "I really could go for some more pie," he said as he picked up his fork with resigned determination.

"You ate an entire pie at lunch." Elizabeth pointed out reasonably.

A hound dog couldn't look more mournful than Asa. "That was hours ago."

She picked up her fork. "I suppose, in the interest of protecting your belly from another lecture, I could pitch in."

Her offer didn't inspire any great declarations of gratitude. "Pardon me, darlin', but the two bites you'd manage wouldn't make much of a dent."

"For your information, Mr. MacIntyre, I've developed quite a hunger during our discussion." She motioned with her fork for him to push the plate more to the center of the table. "You may consider yourself lucky if you get more than a bite or two."

He pushed the plate over, but his expression was anything but confident. "Anything you say."

A lesser woman might have taken offense. She, however, felt like laughing in the face of his hang dog expression. He'd find out for himself soon enough. She hadn't felt this hungry in years.

She took the first bite and let it melt on her tongue. Her stomach rumbled loudly, demanding more. Her fork clashed with Asa's. She emerged victorious. As she triumphantly brought the choice piece of chicken to her mouth, she saw the realization that she was serious dawn on his face. From then on, it was a contest made more complicated by the laughter that kept getting in the way. By the time they got to the pie, it was an effort to keep the food on the fork for the shaking of their hands and bodies.

As Elizabeth took the last bite of pie, she looked across the table. Asa was doing his level best to keep a straight face while chewing the bit of apple he'd swiped off her plate. He was failing miserably in that and his attempt to appear innocent. He caught her stare and had the gall to wink. In a heartbeat, the truth broke upon her. Hell had surely frozen over because Elizabeth Coyote MacIntyre was falling in love for the first time in her life.

Chapter Fifteen

જી

They rode double back to the ranch. Elizabeth's shawl was no match for the falling temperature. She'd fought a bit, but, by applying sense to her practical side, Asa'd managed to get her to sit in front of him on the saddle. He'd wrapped his duster around her, and now they were both as snug as a bug in a rug. Asa grimaced as Shameless stumbled over a dip in the road. Elizabeth's soft buttocks pressed harder against his erection. If he didn't get a chance to adjust things soon, he was going to be permanently bent double.

Shameless whinnied to Willoughby who nickered back. Elizabeth stirred in his arms.

"Welcome back," he said.

"I'm sorry." She yawned, and pushed her hair back from her face. "I fell asleep."

He could tell from the way she fussed with her hair and clothes, she was embarrassed. "No problem."

She tried to sit up. The coat jerked her back against his chest. She sat there a minute, not sure what to do. To help her into acceptance, he hitched her back against him with the arm around her waist. She wasn't going anywhere.

That prompted another second of stillness as she registered the state of his arousal. After a heartbeat, she relaxed infinitesimally against him. "How did it go at the bank?"

"Fair enough."

From all her squirming, he guessed she was trying to twist around to see his face. "What do you mean, fair enough?"

He shrugged. "You know the Rocking C is in a pickle."

"Yes."

"Well, it's going to take time to get the pickle out of the barrel." A lot of time.

"But everything's all right?"

"I've got it under control." That wasn't an outright lie. With his life savings, he'd managed to buy a month's extension on the note. If he made the railroad beef contract, they'd be fine. If he didn't...well, that was a line of thought he wasn't pursuing.

Her struggles continued. He sighed, unbuttoned the coat, and lifted her up. She didn't seem to get the hint. "Swing your leg over."

"Oh." She did as he instructed, wiggling and shifting until she was straddling his lap, facing him. As soon as she was settled, she all but dove back into his coat. She landed against his chest with a little sigh. He buttoned her in.

"I forget you're so strong."

"You'd best remember that next time you feel like getting sassy."

"Are you threatening me?"

"Just a little friendly warning."

"Uh-huh."

There was a smile in her voice. He looked down. Her green eyes were shadowed. Impenetrable. "You got something to say?"

"You're not going to provoke me," she informed him.

"Who says I was trying?"

"I do, but—" She wiggled a hand up between them and touched the corner of his mouth. "This crease right here tells me you're smiling, which means you're not serious."

He resisted the urge to nip her finger. "Can't rightly see the sense of a man provoking his wife for no good reason."

"I know." She shook her head. Her gaze dropped from his. "It doesn't make sense, which is why I've been trying to figure out the why of it."

"Could be you think too much and there's nothing more to it than I'm the ornery sort."

Another snort, this time stronger, indicated she wasn't buying that line. The finger she wagged under his chin stirred a little breeze. "I will figure you out."

"That a threat?"

Her hand retreated into the warm cocoon of his coat. "No," she sounded content. "More of a warning."

He smiled. The woman did like a challenge. "I'll take note."

He wrapped the reigns around the saddle horn. Elizabeth looked at him askance as he slid his hands inside the side slits of the duster.

"My hands are cold," he explained.

His fingers climbed the ladder of buttons on the front of her shirt. When he reached the top, he started working backward, slipping buttons from their holes as he went.

"And my cock is hard," he added as he undid the fifth one.

She didn't move. He wasn't sure if she was horrified or intrigued until he felt her little hands working the buttons on his fly.

"We can't have that," she murmured as she freed him from his pants.

Her hard nipples grazed the side of his hand as he spread her shirt. She gasped at the slight contact.

"Sore?" he asked, rubbing them with his thumbs through her camisole.

She shook her head. "Sensitive."

"How sensitive?" He scraped one with his thumbnail. She jerked against him, her grip on his cock tightening to near pain. The move left her listing slightly to one side. He repeated the move on the other nipple, purely in the interest of straightening her up.

"Very, very sensitive," she gasped as she lurched against him.

He noticed she didn't pull away.

"Good." He bent down until his lips rested near her ear. "And how about your pussy? Is that sensitive too?"

She pressed her head against his chest. Her answer was just a breath of sound.

"Yes."

"I came in you twice today. Buried my cock deep in your sweet pussy and pumped you full of my seed."

"I could feel it."

"When?"

"All day."

"Did you stay wet?"

"Yes."

"Did you like it?"

This time, there was a pause. "Yes and no."

He squeezed her nipples, keeping the pressure steady, knowing she liked it, from the way she threw her head back and pumped his cock. "Explain."

"I liked the way I felt, knowing what we'd done, but every time it leaked out…"

He pinched sharply. "It?"

She squirmed and gasped, "Your seed. Every time your seed leaked out, I would ache."

"Where?"

She hesitated and he pinched again. "My clit. My clit would ache."

"You wanted me to fuck you again."

"Yes."

He began the milking motion she liked, drawing her nipple up and out before sliding back to start anew.

"You wanted my cock coming hard and high in your pussy, and you couldn't have what you wanted because we were in public."

She ground her forehead against his chest while her hands frantically jacked off his cock. "Yes."

He released her nipples, ignoring her moue of protest. "I'll have to check this out."

He gathered her skirt up around her waist. Her pantaloons were in the way, so he simply grabbed and tore. The cotton ripped in two. He angled his hand so his fingers could graze the top of her pussy.

"No lie, your little clit is all hard and hungry. Wet."

He traced the throbbing head with his finger, gathering the moisture there. He brought his hand up in front of her face. "Is this my come that's got you all excited?"

She looked at him helplessly. "I don't know."

"Open your mouth."

She did, taking his finger inside, licking it clean.

"Well?"

"Yes. That's your come."

"Do you want more?"

"Yes."

"Where?"

"In my pussy. Please."

"How much?"

"Until I can't take anymore."

He smiled. "Good answer." He moved his hand to the small of her back. "Tilt back and put your legs around my waist."

Shock had her gaze flying to his. "On horseback?"

"Oh, yeah"

She teetered as she got her legs around his hips. He caught a hand under her left hip and held her steady.

"You're going to have to get used to that. "

"What?"

"No control." He sank his fingers into the soft flesh of her buttock.

"Why?" She didn't look upset by the possibility. Just curious.

"Because for the next hour, you're not going to have any." He lifted her hips, and aligned his cock with the opening to her pussy. He let her drop, catching her hands in his to prevent her mitigating his possession. Her flesh grabbed and pulled at his cock as he forged a path deep into her hot pussy.

She groaned and threw her head back. Her torso jerked. Her teeth sank into her lip. Her pussy accepted another inch. He pulled her hands behind her back, anchoring them with one of his as he kneed Shameless into a trot.

Shameless had a canter as smooth as butter, but his trot could jar the teeth from his rider. A fact Asa intended to take full advantage of.

The first lurch had Elizabeth landing against his chest. Her eyes flew wide on the second as she bounced on his cock, and he slammed home. Her small scream was a mixture of high pleasure and uncertainty.

"That's right," he groaned as her pussy grabbed at his cock, the muscles clenching and releasing as they struggled to adjust. Another jarring step and she bounced up, the dragging pull of her tissues along his sensitive length as she was wrenched off the thick stalk of his cock had a firestorm of sensation burning through his groin. When she sheathed him again, coming down hard on his thighs, it was only a minor relief. He needed more. On Shameless' next step, he lifted her with the motion of the horse, and then released her. She came

262

down hard, his cock driving up into her wet flesh in a ruthless pursuit of pleasure. His groan covered her gasp as her pussy slammed against his thighs.

Her gaze flew to his as he arched his hips up to press higher, deeper. Understanding showed in her eyes as the base of his cock spread her impossibly wide. "You'll ride my cock as I ride Shameless. We're not going to stop until I've come twice. Maybe more. And you're going to take every inch I give you, no matter how hard, no matter how deep."

"God, yes!" she sighed, tightening her thighs around his hips.

He tightened his knees on Shameless, picking up his pace. At the same time, he tightened his spine, fighting Shameless' movement rather than flowing with it. Elizabeth bounced like a rag doll in his lap, her pleasured moans a continuous accompaniment to the wet slap of their bodies slamming together. She was tight, her grip on his cock merciless, the rhythm set by Shameless, erratic and furious, and the resulting friction created a mindless need for completion. He came within minutes, wedged to the hilt in her grasping channel.

He pulled Shameless to a stop and pumped her full. His fingers clenched on her buttocks, pulling her harder against him, his hips jerking under her as spurt after spurt of his seed boiled out of his balls to fill her hungry cunt. Her head fell against his chest. With each splash of come in her pussy, she moaned, her inner muscles clenched, and she twisted against his restraining grip. Come spilled out from between her thighs, seeping through his denims. Her hips rocked on his. Her pleas for release bled into what had been mindless gasps. She struggled to get her hands free, but he shook his head.

"Oh no." He kneed Shameless back into a walk. "You get off like this or you don't get off at all."

"Please Asa. I need…"

He knew what she needed. She wanted his teeth on her breasts, her clit, because she thought that was the only way she could find pleasure. By the end of this ride, she'd find out differently.

"All you need is my cock in your pussy."

He kicked Shameless. The horse surged forward, throwing Elizabeth forward and back. Caught off guard, she didn't have time to tighten her thighs. Her pubic bone slammed against his as she took so much of him, he thought she'd swallowed his balls. Her scream was one of relief and then frustration as Shameless set into his bone jarring, erratic trot.

He didn't plan to offer her relief. He was still hard, and this was a long time fantasy with him. He stiffened his body again and enjoyed the hot glide of her pussy up and down his cock for the next two miles. Elizabeth's face was red and sweating. Her eyes wild as she fought his hold. He knew she loved the bite of pain with her pleasure, that it set her off. He knew the pounding her pussy was taking had her on the edge, but she needed something more to get off. He could feel another orgasm building. She held him too tightly for him to last forever. He decided to take pity on her.

He slid his free hand under her hips. Her juices spilled over his hand, moistening it. As she bounced up, he aligned his thumb with her anus and pressed. Her eyes flew wide as the muscles began to give. If she could, he knew she would have fought the strangeness of the invasion, but he didn't give her the opportunity. As her body came down, as his cock speared through her hungry pussy, he pushed hard. His thumb popped through the tight ring into the silken depths of her ass.

"Oh! Oh!" she gasped, her eyes flew wide with distress, shock. Her thighs clenched on his waist. Her hips twisted. He pulled her down, not letting her dislodge him from that sweet, dark channel. He kept his thumb buried as she bounced up again, letting her get used to the feel, for her muscles to adjust to his width.

He could feel his cock driving into her vagina as she rode Shameless' rhythm. He imagined he could see his thumb possessing her ass. He leaned back, silently ordering Shameless to stop. Willoughby pulled up alongside, with a snort and a shake of his head.

"Okay?" Asa asked as Elizabeth came to a shuddering rest against his chest.

Her nod was frantic. Her fingers dug so deeply into his side, he could feel her nails bite into his skin through his shirt. She squirmed on his cock and finger. He stroked the smooth length of his cock through the tightly stretched membrane separating her ass from her vagina. Her moan echoed his. God, she was perfect.

"I'm going to have Shameless trot again, and I want you to keep your ass loose and ready," he whispered darkly in her ear, his voice reduced to a hoarse growl with the effort it took to speak through the lust tearing at his control, "because every time you come down, I'm going to be stuffing your ass as full as I can."

He paused to nibble on the side of her neck. He pulled his thumb almost free, pressing against his shaft through the membrane as he did, pushing it back in, feeling her pussy writhe and his cock throb as his calluses dragged against her tender inner flesh. "Do you understand?" She tilted her head to the side, facilitating his caress. "Yes. Oh yes."

"Good." With a click of his tongue, he urged Shameless forward.

He came twice more before finally drawing Shameless to a stop. He'd lost count how many times Elizabeth had come. Once she'd started, she hadn't seemed able to stop. The pulses of her last orgasm were still shuddering through her body, and her anus was clenching on his thumb as he tried to pull free.

Her protest was immediate. "Not yet. Please. Not yet."

"You want a little longer?" he asked against the top of her head.

"Please."

He slid his thumb almost all the way out, and then slowly pushed back. Her pussy clenched around his softening cock, massaging it gently as he fucked her ass with his thumb.

"Like that?"

She shuddered and pushed down. "Yes. Perfect."

He made a mental note of her enjoyment as he fucked her gently, bringing her down slowly. Her climax, when it came, was easy and sweet. When it was over, he slid his thumb from her ass and eased her off his softening cock.

She sagged against him breathlessly. Boneless and replete. She didn't even protest when he unbuttoned his duster to lift and seat her crosswise over his lap. As he buttoned her back in, he felt her hands at his fly, returning the favor. Her task was complicated by material that was damp from their combined releases.

When she finished his pants, she worked on the front of her shirt, relying on his strength to keep her in the saddle, she asked, "Do you think Cougar will be happy with that Emily Carmichael?"

He shrugged. "I don't know either of them, so I couldn't say."

She resettled her cheek in the wake of his movement. "I hope so."

"You used to be sweet on this Cougar fella?"

"He's a very decent man."

When he thought of a decent man, Asa pictured someone harmless enough not to have options. Cougar McKinnely had the look of his namesake. Savage. Unpredictable. Dangerous. "That doesn't answer my question."

"When I was sixteen, I thought he was my hero."

"Sixteen, huh? How old was he?"

"Nineteen."

He refused to acknowledge the slight clutch in his stomach as jealousy. "What happened to change your mind?"

"I grew up and realized life doesn't allow heroes."

"He didn't live up to your expectations?" Not surprising for a nineteen-year-old faced with the worship of a sixteen-year-old.

"He almost died for trying." She seemed willing to let the conversation end there.

"Whoa, darlin'!" He tipped her chin away from the haven of his chest. Her expression was stubborn. Her lips pursed mutinously. "You can't just drop things there."

"Why not?"

"Because it sounds like I owe McKinnely."

"It happened long before I met you."

"You're still my wife."

She sighed. "I don't want to talk about it."

He could be as stubborn as she. "I do."

She folded her arms across her chest and pressed her lips so tightly together, they all but disappeared.

Shameless tripped in a hole, jerking them a bit. As rigidly as Elizabeth was sitting, she almost popped off. Lucky for her, he had quick reflexes. "Got ya."

"I never had any doubt." She probably hadn't as she hadn't made a move to save herself.

That bit of trust went a long way to soothing his irritation. "You really going to leave me hanging like that?"

"There's no need to go into something that happened long ago."

Apparently she thought so, but there was more than one way to skin a cat. "I guess if you're so set against finishing the story, I'll be dropping the subject."

Her "thank you" was carefully controlled, telling him she had a lot of emotions packed into it. Probably thought her secret was safe. He felt like smiling but didn't. The woman really had to spend more time studying his nature rather than assuming she knew him, 'cause sure enough, he wasn't letting this go. He was just going to change his angle of attack. McKinnely probably wouldn't be as tightlipped. He'd just ask him.

They rode in silence for awhile. Though he had his wife in his arms, Asa felt her withdrawal like a windstorm from the north. He'd always dreamed marriage would be an end to being alone, but he was discovering it wasn't a cure for loneliness. Just the opposite. It could, he decided on a sigh, serve to point out how far a desperate man could grasp.

Elizabeth broke the silence. "Millicent said Emily wanted no part of Cougar."

Apparently, they were back to the original subject. That strange knot took root in his stomach again. "Uh-huh."

He felt her cheek working against his chest. He wondered if she were biting her lip. Through the gloom, he could see the ranch house.

"She said it was obvious because Emily pulled away every time he touched her."

"Uh-huh." He put as much boredom as he could into the phrase. He didn't want to hear how wonderful McKinnely was.

"I don't think that's true."

She didn't? Despite his urge to avoid talking about good-looking-once-a-hero McKinnely, he had to hear this one. "You don't?"

"No."

"You don't think a woman scooting a man's touch is a sign she's not too sweet on him?"

"No."

"Why?"

Her shoulder pushed into his stomach as she took a deep breath. Had she been facing him, she would have blown him over when she let it out. "Because I used to pull away from you."

It took him a minute to recover from the shock of dragging this particular subject into the open. He finally found his voice. "Not anymore."

"It's a fact I'm not proud of."

"It doesn't bother me."

"Yes. It does."

"You ever hear a wife shouldn't disagree with her husband?"

"Yes."

"So why are you disagreeing with me?"

"Because I think you like it."

"I'd have to be a perverse S.O.B to like arguing."

Shameless picked up his pace. Asa guessed he decided they were close enough to home to push the rules. Apparently, Elizabeth did, too, because she said, "But you do."

He smiled. She was hanging in there despite the nervousness betrayed by her voice. "Why is that do you think?"

"I haven't a clue."

"But you've decided to humor me?"

"Not exactly."

Her spine was stiffening up. As a result, she wasn't moving with the horse, but more like bouncing on it. He waited. Three bounces later, he was rewarded.

"I've decided to use it," she admitted.

"Anything in that fancy school say that's a bit underhanded?"

"Yes."

"And you're not feeling guilty?"

"No. I'm being honest." She took a breath, and he could tell she'd been thinking on this for awhile. "If I tell you, then it's not trickery."

"Some might call that hair-splitting," he pointed out, not really minding.

"But not you?"

She sounded so hopeful, he didn't have the heart to tease her. "No. I guess I can live with fair warning as long as you answer me one question."

"What's the question?"

"Why?"

"I'm not happy with our marriage."

If Shameless hadn't pulled up short in front of the hitching post, he probably would have jerked him to a halt. She'd blindsided him. He hadn't seen it coming anymore than he'd anticipated the hurt. He kept his voice calm. "You're not happy with our marriage, so you're going to argue with me to improve it?"

He must not have been successful in covering his irritation because the hands that had been folded in her lap were stroking his forearm as if to soothe him. "Sort of."

He tipped up her chin, but beyond a blush to her cheeks, her expression gave nothing away. He shook his head. "You're going to have to explain that one, 'cause, sure enough, you lost me in the twists and turns."

Her chin butted his finger, but he didn't heed the silent demand. Given no other option, she evaded his searching gaze by lowering her lids. "I can't."

He pondered a minute. The whole conversation had started out with the way Emily evaded Cougar's touch, and how Elizabeth didn't feel that was a sign that a woman didn't like the touch of a man. Shameless snorted and stomped his foot. Willoughby echoed the impatient sound. Asa ignored both. "Are you saying you don't dislike my touch?"

He might not have been successful in hiding his astonishment. Her whole body winced at his shout. "Lower your voice!"

"Well," he asked, keeping his voice down, "are you?"

"It's hard to say."

"I think we'd better go into the house and discuss this."

"No!"

"You want to sit out here in the cold when there's a perfectly warm house a few feet away?"

"Please. Just let me say this before I lose my—"

He leaned back in the saddle. "Never let it be said I'd interrupt a lady."

Her "You just did" was a muttered aside. For once, he didn't feel like smiling when the real Elizabeth snuck past her prim disguise.

"I'm not used to being touched. My father wasn't very…demonstrative that way." She cut him a quick glance from under her lashes. "You touch me a lot."

He shrugged. "You feel good."

"I'm not saying it's bad. I'm just not comfortable with it."

"You seemed damned comfortable a few minutes ago."

"That's not what I'm talking about." She took an audible breath. "The truth is, I'm afraid of how much I like it when you touch me!" she confessed in a breathless rush.

The blurted-out truth hung between them. The knot in his stomach that had been there since she'd mentioned McKinnely and her dissatisfaction with their marriage started to loosen. "Why?"

"You'll stop and I'll be used to it."

And she didn't want to he hurt. That he understood. "Why would I stop?"

"When I disappoint you, you'll stop."

"You know, I'm getting darned tired of everyone telling me what I'm going to do and not do."

"I wouldn't presume!"

"Like hell!" He reached for the buttons of the coat holding them together. Who did she think she was kidding? "First, you decided I'd sell my soul for a ranch. Then you decided I needed to be tricked into finishing a marriage. Then you decided I was a cheating sort." His anger built as each button of the coat popped open. "Next, you assumed I had no control over my needs and you had to bargain against cheating, and now, you've come up with the fact that I'm tricking you every time I act less than a monster?" He swung out of the saddle. "Well, I'm tired of being insulted."

"I didn't mean—"

He placed her on the ground and pointed her to the house. "You never do, but every time you get thinking, I get insulted, and I'm damned tired of it."

She ignored his push and turned around. "Where are you going?"

"I'm going to settle Shameless and Willoughby for the night."

She bit her lip. Her expression was barely discernible through the light. "Are you coming up to the house?"

"Where else would I go?" He pulled the horses around. "We have a deal remember?"

"Would you let me explain?"

"I don't think my sensibilities can take another of your explanations."

He turned and headed for the barn, seething inside. He'd done nothing but treat the woman with respect, and she persisted in seeing him as vermin. It wasn't going to change, and he'd best get it through his thick skull, because, dammit, it was beginning to hurt. He could feel her eyes watching him as he entered the barn. Without turning around, he closed the door.

Elizabeth stared at the closed door until a voice from the shadowed end of the porch spun her around.

"He's right, girl." There was the creak of the swing, and then two disjointed steps before Old Sam stepped into the light. "You've been trying to slip that man into a crevice since he got here."

"I don't understand him," she burst out.

"You probably would if you'd just see he isn't your Pa."

"I don't think he is."

"If that's the case, why are you expecting him to change into something else?"

"I'm not."

Old Sam spat over the side rail. "And I was born yesterday. Ever since your Dad changed after your Mama died, you've had this fear of men. Like everything good inside one is just fool's gold."

"That's not true!"

"If it's not, then you'd better start thinking before you open your mouth." He came up bedside her, and, for the first time in sixteen years, there wasn't any sympathy in his faded blue eyes. "'Cause that's the picture you're painting."

"I'm not…" But she couldn't finish the denial.

Old Sam laid his hand on her shoulder and squeezed gently. "It's time to grow up, Elizabeth."

"I'm scared," she confessed on a whisper.

He snorted impatience as his hand dropped away. "Who isn't?"

"What if I tell him and he doesn't care?"

"What if ya don't and he does?"

She had no response for that.

"You can make a choice by not opening your mouth as easily as you can by speaking your mind, girl."

"I know."

"Then prove it." He pointed to the barn. "Talk to that man."

"I will."

She mustn't have been too convincing, because Old Sam stared for a long silent moment, his expression as murky as the twilight gloom. His mouth worked. She couldn't tell if he was chewing or working up to a lecture, but then he sighed, slapped his thigh and said, "If it'll help, I'll tell ya I didn't ever think your Pa had it in him to shoot your Ma. He loved her too much for that."

She wished she could be so sure. "Thank you."

He shuffled his feet before settling his weight into his boots and meeting her gaze square on. "I always thought that, if the two of them hadn't been so dead miserly on protecting their hearts, they might have made a happy marriage."

That was something she'd never heard before. "I don't understand."

"Your Pa ever talk to you after your Mama died?"

"About her?"

"About anything beyond ranching?"

"No."

"Well, he wasn't any more chatty before, and assuming your mother knew how he felt, didn't do much to get 'em across misunderstandings."

Elizabeth stared at Old Sam as the truth sunk in. She remembered her mother with her smiles and laughter. She remembered her father with his stern face and total control. "Oh God!"

"You got a choice to make, girl."

"I don't want to be my father," she whispered.

Old Sam slapped his thigh and started to walk away. Three steps into his departure, he stopped and turned around. "Then I guess you'd best be making a new choice."

* * * * *

From the way the door slammed, Elizabeth was pretty sure that Asa hadn't calmed down. She sat in her bedroom and fiddled with the lace-edged collar on her nightdress. She hadn't meant to hurt his feelings. She'd been trying to tell him she'd wanted him to do more than just lie beside her in bed, but how was she going to approach the subject now? The man was convinced everything she did was a scheme to trick him.

Which was really unfair. He was the one always hiding behind words and silence, making her work to understand him. Teasing her when she did, laughing when she didn't.

His booted footsteps on the stairs cut off her budding anger. With each creak, her breath grew shorter until she stopped breathing entirely when the steps paused outside their door. Air rushed into her lungs on a furious gasp when he moved down the hall without even calling a good night. She heard the door on her father's bedroom open and close. There was the sound of water being poured in the wash basin, a fire being built, the creak of bedsprings, and then nothing. The quiet progressed for ten minutes before she admitted he wasn't coming to bed in their room. Which meant any moves were up to her.

She pulled the covers over her bent legs, rested her chin on the plateau of her knees and slowly let the anger build. How dare he cut her off, accuse her of unladylike behavior, and then proceed to break his word by sleeping in another room. So maybe she wasn't the best at getting out what she wanted to say, at least she was trying. The least he could do was shut up and listen.

She threw the goosedown comforter off. She reached for her robe and then left it hanging. The distance to the door had never been spanned so quickly. She made it to the guest bedroom before she understood the reality of her plan. When his door hit the wall under the force of her shove and she was face-to-face with his bare-chested specter in the big four-poster, she started thinking. Unfortunately, it was too late for prudence. Taking her courage in hand, she proceeded.

"I'll allow that I've been a bit hasty in some of my assumptions." She kept her gaze on his forehead because the sight of all that lightly-furred muscle was unsettling. "But you have no right to berate me for it when you're part of the cause."

His arms folded across his chest. "You saying all this is my fault?"

A log crackled in the fireplace. She took a breath to keep her focus and picked up the challenge he'd thrown down. "Yes."

"You've got nerve, darlin'. I'll give you that."

"Yes, I do, and I'm probably using the last of it right now." His right eyebrow shot up, but he didn't offer any further sarcasm, so she plunged on. "I wasn't accusing you of tricking me. I was trying to explain that...that..." God, this was so humiliating to admit. She finally managed in a cold rush of honesty. "I'm not used to anyone being nice to me. I don't know how to react."

"Surely that school taught you the value of a 'thank you'."

She shifted her gaze to the window. Her own reflection stared back at her, a ghostly shadow of white whose only distinguishing feature was the shadowed impression of her eyes. At this moment, she felt as substantial as that reflection. She bit her lip and pressed on. She'd say her piece and put this behind her. However it played out, she'd build her marriage on the remnants. "It's not easy to forget the way I was raised."

He looked impossibly big and stubborn propped up in the bed. He didn't sound the least patient or understanding when he said, "No one's asking you to."

But he was. With every act of kindness, he was. She couldn't put that into words, though. His gaze, when he looked at her, had a measure of respect. It wouldn't, though, if she told him everything. It wouldn't, but she couldn't live this lie anymore. She licked her dry lips and continued, "My father was very strict."

"I gathered that."

She licked her lips again, but she didn't have enough spit left to moisten them. "He had very rigid rules." Nausea churned with the memory.

"Seems like everyone around here had rules from what I can see. Leastwise, they felt like they had a right to boss you around."

"Yes, well, my father was the strictest."

"Most fathers are."

An involuntary shiver shook her. "Mine more than most. I failed him quite regularly." The cold from the floor seeped into her feet. She shivered again. She closed her eyes against the impatience in Asa's gaze. "I know it sounds like I'm making excuses. I'm not." She put the lamp on the table. He was never going to look at her with respect again. "He wanted a son."

"A lot of men do. They make do with daughters."

"When I turned out to be his only child, my father decided to teach me what was necessary to keep the ranch. I wasn't very good at it."

His "of course not" struck her in the heart. She'd been hoping he'd see her as more than she was. Sheer force of will kept her head up. She unbuttoned the top two buttons of her night rail. "I failed him repeatedly. I tried, but I just couldn't be as good as he needed." She swallowed, wishing she dared to look at him. Another two buttons came undone. "I don't want to spend the rest of my life failing you."

"Darlin', I'm sure you weren't a disappointment to your Pa. Little girls are special to their fathers."

Tears stung her eyes. She turned around and let the night rail drop to her waist.

His curses were harsh. Angry. She kept her head up and her back straight. She knew what he was seeing. The three white scars crossing her back. Marks of failure. Marks no father would put on a child he was proud of. Marks she'd earned with her impulsive nature. The swearing behind her stopped. The silence was oppressive. The bed ropes creaked. A log popped and hissed in the fire. She couldn't stand the tension anymore.

"I didn't do my father proud." She took a breath, counted to three and then explained, "I don't want to fail you, too. I just don't know what you want, how I'm supposed to act. You seem happy when I'm arguing, but I don't think I can argue with you all the time…"

The feel of cotton rising up her back silenced her words. She hadn't heard him move, but he was behind her. His hands on her shoulders turned her around.

"Why?"

One grated word and she had to bare all, exposing her weakness, her foolishness, maybe forever ruining his opinion of her. Her gaze was level with the center of his chest. She held onto her dignity by counting the hairs as she explained, "I told you I knew Cougar."

"Yeah."

Was that suspicion she heard in his voice? "I got kicked by a calf in the face during branding. It was hard to eat. Cougar brought me soup."

His silence was deafening. She finished the bottom row of hair. Twenty-five.

"He was very nice. Kind." She kept her gaze on his chest, almost desperately counting. Her fingers clenched to fists. At fifty, she had to resume speech. Oh God. "I let him kiss me." She held her breath and waited for the outrage, the disbelief.

"And?"

Seventy-five. Seventy-six. Seventy-seven.

"My Father saw. He was furious."

"Over a kiss?"

Oh, yes. Over a kiss. She remembered her father's face. His rage. Her terror when he'd turned into someone else. Turned on her.

"He called Cougar a dirty Indian. Called me a fool for throwing myself away on him."

No response. Not by a twitch of a muscle did Asa give his thoughts away.

Eighty. Eighty-one. Eighty-two.

"He said I couldn't be trusted."

Finally, he moved. His hands slid down her shoulders. In an agony of hope, she waited for him to catch her hands in his. To offer her one sign of comfort. Of trust. While their fingers brushed, he didn't take her hand, didn't tell her it didn't matter, and he didn't say the words she'd so pathetically hoped for. She had no option but to confess the last. "He sent me away."

God! How could that still hurt?

"Damn!"

Asa's harshly spat word shattered her concentration. She was either at one-hundred-and-one or one-hundred-and-ten, but what did it matter? The anger in that one word told her what he was thinking. If it had been just a kiss, why would her father have sent her away? She knew because, for every day of the four years she'd spent at Miss Penelope's, she'd been reminded of what crime she'd been making up for. It didn't matter how many times she'd protested her innocence. Or to whom. The doubt was always there. There was no reason to expect Asa to react any differently.

She wanted to whither into a defeated ball at the realization. Instead, she cleared her throat and locked her gaze on the bunched muscles in his cheek. She needed to finish this. She needed to tell him the truth. Whether he believed her or not, she had to try.

"I swear it was only a kiss, and I never, ever let anyone kiss me again."

The declaration hung for a breathless moment in the silence.

Asa was the one to bring an end to the standoff between them. But he didn't use the words she hungered for. Instead, with a move too slow to be startling, he reached for her. So desperately attuned to his response, she swore she could feel the slight breeze ruffling her gown as he did. Her night rail rustled and shifted against her body as he did up the buttons at her waist. His knuckles brushed her breast impersonally as he fastened the buttons over her chest. Slow and deliberate, there was no way she could interpret his gesture as anything but disinterest. The realization was like a knife wound to her soul.

"Now you don't even want me anymore." It was a simple statement of the inevitable.

He stopped, the backs of his hands resting on her collarbones. "Why do you say that?"

It was a logical question. She made her response just as rational. "If any other woman was standing here half-naked, you wouldn't be putting her back into her clothes."

No. Asa decided. He'd be riding out to kill the son of a bitch who'd put the marks on her back, but he couldn't put her father in the ground twice. "I'm sorry. Seeing that my wife has been savagely beaten has a way of taking the starch out of me." The skin beneath his hands was icy and riddled with goosebumps. "You're cold."

"I didn't wear my robe."

"You'd best come to bed, then, so we can warm you up."

He scooped her into his arms. She was still stiff as a board, but she wasn't fighting. He looked at the four-poster. "Was this your father's room?"

"Yes."

He spun on his heel and headed out the door. Once in the hall, he kicked open the door to her room. He placed her on the bed. While she stared at him with those big green eyes, he pulled the comforter over her shoulders and struggled with his anger. Lord, he'd suspected her father had been mean, but he'd never suspected this. He scooted her over with a push of his hip.

"You're naked!" she exclaimed as he slid under the covers beside her.

"Uh-huh." He guessed that would be a bit of a shock since he'd always been careful to wear his long johns when they'd been 'courting'. "I wasn't planning on sleeping with you tonight, so I wasn't worried about sparing your sensibilities."

"I didn't know how to tell you I wanted you to touch me, but that I didn't know if I could handle it."

"All this fighting because you wanted me to touch you?"

"I thought it would make you happy," she admitted.

"And that's why you decided to do it?" He slid his arm under her neck, preventing her from falling off the bed. With a curl of his forearm, he had her turned into his side.

"No."

He waited, adjusting the covers over her shoulder. He flexed his toes to get some warmth back in them. If the floors were any indication, winter was coming early this year.

"I thought things could be normal between us," she said softly.

"Can't get more normal than two folks sleeping together."

"I want babies."

He smiled. "Then again, I guess you can."

"You don't have to be nice to me, you know." The amount of pride packed into that statement would have done a cavalry unit proud.

"I like being nice to you." He shifted her elbow out of his rib cage. "I told you when you proposed I had a liking for touching ladies tenderly."

"I thought you were talking about..." She waved her hand descriptively.

"You thought I was talking about between the sheets," he clarified. "Gotta admit, I have a penchant for that, too." He felt her blush heating her chest on its way to her face.

His grin widened as he went on, "Thing is, I flat out like having a wife to spoil. I'm enjoying being married."

She didn't have anything to say to that. He took the opportunity to get to the meat of the matter. He tipped up her chin so she'd know he wasn't lying. "I know what it's like to be beaten, Elizabeth. Don't you ever think I don't know how ashamed you feel. A shame that goes bone deep when it's someone you love doing the beating. My ma used to whip me daily to drive the devil out."

Her eyes widened in surprise.

"You ever get the urge to look, you'll find marks on me, too. Probably not as much as you're thinking as I grew big fast and could put an end to it, but it's not something I'm proud of or likely to forget."

"I didn't realize..."

"No reason you should. It happened a long time ago."

A hairpin jabbed his thumb as he slid his hand over her hair. He pulled it out, then went in search of more. "Thing is, when I was little, I could never figure out how I had the devil in me when she was the one sinning daily. I used to check the mirror for some sign that everyone else could see and I couldn't." By the time he had the sixth pin free, her hair began to uncoil. With a few passes of his fingers, he aided its surge for freedom. He shrugged and continued. "I could never find it, though."

"What?"

"The mark that made them call me devil's spawn."

"You were just a little boy!"

He carefully slid his arm from under her and propped himself on his elbow so he could see her face. "And you were just a little girl who couldn't help it anymore than I could. The only difference between us is I stopped searching for the reason."

"It's not right—"

He cut her off by sliding his hand down her hips and pulling her legs against his. "Right or wrong has nothing to do with it. It's just the way it happened."

"I know—"

He put his fingers over her lips. He didn't want to rehash the past. Not when he had her in bed with him and in an accommodating mood, her soul bare, her defenses down. "I think the best thing for us to do is forget what we 'know' about the other and start fresh."

She yawned against his chest. "Maybe after I've had a nap?"

He stroked her hair, smoothing it back from her brow. "Tired?"

She snuggled into his neck. "Yes."

He suppressed a yawn of his own. He slid his hand over her waist and up the curve of her hip. She seemed to blend into his touch. As natural as breathing, his palm curved over the globe of her ass. She shivered, and it wasn't from cold.

He dipped his fingers into the crease and lightly traced her anus. "Did you like it when I took you here?"

A slight tension stiffened her muscles. "It felt strange at first."

"And then?"

She didn't answer.

He kissed her temple. "Did you like it later?"

"Yes."

He hugged her and moved his hand back to her ass cheek. "I'm glad."

The tension left her muscles. He wondered if she'd thought he would think her enjoyment was improper. He yawned again. "I hope you don't think less of me, Mrs. MacIntyre, but I'm about played out."

She stroked his chest comfortingly. "Me, too."

He reached down and pulled the covers over their bodies. "Then cuddle up here, darlin', and we'll get some sleep."

She was out before he finished talking. With one last stoke of her hair, he closed his eyes and joined her.

Chapter Sixteen

ဢ

Weary and pleasantly worn out after four days of lovemaking, Asa saddled up Shameless. As much as he'd like to spend the next year or so in bed with his wife, he had a ranch to save. The Rocking C meant everything to Elizabeth. If he wanted to hold onto her, he had to hold onto it. It was simple, but it had been his experience that most things usually were. Sift through all the sediment and there would usually be some shining truths. He tightened the girth and dropped the stirrup into position. Of all the things he'd gained in his life, Elizabeth was the one thing he didn't plan on giving up.

"You ready, Shameless?" he asked the patient horse. Dust flew as he patted the sorrel's neck. Not by the twitch of an ear did the horse indicate agreement. "I know what you mean. It's a lazy day, but we've got work to do."

Catching the bridle, he led the horse out the barn door. Shameless protested with a hard blow of his lips.

"You'd best be finding your pepper, old son, 'cause we got to head over to the East Range. Clint claimed there was Rocking C stock running loose there."

He scratched the horse behind his ears. "That means you get to run," he coaxed. As if he understood, Shameless perked up his step. Asa grinned. "Thought that might help you shake off the blankets."

He cast a wary eye to the sky. "Sure enough looks like bad weather moving in." He checked the knots securing his poncho to the back of the saddle. "Damn, I hate getting wet."

"The mighty Asa MacIntyre has a weakness?"

He turned and found Elizabeth holding a sack containing his lunch. In her red gingham dress, she looked as fresh as a spring day and just as inviting.

"Every now and then, one crops up." Like you, he thought.

Her smile was shy. Her hair was back in its prissy bun. Remembering the night before, he hooked his arm around her neck and pulled her close for a kiss. He swallowed her gasp and seduced her mouth like he wanted to do to her body. When she stepped back, red-cheeked, her hair came tumbling down around her shoulders.

She grabbed for the mass, but it slid through her grasp, curling around her shoulders and falling into her face like living silk. "How did you—?"

"Now you look like my Elizabeth."

She shook her head at him while holding out her hand for her hairpins. "Not even for you, husband, will I go around looking like a harlot."

"I could order you to," he pointed out as he combined the pins into one hand.

She swapped his lunch for the pins, then set to work immediately on her hair. "You won't," she mumbled around the pins sticking out of her mouth like quills on a porcupine. She twisted the waist-length strands into a rope and, with a couple of flicks, reestablished the bun on top of her head. Four jabs and her mouth was free of hairpins.

She seemed pretty confident. A more optimistic man might call her cocky. He adopted his most impressive don't-tell-me-what-to-do expression. "I might."

Instead of backing up, she stepped forward until her breasts brushed his chest. "You won't."

"I won't?"

She smiled. "Nope."

"Your grammar's slipping," he informed her.

"So's your ability to give orders, but I'm not lecturing you on it."

"You're probably just waiting on a better moment." He shifted his grip on his lunch. "So," he asked, raising his arms slightly so she could slip hers around his waist. "Why am I not going to order you to wear your hair down?"

His hands naturally skimmed her body to land at the base of her spine. She smiled and slid her hands up his chest. "Because I don't want anyone but you to see it down."

Neither did he, he realized. It was one of the pleasures he hadn't considered when he took a wife, but all their private moments were just between them. No one had ever come before him. No one would come after him an hour or week down the road. What they did was theirs alone. He liked that. "You're right. I'm not going to be ordering you."

Her smile was full of sass without a bit of propriety. He liked that, too.

He meant to kiss her quickly, but the instant his lips met hers, all thoughts of goodbye sighed away on the breeze. She moaned. He stepped closer. She squeezed nearer. Like wildfire set loose in a windstorm, the passion flared between them, making a mockery of his goodbye intentions. This was a welcome-to-my-bed kiss. And he was participating fully, in the yard, in full view of the hands. Damn! He had to get himself under control, but first, just one more kiss. Just one more time to savor the sweetness of his wife. His wife. His.

He pulled back before he lay her down in the dirt. "Lord, woman! You're as potent as Kentucky sippin' whiskey!"

If anyone was drunk from that kiss, Elizabeth decided, it was her. She opened her eyes slowly. Leather creaked as Asa swung up into the saddle. Shameless half-bucked, half-hopped in his impatience to be off. Asa pulled him under control. His "You take care of yourself" was gruff.

He sat on the horse, tall and proud. Behind him loomed the mountains. He seemed so much a part of them in that moment. So big. So wild. So aloof. "You, too." Tears welled, unexpectedly.

"You crying?"

"Of course not." She blinked the tears back. She wasn't the weepy sort. The man was only going to be gone for a couple of days, for goodness sake.

He pulled back in an exaggerated movement. "No need to nip my head off."

"I wasn't nipping anything."

His smile was as wide open as the shot she'd given him. He rubbed his shoulder. "No. A man tends to remember where you set your teeth."

Heat flamed her chest and neck, surging into her cheeks. She'd bitten him last night in that very spot. He'd been driving her crazy and she'd bitten him to get his attention.

"Yup. Pretty as a picture."

She would have shot him if she'd had a gun handy. Instead, she had to settle for grinding her teeth and enduring his smug, male grin.

"Don't be mad, Elizabeth." He reined in Shameless beside her. His fingers grazed her hot cheeks. She could have jerked away, but there was so much tenderness in his touch. So much emotion. She closed her eyes and leaned her cheek into his fingers.

"You please me, wife," he whispered hoarsely, right there in front of God and half the hired hands. "You please me to my bones."

"Be careful," she whispered.

"You bet."

One last stroke of his fingers and he was gone. She opened her eyes and watched him thunder away. For a moment, it looked as if man, horse and mountains were one. Foreboding snaked down her spine.

"Take care of him," she murmured to the Guardians.

The moment was broken when Clint and Luke galloped after Asa. She shook her head and chided herself for her foolishness. Asa would be fine. He was too big, too mean, and too good for anything to happen to him.

* * * * *

"Easy now." Elizabeth coaxed the young stallion back into the restrictions of the lunge line. "That's it, Prince," she murmured as he reared and pawed the air, but didn't bolt. "This is just another way to play."

He rolled his eyes at her and she couldn't help but laugh.

"Okay," she agreed, pulling a carrot out of her pocket. "Maybe it's not as much fun as frolicking with your friends, but you're going to like it."

He snorted, pawed the ground, and then pranced closer for the tidbit. "Good boy," she crooned as he took it from her hand. "With your brains, speed and agility, you're perfect."

She eyed him and felt a renewed surge of pride. Jet black with a flowing mane, he was the picture of elegance. Just for pretty, her father had mocked her when he'd seen this colt, the first of her breeding program that combined Arabian and thoroughbred with a touch of mustang.

She had to agree. The colt did give that impression until a body looked at his conformation. At sixteen and a half hands, Sir Prince was pure speed and agility. Too big a mount for her, but a perfect mount for a big man. She grimaced. Who was she kidding? She was breaking this horse for Asa. Shameless was a great horse, but the Rocking C wasn't a three-up outfit. A man needed a variety of mounts to get the work done. Sir Prince would be a perfect Christmas present. And he was coming along great with his training. Depending on how well he took to the saddle today, Asa might get his present early.

She picked up the blanket from the ground and held it out to Sir Prince. He sniffed it, but went immediately back to chomping his carrot. It was the perfect reaction, and why she'd decided it was time to step up his training. She settled the blanket on his back. His skin twitched, but nothing more than that. She patted his shoulder. "Good boy."

She swung the heavy saddle into her arms. The strain on her muscles felt good. So did being in the open air and working with her horses. Giving up this aspect of her life had been the hardest thing about becoming a lady. Mrs. Asa MacIntyre might not welcome smelling like a horse, mucking out a barn, or the sometimes bone-crunching results of breaking a horse, but Elizabeth Coyote, Coyote Bill's crazy daughter, did with a devotion that went beyond liking. She needed it as much as she needed to breathe. The only time she came close to the same satisfaction was in Asa's arms with the darkness cloaking them in an otherworldly peace.

She showed Prince the saddle. He sniffed it, then went carrot-hunting in her coat pocket.

"Not yet, big boy. First, you've got to show me how smart you are."

She tossed the saddle onto his back and held her breath. She would have preferred to ease it on, but, at her height, that wasn't possible. He sidestepped and snorted, his breath forming steamy clouds around his muzzle. He swung his head around to inspect the unfamiliar source of weight. He sniffed twice. Her familiar scent must have soothed him because he swung his head back and accepted the carrot she held out.

"Good boy." She took his halter and urged him forward a step.

Beyond a flicking of his ears, he didn't protest the weight on his back. She patted his neck again. "Let's see how you take to the cinch."

She was pushing it, she knew, but she didn't have much time. Asa would be back tomorrow and, if she wanted to keep this a secret, she had to make the most of the time she had.

She unhooked the cinch from the saddle horn, then reached under Prince's belly to pull it up the other side. Like he'd been doing it all his life, he stood still and munched his carrot while she tied the cinch. She pulled it tighter. Not by a sidestep or a snort did he exhibit any displeasure. Exhilaration shot through her.

"You are a bright one." She patted his neck. "Then, again, you probably know I'd never hurt you."

She pulled the stirrups down. Catching his halter, she led him around the corral twice. Beyond a few ear flicks at the stirrup's sway, he didn't seem to realize he bore a saddle on his back. She pulled him up to the hitching post. He was coming along nicely.

She checked the cinch. It was tight enough to hold the saddle and a rider. She patted his neck again. She'd never had a horse come so far so fast, but Sir Prince had been exceptional from the beginning. He was ready for the next step. She'd need a mounting post, she thought, eyeing the distance from the ground to the stirrup. Short of that, there wasn't anything between her and the next step of Prince's training, which was bearing the weight of a rider. She bit her lip and weighed her decision. She didn't want to ruin a good horse by pushing, then again, she didn't want to lose anymore time than necessary.

"You even think of getting on that animal and you won't sit down for a week."

There was no question who that drawl belonged to.

"Asa." She spun so fast, Sir Prince whickered in concern. She sighed. "You're back."

"And none too soon by the looks of it," Asa said.

He wasn't alone. Beside him rode Cougar McKinnely. Both men stared at her with grim expressions. If she had to weigh between the two, Cougar's held more compassion.

She patted Sir Prince on the shoulder. Wind blew hair out of her bun. She caught it before it could blind her. As she tucked the strand behind her ear, she weighed her options. She could apologize and placate, which would be sensible. She could play dumb, which would no doubt anger him. And from the whiteness of his cheeks and the way his lips were compressed, he didn't need much of a push to go over the edge. Prudence had always been her specialty.

"I hope you're happy," she accused. "You've ruined the surprise."

Both men looked startled and well they should. How were they to know she'd decided just yesterday that prudence was boring?

Asa found his voice first. "Can't see how coming home to find my wife trampled by a hot-headed stud is something I'd mind ruinin'."

"Sir Prince is not hot-headed." She looped the halter string around the hitching post. Training was clearly over for the day.

"Yeah, and the door I replaced last week in his stall was because his sweet nature got the better of him."

She scratched the stallion behind his ear. "Poor baby. Were you trying to get my attention?"

"He was trying to get something," Asa agreed.

She shot him a glare. "He was only trying to get out and stretch his legs. I haven't been down to work with him for awhile."

"Uh-huh."

Asa exchanged a meaningful glance with Cougar. It was one of those glances she'd seen the banker give the lawyer after her father's death. A purely male look that suggested the female in question was losing her mind. "I don't know why you're so annoyed."

"I passed annoyed about ten minutes back," Asa drawled.

"That's the truth, ma'am," Cougar obliged. "Thought the man was going to drop his heart along with his good sense when we came over that rise and saw you working that stud."

"There was no need," Elizabeth said. "I've been breaking horses for years." She shot a glare Cougar's way. "As you well know."

"And this is the first time you thought to mention it?" Asa cut in.

He wasn't backing her into that corner. "I explained to you a week ago that my father taught me everything about ranching."

"You said you didn't learn too well."

"I never said I had trouble working horses."

"No, you were real careful to leave that out." He shifted in the saddle. Leather creaked and the silence stretched. She wondered why he didn't get down.

"It's a fact your wife's not good with cows," Cougar offered, no doubt in an effort to be helpful. "Give Miss Coyote a cow and she can't tell one end from the other, but put a horse in front of her and she's pure magic."

"It's Mrs. MacIntyre," Elizabeth corrected, only to have her voice drowned out by Asa's simultaneous snarl.

Beyond a slight smile, Cougar didn't give any indication he'd heard either of them. "Fact is, Mrs. MacIntyre trained old Bucky here." He patted Buck's neck. "He tossed her a couple of times, but she didn't quit until she made a top cow pony out of him."

The accolade was nice, Elizabeth thought, but did the man have to go and remind Asa that she sometimes got hurt? Couldn't he see Asa's lips were getting tighter by the minute? "Thank you, Mr. McKinnely."

"No problem."

With a sweep of his hand, Asa included Cougar and Sir Prince in one gesture. "Do you think you could stop admiring my wife enough to take that brute back into the stable?"

"I can do it," Elizabeth said.

"I'd prefer McKinnely handle it." And that, apparently, he thought, was that.

Elizabeth had news for him. "For your information, Mr. MacIntyre, I like to train horses. I like training Sir Prince."

"Then you're going to have to unlike it."

She most certainly did not. Fury bubbled and frothed. "I don't think so." She kept her tone even as she placed her hand on the horse's neck. "I need this."

"You've got the house to take care of."

"You ever take care of a house, Asa?" She didn't wait for his reply. "It's boring, and if I have to clean one more thing, I'll go coyote-mad." That was the honest truth.

She untied Sir Prince's lead rope and swung around to head to the opposite side of the corral.

"Elizabeth—"

She heard the warning in his tone. She ignored it.

Three more steps and his voice went up a notch while his drawl lengthened, "Elizabeth, pull up right there, or I'll have to—"

She stopped dead, but didn't turn around. "Don't say it." She warned him in the most level voice she could manage. "I've had it up to here," she slashed her hand across her throat, "with people telling me what to do. Don't you dare order me to let go of this lead."

He'd heard that tone before, Asa realized. Right before Elizabeth had pole-axed that fancy gambler with the stool, she'd been just as precise. Just as unnaturally calm. Still, a man didn't take orders from his wife.

McKinnely chose that moment to sidestep his horse hard into Shameless who half-reared and pranced away. Pain lanced out from Asa's damaged ribs. Instead of the "Or what?" he'd intended, all that came out was a low groan.

He glared at McKinnely. "Stay out of it."

"I'd be more than happy to, but it wouldn't be neighborly of me to let those ribs drive you to ruffling your wife's feathers unnecessarily."

Asa watched Elizabeth proceed to the barn, stiff-spined, as if expecting him to swoop down on her. "Ruffle nothing. I'm going to tan her backside."

The look McKinnely shot him was wry. "And when you're done doing that?"

"Things will be back to normal."

This time, Cougar's look was pure pity. "Haven't known you long, and, sure, I'm still learning about you, but..." He shook his head sadly. "I'm pure disappointed you're turning out to be such a fool."

"Remind me when these ribs heal to meet you behind the barn."

Cougar pulled out his makings and rolled a cigarette. Asa had to wait for the man to put it between his lips before he answered. "Don't think I'd mind meeting you there." The glance he ran over Asa was assessing. "We're about a straight match." He lit the cigarette and shook out his sulfur. "Can't say the same about you and Elizabeth."

"How I handle Elizabeth is my business."

"I understand what's between a husband and a wife is a private matter, and, plain as day, I'll be answering to God for it, but you go spouting asinine orders to Elizabeth, she's going to fight back."

"Asinine mean stupid?"

"Pretty much."

"Keeping the woman safe is not stupid."

Cougar tossed the match to the ground. It smoked harmlessly in the dirt. "Putting Elizabeth in a pretty cage is asinine. Expecting her to be happy about it is sheer stupidity."

"Ladies do not break horses."

"Elizabeth wasn't raised to be a lady. Look around you, man." Cougar waved his arm in a descriptive arc to encompass the mountains and the wilderness. "This isn't Boston or San Francisco. Elizabeth was born and raised here. Sure, she can act the part of a lady, but she's still a Coyote with their wild nature and hatred for rules. Part of her will always be wild. Different."

Asa ran his hand down his face. For all he didn't want to hear it, his fairer side said there was truth in Cougar's words. His less savvy side was already halfway to town to buy a wagon load of cotton batting to wrap Elizabeth safely in.

"You said I could ask anything I wanted in return for the debt you owe me," Cougar continued.

Asa grit his teeth. He knew what was coming. "You planning on tying my hands with my own honor?"

Cougar's lips flickered up in a ghost of a smile. "Not only that, but tail-flipped and hog-tied."

"Let's hear it."

"You go in that barn and tell that woman she can't work that horse and she's going to balk. More than likely, you'll be arguing in the bedroom." He took a long drag on the cigarette. The tip glowed red, then faded. "Arguments like that can get nasty."

Asa watched Elizabeth finish unsaddling Sir Prince. "I guess I couldn't blame her if she did."

"Women don't have much else to fight with," Cougar agreed.

Asa thought of the promise of obedience he'd made Elizabeth give. Hell, she didn't even have that.

Cougar took a final drag on his cigarette and tossed it to the ground. "You turn ornery as a result of her fighting back and I'll have to kill you, which would be a shame as you seem the likable sort."

Asa laughed, and immediately regretted it as his ribs screamed. His "you'd like to try" was rather pitiful in the way of challenges.

"I'd like not to put it to the test, but women can drive a man crazy with their ways."

Asa wondered if he was referring to his relationship with Emily. "You have my word. I won't forbid her."

"Guess that'll have to do." Cougar sat straight in the saddle as the barn door closed behind Elizabeth. "You want I should tell her you're pure busted up?"

"Hell, no! Let's just get me into the house. If we're lucky, she'll sulk in the barn and we can inspect the damage before she comes in."

"You thinking she's going to start screaming?"

"I don't want her worried."

Cougar swung his horse to the right, urged him around the corral, and chuckled. "So you're not planning on telling her about the trap you fell into?"

"It's not something I'm proud of," Asa grumbled.

"It was well done." Cougar pointed out, looking back the way they'd come. "Like every thing else that's been going on for the last year and a half. It's no accident that bullet creased you and those cattle stampeded the way they did."

"Yeah."

"If you're not going with the truth, what are you planning on telling her by way of explanation?"

"I'm going to tell her I fell off my horse."

If Cougar's previous chuckle had been irritating, his full blown laugh was pure insulting.

Holding his ribs, Asa nudged Shameless in Buck's wake. As soon as his ribs healed, he and his neighbor were going to have to get some things settled. If a little dust flew, so much the better.

Chapter Seventeen

❧

"You fell off your horse?" Elizabeth stared at Asa where he lay on the bed, his upper torso wrapped tighter than a corseted spinster. Hoof marks were clearly visible on his shoulder. Blood seeped through one of the bandages on his side.

"It's not something I'm proud of," Asa muttered in response to her disbelief.

"That whopper is another thing you'd best not be proud of." His head snapped up. She shook her head. "I am not a stupid woman, Asa." She jerked off her leather gloves. "Why you persist in treating me as one, I fail to understand."

She wanted to examine Asa's wounds, but she'd come straight from the stable. She needed to clean up. She went to the wash basin beside the bed.

"Don't get prissy on me, Elizabeth."

"Then don't go telling me you fell off your horse when it's as plain as the nose on your face you were trampled." She poured water into the bowl and scrubbed her hands with lye soap.

"What are you doing?" He was eyeing her suspiciously.

"I intend to see how badly you're hurt."

"I've just got some busted-up ribs."

"Good." She dried her hands on the towel. "Then this won't take long."

Behind her, she heard Cougar chuckle.

Asa tried to scoot up. No doubt in an effort to intimidate her. His glare was ruined by the moan of pain his action elicited.

She flicked the sheets and blankets down. He tried to grab them back, but the stiffness from his injuries pulled him up short. She bit back a smile as he made another stab at dissuading her. "Cougar tended to everything. There's no need."

She worked the knot of the highest bandage. "Not more than an hour ago, you were reminding me of my duties. I wouldn't be much of a wife if I didn't see to your health."

"Seems you're mighty choosy about when you're wifely."

"I disagree. I'm always wifely."

"But not very obedient."

She shrugged. "You've got to take the good with the bad."

"Uh-huh."

"You never forbade me to work with the horses," she pointed out as she eased the bandage away from his chest.

"Because I wasn't aware there was a need."

"You're right," she countered, not one bit intimidated by his scowl. "There wasn't a need."

"That's where we need to blow off the smoke."

She gently urged him forward so she could unwrap the bandage. His breath hissed between his teeth, but he didn't let on by anything else the agony he had to be in. She wanted to kiss his forehead in comfort. She didn't. Instead, she gave him something he'd appreciate more. A distraction.

"There's nothing to clear. I like to train horses. I've been doing it for ten years. I'm darned good at it and I won't be forbidden to do it."

"You won't?"

She recognized the plan to argue in his low drawl. She took it into full consideration in the second it took to answer. "No."

"What if I see this differently?" he asked.

She unwrapped the last layer of bandage and knew his anger for bluster. The man had to be in too much pain for anything else. "Then you're going to have to change your mind."

"Or else?"

"There is no or else." She winced as she peeled the cloth away from an open wound. She looked at him. "This looks like a bullet crease."

He shook his head. "I hit a branch."

Stubborn man. She turned to Cougar. "What happened?"

"I'm sure I wouldn't know, ma'am. If the man says he hit a tree and fell off his horse, I'll not be the one to call him a liar."

"You don't have to be. I'm calling him one."

The smile that shadowed her neighbor's mouth was a faint simile of a grin. "All I know is I found him like he is, struggling to get back on his horse."

"Naturally, you did the neighborly thing and saw him home."

He took his fixings out of his pocket. "Yup."

"And you two didn't talk the whole way?"

"Nope." He pulled out a paper. "Your husband didn't seem the talkative sort."

And pigs flew. "If you're going to smoke," she interjected before he could shake tobacco onto the paper, "I'd appreciate it if you took it outside."

"I'll wait then." He settled in the wing-backed chair.

"If that's your choice." Elizabeth looked at the deep wound again. "This is going to need stitches."

"Like hell," Asa growled at the same time Cougar said, "I told you so."

To Asa, Elizabeth merely said, "Yes. It does." To Cougar, she had a bit more to say. "You mean to tell me you bandaged him up like this, knowing he needed stitches?"

"Yup. He seemed ready to come to blows over the issue." He shrugged. "Didn't see any harm in it. No wife worth her salt was going to take a neighbor's word for how her husband's faring."

She eyed him, the way he slouched in the chair, and wondered why she was surprised. Asa and Cougar were a lot alike. Neither wasted a lot of time arguing. Not when they could accomplish their goals through other means.

"If you're going to stay, I suppose you can hold him down while I stitch."

"Be happy to."

From the broad grin across his face, Asa just bet McKinnely would. "No one needs to hold me down."

"I'm your wife." Elizabeth informed him in a tone he wasn't used to hearing. "You don't need to worry about impressing me."

Like hell he didn't. "No one's going to have to hold me down because no one's going to stick a needle in me."

He could have been a fly on the wall for all the attention she paid him. "I'll be back in a minute."

"Where you going?"

"To get the needle and silk."

"I don't need stitches." He was talking to air.

"Lady says you need stitching," Cougar said, coming over to the bed.

"You don't have to sound so all-fired cheery about the prospect," Asa muttered.

"Just being neighborly."

"Uh-huh." Asa pointed to the door. "Why don't you try being neighborly back at your place?"

McKinnely didn't take the hint. Instead, he rolled up his sleeves. Elizabeth came back in the room, a brown wooden box in her hand. He didn't need to ask what was in it. Every ranch had its medical supplies. Just as no cowboy ever wanted the lid lifted.

"Elizabeth, I forbid you to come near me with that stuff."

As if she hadn't heard, she proceeded to pour whiskey into a cup. She handed it to him. "Drink this."

He sniffed. Pure, unadulterated whiskey scoured his nostrils with its scent. He sniffed again. Real whiskey. Maybe even Kentucky sipping stock. He tossed the contents back and held out the glass for a refill. From the corner of his eye, he saw Cougar perking up with anticipation.

"That your father's stock?" Cougar asked, as soon as Elizabeth had topped off Asa's glass.

"I assume so." She threaded silk through a needle, then dropped thread and all into a bowl of the whiskey. "I found it in his study after his death."

"Just the one bottle?" McKinnely asked.

"No." Elizabeth poured more water over her hands. She hadn't even gotten the soap into a good lather before McKinnely was asking, "Want me to toss that for you?"

Elizabeth's "that's all right" had no more influence than Asa's initial refusal of help had. McKinnely could be mule-stubborn when he had his own agenda. He poured water over Elizabeth's hands. He didn't stop until the basin was near to overflowing and Elizabeth was doing her best to conceal the concern for her floors. "That's fine, thank you."

"No problem."

"You can just toss it out the window."

"It's no problem at all to take it out back."

"That's really not necessary."

Elizabeth could have saved herself the breath. Asa wasn't fooled about why McKinnely wanted the trip downstairs. A body had to pass right by the study while coming and going. His opinion of his neighbor went up another notch. It took a smart man to think on his feet.

Elizabeth pulled some white rags from the box.

"You're not sewing me up," he told her again.

Yes, she was. "The wound needs cleaning. There's dirt embedded in it."

She'd be lucky if he didn't get an infection. Tears stung her eyes at the thought. To her astonishment, Elizabeth realized she wanted to cry. Because a man had been hurt of all things. She blinked quickly to dispel the moisture. She didn't want Asa to see. He'd probably decide weepy women were too delicate to ride a carriage into town.

"That's what McKinnely said," he admitted.

"And you didn't let him clean it?" She wanted to cuff him over the head for such stupidity.

"The man's got the touch of a bull."

She bent her head to hide a smile. "I'll endeavor to be gentle."

"Being as you're a woman, it can't help but be an improvement."

She rose from the side of the bed and walked to the foot. As she opened the chest, she said, "For a man who grew up with some pretty poor examples of women, you seem to have definite opinions on their qualities."

She grabbed a sheet and stood straight. That half smile on his lips told her he was going to make her laugh. Probably because her eyes were still stinging. As observant as he was, it was too much to hope he wouldn't notice.

"I spent a goodly portion of my adult years studying the matter," he informed her.

"I'm sure you did." And she didn't want to hear about it.

"Where is Cougar with that basin?"

"He'll be along presently," Asa answered. After he sampled some of that whiskey. He patted the bed beside him. "Come here."

Elizabeth did, only because she wanted to slide the wadded sheet beneath him to catch the water from cleaning his wound. She leaned over to do just that, and he caught her wrist and tugged. By nearly twisting full around, she managed to avoid landing on his side. As it was, she plopped on the bed hard enough to jostle a groan from the man. Her apology was instantaneous. As was her anger. "What are you trying to do, kill yourself? I could have landed on you!"

"A little feather like you couldn't make a dent on a cushion."

"Huh!" Ladylike or not, there wasn't anything more eloquent she could come up with in the face of such nonsense than an inelegant snort. She pushed herself straight. The effect was immediately ruined as his hand slid across her cheek. His fingers curled around the back of her head.

"I missed you, darlin'."

"Before or after you met up with rustlers?"

He grimaced. "Not buying my story, huh?"

"A two-year-old wouldn't buy that story."

"It'd be real helpful if you could see your way to pretending."

She resisted the downward pressure of his hand. "Not likely."

He pulled harder.

"What are you doing?" she asked. "You're going to hurt yourself!"

"Darlin', if you don't know I'm working on stealing a kiss, I haven't been doing my job right."

Heat surged into her face, but it didn't deter her from pointing out the idiocy of the statement. "You can kiss later. Right now, you need to be sewn up."

"I want to be kissed now."

She was weakening, which explained how her last token protest ended with a whisper against his lips. "This really isn't the best idea—"

He opened his mouth and she lost all thoughts. His breath, his taste, it was all so dearly familiar. She braced one hand on the other side of his body. With her free one, she cupped his cheek. Her mouth opened over his and her defenses scattered like flies. She'd come so close to losing him. One more inch and the bullet would have insured she'd be alone forever. More desperation than passion poured into the kiss.

He pulled back a fraction. "I missed you, darlin'."

"You could have been killed." It came out on an anguished moan.

"Nah," he whispered.

She closed her eyes. She felt his lips graze each lid before brushing her cheeks. "I just got me a wife." His hand cupped her belly. "Maybe even got a start on a little one." He absorbed her start with his touch. "You can stop your fretting. I'm not going anywhere, Elizabeth."

As irrational as it seemed, she took great comfort in his conviction. For a few precious moments, they rested forehead to forehead, hand to belly, and let time drift. He was here now, she told herself. She'd take care of him and he'd be fine. That's all she had to do. Just take care of him.

The stairs creaked. Boot heels reverberated on the hall floor. While Asa watched, a small, satisfied smile on his face, she repaired her appearance. When there were two quick knocks on the door, Asa called an immediate "come in". She shot him a glare. She would have preferred a few more moments.

Clint came in, carrying the empty porcelain basin.

"Cougar get sidetracked?" Asa asked.

Clint nodded to Asa and tipped his hat with his free hand to Elizabeth. "He sent me up with this, ma'am. He said you might need help?"

Elizabeth took the basin. The roses, painted in pink, cream and blue, looked so pretty. Cheerful. A direct contrast to what she was going to do.

She put the basin on the night stand and poured in some water. With her hands, she worked soap into the liquid. She dipped the cloth into the soapy water. Turning to Asa, she said, "I've got to clean the wound."

Asa shrugged as if he hadn't a care in the world. "We're not going anywhere." He touched the sheet she'd dropped by his side. "This to catch the water?"

And blood. She'd cleaned enough wounds in her time to know there'd be fresh blood. "Yes."

Without her asking, he shifted his torso so he was half on the sheet. When he was done, his breath was coming in harsh pants. "That work?"

"Yes." She'd replace the mattress if it didn't.

Clint appeared at her side like magic. "If you hadn't been in such a hurry to impress your wife with how tough you are, I could have helped you."

Asa's response was a glare.

Elizabeth felt Clint needn't be so provoking. She was going to reprimand him for it when, in a miraculous move, he had Asa re-positioned without a groan of pain or further whitening of his countenance. Instead, she looked at him in amazement. "How'd you do that?"

"My uncle was a doctor. A body tends to pick up a few tricks here and there."

"You probably need to be real strong?"

His smile was gentle. "I'll show you the trick later."

"Thank you." She couldn't put it off any longer. The step to the bedside seemed like a leap across a chasm. She'd done this literally hundreds of times without a qualm. There was absolutely no need for her to be squeamish now, she told herself.

It didn't help.

Before she could touch him, Asa grabbed the last of the whiskey and tossed it down in one swallow. He closed his eyes and braced himself. "Go ahead."

She didn't start immediately. She waited until his breath evened out. When she thought he was ready, she gently touched the cloth to the top of the long tear.

His breath hissed. Hers stopped. A trickle of blood started to flow. She dipped the cloth into the wash basin again. The water tinged a hideous pink. She wrung the cloth until it was short of dripping. She took a breath and applied it again. Asa didn't make a sound this time, but his eyes closed and his whole body clenched. With broken ribs, that couldn't have been comfortable. As if in testament to her assumption, sweat popped out on his brow. She left the cloth on the wound to soak out the debris.

She stared at the cloth and the wound without really seeing them. Her mind she kept focused within, in order to prevent the nausea. She took deep breaths as she repeated the process. Never had treating someone affected her to this degree. She'd even amputated a foot once. She'd been nauseated then, but it had been the practical thing to do. If she hadn't amputated the foot, the cowboy would have died. The same rule applied here. There was no need for her to be nauseous now. It was just a simple cut.

She told herself that repeatedly, but it didn't help because, truth be told, she'd never had to work on anyone she'd loved before.

She paused in wringing out the cloth. The enormity of the realization sank in. God help her, she loved this man. Her hands shook as she replaced the cloth again. She loved him and he'd married her to get a place of his own and respectability. She closed her eyes against the pain. Against the vulnerability. Her father was right. She was a born fool.

She opened her eyes and checked his wound. As best as she could tell, it was clean. She gently placed the cloth in the basin. She dipped her hands in the bowl of whiskey. She caught Clint's eye. The wing-backed chair rustled a protest as he got to his feet. She tipped her head in Asa's direction. "Hold him."

Asa's eyes popped open. "You're not sewing me up."

His gaze collided with hers. She braced and reminded herself this was the practical thing to do. The only thing. "Yes. I am."

"You touch me, and you'll be saying howdy to next week before I do."

It was a nonsense threat. Asa knew it. There wasn't a thing he could do to stop the other man from holding him down. In his current state, he probably couldn't stop Elizabeth. Clint halted and looked at Elizabeth. All Asa could see was her profile. There was no softness to play on. He didn't find any in her voice either as she declared softly, "I'm sewing him up."

"The hell you are!" he growled.

She held the wicked looking needle high and straightened out the thread. "You can settle up with me later for my disobedience," she told him in a very precise voice, "but right now, I'm closing that wound. If you think on it, you'll see it's reasonable."

"There's nothing reasonable about setting a needle to a man's flesh," he snarled, his stomach churning at the sight of it. Jesus, he hated needles.

Elizabeth paused. "You can't expect me to believe you've never had a cut stitched before?"

"The hell I can't." Pain whipped through his body, reminding him that forceful speech was not on the agenda. "I don't hold with needles," he added in a more normal drawl.

"You mean you're afraid of them," Elizabeth corrected in a voice he thought too likely to carry.

"Grown men are not afraid of needles."

She stared at him the longest time, her expression unreadable. Clint stood by her side. Asa didn't fool himself thinking that the man was caught in any sort of indecision. If Elizabeth wanted him held down, Clint would do it.

Something shifted inside Elizabeth. Emotions flashed across her face, too quick to be deciphered, but when all was said and done, the final expression was a resigned practicality. She was going to stitch his wound and that was that. For the first time, he didn't admire her perseverance in the face of adversity.

"Please hold him," she said to Clint.

Asa held up his hand. "You dead set on doing this?"

"Yes."

"Even though you know I don't want it and the only way you're getting away with it is because I'm too busted up to arm-wrestle a gnat?"

"Yes."

"And you don't feel the least bit guilty?"

"No."

"Now that's a sad, sorry state of affairs." Asa waved Clint back. "You won't need to hold me."

It was bad enough Elizabeth had seen him so weak that he couldn't enforce a solid "no." He wasn't going to drop anymore in her estimation by needing to be hog-tied like a green boy.

"It might be better if Clint held you." Her placating tone of voice set his teeth on edge almost as much as the sight of that needle. "I need you to be perfectly still."

He glared at her. "I'm not some whining kid who needs to be forced to stay put."

She flinched, immediately making him feel guilty, but not nearly as guilty as the tiny "I'm sorry" she whispered when she pressed the needle to his side.

He swore loudly as it pierced his flesh. Her hand jerked and he swore again.

Another "I'm sorry" drifted between them. A drop of wetness splattered on his chest. He swore, for no other reason than it felt better than the needle.

"Shut up," Clint growled, sounding as if he were the one under the needle.

Asa opened his eyes. Elizabeth's face was inches from his, and she was crying. Another tear rolled down her cheek to tumble from her chin onto his chest.

Her throat worked as she pressed the needle tip into the other side of the wound. He wasn't thinking. He swore anew. Tears overflowed Elizabeth's eyes. She swallowed hard. Her lips moved. Another "I'm sorry" slipped out before she bit her lip.

The truth was hard to ignore. Sewing him up was killing her. He didn't need Clint's glare to smother the next curse before it could escape.

During the last month, he'd wondered what it would take to make Elizabeth cry. Now he had his answer. All it took was hurting him. He thought she was going to burst into sobs as she pulled the thread through, and he couldn't control his involuntary wince. He caught her hand in his before she could tie off the stitch. Surprise had her gaze flying to his.

"Clint can finish."

Her face set in stubborn lines. "No."

"It's all right, ma'am," Clint concurred, reaching for the needle. "I've sewn up more wounds than most doctors."

Elizabeth's expression turned feral. "Don't you touch him."

Clint jerked his hand back so fast, a body would have sworn he'd been bitten. "I wouldn't think of it."

Elizabeth didn't look appeased. "It's all right, Elizabeth, Clint'll do a fine job."

She shook her head. "No, he won't. You said so yourself. Men are ham-handed."

He wished he'd been smart enough to bite off his tongue earlier. "McKinnely was as gentle as a lamb. I was just spouting nonsense to get out of getting stitched." He kept his grip on her hand and nodded to the door. "Go get McKinnely."

"No problem." Clint all but bolted for the door.

"He's not touching you," Elizabeth informed him in a tone that belied the tears on her face.

"Be reasonable, darlin'," he coaxed. "Stitching me is hurting you more than me. Poking me with a needle won't bother McKinnely a bit."

"We both know he's down there drinking," she told him, keeping a death grip on the needle and thread. "By now, he's so drunk, he'll probably think he's working with two needles."

Asa shook his head at her vehemence. "You really do have a thing about drink, don't you?"

"It turns men into animals."

Well, at least he knew why he'd been rationed to a scant two fingers, which wasn't enough to kill the pain in a tadpole, let alone a grown man. He touched her hand. "Not all men are mean drunks. Some of us get downright happy."

The look she shot him was rank with disbelief. He dropped that line of argument. "It'll take more than a few drinks to affect a man of McKinnely's size."

"He's not touching you."

And that was that, Asa realized. He slid his thumb across the back of her hand. He didn't have much hope of it soothing her, but he figured it was worth a try. "You dead set on finishing this then?"

She bit her lip. The color fled her cheeks, but her answer didn't waver. "Yes."

He relaxed into the pillows. "Have at it, then. I won't say a word."

On another "I'm sorry" that ripped his insides, she tied off the stitch.

While her expression remained perfectly controlled, she couldn't extend that rigid control to her eyes. All the agony she tried to hide from him rested there.

He touched her cheek with his clear hand. At first, he thought it was his imagination, but then he changed his mind. She was leaning her cheek into his hand, taking comfort from his touch even as she insisted on sewing him up and causing herself agony in the first place. He shook his head. The woman was a born contradiction.

"It's all right," he found himself saying as she applied the needle again. In response, she apologized. He looked to the door, wondering where McKinnely was. Apparently, the job of comforting his wife was being left up to him. "We're a fine pair, Mrs. MacIntyre," he whispered, brushing a fresh tear off her cheek. "Too stubborn for our own good."

"I'm not stubborn," she growled, then ruined the effect by biting her lip.

"I can see that." What he could see was her feeling protective. If she weren't bawling her eyes out while she was feeling it, he might have enjoyed the experience.

"McKinnely and Clint wouldn't do it right," she informed him.

"Doc is Cougar's father and Clint's uncle. What makes you think they couldn't do as good a job?"

She paused as if weighing a decision. "They don't know you like I do. They'd probably take something you said personally and do a lousy job."

He laughed. "You saying I'm the provoking sort?"

"You know you are."

She tied off the knot, and he took the brief interlude to relax his muscles.

"If Clint's Cougar's cousin—" she began.

"You didn't know?"

"No." She retied the knot in the end of the thread. "If Clint's Cougar's cousin, why isn't he over at the Tumbling M?"

"McKinnely's been a bit suspicious of things going on here." He cocked an eyebrow at her. "Apparently, you refused McKinnely's offer of help?"

"That didn't give him the right to assign spies!"

"Hey!" Asa warned, watching the way she jerked the knot on the string. "Don't get your feathers in an uproar. He just wanted to make sure you were all right."

"He should have respected my wishes."

"He did. Clint came on a just-in-case scenario."

She glared at the door. It didn't take a genius to figure out she felt betrayed. "He just wanted the ranch."

"Use your head, woman." His response was curt. "The Tumbling M is a prime property of over three thousand acres. There's no way the man would want the headache of the Rocking C on top. Hell, your land doesn't even abut his."

She didn't look convinced.

"McKinnely's a good man who was concerned, rightly enough, about a woman alone being taken advantage of." He glared into her mutinous expression. "I respect him for it, even if you don't have the sense to. He did what any honorable man would. He's the only one of your neighbors who did anything remotely helpful."

This time, she put the needle into his flesh without a quiver. He figured she'd caught his slight to Aaron. Her next sentence confirmed it. "Aaron came over often."

"No doubt trying to prey on your emotions."

"I am not an emotional woman."

"You're one of the most emotional women I've met, whether you show it or not."

She stared at him in shock and horror. Hell, did she really think him that much of a fool? "I wasn't insulting you," he tacked on gruffly.

"I can be as hard-nosed as any man."

"I never said you couldn't be," he backtracked, "but that doesn't mean you don't have feelings."

"With an ounce of cooperation, I could run this ranch as well as you."

"I've never doubted it."

"Yes, you have."

"Just because I don't think you have to do a man's job doesn't mean I don't think you could manage a fair approximation."

She pulled the thread through another stitch. "There you go."

"There I go where?"

She tied off the knot. "You just admitted you think I'm useless."

"Hell, you're determined to twist everything I say!"

"Don't swear, and I am not."

"You saying you can tail a full grown cow?"

"Well…"

"You saying you can wrestle down a bull for castrating and branding?" Her "no" was long coming. He pressed on. "You saying that, when you ride the range, men don't see you as fair game?"

"Men get robbed, too."

"But they don't get raped and they don't become targets just for the opportunity." She didn't have a ready argument for that. "And before you trot out some lame argument that you're not afraid of being caught and violated, reconsider. You're too damned smart not to have sweated the possibility."

She closed her mouth. He had to suffer another stitch before she responded. "It doesn't mean I'm useless."

"I never said you were, but you're not a man, and whether you see it as fair or not, that's the bottom line."

She didn't have an answer to that one either.

"When Aaron came over, I bet he didn't talk about branding or the roundup."

"No, but he was concerned. He knew we were being rustled. He wondered how it was affecting our ability to pay the bank note."

"He knew about the note?"

"Of course he knew. If he hadn't spoken for me, Mr. Dunn would have never honored his agreement with my father."

"Your father negotiated the bank note?"

"Yes, but he died before the paperwork was done. Mr. Dunn didn't want to honor it."

"What would have happened if he hadn't?"

"Do you mean would the ranch have gone under?"

"Yeah."

"No. We were solvent."

"Then why the hell go through with the deal?"

Pain made the exclamation sharper than he wanted. He'd be damned glad when they were done with this stitching.

"I'm sorry." She didn't look that sorry to him. "My father wanted to expand the breeding program. A lot of ranchers have been talking about crossbreeding Herefords with Longhorns. With the railroad coming through, he saw it as a way to capture the beef market back East."

"What does Aaron have to do with that?"

"They were partners."

"And he didn't talk you out of it?"

She gave him a pitying glance. "You just got done pointing out how I can't work a ranch like a man. If my father's and Aaron's plan worked, in a couple of years, I'd have enough money not to have to scrape."

The needle touched his flesh again. "How many more stitches we got left?"

"Two." Her voice was tight. No doubt because she'd just put the damned thing through his wound again.

"So Aaron and your father worked together on this?"

"Yes."

Wheels began to churn in his brain. "Water would be pretty important to a plan like that."

"Yes. The drought made it tough for Aaron. The cross isn't as hardy as longhorns."

"I noticed your father let Aaron use the waterholes here."

"Yes."

"There isn't a written agreement?"

"No, but Aaron knows he'll never be denied water."

Aaron hadn't struck him as that trusting a sort.

She eyed him suspiciously. "You haven't been thinking of cutting him off?"

"The thought hadn't crossed my mind." Today, he added silently.

"Did Aaron have to borrow to finance his side of the operation?" he asked.

She frowned. "I don't know. Probably not." She made quick work of the next stitch. "He always seems to have plenty. Rumor is his wife has money of her own."

Asa made a mental note to check that out. A man who could lose everything if water rights were taken away, was a man who bore watching.

"There." Elizabeth sat back with a huge sigh of relief. "It's done."

He looked at the neat row of black stitches angling up his side. "Neat as a pin." Not by a flicker of an eyelash did he let on how obscene he thought it looked.

She dipped the needle back in the bowl of whiskey. "As long as you don't get an infection, you should be right as rain in no time." She reached out and placed her hand on his forehead as if she expected a fever to conjure itself on suggestion alone.

"I'm too mean to catch a fever," he told her, completely confident in his assertion. "One look at this ugly mug and fevers tuck their tails in pursuit of easier game."

Her smile was weak. Uncertain.

He motioned with his fingers. "Bend on down here and give me a kiss."

"Don't you ever think of anything else?" she asked, yet doing as he bid.

His smile broadened as her lips touched his. "Not when you're around, darlin'. Not when you're around."

Chapter Eighteen

He was burning with fever. Elizabeth bit her lip and dipped the cloth in the cool well water. She ran it over his face, then down his neck to his torso. Too ugly for a fever, indeed. Ha! The man was more like a God than a troll, and the proof lay in his festering wound.

Footsteps on the stairs indicated the return of Clint. A slower step followed and she figured it was Old Sam.

"Doc's at the Hennessy's," Clint said after a soft knock.

She bit her lip. "He's not coming?"

He shook his head. "Can't, ma'am. Seems like Mr. Hennessy's got some kind of poisoning. They don't know if he's going to make it through the night."

She placed the cloth in the water. "Poor Jenna." Hennessy wasn't worth much, but he was still worth more alive than dead.

"Dorothy's with her," he said. "Jenna'll be fine."

She probably would, Elizabeth decided. Doc's wife Dorothy was a beautiful woman who radiated caring and warmth. She'd see Jenna through.

"Elly?"

She took a breath and faced Old Sam. "Yes?"

"McKinnely sent me up here to tell you he's going to take over rounding up those brush tails."

God! She hadn't even considered the cattle. "Would you thank him for me?"

"Already been handled." Old Sam crushed his hat in his hand. "I'll be going with them."

"Of course."

He looked distinctly uncomfortable in the bedroom door. "You gonna be all right?"

Before, no matter what the result, her answer would have been an unequivocal "yes". Now, she wasn't sure. If Asa died, would she be fine?

Her silence dragging long enough, Clint answered for her. "She'll be fine."

"Glad you think so, young'un," Old Sam snapped, "but last I saw, Mrs. MacIntyre had a mouth on her face. From that, I figured she could speak for herself."

"Can't you see she's busy, you old coot?" Clint shot back. "She's got more on her mind than—"

Elizabeth pasted a smile on her face and leapt into the middle of the fray before it could become an argument. "I expect Asa's fever to break tonight." Old Sam cast Asa's supine body a skeptical look. She firmed her voice with an extra dose of conviction. "Everything's going to be all right. Thank you for asking, Sam."

He smoothed the brim of his hat. "Guess we'd better get those critters gathered up then. Asa'll be screaming blue thunder if we don't."

"Yes." She looked at Asa's flushed face, damp from her sponging. She'd give anything right now to see him rumble, let alone generate thunder. She infused all the confidence she could fake into her voice. "He will."

He slammed his battered hat back on his head. "Then I'll be getting those boys moving. No doubt they've been lazing about rather than packing. Can't leave 'em alone for a minute." He was still muttering as he disappeared down the hall.

Elizabeth looked at Clint. He stood twirling his hat in that way he had, slow and unhurried. "Aren't you going with him?"

"Nah."

"Don't they need you?"

"We figured I'd be better served here, what with my doctoring knowledge and MacIntyre being sick."

He made it sound as if it were a reasonable decision based upon illness. It didn't ring true. She looked at him again. "For this, you've come into my house wearing guns?"

Her question didn't disturb the laconic twirling of his hat. His answer reflected the same unconcern. "Must've forgotten to take them off in all the excitement."

She didn't believe that for an instant. "Mr...?"

"Just Clint, ma'am."

"Mr. Clint. I am not a fool. I don't believe Asa fell off his horse anymore than I believe you forgot to take off your guns."

"Asa said you kept a man on his toes, ma'am." His hat continued to twirl at the same lazy pace.

"I'm not finding it particularly difficult when you all persist in treating me like a child."

His chuckle at her wry statement was as easy as his manner. He was really beginning to irritate her.

She took another breath, picked up the cup of willow bark tea and coaxed a bit down Asa's throat. "Mr. Clint?"

"Yes?"

"Are you any good with those guns?"

"Fair to middlin', ma'am."

Which she took to mean he could hit whatever he wanted. "I want you to do me a favor."

"Uh-huh."

"If anyone approaches this ranch, I want you to shoot them."

"Any particular place?"

"Between the eyes would be nice. If you can't manage that, try for the heart."

There was a slight jarring in the twirl of the hat before he answered in his usual calm manner. "I take it we're not asking questions?"

"If you do your job right, there won't be any need."

"No disputing that."

She lifted the poultice over Asa's stitches. If anything, the flesh looked angrier.

"Any improvement?" Clint asked.

"I think the swelling has increased and there are red streaks beginning."

His resigned "damn" said it all.

Crossing to the hearth, he put another log in the fire. With the hand bellows, he pumped the flames high and hot. The three steps it took Elizabeth to reach his side seemed like an eternity. She handed him the long straight knife. He took it from her, his expression grim.

"I was hoping the poultice would work," he said as he put the knife in the fire.

"So was I," she admitted.

"We're going to have to cut and burn out the infection."

It was an unnecessary statement as they were halfway through the procedure. She watched the blade heat. The tip glowed red. Soon, the whole blade would glow and she'd have to lay it against Asa's flesh. Listen to him scream. Smell his burned flesh. Her vision blackened at the corners. Her stomach rose.

"You want me to do it?" Clint asked.

She pushed back the nausea. "We've already been over this. I'm not strong enough to hold him down. You are. Therefore, I've got the job." She took a deep breath. "We're going to have to do it twice due to the way the wound curves."

"You checked?"

At least five times. "Yes. I can't get a clean line in one try."

"Damn," he muttered. "Wish that bullet that creased him had stayed flat rather than bouncing off that rib."

"If it hadn't bounced off that rib, he'd be dead."

Clint pushed to his feet. "You got a point."

Part of her wished she didn't. She didn't know if she could do this.

"I'll hold him down," Clint said. "You cut out the infection."

Elizabeth picked up the smaller knife. Working carefully, she cut away the dead and angry tissue, blocking her ears to Asa's moans, knowing what she was going to do next would make this seem like a picnic. As she wiped at the fresh blood running down Asa's side, she glanced at Clint. His face was as white as hers felt. "Thanks."

"No problem." He handed her another cloth to replace the one she'd dropped on the floor. He nodded to the fireplace. "As soon as that blade's red to the hilt, you grab it up and place it over the cut."

She wrapped her hands in thick strips of sheet. "I know what to do."

She just didn't know if she could. What if she passed out? What if she failed? The quivering started deep inside. She swallowed hard and beat it back. She'd do this because she had no other choice. She thought of Asa, the way he stood up for her. The way he smiled when she lost her temper. The way he treated her, like he actually thought she was fine just the way she was. His tenderness and desire for her. She squeezed the tremors into silence. She would do this.

The blade glowed red. She took a deep breath. She grabbed the handle, stood, and swung around. The room spun. She bit her lip, but the black encroached. Pain seared her hands from the heat. It was enough to help her stay focused. She hurried to the bed. She had to do this right. She didn't want to do it more than twice.

Clint pulled the sheets back. "Now," he ordered. "For the count of ten, hold it there."

She told herself she was just searing meat. She applied the knife. The scent of burned flesh rose with Asa's howl of agony. It seemed an interminable amount of time before she hit ten. She removed the knife and returned it to the fire.

Black crept further into her vision. She knew she was seconds from passing out. It was too much. All of it was too much. She took a deep breath. The horrible scent filled her nostrils. She barely made it to the basin in time.

When the last of the spasms passed, she turned back to the fire. The knife blade glowed red hot. Ready. She moaned despite herself.

"You all right, ma'am?"

It didn't matter if she wasn't. She had to be. "I'm fine," she responded.

She glanced at Clint. He was definitely green around the edges, but he was hanging in there, holding Asa steady. Doing what had to be done. She could do no less.

"Jut one more time," she breathed. She could do that. One more count of ten and she'd be done.

Clint's voice was a soft echo. "Just one more time."

She picked up the blade, welcoming the heat this time against her palms. It gave her something to focus on rather than the suffocating wall of black. Her vision was reduced to a small circle that consisted of the wound she was cauterizing and the blade she was going to do it with. She placed the blade across the wound and resolutely counted through Asa's low groaning agony and Clint's swearing. By the time she got to ten, she could barely see.

"Looks good," Clint declared with obvious relief.

She took a blind step back. "We don't need to do it again?"

"No."

The last thing she remembered was asking Clint to take the knife. Then all went mercifully blank.

* * * * *

A week later, Elizabeth came down the stairs to find Bryce, the youngest hand, waiting in the parlor.

"How is Mr. MacIntyre?"

She gritted her teeth and forced a smile. "He's fine. Almost ready to be up and about to hear him tell it."

The boy grinned ear to ear. "I bet he's not much fun laid up."

If she didn't murder him by sundown, he'd be fortunate. "What makes you say that?"

"My pa was the orneriest thing on two legs when he got laid up with a busted leg," the boy added cheerfully. "My ma swore he was going to drive her mad trying to do more before it was time."

"Mr. MacIntyre is a bit ambitious in his recovery."

"But he's going to recover?"

"Oh, yes." Maybe not from the wounds she'd be inflicting, but from the gunshot, definitely.

"We're real happy to hear that."

She assumed he meant the hands by "we". "Did you need something?"

"Yeah." He blushed a fiery red that went with his hair. "Mr. McKinnely brought in those brush tails. We figured on keeping them close to home, but we need a big fenced-in area."

"Why don't you take that fencing we set aside for the north pasture and put it around the back meadow? If there's enough posts, we might be able to corral all of them."

The boy flushed deeper. "That's a good thought. Do you think Mr. MacIntyre will think so?"

"I imagine so."

From the way the boy stood there, she assumed he wanted her to go ask. Frustration ate her innards. What did the boy think Asa was going to say? They had the same materials to work with. The same open amount of land. The same water supplies. He continued to stare. Finally, she said, "I'll go ask."

She stomped up the stairs, walked past Asa's room, and then stopped. There was no way she was going in there. The first question and he'd be struggling out of bed to supervise the construction of the corral. He was nowhere near healed enough, but, like a typical man, he wasn't hearing that. She waited two more minutes and went back down the stairs.

"Did Mr. MacIntyre agree?"

"It's a fine idea. Go with it."

As the boy loped out the door, she told herself it wasn't strictly a lie. It was a good idea.

"Elizabeth?"

The bellow came from upstairs. She ignored it, went into the kitchen and made up a tray of soup and bread. She added a glass of water. The apple pie, she ignored. The man didn't deserve any sweets.

As soon as she cleared the top of the stairs, Asa bellowed again.

She shot him an exasperated look as soon as she cleared the door. "You hollered?"

He had the grace to drop his gaze from hers. "Was that Bryce I heard downstairs?"

"Yes."

"Guess there isn't trouble or it'd be Clint or Old Sam."

"Exactly," she agreed.

She had trouble putting the tray down without spilling the soup. Asa, reaching to help, didn't improve the situation. She blew her hair off her face in exasperation. "Would you stop that?"

"What?"

"Stop trying to help. Stop trying to get out of bed. Stop trying to make yourself sick again!" The last sentence came out as an angry yell.

Asa relaxed against the pillow. He eyed her as if she were some strange new species of animal. A potentially dangerous one. "Don't think I've ever heard you shout before."

She gnashed her teeth and didn't answer.

"Gotta admit, you don't sound much like a lady when you do."

She permitted herself the luxury of glaring at him.

"That's quite a screech you got there."

He sounded amused. She contemplated dumping the soup over his head.

"I kind of like it when you let go," he went on.

"Excuse me?" Pure shock halted the inclination. She slowly lowered the tray.

"Ever since my fever broke, you've been marching around here all controlled, doing what's necessary, nothing more."

She moved her hands to the soup bowl. "And your problem is?"

"I haven't even gotten one good morning kiss."

She tightened her grip. In the midst of her argument with herself that she'd only have to wash the bed linens if she chucked the tray at his arrogant head, she paused as what he said sank in. He was out of sorts because she hadn't kissed him?

"Clint told me how you cauterized my wound yourself. I'm sorry I carried on as I did. Don't rightly remember it, but I understand it wasn't pretty."

She slowly digested his words. She wondered if he knew she'd fainted like a baby afterwards. "Cauterizing a wound isn't pleasant," she agreed.

Red tinted his cheekbones. His gaze locked to something on the hearth. "I wouldn't have carried on had I been conscious at the time. A man can't help the way his mind betrays him when he's out of his head with fever."

She released her grip on the bowl. He was embarrassed because he'd cried out when she'd put a red hot knife to his flesh?

"Don't imagine the scar's none too pretty," he added, still staring at the fire.

"Are you aware," she asked, "how close you came to dying?"

At least she'd pulled his attention from the fire. His silver eyes skated around the vicinity of hers. "Understand it was close for a bit."

"It was more than close."

"That must have been scary for you."

It had been more than scary. It had been soul-revealing. Terrifying. "I thought I was going to lose you."

She couldn't believe she'd let that sneak out. She'd avoided dealing with that revelation for a week. She'd been avoiding *this* for a week.

The hoarse whisper yanked Asa's gaze to hers. In their green depths, he saw only a reflection of what she'd endured.

"I told you I wasn't going anywhere," he said. "Besides, even if you did lose me to the undertaker, McKinnely would step in and get those cattle to the railroad. Ranch'd be in the black and you'd be sitting pretty."

The bowl of soup came at him so fast, he didn't have time to duck. It half-hit the pillow and his face.

"How dare you?"

He wiped his eyes and plucked a piece of chicken out of the corner of one.

Elizabeth stood next to the bed, her chest rising and falling under the force of emotion. "How dare you suggest I

327

wanted you dead!" She threw up her arms. "You come waltzing in here, ruin our deal, play on my honor, and then you lie there suggesting I'm so shallow, one little cry of pain and a new scar is going to drive me away?"

She grabbed the bread. "Not too long ago, you were accusing me of selling you short." The bread came hurtling at his head. "Let me tell you, Mr. High and Mighty MacIntyre. You may be as handsome as the devil, but you're a poor example of a husband."

"I am?"

"Yes. You are! You're worse than Brent." The napkin came hurling his way. It landed in a gentle plop on his chest. "You're worse than my father!"

He felt a small kernel of hope blossom. "How so?"

"At least they never bothered to try to make me love them." She took one step toward him, then another. "They were content with my cooperation, but not you. You had to have it all."

"Yup," he agreed unrepentantly. He watched her carefully. One more step and he'd have her.

Her slap, when it landed on his arm, was gentle. Full of emotion, but guaranteed not to hurt. "You kept pushing for more and now make fun of me when you get it," she whispered.

"I didn't make fun of you, darlin'."

"Yes, you did. You said I hadn't kissed you."

He caught her wrist and tugged. "You haven't."

She sat on the edge of the bed, stiff-backed and ready to fight now that she'd exposed herself. He touched her hands, then raised his hand to her cheek. "I thought maybe you thought I wasn't useful to you anymore."

"I don't understand."

"I've been lying here, trying to figure out why you haven't been very wifely for the last few days."

"I've been taking care of you!"

"Yeah, I know, and it's been no different than if McKinnely had done the caring."

"I beg to differ. McKinnely would have punched you."

His chuckle sent pain though his ribs. "You threw soup."

"And now I have to clean it up." She made to get up.

He anchored her with his grip on her wrist. "Later. I want to explain."

Her green eyes stared at him. Her lips pursed tight. Her whole demeanor said he'd better make it a good one. "It occurred to me that you married me thinking you were getting a strong man. What happened here a few days ago might have changed your opinion on what you'd married up with."

"That's nonsense!"

She looked so outraged, he had to smile. "Just goes to show how addled a man can get when he's forced to live on gruel."

"I have not served you gruel."

"It's been a long way from steak."

"Your stomach's too weak for steak."

"My stomach's too weak for gruel."

She sighed and looked at the mess on the bed. "Well, looks like you're back to gruel."

"Uh-huh." And they made snowballs in hell. He let his fingers flirt with the collar of her shirtwaist. "So you were fretting on losing me, huh?"

"I was concerned." Her gaze moved to something outside the window.

He smiled, amazed she could sit there so prim and proper while he unbuttoned the top two buttons of her dress. The pulse in her throat came into view. It was tapping fast and hard. "Truth be told, darlin', were our positions switched, I'd have been nervous about losing you, too."

He watched as she swallowed hard, her gaze still fixed on the view outside the window. "You would?"

"Uh-huh." He pressed his finger on her pulse and smiled when it took off racing. "I've gotten used to having you around."

"Oh."

"You honestly find those clouds so attention-getting?"

"No." Honest as always, yet he noticed she didn't drag her gaze away.

"'Cause, if you could see your way to dragging your attention back here, I've got a mind to do some sparking."

That had her jerking her whole body his way. "Are you out of your mind?"

If he hadn't known how concerned she'd been, her outrage would have put canyon-deep holes in his pride. "Nope."

He got another button free before she caught onto his game. She grabbed his hand, stopping him from getting to the flesh he wanted to pay some attention to.

"You can't. I mean, we can't…" She sputtered to a halt, no doubt searching for a polite term for what he wanted. She finally gave up and settled for logic. "You're hurt."

He rubbed his knuckles up and down the prim row of buttons she was guarding so diligently. "I'll allow we'll have to curb your wild side a bit."

"I do not have a wild side!"

"Sure enough, you do, darlin'," he countered. "And I count myself a lucky man for it."

She stared at him, obviously looking for a reasonable argument that would dissuade him from what she saw as idiocy. He couldn't help a smile. After having her care for him for the last week, her hands continually touching his body, her sweet scent always around, her near admission of love. Hell! Short of a bullet in the brain, he wasn't about to be dissuaded.

"The bed is a mess," she huffed, not yet recognizing the futility of arguing with him.

"Can't argue that."

He shoved the covers down. She sprang off the bed as if he'd lit a match to her posterior. "What are you doing? Get back in that bed!"

Lord, she was cute when she hovered. "You know, darlin', I always thought nagging women were like crows, nothing but an irritation."

Her hands landed on her hips in a battle stance. "I do not nag."

"I have to argue there, but I've decided I like it."

"I couldn't care less." The lace of her collar fluttered against her throat with the deep breaths she was taking. "May I ask what you're doing?"

He eased his legs over the side of the bed. "I'm heading to your room."

"Any particular reason?" She reached up and began re-doing the buttons he'd undone.

"Yup." He took a steadying breath as he pushed his torso upright. "Seeing as you won't lie with me in a puddle of soup, I thought I'd switch beds."

"I am not lying down with you, period, so you might as well get back in that bed."

Pain laced his side. He took a few breaths to control it. He wanted to wrap his arm around his ribs, but he knew, if he showed such weakness, she'd use it against him. "You can't have any argument against a clean bed."

She got the last button done up proper. As soon as the button landed in the hole, her spine snapped tight as if welcoming reinforcements. "You're a hard-headed man, Mr. MacIntyre, but I can see you need to attempt this foolishness in order to see the sense in staying put."

He eyed her under his brow. "That a challenge?"

"Merely a call to common sense."

"Uh-huh." He braced his hands on the bed. "And, if I take up this challenge, what do I win?"

"Your health."

"And if you win?"

"You stay in bed and give up this outrageous behavior until you're better."

Did him a world of good to know she didn't want him giving up the behavior altogether. "Not much incentive for me to stay put."

Her sigh was long suffering. "I suppose you have a better wager?"

"Heck, yeah."

Her hands were back on her hips. "I suppose you're not going to lie down until you have your say?"

"Nope."

She made a quick motion with her hand. "Let's hear it."

"If I make it to the other room, you curl up beside me for a little sparking."

"You're too ill for sparking."

"Lucky for you, I see it differently."

"So I see." She stared at him a minute, her expression unreadable. "All right. You make it to the other room, and I'll do what you want."

"The term I used was sparking, but I can settle for what I want."

She shook her head as if at the end of her rope, but he noticed her eyes crinkled at the corners while she did it. The woman wasn't as set against the idea as she let on. Before he could push to his feet, she held out her hand and halted him. "If I win, you do as I say for the duration of your recovery. Until I say you're recovered."

He held out his hand. "Deal."

She shook it. "Deal."

She stepped back. He took long, slow breaths in preparation for the ordeal of standing up. On the fourth, he pushed himself to his feet. He made it in the direction of up, but his ribs forced him to stay humped over like an old man. Before he could stop it, a groan snaked from between his lips.

Elizabeth stood as still as a statue, watching his shuffling progression to the door. Opening the damned slab of wood was almost his undoing. The only thing that kept him moving through the mind-numbing pain was his refusal to act like a baby in front of his wife. She already had a low enough opinion of his strength. He had to brace himself on the door latch of the next bedroom. It gave unexpectedly under his hand. The jerk knocked him off-balance. Black agony swept over him. He stumbled and would have fallen, except for the shoulder inserted under his arm.

"You're the most stubborn man."

"Just determined," he groaned.

"Why?"

He opened his eyes and stared at the bun bouncing along beneath his chin as they shuffled to the bed. "Sad fact is, I got this never-ending hunger for my wife, and stubborn woman that she is, she won't appease it unless I prove myself to her."

The little quiver that shook her bun, he put down to outrage. She didn't respond to him, however, until she levered him onto the clean bed.

Her face was cherry-red when she did. "I don't know why you persist in this ridiculous teasing. There's no way you can...uhm, hold yourself, I mean..." She pushed her hair off her face in exasperation, then blurted out. "You know what I mean!"

He pulled her down beside him and went to work on the buttons of her dress.

"This is one of those times when a woman has to take charge." He could see from her frown that she didn't take his meaning. The angle of their position made it impossible for him to undo more than five buttons. "Like you did in the meadow."

"Oh."

"Though you might want to take off your dress first."

She paused, seeming unable to take a breath.

"Please," he added.

She sighed, told him he was a scandalous man, and went to the door and locked it before coming back. Halfway to the bed, she stopped, reached up and released her hair from its bun. It spilled in auburn glory past her waist.

He knew he was grinning like an idiot. "Lord, you're something, darlin'."

Her smile was shyness tinged with confidence. It took a long time for her fingers to get those buttons undone. By the time she let the dress slide down her arms to pool at her feet, he was panting like a winded race, horse and the shyness had left her smile to be replaced with sheer witchery. She stood before him in her lacy camisole, pantaloons, and delicate white stockings.

"You liked that," she said, a wealth of satisfaction in her voice as she approached the bed. As she stepped into a beam of sunlight, he could clearly make out the curve of her waist, the soft pink of her nipples and the tempting triangle of her pussy.

He managed an eloquent, "Yeah."

She leaned over, careful not to jostle his side. He reached up and curled his hand around her neck, urging her into his kiss. Her mouth felt good over his. She tasted hot and spicy. Womanly. "I missed you, Elizabeth."

He felt a fool for such an emotional admission. He hadn't meant to say it, but it had just sort of popped out. Instead of withdrawing or laughing, she sealed her mouth tighter to his. The ardor in her kiss increased tenfold. He took full advantage, sliding his hand to her breast, smiling when she gasped and pressed harder into his hand. Her nipple was already hard. He rubbed it with his thumb. It pulled up tighter. Harder. Begging for more. Her gasp whispered past his ear. Her eyelids drifted shut.

"You like that," he whispered into her mouth, no less satisfied than she'd been.

She nodded, squashing her nose into his cheek.

"Ease up here, and I'll make you feel even better."

He didn't have to tell her twice. The bed dipped as she braced first one knee and then the other beside his hip. Her hands straddled his torso. She smelled of sunshine and vanilla. Of woman and rising need. He could never get enough of her. He stroked her breasts with his fingers, smiling as the calluses caught on the delicate material of her camisole. Her gaze met his. With taunting slowness, she lowered her head, letting him feel the whisper of her breath, the heat of her body, the promise in her emerald eyes. Her hair fell around him, a silky curtain as she slowly, delicately, traced his smile with the tip of her tongue, sending a frisson of sensation licking through his body. When she raised her head, his smile rested on her full lips, but there was a provocative quality there now. A sultry cast that had his heart pumping and his cock pounding with anticipation.

Keeping her eyes locked with his, she eased her breast toward his mouth. It hovered just out of reach. He couldn't lift his head to capture her pouting nipple. He waited for her to realize she had to lower herself more. If possible, her smile grew broader as she daintily prodded his lips with the swollen tip. He opened his mouth and accepted the sweet offering against the cushioning softness of his tongue. She tasted all the sweeter for the anticipation. He plumped her breast with his fingers, bringing her harder against his mouth, laving her through the cotton of her camisole, using the damp material to increase the friction of his caress.

Her soft moans were sweet music to his ears. When she threw her head back and groaned, he pulled the cotton underthing away. She was hot against his tongue. The slightest hint of salt tanged her flesh. He swept the crest of her breast, catching more of her essence before drawing her deeply into his mouth. He suckled strongly, discovering what she liked. Her cries of delight and then protest when he pulled back, had him hotter than the Fourth of July.

"Just switching sides," he explained.

She adjusted her position to make it easier on him.

Her moans were pretty constant by the time she said, "I want you."

He kissed the hard nipple hovering above his face. "Not yet."

She pulled back. Her hands at the buttonfly of his long johns made mincemeat of his determination. As each button popped its hole, his cock received a dancing caress.

"Now." She clearly wasn't in a mood to be denied.

He slid his hand from her breast to the slit in her pantaloons. The material was wet with her juices. His fingers slid smoothly through her thick cream. He parted her folds, stroking her as he swirled a path to her vagina. As his finger breached the tight portal, she freed his cock. The cool air of the room was both a balm and torment on his heated flesh. The tips of her fingers glided up and down his length in a gentle demand that tore another moan from his throat. He gritted his teeth against the fiery demand that he take charge. Instead, he braced himself to endure. There was a lot to say for letting a woman take charge. He slid a finger into her pussy, groaning when her muscles clenched hard on him. He wanted in her now.

"Straddle me and then lean back against my knees so you won't hurt your palms."

She didn't immediately move into action. She stared so long at his arousal, trapped so gently in her hand that he thought he'd embarrass himself from the enjoyment he got from her pleasure.

"I like you like this," she informed him.

"You'll like me a lot better in a minute."

She chuckled and petted him. Actually petted him while he strained and jerked. She moved away, took off her pantaloons, and then, light as a feather, she straddled his hips. He curled his fingers around her ribs, supporting her. As if she'd been riding him all her life, she fell into position. With exquisite care, she settled on him, taking him in slow, delicate increments until he thought she might tear him apart.

She looked into his eyes. Her expression fierce. "You're mine."

He couldn't believe it, but a laugh found its way through the searing pleasure. "No one here's arguing."

She repeated it again, a bit desperately. He wanted to respond, but she suddenly took his cock fully into the clenching grasp of her pussy, and his world narrowed to a tight, hot focus of building desire that allowed nothing but response to the woman who held him so close. She was in control and loving it. He could do nothing but surrender and glory in the wildness she denied having.

Chapter Nineteen

❧

She felt like an intruder entering the office. Elizabeth hesitated, called herself a fool, and crossed the threshold. Book work needed to be done. Just because Asa had been much more eager to stay in bed since that afternoon two days ago, didn't mean the rest of their problems had disappeared. As depressing as it would be, she needed to see exactly where the ranch was financially. And that meant she had to not only step one foot past the door, she had to go all the way into the room, seat herself at the desk, and finish what needed to be done.

As she opened the drapes on her way to the desk, she looked around. It was distinctly male terrain. It was all so familiar; the dark paneling, the ink-splattered leather blotter, the heavy desk, the big chair stationed so impressively behind it. First her father's and now her husband's, the study was a room designed to reflect power. She waited for the feeling of suffocation to swamp her as it usually did. She stared at the desk a good two minutes before she realized it wasn't happening and why.

For the first time since she could remember, she didn't see, in her mind, her father sitting in that big chair, a frown on his face, eager to hand out the list of today's failures. Instead, she saw Asa's image, half-smiling, patiently waiting while she stumbled through an explanation. Never rushing, never hurrying, simply waiting her out. The man was truly a magician. She didn't think anyone could dispel her unease with this room, but he seemed to have done it.

She trailed her fingers over the desk. It was tan, smoothed by age and hard. Just like Asa. As she flipped open the ledger, she looked around the room with new eyes. Instead of seeing the past, she saw its potential. With some redecorating, the office could actually be a pleasant place. Maybe even pleasant enough that she'd consider seducing her husband here. Creating some nice memories would go a long way to shedding the old.

She shook her head over her licentious thoughts. She was turning into a scandal all right. She settled into the big wing-backed chair behind the desk. She closed her eyes and breathed in the scents of leather, man and ink.

She flipped open the ledger on the desk and ran her fingers down the entries. She was so lost in thought, she didn't immediately recognize what she saw. When she did, she saw red. Not only was her husband the sexiest man in the territory, he was also one of the most conniving sons of a bitch she'd ever met.

A squeak of the wood floor jerked her eyes from the books. Asa stood in the door. Pale but resigned.

"You son of a bitch," she said.

"You know?"

"Were you ever planning on telling me?"

"Not if I could help it," he admitted.

"You lied to me." She thought the pain would split her open like a ripe melon.

"I never lied to you."

"You didn't tell me we're going to lose the ranch."

"We're not losing the ranch."

"You didn't tell me the bank didn't extend our note."

"I didn't want to worry you."

She sat as still as stone, feeling like she'd break apart inside. "You didn't trust me."

"Dammit, Elizabeth, you knew we were close to bankruptcy. That's why you married me."

"You said we were partners."

"We are."

"No, we're not." They could never be equals if he could keep something like this from her. "We're nothing more than a man and his paramour."

"If you don't want your mouth washed out with soap, you'd better be watching your language."

She looked at him. God, did he think he could scare her now? "Don't you try and threaten me."

"I never make threats."

"No," she agreed. "You don't need to. You just spin fairy tales out of half-truths, and then, when you're caught, you claim you never lied." She stood slowly. Carefully. Not much of her dignity remained, but she was going to hold onto what she had left. She crossed the room until she was only two feet away from him. She tilted her head back until she could look into his eyes. Eyes that were storm gray, reflecting a determination she felt pulsing in her own veins.

"You had me," she told him. "You had me cold. I believed everything you said and did. I thought you liked me as I am. I thought—God help me for my stupidity— that you respected me." A hoarse laugh escaped before she could smother it. "My father was right. I am a fool."

"Your father didn't know squat."

"He knew enough to know that a man would use my weakness against me."

Asa crossed his arms over his chest. His splayed feet and broad shoulders blocked the doorway. His message was as clear as the anger on his face. She wasn't going anywhere until he had his say. She settled her weight evenly between her feet and forced her arms to relax at her side. Two could play this game.

"Sure enough," Asa said, "your father got you twisted up inside. To the point you'd marry two complete strangers to hold onto a piece of land you'd be better off selling and living off the proceeds, but you wouldn't do that."

"I made a promise."

"Yeah. The kind of promise that lingers. The kind bound up tight with guilt and failure." Her surprise must have shone through because he nodded his head. "Yeah. I've made a few of those myself. Back when I was a kid, lying in the alley, bloody from a beating, whining because no one ever told me 'Welcome home.' I made a promise to whatever God was listening, told him that, if he could see his way to getting me a home, a lady and a bit of respect to go with it, I'd do what I had to not to let him down in the meantime. I never thought anyone was listening, but then you came along and that promise was dropped in my lap."

"I don't understand."

"Yeah, I know. You're so busy tarring me with your father's brush, you can't credit me with common decency."

She crossed her arms against her chest. "Now you're saying it's decent to lie?"

He snorted. "I'm saying I never thought you'd ride this mustang through to the finish, but I expected better than this."

"You thought I'd be so bowled over by what you make me feel in bed that I'd overlook your highhandedness?"

He pushed away from the doorjamb. "I expected you to understand that I was trying to spare you this worry on top of all the others you'd taken on."

"You didn't think I'd want to know?"

"What difference would it have made?" he asked, pinning her with the truth. "What would you have done differently than I did?"

He waited, clearly expecting an answer, but she didn't have one. She didn't know what she would have done differently. She didn't even know what she was mad about. She just knew. "You should have told me."

"So you said." He motioned to the books. "I've got to see a man about a contract. You have a good look at the books, and when I get back, you can give me an earful about how else I've let you down."

He spun on his heel. While she'd never seen the man do more than amble, today he stalked to the front door. Granted, he favored his right side due to his half-healed ribs, but he was the absolute picture of male outrage. Lord knows, she'd seen it enough to recognize it.

Something she didn't initially recognize then registered as guilt pricked her conscience. How had she ended up the guilty one? The front door slammed. She crossed to the window and watched as Asa stormed toward the barn. The stupid man hadn't even put on a coat. He got to the big oak in back and stopped, leaning against it for support.

She thought maybe his ribs were screaming, but then his shoulders, those broad shoulders she'd never seen anyway but squared, drooped. His head bowed. He took off his hat. She couldn't see exactly what he was doing, but she'd seen him run his hand down his face enough times to recognize the gesture for what it was. Pain.

Unease tore her insides. The prickle of guilt developed claws. She'd hurt him. She'd honestly hurt the man. Oh God, more than she didn't want the ability for him to hurt her, she didn't want to be able to hurt him. Dammit! This was all his fault. If he'd trusted her. If he'd only told her the whole truth, she could have understood. She would have been fine. They could have faced it together.

But this was… She sighed as he pushed away from the tree. This was… She stopped and admitted the truth. *This* was totally in character for the man.

Come here.

How many times had he said that to her and then offered his shoulder as comfort? How many times, in their brief acquaintance, had he stepped between her and something he felt was a threat? Brent. Aaron. Millicent. He had shoulders as broad as the mountains that guarded her home. Since the day they'd met, he'd done nothing but use them to shield her. Heck, he scooped up problems and discarded them the way other men picked up stones. So why had she expected him to act any different when it came to bad news? He'd been upfront from the beginning that he thought ladies needed tender touches and gentle handling. Keeping bad news from her was nothing more than another protective gesture.

She bit her lip as he disappeared into the barn. No doubt he intended to ride Shameless to the railroad to get the contract. The ride would kill his ribs. Clint could handle the asking, but this was too important to the ranch for Asa to risk it to anyone else. He'd made her a promise. He clearly intended to keep it.

I never expected you to ride this mustang through to the finish.

What had he meant by that? He couldn't mean he hadn't expected her to keep to her end of their agreement. That didn't make any sense. They were married. Something like that couldn't just be set aside. She watched as Shameless trotted out of the barn, Asa on his back. She held her breath waiting—no, hoping—for a glance, but, without so much as a turn of his head, Asa rode out. She let the curtain drop back into place.

Oh Lord, she didn't know what to feel inside. She was mad, confused and guilty. The ledger, lying open on the desk, beckoned. Maybe she'd find the road out of this mess in there. Maybe, when Asa got home, they could talk. If they couldn't put this misunderstanding behind them, she could at least apologize. She crossed to the desk, sighed, flopped down in the chair and spun the ledger toward her. Son of a bitch, she was a fool.

* * * * *

Asa pulled up Shameless in front of the house just as dusk was falling. He couldn't remember a time when he'd felt worse. And not because his ribs were screaming. That he could live with. The knowledge that he was failing Elizabeth, that was a whole different animal altogether. A big-clawed, ugly-toothed monster he couldn't beat back.

Someone had gotten to the railroad. There was no earthly reason why they couldn't take the cattle two weeks early. No reason for them to have changed their minds from yesterday to today, but they had. Irrefutably. No amount of reasoning or threats would change it. Lord above, he'd tried everything in his considerable repertoire. Shameless pawed the ground, anxious to get to the barn. Asa reined him in. He looked up at the mountains looming beyond the house.

"If y'all are planning to do some guarding, this would be the time to do it."

The only answer he got was a storm cloud cresting the peak. It wasn't a comforting sight. He looked around the ranch. It was a damned nice lay. He could understand the desperation Elizabeth's pa had felt to hold onto it. He could never agree with what he'd done to Elizabeth. For that, he'd like to shoot him on sight, but he could understand what drove him. The same desperation festered in his own innards. Not for the land, though. He wouldn't kill a man for land. He looked to the house where the lights burned bright and beckoning. For the loss of Elizabeth, he'd kill twenty men. That kind of pain was going to take some getting used to. Probably a lifetime.

She was never going to forgive him for not holding the ranch. She saw him as a hero, someone who could beat all the odds. Only this time, the deck was stacked against him. This time, he wasn't going to pull it off. And when she learned the truth of it, she'd leave him eating her dust so fast, he'd be choking for a month of Sundays. He nudged Shameless into the barn. It had been sweet while it lasted, though. Mighty sweet.

He settled Shameless, then stood in the barn door and braced himself for the tongue-lashing awaiting him at the house. He deserved every angry word. He should have seen this coming earlier and taken more aggressive steps to halt it. Hunching his shoulders against the cold encroachment of night, he made his way to the kitchen door. Rich scents of dinner swept his way on an errant breeze. His stomach growled and his mouth watered. Damned, he was going to miss eating regular, too.

As soon as his boot hit the top step, the back door opened. He suppressed a groan. He'd been hoping she'd spend the evening avoiding him. He wasn't in the mood for another argument. He should have known better. Elizabeth had a penchant for facing life head on.

"You've got to be freezing."

As first words went, those weren't the ones he thought he'd be hearing.

"I'm fine."

Her hand went to his upper arm. "Come on in."

He eyed her warily as he crossed the threshold. Like she'd done every day for the last six weeks, she took his hat and set it on the hook on the wall.

"Thank you." What else could he say in the face of this concern that didn't make sense?

"Supper's ready. I hope you like chicken fricassee."

He sat in the chair, but not before checking it unobtrusively to see if the legs were sabotaged. It was as solid as a rock. "I'm sure it'll be fine."

She placed a mouth-watering concoction in front of him. Two seconds later, she served herself. He'd watched her serve both, so that left out poisoning.

He applied himself to his meal like it was his last, 'cause, sure as shooting, it was. He was halfway through his plate when he realized she was eating, too. Not picking at her food like he expected, seeing as the way they'd parted, but actually eating. And with enjoyment. He was so shocked, he stared.

She noticed. "Is something wrong?"

Not one for beating around the bush, he said, "You're eating."

"It's supper time."

"You never eat when you're upset."

"That's true."

"When I left here this afternoon, you were mad enough to have target practice with my heart."

She took a delicate bite of chicken stew. Washed it down with some milk, and then took a bite of biscuit. He watched her. His gaze lingered on her lips. A predictable response started trickling through his body. Damn! The woman could heat his blood just by eating.

She ran her tongue over her lips, scooping crumbs and butter as she went. The trickle of desire roared into a flood. He dragged his gaze from her lips and found her staring at him. In her eyes, there was humor, knowledge, and something softer he couldn't name. When she finally deigned to answer him, her response cleared up nothing. "I admit I was mad this morning, but you're overreacting. I was thinking more along the lines of buckshot in your posterior."

God help him, he could picture it—her with a shotgun and him with a stinging butt. "Buckshot, huh?"

"I wanted to make a dent in your arrogance."

"And you figure I keep my arrogance in my hindquarters?"

She shrugged. "It seemed as likely a spot as any."

"I'm going to miss your sense of humor, darlin'."

"You're admitting I have one, finally?"

"I've always known you have one. It's just been a darn shame the care you have of it."

She answered his smile with a sigh. "I admit I wasn't the best of wives for a while."

"You came along just fine," he answered, as serious as she was.

"I was thinking while you were gone."

"That when you came up with the buckshot plan?"

She shook her head and motioned for him to eat. "No. That's when I realized how unreasonable I've been."

"You, darlin'?"

"Don't go teasing, Asa."

"I am serious here."

"No, you're not. You're in a strange mood, but I'm hoping you'll be back to your old self by the time we finish our conversation."

"Must have been some understanding you came to."

She shrugged. She didn't speak, just waited. From the way her eyes were glued to his plate, he figured she was waiting on him to eat. He took a bite. As if on cue, she started talking. "Ever since we married, you've been taking care of me."

He shrugged, hampered to do more by a mouthful of food.

She didn't seem to mind his lack of response. "After I got over my mad this morning, I started thinking on what kind of man you are." She patted his hand. "You're a taking-care-of man. You handle everything by yourself. You always have. It was unreasonable of me to expect that, just because we're married, you'd automatically understand you no longer have to do things on your own."

"I don't?"

"No," she said gently, as if she thought this was going to hurt. "I blame it on a lack of family life that you don't know you're supposed to treat your wife like a partner rather than a child."

"And your family taught you this?"

She shook her head "No. Millie and Doc did."

"And I need to follow their example?"

She nodded earnestly. "Yes."

And she thought he was in a strange mood. She sat there across from him, looking as delicate as a flower in a white lacy-necked blouse tucked into a blue serge skirt, and she didn't want him to protect her? The woman was clearly out of her mind.

"You spent all morning thinking on this?"

"Yes." This time, after she patted his hand, she ended the motion by curling her fingers around his. "We can do this, Asa."

He stared into her earnest face. Her beautiful green eyes framed by their sooty lashes glowed like gems in the lamplight. She was the most beautiful thing in the world, and, for a few precious weeks in his life, she'd shown him heaven, but she was looking for a hero. God, he hated to be the one to break the news to her. "You were right when you said there aren't any heroes."

She looked confused.

He pulled his hand from hers before she could do the rejecting. "I promised you I was going to save this ranch, Elizabeth, and I aim to do it."

"I know you will."

He pushed his plate away, his dinner half-eaten. "This isn't one of your books, Elizabeth. You'll keep the ranch, but it won't be clean or pretty. There are going to be sacrifices."

She frowned at his plate, then at him. "I told you, Asa. I'm not a child. I understand responsibility and sacrifice."

"Even if your pal Aaron is one of those sacrifices?"

She sat back in her chair, guard up. "What are you talking about?"

"In order to save your ranch, I'm going to take Aaron down."

"What does Aaron have to do with anything?"

"He's the one who's been driving the Rocking C into the ground."

She bristled immediately. "That's absurd. Aaron is my friend."

"I know you see it that way, but, as I mentioned before, with friends like him, you don't need to be hunting up enemies."

"You don't know what you're talking about."

"Darlin', the one thing I know is that, if you're counting Aaron as a friend, you'd best start packing something against snakebite."

"You don't know him as well as I do."

"I know him well enough."

Her hands balled into fists. Her voice dropped from warm to icy politeness. "I know you've always been jealous of our closeness, but you're going too far."

Her withdrawal struck him like a slap. He shook his head. "Got to disagree with you there. I'm saving that for tomorrow."

Fact was, he was saving a lot for tomorrow. Including his goodbyes, because, sure as hell, when he called out Aaron for his back-stabbing, Elizabeth wasn't going to waste a lot of time sending her husband packing.

She interrupted his thoughts. "I know from your notes in the books that you suspect someone of sabotaging the Rocking C."

And she wanted him to tell her he didn't suspect Aaron. He ran his hands through his hair. "There's no sense dancing around the subject. Aaron's the one behind the Rocking C's troubles."

"My father made some mistakes...?" Her hands disappeared from the tabletop. He assumed from the way her spine was razor-back sharp, she was clutching her fingers in her lap. "Number one being taking Aaron on as a partner?" she asked, and then went on before he could answer. "Do you have proof?"

She looked at him. It was clear in her eyes she was hoping against hope that she wasn't going to lose another dream to reality. He swore long and hard. Why did he have to be the messenger? Why couldn't her father have had the brains God gave a rock, and seen Aaron for the snake in the grass he was?

"Nothing the law would cozy up to," he hedged.

"Which means you don't have proof."

Christ, he could feel the knots that bound them together unraveling. The small part of him that hoped she'd believe him, despite her lifetime belief in Aaron, started to die. "I've got the facts. Whether they'll hold up in a court of law isn't the point."

"It is to me."

"Yeah. I figured that."

"What are these facts?"

"First off, Aaron's set to lose everything without the water rights you grant him."

"So? He knows those aren't in danger."

"He set you up to lose the ranch by furthering that bank note when any prudent advice would be to hold tight while you were solvent."

"I don't agree."

The last drop of hope in him died. "No shock there." Wanting this over, he pushed on. Words fell over words as he let the explanation spew forth. "Then this fancy pants Brent comes along. Man goes out of his way to hunt you up and, from what Old Sam says, seemed to know exactly what to say to you to make you tumble like an old stack of hay."

"I was stupid."

"You were set up."

"Who says?"

"I do, and so do the men."

"What do you know?"

"More than you, apparently, because there was no danger of you losing the ranch until you married me." He shot her an amused glance. "Appears you spiked their guns when you took matters into your own hands. The way Cougar and I figure it, they couldn't be sure I'd continue to allow the water, so they had to drive it under."

"They called in the note." Desperation entered her voice.

"Yeah. They delivered the news when you and I were in town that day. And guess who was walking out of the office right before I walked in?"

"Aaron, but that's not surprising. It is the only bank in town."

"It's mighty strange that, a week before, they were willing to extend the note until spring with my savings against the balance. But, when I brought the money in, all I could manage was one month."

"That doesn't mean Aaron had anything to do with it."

"No, it doesn't, but it does point a finger that way."

"But Aaron—"

He didn't want to hear her defend good old Aaron. He cut her off. "As soon as it looked like I was going to get the cattle rounded up for the railroad deal, I got bushwhacked."

"That could have been anyone."

"Except that foreman of Aaron's was there when I made the deal."

"It's still supposition."

Asa threw his napkin on the table. "Yeah. Just like today, when I went to deliver the cattle a week early, and I find the railroad is wary of taking them. Seems a rumor's been spread that the reason I want to bring them in early is because they're sick and I want to unload them before it becomes obvious."

Her rigid posture collapsed. "Oh, no."

"Yeah. Oh, no."

"What are we going to do?"

They weren't doing anything. "Tomorrow, I'm going into town and settle this."

She caught his arm as he was trying to pass. "You're not going to do anything foolish, are you?"

"Depends on what your definition of foolish is."

"Asa..." All the uncertainty in the world rested in her gaze. He felt her lack of faith like a blow. Not because he expected her to believe in him blindly, but because she'd believed in him at all. He'd been a fool reaching for rainbows. He'd had no business taking her with him.

"I'm sorry, Elizabeth. I should have negotiated a sale for you."

She looked at him, confused. "That wasn't part of our deal."

"It should have been. One look at the books and I should have done the right thing."

She stood. Her hands on his chest prevented his leaving. "You did what I wanted."

"Yeah, that's the hell of it. I used what you wanted to lasso a dream."

"Asa."

He stepped back. "You were right to distrust me."

She stared at him for a brief moment, leaving him feeling like he hung over a cliff with nothing to break his fall. "No. I don't think so."

He shrugged, facing the inevitable. "You will tomorrow."

"Because you're going to confront Aaron?"

"Yes." She wouldn't be safe until the man was out of the picture. By the time she realized it, he'd be gone.

"Asa, I don't believe Aaron would betray me like you say, but I agree it looks bad."

"Uh-huh."

The breath she took was audible. "I want to be there tomorrow."

"No."

"Why not?"

"It's not safe."

"Even if you thought Aaron would hurt me, which he won't, what do you think is going to happen with people all around?"

"I don't want you there."

"Tough."

She caught his arm before he could slip out the door. "I'm going to be there."

"I'm not arguing with you."

She didn't seem put off by the finality in his tone. "You can be a bear, Asa MacIntyre."

"You're not the first to tell me that."

Angling out the door, Asa heard her footsteps behind him as he headed up the stairs. The woman was as tenacious as a badger. He paused outside their bedroom door. Somehow, it seemed wrong to sleep with his wife when he knew she'd be kicking his sorry butt out the door in the morning. Two heel clicks and he knew she was right behind him. Asa could smell her scent—woman, vanilla, and a touch of something he had never figured out—as he wrenched open the door to their room. To hell with the right thing. Asa wanted one last night. He'd be paying the rest of his life anyway, what was one more infraction? She wanted a hero? Give him a feather tick and he could be all the hero she needed. It was outside the bedroom he was having trouble.

She was right behind him as he entered the room. No doubt high on indignation. A smile tugged. Sometimes the woman didn't know when to quit.

He turned and scooped her into his arms when her momentum would have caused her to shoot on past. "There's a point when you ought to pull back and regroup."

There was nothing of the turbulence he expected to see on her face. Just a bone-deep satisfaction that softened the edge of her determined smile. "Why?"

Now there was a question he didn't want to answer. "Because, sometimes, it helps you to see things clearer."

She looped her arms around his neck. "And here I thought you were going to pout."

"Men don't pout." They pounded walls, or even took advantage of sweet, misguided women, but they never pouted.

"I'm glad to hear it." She snuggled closer. "Everything's going to be fine, Asa. When you talk to Aaron, you'll see."

"And if I don't?"

He felt her shrug all the way up his body. "It'll still be fine."

He wished he could be so sure. His body reacted predictably to the closeness of hers. His hands, instead of putting some distance between them like he told them to, encouraged her to arch so her hips matched his better. He really was sinking to an all-time low. He hummed as she snuggled closer. "You got something on your mind?"

"I thought a little distraction might be in order."

Damn. When had she learned to purr like that?

"Distraction?" he asked. He tried to revive his honor, but, as fast as she was slipping buttons through the holes on his shirt and undershirt, he didn't think honor stood a chance. Elizabeth could be mighty determined.

"All right, not a distraction." She sighed in satisfaction as she spread his shirt and longjohns off his shoulders. "More of a reminder."

"Reminder?" That hoarse croak wasn't much of a deterrent, but damn, she was a quick study when it came to pleasing him.

"Yes," she answered, her voice strong and confident. "You're in a strange mood. I don't like it."

"You figured seducing me would fix that?"

"Maybe." She smiled a witchy smile that sent his blood surging through his veins. "But it will surely remind you where you belong."

As if he needed reminding. He stroked her hair. Her bun slipped to the side. He undid a few of the hairpins as she pressed her lips dead center on his chest. Her hair tumbled down. Her tongue touched his flesh. His breath hissed between his teeth. He dropped his good intentions like a hot potato. "I should be reminding you that things don't always work out like we plan."

She kissed her way to his navel. "But?"

"But I've never been that long on honor."

"Uh-huh." She dipped her tongue into his belly button. His stomach jerked inward.

"Hey! That tickles."

She grinned. He could feel her lips stretch across his stomach. "Sorry."

"You don't sound sorry." His hands, in direct contradiction to his words, were urging her to do it again.

"If you promise to be quiet, I'll apologize."

Her lips wandered further south.

"If you're planning on what I think," he croaked, "you'd best save your apologizing until I get a wall at my back."

She shook her head emphatically. Her fingers worked the buttons on his denims. "You're just going to have to stand tall, Mr. MacIntyre."

The last button popped free. With a move he had no idea she knew, she slid his pants down his thighs. Her breath brushed his straining cock through his long johns, setting fires raging. "Because I'm not giving up until I get what I want."

God help him, she sounded as stubbornly petulant as a kid refusing to leave a candy store. "I wouldn't want to deprive you of something you like," he countered.

Letting go of her hair, he unfastened the buttons on his longjohns. He wished he could see her expression, but she was staring hard at his hands, her hands on her thighs, her fingertips twitching as if she wanted to be doing the job.

When he had the last button on his fly free, he cupped the back of her head in his hand. With the other, he eased his painfully hard cock into the light.

"Oh, my goodness."

He hoped that note in her voice was awe. With steady pressure, he urged her forward. Her breath reached him first. Warm and moist, it blew over the sensitive head in a sensual caress. The vertebrae in her neck were a delicate ladder beneath his fingers. The flesh under her chin, soft as down as he applied pressure, tilting her head back.

The look she sent him was questioning.

"I want to see," he explained. From this angle, he wouldn't miss a thing.

"How do I do this right?"

He couldn't believe she was turning shy after taking the bull by the horns. "I don't think you can do this wrong."

She sat back on her heels. "You don't think?"

"I'm as green at this as you."

Her small smile told him that pleased her to no end. "Do you like it when I touch you?"

"He'd be mighty grateful."

She ran two fingers down his shaft, stopping when they collided with his fingers.

"He?"

He shrugged. "Nothing that ugly could be female."

"Oh, he's not ugly." She stroked him again, her voice as soft as her touch. A featherlight caress that had him gritting his teeth. She paused again when she reached his hand. "Does he have a name?"

He slid his hand over hers, showing her he liked a bit more pressure. "Johnny."

"Why Johnny?"

"Cause when I was of an age to be naming things, he had a tendency to be always jumping up."

He couldn't believe how good her laugh felt against his skin.

She leaned forward and placed a chaste kiss on the tip of his cock. "Hello, Johnny."

He shuddered as fire shot down his shaft and spread like a conflagration up his spine. Sheer pleasure drew his balls tight.

The smile she gave him left him in no doubt that she knew what she was doing to him. A drop of pre-come beaded the tip of his penis.

Elizabeth eyed it speculatively. "You liked that."

"Yeah."

His reward was a squeeze of her hand. "I could do it again."

He had to struggle to find his voice. When he found the words, they came out as more growl than drawl. "We'd be obliged."

This time, the kiss wasn't so chaste. This time, she used her tongue, sweeping it around the swollen crest, lapping up all the creamy moisture she found there. When she pulled back, her expression was considering.

Though he knew he might regret it, he had to ask, "What?"

"You taste good." She ran her tongue over her lips as if searching for more. The expressions that crossed her face traveled the distance from surprise to interest.

It was the interest that had him throbbing in her hand.

Shit! She was going to kill him for sure.

"What else would you like?" she asked.

Now, that was a loaded question. Another bead of come appeared on the head of his penis. As much as he loved the feel of her tongue lapping him with the delicacy of a cat, he had another fantasy he'd like played out.

When she would have leaned forward, he forestalled her. "Wait."

He didn't answer the question in her eyes with words. Using his hands on her shoulders to keep her still, he leaned forward until the tip of his penis brushed her lips. When she would have parted them. He shook his head. "Just stay still."

Using the lush curves as a guide, and using only the tip of his cock as a brush, he painted her pouting lips with his pre-come, taking great care to cover every inch of that exotic mouth with his essence. All the while, she watched his expression with those big, unfathomable eyes. When he was done, her lips glistened and her breath came in short pants.

Lord above, she was a gorgeous sight with his come on her lips, her hair curling about her face and her dress buttoned prim and proper to her chin. And selfish bastard that he was, he wanted more.

"Unbutton your dress," he ordered.

She cast a quick glance at the window.

"No one can see," he assured her. "I want to see your breasts while I fuck your face." Leaning forward, he smoothed another drop on her generous lips.

The sensation was exquisite. Like fire encased in luxurious silk. He only lasted until her fingers got the fifth button free before he pushed forward. There was an awkward bump on her teeth as she struggled to open wide enough to admit his cock, and then he was buried in the molten heat of her mouth.

He closed his eyes against the need to pump hard and deep and moaned, "God, darlin', your mouth feels good."

Her hands settled to the backs of his thighs. She flicked him with her tongue, by accident or design, he didn't know. His body didn't care. His knees went week. His palms fell flat back against the wall. He braced his weight on his forearms while she suckled his cock.

He tried to hold still, to let her adjust to his size and presence, but the soft swirls of her tongue over his sensitive flesh had his balls on fire. He had to move.

His sudden surge into her mouth caught Elizabeth by surprise. One moment she was pleasantly sucking on the tip of his cock, and the next, she was struggling to breathe as his huge cock forced her jaws wide and hit the back of her throat. She gagged. He groaned, pushed deeper, and then withdrew. He pulled back until his cock pulsed against the inner lining of her lips.

"You okay?"

She took a breath through her nose and nodded.

Before she finished the gesture, he pushed forward again. She tried to slow his progress, but the power of his hips slid his cock inexorably deeper until he once again hit the back of her throat. This time, she was better prepared. She struggled not to gag. As he held his cock there, she rolled her tongue over the smooth, salty skin. Her lips tingled where he'd brushed them. Her pussy burned and moistened. Her breasts ached.

Almost helplessly, she felt him move. Her jaws ached to take this much of him, but she wanted more. She wanted all of him. She dug her fingers into the back of his thighs and pulled him toward her.

"You want more?" The question came from above her head.

With her mouth stuffed full of his cock, she couldn't speak or nod. But she could entreat with her eyes.

One big hand swung around to cup her taut cheek. His thumb traced the corner of her mouth. Tiny nerve endings she didn't know she had shivered with delight. Her eyes closed. Her pussy flooded with creamy moisture. She clenched her thighs to control the throbbing between them.

"I don't know." He stroked the tight skin with his thumb. Once. Twice. His voice was gravely with his need. "I don't know if this sweet mouth can hold anymore."

She curved her tongue around as much of his cock as she could. She worked it back and forth before she started sucking. All the while she watched his eyes. They went from light to dark. From open to slumberous before his head fell back and he conceded defeat, responding to the demands of her hands, sliding his cock in and out of her eager mouth at the pace she wanted. At the depth she wanted. Giving her control. Giving her pleasure.

"I want to see your breasts."

It was an order and a plea. Releasing his thighs, she balanced on her knees and let him set the pace while she undid the last four buttons of her blouse. His cock almost slipped from her mouth as she shrugged the blouse off her shoulders, but with a twist of his hips, he maintained the connection. She pulled the lace-edged camisole down so it tucked under her corseted breasts, pushing them higher.

"Cup them in your hands," he whispered, shoving his cock in as far as he could and holding it. The flared head throbbed against her throat. Elizabeth struggled to breathe through her nose as her aching jaws stretched further. She cupped both breasts in her hands, shivering at the darts of fire that raced down her spine.

"Roll and pinch your nipples between your fingers."

She did, lightly at first, but as his cock picked up the pace and his breath came short and hard, it wasn't enough.

"God, you look gorgeous," Asa murmured, burying his fingers in her hair, holding her head still for the rampant pillaging of his cock.

Nerve endings in her breasts seemed directly connected to the area throbbing between her legs. The harder she pinched, the better it felt. Soon, she was tugging and squeezing as hard as she could as his cock wildly pounded her throat. His hands in her hair pulled her face harder into the thrust of his hips. The sensation was both torment and pleasure. On the last thrust, his cock popped through the resistance of her throat, sliding deep. There was nothing she could do to prevent it. She couldn't breathe. She couldn't resist. All she could do was relax her throat and try to take it all as, suddenly, his cock throbbed and then spurted. Again and again. She swallowed all of his creamy essence, unable to get enough of his uniquely masculine flavor. Finally, after an eternity, he pulled back until he only filled her mouth. She sucked deep breaths through her nose. His hands dipped to her breasts. His fingers replaced hers. Another silky spurt of fluid coated her tongue as he started working her nipples.

"That's right, darlin'," he encouraged as she swallowed. "Take it all." His shin pushed between her legs, pressing against her straining clit as he started milking her breasts, pulling and pinching the nipples, before drawing them out, only to release them and quickly start over. "Lord, you're beautiful."

She suckled his cock harder, loving his taste and the fact that she could put that desperate tone in his voice as she rode his leg. She was close. So close.

"C'mon, darlin' go with it," he whispered above her. "Let go."

And suddenly, she was flying. Without wings, without care, just riding a maelstrom that consisted of nothing but Asa's hoarse encouragement and her own spiraling climax.

When it was over, when she found her balance again, she found herself staring into Asa's strained face. With a last groan, he slid free of her mouth. Falling to his knees in front of her, he cupped her cheeks in his big callused hands and rested his forehead against hers. "Elizabeth, darlin', you are somethin'." His labored breath fanned her heated cheeks. "And I am one lucky man."

She wouldn't—couldn't meet his eyes. "I did it right?"

"You smoked the soles off my boots."

For some reason, his praise made her feel self-conscious.

"Now you're shy?" he asked disbelievingly.

He smoothed a stray smear of come from the corner of her mouth. "You have your wicked way with me, and then you won't look me in the eye?"

She swallowed and sighed. "That's about it."

She wrapped his hand in hers and rolled her forehead against his. "You going to hold it against me?"

His laugh, as he got to his feet and held his hand down to her, was unsteady. "Not in this lifetime."

Placing her hand in his and rising to her feet, she smiled. "Nice to see you're thinking long-term."

He stepped out of the remains of his clothes and swung her up in his arms, "What makes you think there was a time when I didn't?"

She didn't have an answer, and from the way his mouth ravaged hers, she didn't think he was expecting one.

He stopped beside the bed. His hand slipped from beneath her legs. She tightened her grip on his neck, holding his gaze with hers as her thighs slid down his. Her skirt rode up with her descent. As she twisted to free the bulk, he bent over, letting her feet touch the ground. Her skirts slid back into place. His hands caught hers, releasing first one and then the other from his neck and holding them against his shoulders. He didn't move then, just stared at her, the silver of his eyes darkening to pewter. Anticipation shivered down her spine. Things were always wild when Asa got that hard, intent look on his face.

His smile started out slow, a wicked lift to the corners as he kissed her palms and released her hands.

"Undress for me."

His drawl was low and deep, temptation itself. She took a step back. His eyes never left her as she reached for her buttons. She paced herself. One button for every two of his breaths. By the time she had her blouse open all the way to the waist, his breath was coming twice as fast, and she had to rethink her plan. She settled for just letting it slide off her shoulders, no particular rhythm, just let it slide. He stopped breathing altogether. She toyed with the lacy strap on her camisole. Asa's breath whooshed out on a sigh as she dropped it to her elbow. She slid her arm free, and then let her fingers meander to the other side.

"You're killing me, darlin'," he groaned, his gaze a hot licking incentive to continue.

She shrugged her other strap down, keeping her expression as innocent as possible. "And here I thought I was teasing you."

Her camisole hung on the tips of her breasts. The slightest movement on her part would have it tumbling down. Asa licked his lips.

"You admitting it?"

She raised her eyebrows, turned her back to him, and threw a coquettish smile over her shoulder. "Yes."

The camisole slid to her waist.

His "Son of a bitch," slid just as softly into the sudden silence.

She smiled when it reached her. She raised her arms and lifted her hair off her back, holding it high, feeling wickedly powerful as she heard his breath catch and a floorboard creak beneath his foot. Slowly, little by little, she let the silky strands drift through her fingers to slide over her back, falling below her buttocks and once more shielding her curves.

She reached for the sash of her skirt. She knew Asa couldn't see what she was doing, yet she knew he was hoping. She took her time undoing the button beneath, gauging the proper time to release it from the hard rasp of his breathing. When she deemed him sufficiently eager, Elizabeth untied the tabs to her petticoats, and pushed skirt and all to the floor.

Glancing over her shoulder, she stepped out of the pile. He was a feast for the eyes where he stood in the middle of the room, his face hard, eyes dark, his fists clenched at his sides as if to keep from grabbing her. His skin glistened with a sheen of perspiration. The soft glow of the lamp threw into sharp relief the angles and hollows of his lean, well-muscled body. Between his legs, his cock surged hard and solid. Straining. For her. She blew it a kiss before turning away and bending over at the waist on the pretext of untying her shoes. Her hair fell in a curtain around her, blocking out the light, but nothing could block out the sound of Asa's sharp curse and rapid approach. She giggled as his arm wrapped around her waist and he tossed her face down on the bed.

"Think it's funny to tease your husband, do you?" he growled in her ear, his body covering hers, his hard chest pressing her torso into the mattress.

She wiggled lower in his grip until the side of her hip connected with his cock. The tip was hard and damp. For her. Anticipation shivered down her spine. "Yes."

The mattress sagged as he moved completely over her, his elbows braced on either side of her head, his strong thighs bracketing her softer ones, as his cock nestled its length along the crease of her ass. He slid her hair off the side of her neck and whispered in her ear, "Little girls who play with fire sometimes get burned."

She arched her neck so his lips found the spot behind her ear that she liked. "Lucky for you, I'm not a little girl." He sucked the flesh into his mouth before releasing it with a little popping sound. She felt it all the way to her pussy, which clenched and spilled in response. She had to catch her breath before she could finish, "And I like it when you get hot."

To prove her point, she used the little leverage she had to wiggle her ass against his cock.

His breath puffed against her neck. Out of the corner of her eye, she could see his fist clench in the brightly patterned quilt.

"Very lucky me," he agreed. Cool air wafted over her back as he drew away.

Her protest died in her throat as he bent his knees. He dipped the head of his cock in her slick juices, and then slid it easily over her pussy lips, nudged into the valley of her vagina before sliding firm and thick back up between her buttocks. As the velvety head caught on the puckered opening to her anus, a bolt of sensation, dark and foreign, shot up her spine. Convulsively, she pushed back, seeking more.

But he was already back at her pussy, retracing his steps, gliding over familiar territory. When he got near her rear, she tensed, wondering, anticipating. This time, when he reached her anus, he paused, lingered, and then slowly, almost delicately, aligned the broad head with the sensitive opening. And pressed.

"Oh my God." It was like nothing she'd ever felt before. Hot. Forbidden. Intensely erotic, it shot through her inhibitions and awakened something wild and dark into life.

Above, Asa froze. "You like that?"

She didn't know how to answer. He flexed against her and she didn't need to, her helpless moan and shifting hips spoke volumes.

He pressed harder against her as he leaned across the bed. She arched back against the pressure, wanting more, the bite of pain as his ungreased cock started to win the battle with the tight ring of muscle, only served to make her ache with a mindless need to be taken. Deep and hard. She didn't understand it, but she was helpless against the carnal need to have his cock buried in her ass.

There was the sound of a jar opening, and then his cock was replaced with the coolness of a cream.

His finger swirled around her anus and then pressed in. "I could take you here," he whispered as her flesh submitted to his insistence. His finger felt alien inside her. Alien but incredibly good. She squeezed tentatively, experimenting with the sensation, gasping when he curled his finger and rubbed her against the agonizingly sensitive flesh, sparking secret nerve endings to screaming desire.

"Make you mine in every sense," he continued.

Fear and desire warred for dominance inside her. "You're too big."

He pulled her to the end of the bed. As her legs dangled over the side, her feet inches from the floor, he braced his arm across her back and pressed two fingers against her opening. "You can take me."

She caught her breath as her flesh parted and muscles struggled to stretch to his demands. It hurt so good, she wept with the pleasure. The demand for more. Suddenly, the battle was over and his fingers were deep in her channel, conquering her muscle's resistance with masculine determination. He held her still as she twisted to relieve the pressure.

"Just relax," he told her, pushing harder. "You want this."

She did. Her pussy was gushing with her pleasure. For all the burning at his first possession, there were other sensations coming to the fore. Ones that had her wanting to move her hips. Take him deeper. Sensations that demanded more.

He pulled his fingers free, and then just as deliberately slid them back.

"Relax," he ordered again when she instinctively fought his possession. She took a breath, and managed to do so. His fingers slid to the hilt. The burn was minimal, but those other demanding sensations were getting louder. She wiggled her torso since she couldn't move her hips. He pulled out completely again, but this time, when he came back, he added a third finger.

"I can't," she gasped as he demanded entrance.

"You can," he countered, his tone brooking no objection.

He pushed and her flesh began to give.

"It hurts," she gasped, straining to relax, but it was too much.

He backed off, and settled for working two fingers in. "If you can't take three fingers," he whispered in her ear, "you'll never take my cock."

He resumed a steady rhythm with his fingers, gliding in and out, stretching her sensitive channel, preparing her.

"Don't you want my cock?" he asked as his ministrations had her pussy clenching on air, demanding to be filled the way her ass was.

God help her, she did. She wanted to be everything to him. To give herself to him in this ultimate way. She bit her lip and nodded her head. His third finger pushed against her ass. She forced herself to relax, to bear back against the pressure.

Her breath caught in her lungs as his fingers slid home. She struggled with the feeling of being helpless and overwhelmed. He was taking her ass whether she wanted it or not, and it was the most erotic moment of her life. She wanted more. He gave it to her.

Holding her hips steady, preventing her from moving at all, he applied strong pressure to the fingers pushing at her ass. Her strength was no match for his. All three fingers to the second knuckle. She could do nothing but accept the pleasure/pain that stole her breath and had her mindless with the need for more. She needed him to move. To fuck her. To give her the rhythm her tightly stretched nerves wept for.

"Beautiful."

It suddenly occurred to her that he was watching what he was doing to her. Watching his fingers claim her ass. Watching her response. Instead of shocking her, the knowledge set off a primitive rush of lust that surged out of control as he began a gentle in and out motion. She couldn't repress her moan.

He stilled. "Too much?" he asked, stroking her back with his free hand.

Heat flared through her body. Her fingers twisted in the quilt. Words were beyond her, even if she'd had the courage to speak them.

His fingers on her back froze. "Not enough?"

She nodded and bit the quilt as he chuckled.

"Not a problem." He found a steady rhythm, working her ass, loosening her muscles and teasing her passion. Her clit throbbed for attention, but she couldn't find relief because of how she was situated. Her breasts felt so swollen, they were going to explode from her body, but the smooth quilt couldn't provide the stimulation her nipples begged for. And her pussy. Her poor neglected pussy ached with an unrelenting desperate hunger that had her out of her mind. And still Asa fucked her ass with that consistent motion that promised everything and delivered nothing.

If he hadn't had her pinned with his arm, she would have come off the bed and scratched his eyes out for torturing her so.

"Stop teasing me," she finally gasped out.

"But I thought you liked to tease." His voice was hoarse and tight as if he, too, were battling his hunger.

He pushed his fingers deep, and held them high, spreading them. The change in rhythm caught her off-balance. He was clearly enjoying being in charge.

She could work with that. Taking a steadying breath, she clenched her muscles on his fingers.

"Don't you want me, Asa?"

He pulled his fingers all the way out and pushed them back in. Rougher this time. "When I'm done playing."

He was done playing if she had anything to say about it. And she did. Lots. "But I need you now, Asa. I need your cock in my pussy. All of it, Asa."

He fucked her harder, forcing a grunt from her lips. She had to struggle for her voice. "I want you to stuff every last delicious inch of that huge cock in me. I want you so deep in me that I'll be able to taste you." His fingers pulled from her ass.

"And then I want you to come. I want to feel you spurt inside me. I want to feel every drop of your seed as you fill me to—"

The words were cut off as he rammed his cock into her dripping cunt, giving her what she wanted, grabbing her hips and pulling her closer, forcing her to take more.

Her shrill cry was pure satisfaction.

"Witch," he chastised as he pulled free and drove deep into her tight pussy again. "Is this what you wanted?"

She nodded.

"Me too," he admitted on a groan. He pulled out. Her inner walls clung to his cock, struggling to keep him within her. "I love this tight pussy of yours."

He reached around and slid a hand under her hips. His fingers grazed her clit. Lightning shot up her spine, jerking her off the bed. "Poor baby," he murmured in sympathy, "all swollen and neglected."

He rubbed his finger over the well lubricated surface as he fucked her hard and fast like she wanted. When she was on the edge, her spine stiff with need, her juices pouring from her cunt, pleas for release tumbling from her lips, he took the sensitive nub between his finger and thumb, and milked it in time with his thrusts. As he drove in, he pulled her clit down, toward him, dragging his fingers along her length. As he pulled out, he let go. Only to repeat the gesture on the next thrust. She came in a blinding rush, ignorant of anything except the fiery explosion that fragmented reality until all that existed was his cock, her pussy, and the insatiable pleasure rushing through her.

She came back to herself a few minutes later. He was still in her. Still hard. His fingers still caressed her clit, though delicately in light of her sensitivity. She wiggled her hips in invitation "You didn't come."

A kiss landed between her shoulder blades. "In a minute."

He pulled his cock free of her pussy. A rush of juices spilled over his hand. He dipped the head of his cock in the puddle, pausing a moment to nudge her clit with the tip.

She purred and tilted her hips in response. He smiled against her back, and stroked her recovering clit a little harder. Her body, which she thought was exhausted, began to pulse anew.

He levered himself up. The air felt cool after the heat of his body. His cock eased down against her anus. Before she could resist, he breached the well-lubed opening with just the tip.

"Oh God!" He was too big. Too hard. Too much.

"Easy darlin'."

He kept his cock where it was, barely in her, poised for possession. Her muscles clenched and released with anticipation and dread. A dark throb of desire took up a beat in her pussy. The echo reverberated in the muscles of her ass. She didn't know whether to push him away or pull him close. Not that she could do either. She was helpless and at his mercy.

He had none. Refusing to give up the ground he'd gained, he began playing with her clit, swirling his fingers over the surface, tweaking it when she got complacent, rubbing it when she moaned. Despite her apprehension, her attention switched from her ass to her clit, needing him to give her more.

Something, anything. He did, pressing harder on her ass, coaxing that forbidden desire into life until she was moaning into the quilt, begging him to take her. To do it.

He did. Pulling her hips up with his hands as he surged hard from behind. With a popping sensation, he was in her, driving up the tight channel, his huge cock dragging against the sensitive nerves, throwing her into overload.

Against her ear, he whispered one word, "Mine."

She didn't breathe, struggling to come to terms with the reality of his burning presence. She hadn't expected to feel so vulnerable. So possessed. He pulled back until only the tip of his cock parted her. His hair brushed her cheek as he put his mouth on her shoulder. She felt his muscles gather, the edge of his teeth, and then he was surging back into her. Deeper than before. He held her pinioned with his body and his mouth as he drove into her. Shock subsided as something primitive began to respond to the elemental possession. Her body relaxed and his cock moved more freely in her passage. She tried to push up, but his teeth tightened on her shoulder as his fingers tightened on her clit.

"Mine," he repeated, fucking her harder, forcing her to take more. To take him.

She turned her face sideways, kissing his hand where it was braced beside her head. "Yours," she admitted, knowing it was true, understanding what he needed.

"Make me yours, Asa."

He froze above her as if he wasn't sure what he heard.

She kissed his hand again, and then turned her face into the quilt. "Make me yours, Asa," she repeated. "Claim me."

"Oh God, Darlin'."

As if she'd lit a fire under him, he went into motion. His hands, mouth and cock were insatiable, demanding her response, demanding she hold nothing back, that she let him do as he wanted, with no restraint.

He wasn't gentle. She didn't want him to be. She wanted him as he was. This was her Asa. Part primitive warrior. Part wild knight in shining armor. The man who saw her for what she was and reveled in it. When he finally buried his cock as deep as he could and pumped his hot seed into her welcoming ass, she buried her face in the quilt and relished each spurt, knowing there was no going back. She'd made her choice. She was his.

Chapter Twenty

ဢ

It turned out worrying about Asa borrowing trouble was a moot point. The next morning, it galloped up to the front door as bold as brass in the shape of Aaron on his blood bay. As soon as he heard the hoofbeats, Asa leapt out of bed. Despite his explicit "Stay there", Elizabeth followed him to the window, her progress much smoother as she wasn't hopping into her blue denims as she went. She merely had to shrug into her robe. By the time he was buttoning the fly of his pants, she was beside him. She ignored his exasperated glance and pulled back her side of the curtains.

She couldn't believe her eyes. The message she'd sent Aaron two days ago had said she needed to speak to him. She hadn't said it was urgent. As a matter of fact, she'd said anytime after breakfast would be fine. The rising sun flashed off the silver conches circling his hat. She flinched from the assault on her vision and the catastrophe brewing beside her. Asa was never at his most cooperative before a full stomach.

"Elly!" Aaron bellowed, the urgency in his voice unmistakable. "Elly! Are you all right?"

Asa let his side of the window curtain drop. "The man seems to have something important on his mind."

"What makes you think that?" she asked, stepping back.

"Might be the way his horse is winded, or the way he's bellowing like a bull."

She strove for innocence. "It might?"

From Aaron's haste, he must not have been home to receive her note, and had worked himself into a lather worrying as a result. She cast another glance at the window. She saw Cougar approaching from the bunkhouse where he'd spent the night. She breathed a sigh of relief. Cougar would keep Aaron entertained while she worked on her husband.

Asa reached out and touched her cheek, the grimness of his expression not matching the gentleness of his touch. "Yeah, it might." He sighed. "What'd you do, Elizabeth?"

She tightened the belt on her robe and avoided Asa's gaze. "What makes you think I did anything?"

Aaron bellowed again. Through the window, Cougar's muffled drawl could be heard in response.

Asa trailed his finger down her cheek, tipping her gaze to his when he reached her chin. "The fact that you're ducking my gaze. The fact that, if you pull that belt any tighter, I'm going to be caring for two wives, and because my gut says so."

She couldn't hold his gaze. "Your gut could be wrong."

His fingers slid along her neck until they anchored in the curls at the base. One tug and she was back to looking at him. "Is my gut wrong?"

She took a deep breath. Instead of the hedge she'd intended, out popped the unvarnished truth. "I sent him a note."

"After we agreed you'd trust me to handle this?"

She was glad she hadn't lied before. "Of course not! I sent it two days ago."

He stared at her a moment before the rigidity left his posture. The fingers still anchored in her hair began to stroke her skin. "I'm glad to hear that."

She put her hands on her hips. "You were ready to believe I broke my promise!"

"Seemed possible based on the situation."

"The situation being your worry that I place more value on Aaron than I do you?"

"You've known him all your life."

"You're my husband."

"I know you've got a strong sense of duty, but—"

"You're my husband."

This time he didn't argue. She stared at him a minute. Downstairs, she heard Cougar ushering Aaron into the study. No doubt he'd be up here in a minute. Aaron wasn't easily put off. He would, however, just this once, have to wait. There was something she needed to get clear between herself and Asa. "Aaron and I grew up together. I know him and I trust him. I think you're mistaken in your assessment of him based on my knowledge of his personality, but that doesn't mean I put him before you."

"You sent him a note."

"Yes. I wanted to know if he saw anyone around. Anyone suspicious. Specifically, your previous foreman, Jimmy."

"You think he's causing trouble?"

She sighed. He didn't need to sound so skeptical. "I think he's vicious enough to do a lot of things behind a person's back." Asa stared over her shoulder, obviously pondering her statement. She touched his cheek, bringing his gaze back to hers. "About this ridiculous fear you have regarding my loyalty…"

"I don't doubt your loyalty."

She continued as if he hadn't interrupted. "You are my husband. The man I trust with my ranch, my life, and the lives of any children we might have together. If you put that on a scale and balance it against my affection for Aaron, you'd see there really isn't any competition."

His expression didn't change. Behind his eyes, emotions surged. She sighed. She was obviously going to have to spill her guts, to borrow one of Asa's sayings. "I don't believe you're right about Aaron, but, if this comes to a confrontation and it doesn't go the way I think it will, when the dust settles, I'll be standing there by your side."

"You mean that?"

"I'm not in the habit of saying what I don't mean."

His response was interrupted by the knock on the door that prefaced Cougar's "Y'all up in there?"

"We're up."

"You got company."

"We heard. Tell him I'll be right down."

"He wants to see Elizabeth."

Asa put his fingers over Elizabeth's lips, preventing her response. He stared into her eyes as he said, "He'll have to make do with me."

"Better hurry." Cougar growled. "Looks like lack of sleep has been hell on the man's patience."

"I'm right behind you."

As soon as she heard Cougar's footsteps leave the door, Elizabeth shook free of Asa's hand. "There's absolutely no reason I shouldn't go down and speak to Aaron."

"Darlin'," Asa drawled in that slow way that said his mind was set. "Until I'm as convinced of that man as you are, you're not getting within shouting distance."

She followed him as he headed for the dresser. "You'll have a much better chance of intelligent conversation if Aaron is sure I'm all right."

Asa opened a drawer and pulled out a shirt. As he shrugged into it, he said, "I'm not looking for intelligence. I'm looking for truth."

"Which," she persisted, "you'd be much more likely to encounter if both of you are calm and rational."

He buttoned the shirt to mid-chest. He looked impossibly handsome and assured. "You're not going down, Elizabeth. The man came here wearing guns."

"Everyone wears guns."

He cocked an eyebrow at her. "You just got done saying you trusted me."

She stamped her foot. "Don't twist my words against me."

He grabbed his boots and sat on the bed. His other eyebrow winged upwards to join the first. "Exactly how am I twisting things?"

"By trying to make me feel guilty so I'll abandon rational argument."

He stomped his right foot into its boot. As he stomped the other one in, he asked, "Is it working?"

She folded her arms across her chest. "Somewhat."

He stood and tucked his shirt into his pants. "There's no somewhat about it, Elizabeth. Either you trust me or you don't."

Part of her wanted to argue, but he was right. . Either she trusted Asa to handle things or she didn't.

"You won't get into a fight?"

"Not unless I'm provoked."

"You promise?"

He paused on the way to the door. "I promise I won't hurt your precious Aaron unless there's no choice."

She really was going to have to take a sledgehammer to her husband's stubborn pride. "I wasn't worried about Aaron." He stopped and turned. While she had his attention, she added for good measure. "And you were wrong earlier."

"About what?"

"I wasn't trying to tell you I trusted you."

His only response was a surprised lift of his right eyebrow. She bit her lip and then risked it all. "I was trying to say I love you."

He stood like he'd been pole-axed. Not a muscle moved anywhere on his body, but his eyes burned almost black with emotion. Her pulse hammered in her ears. Her impetuous revelation might have been a miscalculation, she decided, as he struggled to get himself together. She counted ten beats of her heart before Asa found his voice. If he hadn't been so obviously off balance, she might have been crushed by his reply.

A low drawled, "Thank you, darlin'," as the man slipped through the bedroom door was hardly the response of a woman's dreams.

* * * * *

She stared at the closed door and decided it was a miscalculation making her announcement just then. As much as she wanted him to know he ranked first with her, telling Asa she loved him as he went to confront her best friend whom he regarded as an enemy might not have the calming effect she'd been hoping for. It might, in fact, trigger all those over-protective instincts she was trying to soothe.

She listened to Asa's steps descend the stairs. When he hit the small landing two steps from the bottom, he paused. She pictured him in her mind, getting his bearings and settling his expression into controlled amusement. When his steps didn't resume immediately, her grin spread to a full smile. Poor baby, she must have really thrown him with her declaration of love.

The smile dropped as he continued down the stairs. She heard the study door creak open. She held her breath. If the men were going to drop each other on sight, this would be the moment. Gunshots didn't boom, but voices did. She caught a stray "son of a bitch" and a harsh, "cold day in hell" before the study door slammed closed.

Neither did anything to settle her nerves. She started grabbing clothes willy-nilly from the dresser. She winced when a "the hell I do" shook the rafters. It would be a lot easier to let Asa handle things if she was confident the matter would be settled with discussion and not fists. For all his bluster, Asa wasn't completely healed. Aaron knew it, too, because she'd mentioned the shooting in her note. If he took advantage of that, she'd —

She looked around the room, glanced under the bed, and found inspiration. She'd brain him with the chamber pot.

No more shouts broke through the muffling aspect of the closed door. All she could hear was the rise and fall of incomprehensible murmurs. She sat on the bed and dragged on her shoes. Wielding the boot hook like a weapon, she buttoned them tightly. When she was done, she strained to make out the conversation below. With no success.

She sprang to her feet and paced. They had no right to shut her out. She was as much a part of the problem as any of them. She had a right to be part of the solution, darn it! The rhythmic squeaking of the floor grated on her nerves. Grabbing the pillow she'd just finished embroidering the other day, she plopped into the wing-backed chair. She looked down at the needlework and shook her head. Her fingers traced over the intricate embroidery spelling out 'Home, Sweet Home'. She crushed the pillow between her fingers before dropping it back into her lap. If Asa wanted his home to be sweet in the future, she decided, grabbing hairpins off the small table and twisting her hair up, he was going to have to stop being so darned protective.

A loud crash and a shaking of the floor beneath her feet startled her into jabbing a hair pin into her finger rather than her bun. She jerked her hand away. Every muscle in her body turned to stone as she sat, waiting, finger in her mouth, hoping against hope for a resumption of the shouting.

The floor shook again and she heaved a sigh. So much for peaceful solutions. She got up and jabbed the last hair pin into her hair. Dropping the pillow on the chair, she headed for the door. Her deal with Asa hadn't included sacrificing her heirlooms to brawling.

She winced as another crash shook the walls. Damn Aaron! If he took advantage of Asa's condition, he was going to have to deal with her. She hit the landing just as Aaron and Asa came hurtling through the study door. By leaning over the banister, she was able to save her Momma's favorite vase from the table positioned below. The table was a total loss, shattering as four hundred pounds of angry male collided with it.

"Stop it!" she hollered around the flowers she'd spent a half hour arranging yesterday.

Her shout was lost amid the thump as both men landed on the floor, Aaron first with Asa on top.

"Don't think they heard you."

She looked up to find Cougar standing in the doorway to the study. An unlit cigarette rested between his lips.

"Why aren't you stopping this?" she demanded.

His response was a shrug and a half smile as Asa landed a decent punch to Aaron's face. "Doesn't appear they're through discussing things."

She jumped as Aaron flipped Asa up into the railing. If they kept up this level of discussion, she wouldn't have a house left. "They're through."

She tipped the large vase over, smiling as water and roses spilled onto the two men, conveniently landing in their faces and filling their noses and mouths.

As they spluttered and choked, she rested the vase on the railing and looked over at Cougar. "Do you think I have their attention now?"

His half smile turned to a full grin. "It would appear so." His right eyebrow went up. With a dip of his chin, he redirected her attention. "At least, for the moment."

She looked down to find the two men wiping blood and water from their faces, eyeing each other as if they were contemplating a rematch. "If you even think of resuming your previous unpleasantness, there will be hell to pay," she informed them in no uncertain terms.

Asa's resigned, "Aw, hell!" came on the heels of Aaron's shocked, "Elizabeth!"

She ignored Asa and focused on Aaron. "Don't you dare reprimand me for my language when you come into my house and pick a fight with a helpless man."

"Helpless, my ass!" Asa growled.

Aaron stared at her, then looked at the blood on the hand he'd just pulled from his face. "Have you looked at me? This isn't soup on my face."

She refused to be swayed. "No matter how good an accounting Asa managed to give of himself, the fact remains that you knew he was injured and you picked a fight."

Aaron wiped the blood on his pants, looked at Asa, and glanced over to Cougar who was all but doubled up with mirth. "You can't believe I started this."

"I most certainly do," she snapped. "Asa is too intelligent a man to overlook the disadvantage his injuries present."

Asa leaned his shoulder against the banister. She noted how gingerly he did it, and worried as he groaned and said, "I tried to keep it peaceable."

"I'm sure you did." She glared at Aaron. "I'm well aware of how hotheaded Aaron can be."

"I didn't provoke a damned thing and you know it!" Aaron growled at Asa, looking like he wanted to start up all over again.

The expression Asa turned on her was as eloquent as his see-what-I-mean shrug.

"If you didn't start this fight, Aaron, how did it begin?" She shifted the vase more comfortably on the banister as she waited for his answer.

Aaron wiped his sleeve over his face. "I came over here as soon as I got your note. And, as soon as I stepped over the threshold, your *husband*," he sneered the word, "started flinging wild accusations at me. Accusing me of shooting him and sinking the Rocking C."

"I notice you didn't deny it," Asa piped up.

"Who the hell had time?" Aaron protested. "No sooner had you stopped throwing lies when you started throwing punches."

Elizabeth turned on Asa. "Is that true?"

"Well…"

"I didn't ask for prevarication. I asked if it were true."

"Sorta." Asa pushed a bit away from the wall, held his ribs and groaned.

Since she knew, if he were really hurt, he wouldn't utter a sound, she ignored the blatant ploy to distract her attention. "You promised me you'd keep things civilized unless you were provoked," she reminded him.

"Uh-huh."

The glance he cast Aaron was full of frustrated anger. Her suspicions leapt to the fore. "Were you provoked?"

He shifted his weight and groaned louder.

"You're wasting your time," she informed him at his theatrics. "I'm not going to be distracted." She tapped the vase gently on the banister. "Were you provoked?"

To her surprise, Aaron leapt to Asa's rescue, making her instantly suspicious. "Now that I think back on it, I might have said a few things out of line."

"That is true, ma'am," Cougar spoke up.

She stared at them. All three wore identical expressions of sincerity. All three were suddenly united in a common goal where, just a few minutes ago, they'd been ready to bring her house down around her. What didn't they want her to know?

"I don't believe any of you," she informed them.

All three had the gall to look shocked.

Something was definitely up, she decided. About the only thing that would cause Asa to do an about face was if he was protecting her. She looked at Aaron. A muscle twitched in his cheek.

She leaned her elbows on the banister and said, "You know, Aaron, the last time I saw that muscle twitching in your cheek and an expression that innocent on your face, you'd just told the teacher I was the one who'd put the frog in her lunch box."

Aaron paused from wiping a trickle of blood from his mouth. "That was a long time ago, Elly."

"Just goes to show that some things never change."

"Miss Panetta liked you. I knew she'd go easy on you."

"I'm sure, in your mind, that made it all right."

"You only had to do a little writing. Me, she would have taken out to the shed."

"And rightly so, since it was the fourth time you'd played that prank."

"I didn't like her."

She sighed. "And you thought, if you could drive her away, we'd find someone you'd like better."

"Yeah."

"You always did think you knew best for everyone, but, for your information, Aaron, I liked Miss Panetta and didn't want her to leave."

"That's probably why she stuck around so long."

Elizabeth smiled. After all these years, he was still frustrated at not having his plan work out. "That and the fact she married up with the blacksmith."

Cougar's low laugh filtered into the room. "He wasn't any more successful at preventing that than he was her teaching."

Asa looked at Aaron. "Seems you have a habit of sticking your nose where it's not wanted."

"People don't always know what's good for them."

"And you do?" Elizabeth asked.

Aaron folded his arms across his chest and leaned against the stair casing. "Did the blacksmith regret marrying the school marm?"

"I'm sure Miss Panetta's marriage problems stem from things other than what a ten-year-old boy could foresee."

"That and the blacksmith's weekend habits," Cougar offered, earning him a glare from Asa, which prompted a "begging your pardon" in Elizabeth's direction.

"None of that changes the fact that I knew the marriage was a mistake," Aaron pointed out.

With equal confidence, Elizabeth said, "And none of that changes that I know you've done something I need to know about."

Asa looked at Elizabeth, then at Aaron. He seemed to deliberate before, with a wipe of his hand on his pants, he came to a decision. "Tell her."

Aaron glanced at him like he'd sprouted a second head. "I don't think that's necessary."

Elizabeth was about to argue when she noted the set of Asa's jaw. She settled back on her elbows and amused herself by rocking the vase on the banister.

Asa plucked a flower from where it sat adorning his lap. "I have to disagree with you there." He looked up at her. "You rescuing these?" She shook her head. He flicked the flower to the front door before turning back to Aaron. "The way I see it, I can either climb into bed with you by keeping your secret or I can cuddle up with Elizabeth." He looked Aaron over from head to toe before sending another flower winging to the front door. "No offense, but my wife's got you beat nine ways to heaven when it comes to things I admire."

Aaron looked to Cougar for support as he said, "There's no reason to upset Elizabeth with something dead and buried..."

He didn't find much help there. "I can't say I'm in a position to make a statement. Seems as both Elizabeth and Asa feel you ought to 'fess up."

"It was the only thing to do at the time."

Cougar shrugged. "Maybe."

Aaron turned back to Asa. "What would you have done faced with the same situation?"

Asa stared back. "I can't rightly say, not being there, but now you've got to come clean."

"Could someone please tell me what is so poorly dead and buried that Aaron's still wrestling it?" Elizabeth asked with the last of her patience.

All three men stared at her. Of the three, she felt Asa's gaze the keenest. There was resolution in his gaze that told her he was going to make sure she knew. There was also pain, which told her this was going to hurt. He got to his feet. Aaron followed suit. As she was standing one step below the landing, they were at eye level. Taking a deep breath, she mentally prepared herself. Before she could let it out, Asa said, "It was Aaron here who set Brent on you."

She couldn't have heard right. She glared first at Asa, then at Aaron before repeating the procedure. She couldn't focus on either, but kept bouncing between reassurance and disbelief. She released her breath in an explosive, "What? But you said you wanted me to marry Jed!"

He glanced down and muttered, "That was after Brent turned out to be such a disappointment."

The only word she could push past her anger was, "Why?"

Aaron reached out a hand to her. "You needed a husband, Elly, and you weren't interested in the local boys. You wanted someone prettier with more flash." He shrugged. "I wanted you to be happy, so when Brent passed through, I made him a deal."

Her breath came in hard gasps. "You bought me a husband?"

"I made him a deal. Cash for passing on my orders and keeping you happy."

She remembered Brent's arrogance, heavy fists, and complete disregard for her feelings. No wonder he hadn't cared. She'd truly been a means to an end. Spots of light danced before her eyes. She couldn't get enough air into her lungs. Her words came out in jerky bursts of rage. "You spent six months traveling all over the place, picking out just the right stud for your precious breeding program, but, when it came to a husband for your best friend, you grabbed the first male wandering out of the saloon?"

"It wasn't like that, Elly!"

She launched the vase at his head. He caught it and bent to set it on the floor.

"You couldn't have ridden into Cheyenne to see if the pickings were better there?" she shouted.

She looked around for something else to throw. Asa obligingly handed her a couple of table legs. They bounced off Aaron's shoulder and back.

He jerked upright. "Ow! Dammit, Elizabeth! Cut that out!"

"I don't want to cut it out," she retorted, looking around for something else to throw.

Cougar tossed Asa a book from the study. Asa passed it to Elizabeth. She heaved it at Aaron's head. He deflected it with a forearm.

"Will you stop chucking things at me and listen?"

He took a step forward as if to grab her arm. She swatted him with a flower. She would have hit him again if Asa hadn't gotten between them and slammed his hand into Aaron's chest, sending him stumbling back a step. "Don't you touch her."

A sharp whistle was the only warning she had before Cougar lobbed a humidor her way. She caught it, but she couldn't throw it. Not with Asa blocking her way with his big shoulders. Shoulders that were clearly squared for a fight.

She glanced at Aaron and saw the same itching need to exchange blows reflected in his face. "Get out of my way, Asa."

With obliging quickness, he stepped to the left. "How could you do it, Aaron?" she asked, tightening her grip on the humidor. "How could you do that to me?"

"I thought I was giving you what you said you wanted." He growled, running his hands through his hair. "I asked Patricia what women wanted and— Hell!" He threw up his hands. "Brent seemed heaven-sent. He spoke with fancy words, tossed compliments around like they were candy, and dressed Eastern."

"You asked Patricia?" she asked in horror. Lord, did the whole territory know her best friend thought her so pathetic, he'd bought her a husband?

Aaron shuffled his feet, blew out a breath, then pulled his arrogance around him like a shield. His gaze locked somewhere over her left shoulder as he admitted, "I wanted you to smile again."

"So you bought me a husband you thought would make that happen?"

"Yes."

The humidor was tugged from her grasp. She looked down as Asa's finger's squeezed hers gently. She looked over at Aaron, standing before her. She saw the fear of rejection in his eyes as he stood there, pretending he didn't have a care in the world. She remembered back to her youth, the times he'd stood by her. The times he'd stood up for her.

I thought I was giving you what you said you wanted.

Most especially, she remembered her whispering to him once that she wanted a prince in wonderful clothes who wouldn't stink like cows, and who'd take care of everything so she'd never have to worry about anything again. She'd been so young when she'd told him her dreams. So young and ignorant of her own personality, but he'd remembered and taken to heart his promise to give her all that. He'd had to dredge the bottom of society to find the epitome of a fourteen-year-old girl's dream, but he'd found it and gifted her with Brent. She sighed. Someday, she was going to have to get through to him that she was all grown up now and her taste had definitely changed.

"I can forgive you Brent," she admitted. "Especially as I didn't see through him either." She doubted she'd ever get over the humiliation of that. "But what I can't forgive is driving the Rocking C into the ground."

Aaron's hands clenched into fists, and even the curls on his head seemed to bristle. "I haven't done a goddamned thing to the Rocking C!"

There was no mistaking the sincerity in his voice or his eyes. God, she was so relieved to be able to believe him. "But Asa said…"

"I was wrong," Asa admitted heavily.

"Did I hear you right?" she asked

"I never said I couldn't be wrong."

"Not in so many words…"

He silenced her with a hard kiss. "You want to get into this right now?"

"Not particularly." But later, that was a whole other kettle of fish. "But, if Aaron isn't the one sabotaging the ranch, who is?" she asked.

"That's what we have to figure out," Cougar said, pulling the unlit cigarette from between his lips as he stepped away from the doorjamb.

"And fast from the looks of things," Aaron interjected.

"The look of what things?" Elizabeth asked.

No one paid her any mind.

"Elizabeth mentioned that Jimmy might bear looking at." Asa mentioned, releasing her hand and putting the humidor away.

"He's good with a gun," Cougar offered.

"He doesn't have a reason," Aaron countered.

"Revenge is usually reason enough for most things."

Aaron cocked an eyebrow at Asa. "And you think losing a job would drive him to killing?"

"That and my objections to his treatment of ladies."

Never slow on the uptake, Aaron cut Elizabeth a sharp glance. "Jimmy was pestering you?"

She shrugged. "Maybe he got the impression that, being for sale, I was up for grabs."

"Goddammit, Elizabeth!" Aaron shouted, reaching for his nonexistent hat before dropping his clenched fist to his side. "I did not sell you!"

"That's a matter of opinion," she said with infinite sweetness.

"That still doesn't explain why you didn't come to me for help!" Aaron growled.

"Elizabeth has a real aggravating habit of thinking she can solve things herself," Asa said, giving her hand a warning squeeze when she would have answered for herself.

"She always has," Aaron agreed. He looked at Elizabeth and then at the tall man beside her. He gingerly dabbed at the cut on his cheekbone with his finger. Some of the frustration ebbed from his face as he said to Asa, "I assume that's a trait you'll be working on?"

"I've about got it under control," Asa answered with irritating confidence.

Elizabeth jerked on her hand. "I'm not deaf and dumb, gentlemen."

Asa didn't let go, but his "Of course not, darlin'," was immediate enough to set her teeth on edge. The approving look Aaron gave him finished the job. What was it about men that drove them into an instant fraternity when they had a chance to gang up on a woman? Three minutes ago, Asa and Aaron were looking to kill each other, and, now, they couldn't be more united than if they were brothers.

"You know," Cougar broke in, his tone thoughtful, the cigarette between his lips bobbing like an exclamation point on every syllable. "If I'm remembering correctly, the trouble on the Rocking C started about the time Jimmy hired on."

Aaron looked to Asa for confirmation. He nodded.

"From the books, that looks about right."

"Jimmy might be our man, then."

"Or not," Elizabeth interjected before the idea could gain more momentum. "As much as I hate Jimmy, I just can't see him masterminding a plan as complex as this one."

"The man knows cows and the way a ranch works." Asa shrugged. "Wouldn't need much more than that."

"But why?" she asked. "What did he hope to gain?"

Asa squeezed her hand. "The Rocking C."

"And you," Aaron added grimly.

"Pretty sweet reward for a year of easy pickings," Cougar agreed.

Elizabeth remembered Jimmy's constant pawing. Outright disrespect. Not a moment of his attention had been spent trying to get her to see him as her savior. Just the opposite, as a matter of fact. She said as much. She might as well have saved her breath.

"Never said the man was good at courting," Asa countered.

"Jimmy was probably as ham-handed at that as he was at breaking horses," Cougar agreed.

Aaron pinned her with a glare. "One of these days, you're going to have to explain to me just how ham-handed a beau he was."

Not while she was breathing, Elizabeth thought. All she needed was for Aaron to go looking for Jimmy and have Jimmy find out about it and shoot him in the back. Meanwhile, Cougar's comment played on her memory. The plan to drive the Rocking C under was well-orchestrated, requiring finesse. The same sort of finesse required in courting.

"Brent was excellent at courting," she observed aloud.

Her observation landed in the silence with the startling impact of glass shattering.

All three men stared at her like she'd lost her mind. Asa was the first to speak. "You can't be seriously thinking that little pissant had anything to do with this."

She folded her arms across her chest. "I think the chance bears investigating."

"No offense, ma'am," Cougar offered, "but your first husband didn't have enough meat on his bones to toss a day-old calf."

"It doesn't take muscle to drive a ranch into bankruptcy," she pointed out. Her observation fell on deaf ears.

"You may want to get back at the gambler," Aaron reasoned, "but I met the man, Elizabeth. He was a spineless wimp."

"My point exactly," she agreed. "Just the type to lurk behind the scenes and take advantage of innocent women."

"If that were the case," Asa asked, "how come he didn't kick up more of a fuss when you threw him over?"

"Yeah," Aaron challenged. "He could have tied things up for years in court, rendering anything Asa tried to do useless."

She didn't have an answer for either of them. "I don't know," she admitted.

"Trust us on this one, Elizabeth," Aaron said, reaching for his hat from the floor. "Jimmy had the knowledge and motive for driving the Rocking C under."

"Brent just doesn't have a motive that we can identify right now," Elizabeth cut in.

"None that can be identified at all," Asa countered.

Elizabeth yanked her hand free of Asa's. She knew she was right, but without facts, she didn't stand a prayer of busting through all that male self-importance.

"Anybody up for checking in town to see if anyone's noticed Jimmy hanging about?" Cougar asked, rolling to his feet with an easy movement that drew the eye. He was, Elizabeth realized as he took the cigarette out of his mouth, a very masculine, very good-looking man in his prime.

"Good plan," Asa agreed with a growl. Elizabeth glanced up and saw his gaze had followed hers. She bit back a smile.

"And soon," Aaron cut in as he settled the brim of his Stetson to the proper angle on his head.

Asa waved Cougar ahead of him as he headed for the back door where his own hat was kept. "Yeah. There isn't much time and, with bullets flying, I'm not sure how safe it is for the ranch hands."

"You got any plans for what to do when we find him?" Aaron asked, trailing in his wake.

Asa looked pointedly at Elizabeth. "Why don't we save this discussion for after we wash up?"

Elizabeth rolled her eyes. Did they think she couldn't figure such a thing out for herself? "I repeat, gentlemen. I am not deaf and dumb."

Asa snagged his gun belt off the hook. "Never said you were darlin'. Just can't see the sense in standing here chatting," he wiped his sleeve across his cut lip, "bloodying up your nice floors."

"And I could use a smoke." Cougar gave his unlit cigarette a disgusted look. "Got this poor thing so soggy, it's about useless."

Elizabeth looked at Aaron. "Do you have an excuse?"

He merely smiled and jerked his thumb over his shoulder. "Yup. I'm with them."

She sighed. As if there was any doubt.

United in their misplaced need to protect her, they left the house. She watched as they strolled purposefully to the pump. No doubt all sorts of plots were being discussed outside her earshot. She bit her lip and frowned. Asa may have been right, Jimmy might have the knowledge to hurt the ranch, but there was something about the whole set-up that didn't ring true. Jimmy was a behind-the-back sort of snake, but he'd never struck her as a long-term thinker. He tended to act on impulse and pay the price later. In other words, all brawn and very little brain.

As soon as the thought hit her, so did an image of Brent. He'd been short on brawn, but very, very good at manipulating people. No matter how logical the men's reasoning, she couldn't shake her feeling that they'd misplaced their faith, putting too much emphasis on brawn when they should have been looking for brain.

With a sigh, she headed for the kitchen. They'd be back for breakfast, and, when they did, she'd bring up the subject again. As she pulled out the frying pan, she planned her arguments. Her intuition was telling her she was right and she wouldn't give up until she made them see the possibility.

Chapter Twenty-One

 જી

She was going to kill him. Elizabeth tugged on her gloves, adjusted her bonnet, and grimaced as her corset bit into her side. Killing Asa was certainly justified for him forcing her to wear the contraption again, but, today she was going to kill Asa for slipping off the ranch and sneaking into town like a thief with Cougar and Aaron. Theirs was a partnership based on honesty. If he thought she was going to let him sully it with sly protective measures, he had another think coming.

She opened the door. Cold wind nipped her nose. She sighed, unpinned her wrap and grabbed her wool pelisse. Just as she reached to close the door, she paused and reconsidered. A woman had to be prepared. After retrieving and closing her reticule, she marched down the steps and got into the buggy. Willoughby snorted his protest at being out on a day like today.

"Take it up with Asa!" she informed him as she snapped the reins over his back. "Right now, you just get me to town."

He plodded across the yard. She sighed. At this rate, she'd be too late for dinner, let alone to talking sense into her husband. Clint came out of the barn. He removed his hat and asked, "Heading into town now?"

"Yes, if I can get Willoughby to pick up the pace."

His grin was a smooth motion of his lips. As free and easy as his personality. He slapped Willoughby on the haunch. "He does hate the cold."

"He'll have to get over it."

"I imagine he'll see it your way."

She sighed. "I hope. Thanks for hitching him up."

"No problem." His expression became serious. His hat twirled in the lazy rhythm she associated with the man. He watched it spin. It loped through three revolutions before he said, "Boss man was kind of funny this morning. Seemed almost like he was saying his goodbyes instead of good morning. Boys and I were wondering if you planned on bringing him back with you?"

"Kicking or screaming, in one piece or four, I'm bringing him back."

He looked up. His mouth twitched while his eyes crinkled at the corners. "Begging your pardon, ma'am, but Old Sam said I was to ask if you made any promises, whether it was Miss Coyote speaking or Mrs. MacIntyre?"

She straightened her shoulders and tightened her grip on the reins. She looked up at the Guardians and let her gaze sweep across the plains. Wherever she looked, it was Coyote land. Bought with blood and sacrifice. Not the least of which was her own, but there wasn't going to be any more sacrifice for this land. She was going to keep it, but, through brains, not sacrifice. There'd been enough of that. In her life as well as Asa's.

As she brought her gaze back to the man before her, she identified the strange feeling she'd been trying to place for weeks. Confidence. As if waiting for her acknowledgment to take its rightful place, it sank into her bones and spread its strength through her body until it reached her voice. She smiled and looked down the road to town. "You tell Old Sam I'm going hunting and I'll not be coming back empty-handed."

Clint went absolutely still, another first, as he stared at her intently. "And who'd be doing the hunting, ma'am?"

"Why myself, Mr. Clint." She snapped the reins and clucked Willoughby into motion. "Who else would you be expecting?"

He resettled his hat on his head. As she passed by, he gave her a slight smile and a nod. "I'll be happy to pass that message along, ma'am."

"Thank you."

* * * * *

Her confidence lasted until she got to town and saw the crowd in front of the saloon. Then it transformed into exasperation. What had those fools done now?

She pulled the buggy up in front of the bank. Everyone was so intent on the confrontation going on, they took no notice of her. Deciding if she waited for someone to lend her a hand, she'd be frozen to the seat until spring, she gathered her skirts and hopped down from the buggy. Her right foot twisted in a frozen rut as she hit the ground. She righted herself, checked the angle of her hat and marched through the crowd in time to hear the sheriff say, "Those are mighty harsh accusations, MacIntyre. You got any proof?"

"You've got my word."

That was Asa's voice. Hard, rigid, and packed with enough conviction to set tongues wagging. A large set of shoulders in a black coat blocked her view. She jabbed the man in the back with her finger. He shifted but didn't move.

"I'm sorry you're not able to pull the ranch out of trouble, but I assure you, I have nothing to do with any of this." Aaron's voice was equally easy to recognize. It was also as confident as Asa's.

"Uh-huh." The hairs on the back of her neck stood on end in warning. The men had left the range as tight as coons at a garbage pile, and now Asa was tossing out those provoking "Uh-huh's" like a man with a twelve-prong buck in his sights. What could have happened?

"Tell me, Aaron." Asa continued. "When are you planning on driving your cattle over to the railroad?"

"You surely can't blame me for making a profit?" Aaron asked. "The rail crew has to eat. If the Rocking C isn't going to make the profit, I don't see why the Bar B shouldn't."

"Seems funny that you're right there ready to fill the hole."

That low drawl belonged to McKinnely. She knew he had to be here somewhere. Had he and Asa hatched a plot against Aaron between them? She poked the man in front of her again. She might as well be poking a wall for all the attention he paid her.

"I gotta agree, Aaron," the sheriff muttered uncomfortably. "It's mighty convenient that MacIntyre's been having these problems and the one picking up the profit is you."

Elizabeth took out her hat pin and applied it to the man in front of her. On a howl, he got the point. She broke through to the center of the crowd in time to see Aaron hold his hands up in a helpless gesture.

"The Bar B is the second biggest ranch in these parts. We've worked closely with the Rocking C in the past. Who better to step in and fill the hole? Would you rather have an outsider profit?"

He had a point. A very, very good point.

"Elizabeth!" She winced at Asa's bellow. As one, all eyes fell upon her.

Mustering all the calm she could manage, she re-secured her hat with the pin and gave Asa her best wifely smile. "Hello, Mr. MacIntyre."

"What are you doing here?"

"I told you I'd be along." She smiled at the other ladies present. "You know how men are. Always in such a rush, there's never enough time for a woman to get herself properly together."

Several of the ladies nodded in sympathy. A couple of the spinsters reserved their opinions. From the frowns on their faces, she suspected they'd seen her apply the hat pin to the undertaker's posterior. Rats!

"What in the heck are you up to?" Asa asked.

He needn't sound so suspicious, she thought. "I was just checking out the commotion."

"Check it out from the ranch."

She smiled at him patiently. "But then I'd miss it all."

His response was a growl. Aaron stepped to her side protectively. "I, for one, am glad you're here, Elizabeth. Your husband is operating under a misunderstanding."

She looked into Aaron's handsome face and kept her expression to simple curiosity. "He is?"

Sheriff Mulden stepped forward. He was an aging bear of a man who was shy with every woman except the Widow Foster. With her, he fought like a dog protecting the last bone on Earth. He tipped his hat. "Miss Coyote."

"Mrs. MacIntyre," she and Asa corrected in unison.

The poor sheriff flushed to the white of his hairline. "I'm right sorry for the mistake, Mrs. MacIntyre."

"It's perfectly natural, Sheriff Mulden. Mr. MacIntyre and I haven't been married all that long." She had to think of the scandalous things she'd done to her husband last night to create the proper maidenly blush.

"Yes, well, that's part of the problem. Mr. Ballard is an upstanding member of the community. Mr. MacIntyre, who casts a mighty long shadow himself, is making accusations against Mr. Ballard, which are, quite frankly, hard to believe."

"What sort of accusations?"

"Mr. MacIntyre is accusing Mr. Ballard of running the Rocking C into the ground."

Damn. She turned to Aaron. "How did Asa come to these conclusions?"

"I assure you, I have no idea."

She stared into his blue eyes and wanted to believe him. For all the years he'd been her only friend, for all the childhood dreams she'd attached to him, she wanted to believe what he said, but there was the twitch in his eyelid as he met her gaze. He was lying.

"I don't understand."

Aaron patted her hand while Asa glared daggers. "There's no reason you should."

Elizabeth thanked Aaron politely for his concern, then wiggled her way back into the fray with a simple, "But it appears I must if we want to resolve this unfortunate situation."

"Yeah," someone said from the crowd. A quick glance told her it was the undertaker, looking to get his own back for her poking him with the pin. She sighed. There were days when it didn't pay to get out of bed.

"Let's hear Miss Coyote's side of this."

"That's Mrs. MacIntyre," Asa corrected over her head, ignoring the undertaker. Sheriff Mulden showed no such inclination.

"Now, John," the Sheriff counseled, "don't go taking sides. Right now, we've just got us a misunderstanding."

"There's no misunderstanding," Asa said, his low drawl carrying. "For the last couple of years, Aaron Ballard has been doing his level best to drive the Rocking C into the ground so he can pick up the pieces."

Asa shifted his weight, and Elizabeth saw he had his guns unstrapped. Good God, was this a charade or wasn't it?

"What are you saying?" she gasped, leaning against Aaron with what she hoped was proper, ladylike distress. She needed to stall until she figured this out, and playing stupid was the one gambit wide open to a lady.

"I'm saying that when a man starts taking advantage of women, rustling cattle, and poisoning wells, someone has to belly up to the bar and call a halt."

Aaron stopped patting her hand halfway through Asa's statement. He looked around, and donned the superiority he wore like a cloak. Elizabeth had seen him do it all his life when he wanted to gain the upper hand. It was a very impressive maneuver in a man of his stature. She was so caught up in her admiration that she almost toppled when Aaron took a step to the right.

Aaron caught her, supported her while she found her balance, and then returned to the argument. "And this is what you're doing?" he questioned Asa. He took another step to the right, motioned to the audience surrounding them and continued, "Out here in the street? In front of the whole town? 'Bellying up to the bar'?"

Asa showed no sign he shared Aaron's distaste for such lack of propriety. He merely smiled, leaned back against the doorjamb, hooked one foot over the other and nodded. "Would appear so."

Aaron turned to Elizabeth. "I'm sorry you have to suffer this public humiliation, Elizabeth."

"She wouldn't be suffering anything," Asa drawled, "if she'd kept her keister where I put it."

The crowd gasped at his disrespect. Elizabeth frowned. Did the man think to send her flouncing off in a huff? If so, he had another think coming. "Why are you doing this in the middle of town?"

"That snake in the grass you're cozying up to is dead set on having the Rocking C. While you and everyone else in this town might think he's a lily-white character, I know him for what he is." He ended the statement with a wave to her right. Cozying up to? Aaron was sidestepping faster than she was breathing. She followed the motion and had to swallow a gasp when she saw Jimmy, not three feet from Aaron.

"And that would be?" Aaron asked Asa with a superior smile.

Asa's smile reflected the same arrogant superiority. "Why, a back-stabbing, ruthless, yellow-bellied S.O.B, of course."

"There's no need for name-calling." Sheriff Mulden interjected.

If he'd hoped to head off this confrontation, Elizabeth could have told him to save his breath. When Asa got a bee in his bonnet, there was no stopping him.

Aaron was no better as he said, "I'd be glad to drop the subject, Sheriff, but Mr. MacIntyre seems reluctant to allow it."

Asa pushed his hat back and shrugged. "Go figure."

This was getting ugly. Elizabeth turned to Asa.

"You have no proof," she reminded him. Without proof, they couldn't do anything except embarrass themselves. She stared at him, willing him to let it go until they did have it. Asa didn't seem to be getting the point.

"I have enough to know there's no way you'll be safe until he's six feet under."

"That's pretty harsh words," Sheriff Mulden said.

"It's a harsh world." Asa pushed away from the building. He encompassed the crowd in his gaze as he continued. "Of course, I wouldn't have to dig up false proof against Ballard if Jimmy here would just confess."

Never at a loss for words, Jimmy's "You're crazy!" was as immediate as his bluster.

Elizabeth shook her head. He would have been better served by making a run for it, because, while he was sputtering, Aaron moved in and locked his arms behind his back.

His "Hello, Jimmy," was eminently cordial.

Red-faced and struggling, Jimmy demanded an explanation.

"Yeah," Sheriff Mulden echoed. "I think that might be timely, seeing as you started by accusing Mr. Ballard and now have this one hog-tied."

Asa pushed away from the wall. Elizabeth lost sight of him when someone jostled her. She surged forward with the crowd, trying to get a good look.

"I apologize for that, Sheriff. Needed to pass a little time while I waited."

"Your idea of passing time is getting town folks worked up?" Sheriff Mulden didn't sound pleased.

"He's goddamned loco," Jimmy protested.

Sheriff Mulden didn't appreciate the interruption as evidenced by his scowl. "I'll thank you to remain quiet, Jimmy. I'm basing my listening on how many times I've had the pleasure of a body's company in my jail. Those that don't disturb my Saturday nights get first shot."

A titter of uneasy laughter rippled through the crowd. Jimmy was a regular at the tiny jailhouse. Sheriff Mulden turned back to Asa. "You said you were waiting on something, son?"

"Yeah."

Elizabeth waited with the same breathless anticipation as everyone else.

Sheriff Mulden shifted his feet. "You planning on getting to the point before lunch?"

"You might want to hurry it along," Aaron agreed.

She couldn't see, but Elizabeth bet the reason for the tension in his voice was because Jimmy was objecting to being restrained. Bullies rarely enjoyed being subjected to the treatment they handed out.

"He was waiting on me," Cougar called from somewhere behind her.

Like a scene from the bible, the crowd parted. He passed within two bodies of Elizabeth, carrying a branding iron, a bag of something, and an aura of grim purpose.

She followed his progress until he stopped in front of Asa, who asked, "That what I think it is?"

Cougar twitched the bag. "If you're talking about this, it's pure poison. The kind a man might want to drop in a watering hole if he'd a mind to do some damage."

The crowd's united gasp stirred a little breeze. The person on her left jostled Elizabeth again. She stuck out her elbow in self-defense, but she didn't take her eyes from the drama unfolding.

Sheriff Mulden pointed to the other objects in Cougar's hand. "Could I see that brandin' stick?"

Cougar gave it a toss. The sheriff caught it. He studied it briefly, then frowned. "Where'd you boys find this?"

Cougar jerked his thumb over his shoulder. "Stashed under Jimmy's bedroll at the hotel."

Speculation ran rampant through the crowd, starting with a murmur and rolling into an annoying roar that drowned out everything but bits and pieces of the conversation between the Sheriff, Asa, Aaron and Cougar, but Jimmy's howls of innocence kept overpowering the parts she really wanted to hear. And what they didn't drown, the crowd's repetitions did. The best she could determine, the men were doing the same as the crowd, indulging themselves with drawn out speculation when the person with the answers sat right before them.

Finally, unable to contain her frustration, she called out, "Oh, for heaven's sake, someone ask him why!"

The crowd chose that moment to fall silent, leaving everyone in no doubt as to who'd given the order. Well, spit!

The reactions of the men concerned were predictable. The Sheriff and Aaron frowned repressively at her. Cougar wore that halfcocked grin, and Asa merely offered, "I guess we

403

could do that." He said it like she was taking all the fun out of his day.

"If you don't mind, son," Sheriff Mulden interrupted, "I'll be handling the questioning."

Asa surrendered his role of interrogator with an open gesture of his hands and a nod.

The sheriff accepted the invitation and turned to Jimmy. "You got an explanation for all this?"

"I ain't got no explanation for nothing." Elizabeth still couldn't manage a glimpse of his face, but his voice sure sounded sullen. "I don't know how that stuff got under my bed, but I sure as hell didn't poison good beef and didn't shoot nobody."

The crowd shifted to get a better view. Elizabeth didn't move with them, held up by the disgust in Jimmy's voice as he talked about poisoning good beef. It was genuine. Elizabeth knew it as surely as she knew she was going to have a raw spot from the darned corset. She bounced on her toes, trying to get Asa's attention, but the undertaker took advantage of her dawdling and moved in front of her, leaving her with a bird's eye view of his black wool jacket. She fingered her hat pin, and scouted for a parting in the crowd.

"You saying you didn't run off any cattle or change any brands either?" Sheriff Mulden asked.

"Or terrify my wife?"

That was Asa's voice. She'd recognize that low drawl anywhere, and, from the careful way he was shaping his words, he was furious.

She shifted to the right, but the opening she'd been aiming for closed up as Jimmy shouted, "I branded a few cattle, scattered a few cows, but that's all."

The precisely spoken "I don't think so" belonged to Aaron.

"All right. I hassled Miss Coyote, but only until she married up with him. After that, there wasn't much point."

Now that, Elizabeth thought, was an interesting way to phrase it. The subtlety was lost on Asa. "Bothering my wife was a huge mistake."

"We're already square on that!" Jimmy hollered. The edge of desperation in his voice made her wonder if Asa was advancing on him.

"If we want to nail this," Cougar jumped in, "I got Clint fetching the railroad man."

Clint must have ridden like the devil to get here before she did. She wondered if he'd been given the job of watching her again and, as soon as she'd left the ranch, he'd headed for the shortcut she couldn't take in the buckboard.

"What good will that do?" Sheriff Mulden asked, interrupting her speculation.

"He can verify who told him Rocking C cattle were diseased," Aaron pointed out.

The crowd shifted, and, for a brief moment, Elizabeth had a glimpse of Jimmy, Aaron, and half of Asa's face. Aaron was having all he could do to hold Jimmy. Asa was wearing the quirk-of-the-lips smile that boded ill, and Jimmy — well, he just looked desperate.

"I didn't talk to no railroad man!" Jimmy hollered. "Let go of me, damn you."

"I think we'll wait until Mr. MacIntyre's witness gets here before we do that, son," Sheriff Mulden said congenially.

Elizabeth bounced on her toes again. She poked the undertaker, but he didn't move. Since there was no hope of catching Asa's eye, she settled for shouting, "Ask him why there wasn't any point in hassling me after I married Asa!"

"Yeah!" someone shouted. She thought it might be Millicent. "Why was marrying up with her so important?"

The person behind her bumped Elizabeth again. She spun around to give him or her a piece of her mind and froze. Brent!

"I can answer that for you," Brent said to Elizabeth only, yanking her to him so hard, her hat pin went flying out of her hand. "I was paying him good money to drive you into my arms." He tossed her up and around, slapping his hand over her mouth, cutting off her cry.

She glanced around frantically for help, but her previous hesitation had left her at the back of the crowd. Unless Millicent really did have eyes in the back of her head, no one was going to notice Brent carrying her off, which was what she thought he intended from the way he was backing up.

Her heart pounded in her ribs, leaving a thundering pulse in her ears. She'd been right! Brent was the mastermind behind this. He'd used Jimmy, Aaron, and herself, but the plan and its implementation were all his. She bit down on his fingers just as Jimmy hollered, "Brent Doyle asked me to scare her so she'd look favorably on him. He wanted to speed up the courtship!"

Brent hissed and shook his hand free. He wasn't as bulky as Asa, but he was lightning quick. Her "why" was smothered before she could get it past her throat. So was her scream as he hauled her back against him, crushing the corset into her waist. It turned out she didn't need to scream to get the crowd's attention. As soon as Jimmy yelled, they'd started searching for the new face in this drama. In another one of those biblical moments, the crowd shifted, searched, and then parted when they found their quarry.

For the first time, she had a clear view of Asa's expression. It wasn't encouraging. Along with the dismayed realization as to what was going on, there was also a certain amount of accusation. No doubt, to his way of thinking, her being here was tantamount to walking up to Brent and inviting him to take her hostage. She met his accusation with a glare of her own.

"Let her go, gambler." The drawl was low, more like a growl than speech. Elizabeth had never seen Asa so cold. So dangerous.

Cougar's "You can't hope to get out of here," all but covered Aaron's "You're a dead man."

Brent shook his hand free of her teeth and countered, "Like hell I can't."

Taking a desperate breath, Elizabeth redirected her glare to Aaron. "This isn't the time to be making threats."

"You can think of a better one?" Asa asked conversationally, one eyebrow winging up, shifting his position so he was clear of the door and his hands hovered near his guns.

She felt the cold muzzle of a gun press against her temple. She swallowed carefully. "Yes."

She tightened her grip on her reticule, closed her eyes, and prayed.

"Get back!" Brent warned the crowd, twisting her about as he made sure everyone saw the gun. He switched his grip to her throat, pulling her back against his chest. He waved the gun at Asa before snapping it back against her temple.

"You ruined everything," Brent snarled at Asa, who stood, gun drawn, his face a calm mask of determination. "I would have had the ranch, my revenge, and Elizabeth if you hadn't come along."

"You most certainly would not," Elizabeth protested, testing Brent's hold but finding no weakness. "I don't care how desperate I became; I never would have stayed with a no-account wastrel like you!"

"Shut up, Elizabeth!" Aaron and Asa bellowed simultaneously.

While she couldn't see Aaron's face, Asa's eyes were flat gray with tension and worry. Brent's forearm around her throat made it hard to talk, but she wanted this point clear. "I am not shutting up. This is my reputation the man is smearing!"

"I'm going to smear a hell of a lot more than your reputation if you don't shut up," Brent growled.

No he wouldn't. She knew that. Not until they were clear of the crowd at least. She gathered the cord on her reticule and closed her mouth. Brent started backing away. Behind him, the crowd must have parted because he didn't slow down. She stumbled once and he dragged her until she found her feet. She twisted, but accomplished nothing more than losing her balance and getting dragged again.

"For God's sake, Elizabeth," she heard Asa call. "Don't fight."

She ignored him and tried pulling Brent's arm from her throat. She might as well have been tugging on a tree. As Asa had pointed out before, her weight was nothing to a man.

She checked the crowd for signs of rescue and found no comfort there. All the men had guns drawn and were searching for a shot. Unfortunately, few of those guns were in sober hands. The best she could hope for was that some drunken idiots wouldn't let off a shot by mistake.

She tried to tangle her feet in Brent's. "If you don't lay off, you're going to meet the same end as your mother." He hauled her higher, choking her in the process.

Time stopped. Hardly caring about her lack of breath, she wheezed, "My mother?"

"She wouldn't cooperate either. Killed herself when Coyote Bill caught me at the ranch. Stupid bitch fought me for the gun." As he spoke, he continued to drag her uncompromisingly backwards, toward his safety. Toward her death.

"Why?" She had to know. Even if she died, she had to know.

He shrugged against her back, then she felt his muscles pull as he scanned behind him. "I would have had the ranch years ago. All I had to do was seduce your mother, kill your father, and I could have married into the best piece of property this side of the Mississippi." He stumbled on a rock. The gun rapped her on the temple; pain slammed her eyes closed, but not her ears. "A place like that could fund a man for a good many years."

In her mind's eye, she pictured her gentle mother's face. She remembered her father's devastation upon her death. The suspicions she'd harbored against him. "You killed my mother because you didn't want to work?"

"No." Grunting, he picked up the pace, dragging her around a water trough. "I killed her because she didn't have the sense to appreciate what I offered."

"My mother was a very smart woman."

She whispered a prayer to her father, asking for forgiveness for thinking he had killed her mother, before she opened her eyes.

The first thing she saw was Asa. He was behind Cougar and Aaron, staying back, but following. Waiting. Watching. She met his gaze through the dust kicking up at their passage, and shivered. The man she was looking at bore no resemblance to the easy-going man she'd married. The man she saw now was pure warrior. This was the man who would follow her to the grave if they allowed it.

A strange calm settled over her. "Let me go, Brent."

"In a minute."

"Now."

"You never did as you were told." He made it sound like a failing.

He swore as he tripped in a rut. She could smell the acrid sweat of his fear. Or maybe it was hers. There were a couple of things she was sure of in her life. One of them was she wasn't prepared to die since she'd just discovered how much fun life could be. The other was she was done being tossed about like dandelion fluff on the capricious breeze of a man's whim.

"I'm not going with you, Brent."

"You might want to wait until you're asked," he grunted as her weight began to tell on his strength.

"I mean now," she said calmly, sliding her hand into her reticule. "I'm not going any further with you now. You have to let me go."

"Not likely." He yanked viciously on her throat, hauling her to the left. "Seeing as how you've made a habit of ruining everything, I'll be making the decisions."

"No. You won't," she said softly before letting her body twist into his, closing her eyes, and pulling the trigger on the derringer she'd hidden in her purse.

Chapter Twenty-Two

🔊

Three things happened at once. Her gun went off. Brent jerked backward and the world around her exploded in a hail of bullets. When her shoulder slammed into the hard ground, she opened her eyes. The first thing she saw were the worn soles of a man's boots. Brent.

She closed her eyes, rolled to her side and retched violently. Hands on her shoulders tried to pull her back. She fought. They tugged harder. She moaned, but it was a soundless protest. She couldn't hear anything beyond the ringing in her ears. The hands firmed their grip and willy-nilly, she went up and over.

Something hard propped up her shoulders. That was better. At least the world stopped spinning. Fingers patted her cheeks. She thought she told them to go away, but she couldn't be sure if her lips just shaped the words or she actually said them. The annoying ringing persisted. God! Her head hurt!

She said so.

"I know, darlin', but I'd be mighty grateful if you opened your eyes."

She should have known it was Asa irritating her when she wanted to be left alone.

"How grateful?" she asked, keeping her eyes closed because the sun through her lids was enough to have her gritting her teeth.

Her perch bounced under her shoulders as he laughed, sending more pain shooting through her skull. She moaned. He was properly contrite, immediately stopping, smoothing her hair off her forehead, kissing her brow, whispering things she'd never thought to hear a man say. Sweet things. Ridiculous things. Love things.

She reached up blindly and wrapped her fingers in his hair. She pulled his head down and asked in a hoarse whisper, "Do I look a fright?"

"You look beautiful." This time, his kiss landed on her lips.

"Save that for later, young man," a gravely voice interrupted. "And lay that young woman flat. Don't you know better than to disturb a patient with a head wound?"

As soft as thistledown, she was flat on the ground. She frowned. She'd have much rather had Asa's lips than the cold dirt.

She flailed out with her hand. "Asa?"

"Right here." Her fingers were wrapped in a rough, warm palm.

"My father didn't kill my mother."

A kiss as gentle as a breeze brushed her cheek. "I heard."

"Save the kissing for later, young man." That gruff voice could only belong to Doc. For a moment, a shadow blocked the painful light of the sun. She moaned with relief.

"Hello, Doc."

"How are you doing, Elizabeth?"

"Where's Asa?"

"Stuck like glue to that spot beside you, but that doesn't answer my question," he said in his usual gruff manner.

"My head hurts, but at least my ears have stopped ringing."

'Well, then, I'd say things are looking up." She heard a rasping sound. It was familiar from her youth. He was opening his medical bag.

"No vile medicines," she ordered as he picked up her wrist to feel her pulse.

Doc's "We'll see" was congenial. It overshadowed Asa's "You'll take whatever Doc says you'll take."

"Leave my patient alone," Doc ordered, "or I'll make you go wait a block south of here."

No more commands were forthcoming from Asa, but she heard dirt shuffle beneath his boots as he stood. Elizabeth smiled, imagining indignation drove him to his feet.

"Does anything hurt besides your head?" Doc asked as he probed the side of her skull.

"My shoulder from where I fell."

His touch on her head, though gentle, hurt like the devil and she winced.

"Hurt?"

"Yessss," she hissed.

"I'm not surprised," Doc answered, moving his fingers down her neck, manipulating gently. "That bullet creased you good, but I don't think there's any permanent damage."

"Then why hasn't she opened her eyes?" Asa demanded.

"I imagine she has quite a headache and the sun is hurting her eyes." Doc's fingers reached her collarbone. "No," he warned. "Don't tense up."

His fingers slid down her arm, straightening it as his knee pressed on her chest. Before she realized what he was doing, he snapped her shoulder back into the socket. The scream ripped from her throat as the pain tore through her.

Doc's apology coincided with Asa's "Jesus!"

"That's better now, isn't it?" Doc asked before shouting, "Someone catch that man!"

Elizabeth opened her eyes to see Asa being lowered into a sitting position by Cougar.

Doc shook his head. "It's always the tough ones."

He shifted so his body blocked the sun from her eyes. Unfortunately, he also blocked her view of Asa. All she could see was Doc's grizzled silhouette with his fly-away hair sticking out all over.

"What?" she croaked in response to the question in his eyes.

"I hope you aren't counting on him when it's time to deliver your babies."

She hadn't thought about it, but now that she had, she realized she was. "Why?"

Doc shrugged. "He won't be much use to you if he passes out every time you make a little noise."

"Asa fainted?"

"Got a bit weak in the knees."

"Asa?" She couldn't believe it.

Doc smiled. "Yup."

As if conjured by his name, Asa appeared around Doc to kneel beside her. He was as white as a ghost. "I'm sorry, darlin'."

"For what?" She experimented with her good arm. It didn't hurt when she moved it, so she placed it against his mouth.

He kissed her fingers before desperately clenching her hand in his. "For not seeing how Brent and Jimmy were double-teaming."

"Well, you didn't and it worked out all right." She took a breath and cast a glance in the direction of Brent's body. He hadn't moved. "Is he dead?"

Asa touched her cheek. "Yeah. I'm sorry."

"I never really knew him, did I?"

He silently shook his head.

"None of us did, apparently," Doc said as he closed his bag.

She bit her lip. "Did I kill him?"

Asa shrugged. Doc pushed himself to his feet with a grunt and walked over to the body. "If you did, you'd have to get behind about thirty other folk."

Elizabeth winced at the image. Despite all that had happened, she was grateful she didn't have to bear the guilt of Brent's death.

Asa stroked her cheek with his fingers as if needing the contact. "No one was too fond of the way he manhandled you."

"I wasn't thrilled myself." She glanced over at Doc. "Can I get out of the dirt now?"

"I don't see why not."

Asa immediately slid his arms under her body.

"Handle her easy," Doc instructed.

It was a totally unnecessary warning. Expensive china hadn't ever been handled as delicately as she was lifted. She closed her eyes and rested her head against Asa's broad shoulder.

"Watch her for signs of a concussion," Doc continued. "Don't let her sleep or take anything for the pain for twenty-four hours. After that, you can give her one spoon of this powder in a glass of water three times a day."

She dipped slightly as Asa took the pouch from Doc.

"What about her shoulder?" Asa asked.

"A couple of weeks in a sling and she should be right as rain."

"Thanks, Doc."

"Call me if there's any change, but I don't expect any complications beyond some stiffening." He moved ahead of them into the throng of people. "All right, folks, let's give them a little room."

Elizabeth opened her eyes to see half the town around them. As Asa cut a path through the crowd, a cheer went up.

One unthinking soul slapped Asa on the back, jarring her head. She moaned. Doc whirled on the man.

"Have a care, you fool!"

She closed her eyes and thanked the Lord she didn't look a fright. Her dignity was about all she had left after being made into a spectacle in front of the whole town.

* * * * *

Asa carried Elizabeth up the street to Millicent's boarding house. She felt so delicate in his arms. So fragile. God, he'd almost lost her. It took all his concentration to hold her carefully and not press her into his body, to hold her so close, she'd never be in danger again.

"Where are we going?" she asked in a low voice.

"I figured on seeing if Millicent could put us up. You're in no shape for a ride home."

"Oh."

"Do you have any problem with that?"

"No."

An unreasonable part of him resented her compliance. He sighed, recognizing reaction setting in. He, on the other hand, was itching for a fight. Maybe he'd head over to the saloon later. A man could always find a body there to satisfy such urges.

By the time he got to the front step of the boarding house, Millicent was standing in the doorway. "McKinnely said you were coming," she said. "I made up the bed in the room next to the back parlor. There're bandages and such on the dresser."

"Thanks." He carefully maneuvered the three steps to the porch. As he drew abreast of Millicent, she clicked her tongue and declared, "Good Lord, honey! The first thing we've got to do is get you cleaned up. You look a fright!"

Asa swore under his breath as Elizabeth came alive in his arms, "What?" She turned those big green eyes on him. "You told me I looked beautiful!"

"You do." He refused to feel guilty. Even blood-streaked and dirty, she was gorgeously, beautifully alive.

She twisted, ignoring his efforts to keep her straight, trying to manage a peek in the hall mirror as they passed. She must have caught a glimpse of her reflection because her hiss of pain exploded into a screech of horror. "You carried me through town looking like this?"

"Wasn't much I could do seeing as how no one stepped forward with a comb."

The logic of the argument was lost on her. "I asked you if I looked a fright!" She struggled to lift her good arm to straighten her bun. "You said I didn't."

"I said you looked beautiful." He pushed the bedroom door wider with his foot. It was only two steps to the bed. Millicent rushed forward to pull down the covers.

Elizabeth glared at him as he laid her on the smooth white sheets. "You lied to me!"

"No, I didn't." He eased her head onto the pillow. Her face was as pale as the sheets. "Could you heat some water so I can clean her up?" he asked Millicent without taking his eyes off Elizabeth, who winced and closed her eyes. No doubt screaming at him wasn't helping her headache much.

"I'll do it right away," Millicent answered, heading for the door. "Give a holler when you get her stripped down and settled. It'll be ready."

"Thanks." He breathed a sigh of relief for her tact. He didn't need an audience right now, no matter how caring. He needed a moment to get himself together. Maybe then, his hands would stop shaking. Maybe then, he could stop seeing, over and over in his mind, the image of her falling under the roar of gunfire. Maybe then, he could accept she was alive.

He stared at her as she lay, eyes closed, on the bed. The blood on her skin was obscene. He traced the thin path of dark red as it angled behind her ear and down her neck. With his thumb, he rubbed at the smudge. He lingered over the task, not stopping until the smear was gone. He wished he could erase her injuries and all the events preceding them just as easily. Gently nudging her hair away from her wound, he studied it. Nausea churned. One inch lower and she would have been dead.

"I didn't lie to you, Elizabeth," he said, knowing she was waiting for him to respond to her accusation. "You looked a fright when Doyle had that gun to your head. You looked a fright when bullets started flying and I couldn't get to you before his gun went off. You looked damned frightening when you hit the ground and I didn't know if you were dead or alive." He rested his forehead against hers and confessed, "But, darlin', when you were sitting in the dirt, sputtering nonsense about your appearance, you were the most beautiful sight these eyes have ever seen."

Her hand slid around the base of his neck and she sighed contentedly against his mouth. "You love me."

"More than anything," he admitted, shifting so his mouth could mate with hers.

"More than apple pie?" she asked.

The chuckle came from nowhere, catching him by surprise. "Yeah," he drawled softly. "More than apple pie."

She rubbed her nose against his. "I'm glad because I love you so much, I've been jealous."

"Of pies?"

"It's shameful," she admitted in a voice that said she couldn't care less. "But I begrudge them your attention." She ducked her head, and admitted shyly, "You ogle them with such passion."

He slid his lips to the side of her neck. The swirls of her ear beckoned. "Next time we make love, keep your eyes open," he whispered, kissing his way from her ear to her cheek. "You'll see what I feel for apple pie is nothing compared to what I feel for you."

She shuddered and then groaned.

"Your head?" he asked.

"I'm sorry. I'm not up to playing right now."

Guilt hammered him anew. First, he got her shot, and now, he was rutting on her rather than getting her settled to recuperate. "Hell, I'm the one who's sorry. I'm a little shook up right now and not thinking straight."

She caught his hand as he pulled back. "I love you."

If the words hadn't held him spellbound, the fierceness with which she said them would have. There was no doubt she was serious. When Elizabeth did something, she went whole hog.

"You sure you want to be saying that?" he asked. "As husbands go, I'm not doing much to polish my image. First, I get you shot, and then I can't even follow Doctor's orders."

"You did not get me shot."

"I should have seen it coming."

"And I should have had enough sense not to stand next to a man I suspected of attempted murder."

"You shouldn't have been there in the first place." He started unbuttoning her dress. "As soon as I get this dress off you, we're going to have a talk about your obedience."

"I have no idea what you're talking about. I followed your orders perfectly."

He paused and looked into her eyes. The smile he didn't see on her face rested lightly in their green depths. "Uh-huh."

He eased her up to slide the dress down her back. He broke into a sweat as he worked it off her right shoulder. To distract her from the pain he was likely causing, he asked, "How do you figure that?"

"You told me that, if I continued to deal with Aaron, I ought to pack protection against snake bite." She shrugged her left shoulder. "I just transferred your advice to Jimmy, then Brent."

"And that little pea-shooter was the best protection you could come up with?" He finally managed to get her right arm free.

She smiled and played with the hair at the nape of his neck. "It was the only one that fit in my reticule." She tugged and he looked up. Straight into her love-soft smile. "You can breathe, Asa. You're not hurting me."

He shook his head and admitted wryly, "I don't know if I'm ever going to breathe steady again after this afternoon."

"You'd better."

"How so?"

"Because I want you there when our babies are born."

She wanted babies with him. The thought made him smile. Sure enough, their kids would be terrors. He pictured a toddler with his mother's red hair playing at her feet as she sat on the porch. He pictured her belly round with another child. He imagined her face and saw it soft with contentment. He couldn't wait. He put his hand on her belly, cupping it low where his child would someday rest. He looked up and realized he didn't have to wait to see the contentment.

"I promise to do my best, darlin'," he drawled.

"You'll do fine, Asa."

Guilt ate at him. There was something they had to get straight between them. "Sometimes I think you're looking for a hero and, darlin', I sure fall short of that mark."

She cupped his cheek in her hand. "Who needs a hero?" She lifted her left shoulder in a dismissing shrug. "All they're good for is swooping in sporadically and whaling on the bad guys."

On the pretext of sliding her dress off, he avoided her eyes. God, he wanted to be a hero for her. He wanted to move mountains. He wanted to wrap her in cotton-wool. He wanted to stand between her and all comers. He wanted it so badly, it gnawed at his gut like poison. "I'm not ever going to be a hero, Elizabeth."

She pulled his gaze to hers with a tug on the hair on the back of his neck. "I don't need a hero, Asa. I can handle bad guys on my own." Her good hand smoothed his eyebrows. "What I do need is someone who makes me laugh. Who likes me. Someone who's gentle and loving. Someone who sets me free and laughs with delight when I fly." She stroked her hand down his face until her thumb rested on his lips. With three fiercely spoken words, she made mincemeat of his uncertainty. "I need you."

He kissed her then, wildly, trying to express without words how much she meant to him, because there simply weren't any. She was everything—past, present, future, hope and promise—all rolled into one. She took his kiss and all the emotion he poured into it and gave it back tenfold.

It wasn't enough. She gasped for breath and he let her go, raining kisses on her cheeks, eyes and nose. She slid her leg over his, turning half on her side. He helped her ease her injured arm into a comfortable position against his chest. As her head settled into the hollow of his shoulder, he whispered, "I love you." He couldn't seem to say it enough.

"I love you, too."

She nuzzled her nose into his shoulder. Her eyelashes tickled his skin as she blinked. Her hand fumbled for his at his side. She squeezed it tightly and said, "Welcome home, Asa."

He remembered his prayer that day he lay broken and bleeding in the alley. Just a hurt kid, aching for a home. He remembered his desperate prayer to belong. He remembered the promise he'd made and received. He bent and kissed the top of Elizabeth's head. He squeezed her arm gently with his fingers, looked up at the ceiling and blinked rapidly.

It was funny how promises lingered. Now, not only did he belong, but he was loved, from the soles of his feet to the top of his head, by a woman who didn't have an infant's grasp of what it meant to do anything by half measures. He was home at last and there seemed to be only one thing to say.

"Thank you."

Enjoy an excerpt from:
PROMISES KEEP

Copyright © Sarah McCarty, 2004.

"I'm not going to hurt you, Miss Kincaid."

Thrown off balance, she could only ask, "Why?"

The fingers on the back of her head threaded through the shambles of her bun and massaged small circles on her scalp. "Because it's not my way."

Two hairpins hit the floor with little pings of protest. Mara closed her eyes against the urge to melt into the first kindness she'd experienced in a long, long time. "It's been my experience that men and women define hurt differently."

"I wouldn't base the opinions of a lifetime on the last few months if I were you."

It was probably a trick caused by the way his chest muffled his voice, but somehow his tone sounded kinder and gentler than she'd remembered from their previous encounters. She tried to pull back, but he wouldn't allow it and that fueled her anger more than a slap ever could. "Well, you're not me, and until you've been drugged, torn apart by a man's lust, and then ostracized because of it, you've no right to think anything."

Was that her imagination, or did the man just wince?

"I'm sorry that happened to you."

So was she, but that didn't change anything. "Let me go, Mr. McKinnely."

"I can't do that."

"Yes. You can. All you have to do is drop your hands to your sides and keep them there."

His response to her snapping was a laugh that rumbled up from deep within. "If I do that," he pointed out in a reasonable voice, "you'll fall."

He was right. For all her belligerence, her body was resting against his as if he was the sole support in a world gone awry. Her face flooded with heat. She pushed herself away. Mara ducked her head in the hopes that her hair would hide her embarrassment.

It was a vain hope.

Cougar chuckled and steadied her with a hand to her shoulder. "Doc's back at his place," he said. "We're going to have to get you out there."

She slowly straightened and flicked at his hand with her fingers. "You may go anywhere you like," she snapped. "I'm staying here."

"You are going with me." He slid his hands around her body, lifting her up.

The ease with which he sidestepped her wishes struck a raw nerve. The gentleness with which he accomplished it was even more galling. She didn't understand him, nor did she want to. She just wanted him to go away. Wrapping her fingers in the chest hair peeking between the dangling buttons on his shirt, she twisted viciously, wanting to hurt him the way he was hurting her with his casual arrogance. "Let me down, you, you—"

"Bastard?" he supplied with a lift of his brow. "Son of a bitch?"

"Yes." She twisted harder. She knew it had to hurt, yet he gave no sign. Unless the broadening of his smile could be considered one. Leaning forward, she bit him in the hard muscle of his chest. Let him ignore her now.

He swore and stopped moving. Mara bit down harder, bracing her body for the blow to come.

A thumb and finger surrounded her face and then applied force to her jaw. There came a point when she had to admit his greater strength and unlock her teeth. The body beneath hers was tense, the muscles corded. She could feel him staring at her as he tilted her face up. Finally, she couldn't stand the tension any longer and she opened her eyes. To her surprise, his hand wasn't raised to strike.

She searched his dark face for anger and found none. There was only a strange sorrow and something else. Something so disgusting, she wanted to kill him.

"Don't," she hissed. "Don't you dare pity me!"

He took the bandana from around his neck with his right hand and dabbed at the blood on her mouth.

"Why not?" he asked, transferring the bandana to his chest where he scrubbed with a lot less gentleness. "Nothing much more pathetic than attacking someone who's trying to help."

"I don't want your help," she growled.

"Well, that's neither here nor there, seeing as how I was raised that a man doesn't desert a lady in distress."

"I am not a lady, and I am not in distress."

"Uh-huh."

She was tempted to point out that the only distress she was in was caused by him, but her brief stint with lunacy was apparently over. Angering him while he had her in his arms was no longer desirable. The man was a keg of dynamite. She could tell that from the energy pulsing beneath his skin. She just couldn't figure out what would set him off. An unknown enemy was a dangerous one. She forced the anger out of her tone.

"Mr. McKinnely, I appreciate all you've done for me, but I'm truly all right now. If you'll put me down, I'll be on my way."

If she wasn't mistaken, the look he shot her was reproachful.

"I'll put you down as soon as Doc says it's all right. That was a hell of a shot you took." His eyes ran the length of her body. "And there's not much of you to go around."

Not much to go around? Where on Earth did he plan on…spreading her? She lifted her chin, put on her most off-putting expression, and stated with cool implacability, "I assure you, Mr. McKinnely, I am perfectly fine. Bruised at the most."

A muscle along the side of his jaw snapped tight. "That's something we'll let Doc decide."

"Where do you get this 'we' from? I should know how I feel."

He ignored that. He shot a glare out the window as he hitched her up in his arms. "It shouldn't have happened at all."

"At last we agree on something. Now, if you could just see your way to being reasonable." She pushed tentatively at his chest. Nothing happened.

"I'm always reasonable," he said as he shifted her weight in his arms.

That was debatable. Mara took a calming breath. She could see that he was taking special care not to jostle her more than necessary. Still, it hurt. The minute she gasped, she had his full attention and an apology. She wanted neither.

"Mr. McKinnely, I can see that you are a true gentleman. I'm grateful you stepped in and put an end to that cowboy's insult."

"Sweet talking me isn't going to get you anywhere."

"Excuse me?"

"You're right fond of that expression, aren't you?" He grabbed a black shawl that was hanging on a peg and draped it over her, before continuing, "I'm not putting you down until Doc says it's okay. And leave that on."

Mara kept on pushing at the shawl. "It's hot enough to fry an egg out there."

"You might be in shock."

"For the last time, Mr. McKinnely, I am perfectly fine."

He snagged the edge of the shawl with his fingers, stopping its tumble. "I'm not taking any chances."

"Nobody is asking you to."

"I made you a promise, Miss Kincaid. I intend to keep it."

All this hassle was because of some promise she didn't remember? Lord help her! "What promise?"

He paused in reaching for the door. This close, Mara could see the wrinkles fanning out from his eyes above the sharp plane of his cheekbones. His Indian ancestry was evident in the darkness of his skin and the blue-black sheen of his long hair as it fell on either side of his face in a thick curtain, framing his rugged features. She followed the flow of his hair from his wide forehead to the sharp edge of his cheekbones, down the flat planes of his cheeks to his full, purely masculine lips. And there she paused, her attention caught by the way his mouth lifted slightly at the corners as if in anticipation of a smile. It just seemed so at odds with what she'd heard about him. What her fear said about him. What she knew about him. This was a very, very dangerous man.

She looked at his mouth again and then back at his eyes. At the lines that she knew in her gut were caused by laughter rather than long hours spent in the sun. And adjusted her assessment. Cougar McKinnely was a very dangerous man, but apparently, he was also a dangerous man who liked to laugh.

He dipped his head until his nose tapped hers, bringing her attention back to here and now. She forced herself not to look away from the intensity of his gaze as he uttered with the utmost sincerity, something impossible to believe.

"I promised you everything is going to be all right from here on out."

Why an electronic book?

We live in the Information Age—an exciting time in the history of human civilization, in which technology rules supreme and continues to progress in leaps and bounds every minute of every day. For a multitude of reasons, more and more avid literary fans are opting to purchase e-books instead of paper books. The question from those not yet initiated into the world of electronic reading is simply: *Why?*

1. *Price.* An electronic title at Ellora's Cave Publishing and Cerridwen Press runs anywhere from 40% to 75% less than the cover price of the exact same title in paperback format. Why? Basic mathematics and cost. It is less expensive to publish an e-book (no paper and printing, no warehousing and shipping) than it is to publish a paperback, so the savings are passed along to the consumer.

2. *Space.* Running out of room in your house for your books? That is one worry you will never have with electronic books. For a low one-time cost, you can purchase a handheld device specifically designed for e-reading. Many e-readers have large, convenient screens for viewing. Better yet, hundreds of titles can be stored within your new library—on a single microchip. There are a variety of e-readers from different manufacturers. You can also read e-books on your PC or laptop computer. (Please note that Ellora's Cave does not endorse any specific brands.

You can check our websites at www.ellorascave.com or www.cerridwenpress.com for information we make available to new consumers.)

3. *Mobility.* Because your new e-library consists of only a microchip within a small, easily transportable e-reader, your entire cache of books can be taken with you wherever you go.

4. *Personal Viewing Preferences.* Are the words you are currently reading too small? Too large? Too… ANNOYING? Paperback books cannot be modified according to personal preferences, but e-books can.

5. *Instant Gratification.* Is it the middle of the night and all the bookstores near you are closed? Are you tired of waiting days, sometimes weeks, for bookstores to ship the novels you bought? Ellora's Cave Publishing sells instantaneous downloads twenty-four hours a day, seven days a week, every day of the year. Our webstore is never closed. Our e-book delivery system is 100% automated, meaning your order is filled as soon as you pay for it.

Those are a few of the top reasons why electronic books are replacing paperbacks for many avid readers.

As always, Ellora's Cave and Cerridwen Press welcome your questions and comments. We invite you to email us at Comments@ellorascave.com or write to us directly at Ellora's Cave Publishing Inc., 1056 Home Avenue, Akron, OH 44310-3502.

ELLORA'S CAVE
ROMANTICA PUBLISHING

*Discover for yourself why readers can't get enough
of the multiple award-winning publisher
Ellora's Cave.*

*Whether you prefer e-books or paperbacks,
be sure to visit EC on the web at
www.ellorascave.com*

*for an erotic reading experience that will leave you
breathless.*